Gun Games

ALSO BY FAYE KELLERMAN

Hangman
Blindman's Bluff
The Mercedes Coffin
The Burnt House
The Ritual Bath
Sacred and Profane
The Quality of Mercy
Milk and Honey
Day of Atonement
False Prophet
Grievous Sin
Sanctuary
Justice
Prayers for the Dead
Serpent's Tooth
Moon Music
Jupiter's Bones
Stalker
The Forgotten
Stone Kiss
Street Dreams
Straight into Darkness
The Garden of Eden and Other Criminal Delights:
A Book of Short Stories

With Jonathan Kellerman

Double Homicide
Capital Crimes

With Aliza Kellerman

Prism

Gun Games

Faye Kellerman

HARPER LUXE

An Imprint of HarperCollins*Publishers*

For Jonathan

GUN GAMES. Copyright © 2012 by Plot Line, Inc. All rights reserved. Printed in the United States of America. No part of this book may be used or reproduced in any manner whatsoever without written permission except in the case of brief quotations embodied in critical articles and reviews. For information address HarperCollins Publishers, 10 East 53rd Street, New York, NY 10022.

HarperCollins books may be purchased for educational, business, or sales promotional use. For information please write: Special Markets Department, HarperCollins Publishers, 10 East 53rd Street, New York, NY 10022.

FIRST HARPERLUXE EDITION

HarperLuxe™ is a trademark of HarperCollins Publishers

Library of Congress Cataloging-in-Publication Data is available upon request.

ISBN: 978-0-06-210698-8

11 12 13 14 ID/RRD 10 9 8 7 6 5 4 3 2 1

Chapter One

I t was bad news walking through the door.

They were coming his way: five of them—three guys, two girls—all of them looking older than him by a couple of years but probably still in high school. The guys had some muscle, but none of them was steroidal, meaning he could take any of them one-on-one. Collectively, he didn't stand a chance. Besides, Gabe wasn't spoiling for a fight. Last time that happened, he messed up his hand—temporarily. He'd been lucky. Maybe he'd be lucky again. If not, he had to be smart.

He pushed his glasses up on his nose and kept his eyes on the book until the group was on top of him. Even then, he didn't look up. Nothing was going to happen to him inside a Starbucks . . . staring at the page in front of him, his mind going a mile per sec.

"You're sitting in my seat," one of the guys said.

His dad had always emphasized that if he were about to be jumped, it was best to take on the leader. Because once the leader was gone, the others fell like dominoes. Gabe counted to five before he looked up. The guy who spoke was the biggest of the three.

"Excuse me?" Gabe said.

"I said you're sitting in my seat." And as if to emphasize the point, he pulled back his jacket, giving Gabe a five-second peek at the gun stuck into his waistband—positively one of the worst places to keep an unharnessed weapon. There were only two people in the world that Gabe would take crap from and he wasn't looking at either one of them. To acquiesce would be a mistake. On the other hand, to confront would also be a mistake. Luckily, the dude gave him an out.

Gabe held up an index finger. "Do you mind?" Slowly and carefully, he pulled back the guy's jacket with his finger and stared at the gun. "Beretta 92FS with some kind of a custom grip." A pause. "Sweet." He let the jacket drop. "You know the company just came out with an advanced model—a 96A or something like that. Same thing as the 92 series except it has a higher magazine capacity."

Gabe stood up. Nose to nose, he was a couple of inches taller than the gunslinger, but the height differential wasn't something he was about to flaunt. He took a half step back, giving them both some personal space.

"I like the plinkers . . . like the 87 Cheetah .22LR. First of all, it's got great reliability. Second, it's one of those ambidextrous pieces. I'm right-handed, but I got a real strong left. You know how it is. You never know which hand it's gonna be convenient to use."

They were locked in a staring contest, Gabe's focus on the dude with the piece. As far as he was concerned, the other four didn't exist. Then, with a sudden, fluid motion, Gabe stepped aside and held out his hand, magnanimously offering the dude his seat. "Be my guest."

A few seconds ticked by, each waiting for the other to blink.

Finally, the guy said to Gabe, "Have a seat."

"After you."

The two of them eyed each other, then they both sat down at the same time with the dude taking up the leather chair that Gabe had formerly occupied. He kept his eyes on the guy's face, never letting up for a moment. Dude was around five ten, one eighty, broad chest, strong arms. Brown hair past his ears, blue eyes, strong chin. Under his leather jacket, he had on a gray T-shirt and wore black, tight-fitting jeans. He was a good-looking guy and probably had a posse of admirers.

Dude said, "Where'd you learn about guns?"

Gabe shrugged. "My dad."

"What does he do?"

"My father?" At this, Gabe broke into a slow grin. "Uh . . . actually, he's a pimp." The expected pause. "He owns whorehouses in Nevada."

The dude stared at him with newfound respect. "Cool."

"It sounds a lot cooler than it is," Gabe said. "My dad's a nasty guy—a real mean motherfucker. He also owns about a zillion guns and knows how to use every single one of them. I get along with him because I don't cross him. Plus, we don't live together anymore."

"You live with your mom?"

"Nah, she's in India somewhere. She took off with her lover and dumped me into the care of complete strangers—"

"Are you shittin' me?"

"I *wish* I was shittin' you." Gabe laughed. "Last year was a total nightmare." He rubbed his hands together. "But it worked out okay. I like where I am. My foster dad is a police lieutenant. You'd expect him to be the hard-ass, but compared to my own dad, the man is a saint." He looked at his watch. It was almost six in the evening and night was inches away. "I gotta go." He stood up and so did Dude.

"What's your name?" Dude asked.

"Chris," Gabe lied. "And you?"

"Dylan." They fist-bumped. "What school do you go to?"

"Homeschooled," Gabe said. "Almost done, thank God. Hey, nice to meet you, Dylan. Maybe I'll catch you on the shooting range."

He turned his back to the group and slowly swaggered away. It took all his energy not to glance back.

Once he was out the door, he ran like hell.

Rina was arranging roses when the boy came in, flushed and panting. She said, "Are you all right?"

"Just out of shape." Gabe tried to steady his breathing. He attempted to give his temporary mother a smile, but it probably didn't come out too sincere. He could tell that Rina was scrutinizing him, her blue eyes concentrated on his face. She was wearing a pink sweater that matched the flowers. His mind was desperately trying to figure out small talk. "Those are pretty. From the garden?"

"Trader Joe's. The roses in the garden won't start blooming for another couple of months." She regarded her charge, his emerald eyes flitting behind his glasses. Something was off. "Why were you running?"

"Trying to be healthy," Gabe told her. "I really need to do something about improving my stamina."

"I'd say anyone who can practice for six hours a day has a great deal of stamina."

"Tell that to my beating heart."

"Sit down. I'll get you something to drink."

"I can do it." Gabe disappeared into the kitchen. When he came back, he was holding a bottle of water. Rina was still giving him funny looks. To distract her, he picked up the paper from the dining room table. The front page showed a picture of a boy, the caption stating that fifteen-year-old Gregory Hesse had committed suicide by a single gunshot to the head. He had a round face and big round eyes and looked much younger than fifteen. Gabe started reading the article in earnest.

"Sad, isn't it." Rina was looking over his shoulder. "You think to yourself, what on earth could have been so bad that this poor kid was willing to end it all?"

There were lots of reasons for despair. Last year he had gone through all of them. "Sometimes life is hard."

Rina took the paper from him, spun him around, and gave him her serious eye-to-eye contact. "You looked upset when you came in."

"I'm fine." He managed a smile. "Really."

"What happened? Did you hear from your dad or something?"

"No, we're cool." When Rina gave him a skeptical look, he said, "Honestly. I haven't spoken to him since we came back from Paris. We texted a couple of times.

He asked me how I was doing and I told him I was fine. We're on good terms. I think he likes me a lot better now that my mom is out of the picture."

He took a swig of water and averted his eyes.

"Did I tell you my mom IMed about a week ago?"

"No . . . you didn't."

"Must have slipped my mind."

"Uh-huh—"

"Really. It was no big deal. I almost didn't answer her because I didn't recognize the screen name she was using."

"Is she okay?"

"Seems to be." A shrug. "She asked me how I was." Behind his glasses, his eyes were gazing at a distant place. "I told her I was fine and not to worry . . . that everything was cool. Then I signed off." He shrugged again. "I didn't feel like making chitchat. Tell you the truth, I'd rather she not contact me. Is that terrible?"

"No, it's understandable." Rina sighed. "It'll take a lot of bridge building before you get some trust—"

"That's not gonna happen. It's not that I have anything against her. I wish her well. I just don't want to talk to her."

"Fair enough. But try to keep an open mind. When she contacts you again, maybe give her a few more seconds of your time. Not for her sake, but for yours."

"*If* she contacts me again."

"She will, Gabriel. You know that."

"I don't know anything. I'm sure she's busy with the baby and all."

"One child isn't a substitute for another—"

"Thanks for the pep talk, Rina, but I really don't care. I barely think about her." But of course, he did all the time. "The baby needs her way more than I do." He smiled and patted her head. "Besides, I've got a pretty good substitute right here."

"Your mom is still your mom. And one day, you'll see that. But thank you very much for the nice words."

Gabe returned his eyes to the newspaper article. "Wow, the boy was local."

"Yes, he was."

"Do you know the family?"

"No."

"So like . . . does the lieutenant investigate cases like this?"

"Only if the coroner has questions about whether it was a suicide."

"How can the coroner tell?"

"I really don't know. You can ask Peter when he gets home."

"When's he coming home?"

"Sometime between now and dawn. Do you want to go out to the deli for dinner?"

Gabe's eyes lit up. "Can I drive?"

"Yes, you can drive. While we're there, let's pick up a sandwich and take it to the Loo. If I don't bring him food, he doesn't eat."

Gabe put down the paper. "Can I shower first? I'm a little sweaty."

"Of course."

Gabe could tell that Rina was still evaluating him. Unlike his father, he wasn't an adroit liar. He said, "You worry too much. I'm fine."

"I believe you." Rina mussed his hair, damp with perspiration. "Go shower. It's almost seven and I'm starving."

"You bet." Gabe smiled to himself. He had just used one of the Loo's favorite expressions. He had been with the Deckers for almost a year and certain things just filtered in. He became aware of hunger pangs. It had just taken time for his stomach to calm down for his brain to get the message that he hadn't eaten since breakfast and that he was famished.

It's not that he had a nervous gut. But guns did strange things to his digestive system.

Completely unlike his dad.

Chris Donatti never met a firearm he didn't like.

Chapter Two

S ince the Hammerling case was aired on the TV show *Fugitive*, Decker had been getting calls, most of them dead ends. Still, he made it a habit to probe every single lead no matter how inane the tip. A serial killer was on the loose, and there was no such thing as half-assed investigation. The current tip was a spotting in the New Mexican desert in a small blip of a town somewhere between Roswell—known for its close encounters with UFOs—and Carlsbad, known for its network of underground caves. In the middle of nowhere was always a great place to hide out. Plus that region was in a direct line to Ciudad Juárez, Mexico, where, by some estimates, there had been more than twenty thousand murders in the past decade. The vast majority of the dead had been participants in vicious drug wars. But there was also a large minority of young female victims, possibly five thousand of them, called *feminicidios*, most between the ages of twelve and twenty-five, with no apparent connection to one another. The Mexicans' penchant for violence would provide convenient cover for someone like Garth Hammerling if he could avoid getting killed himself.

Decker raked fingers through his thick head of hair, which retained some bright red highlights among the gray and white. Hannah said the streaks looked very punk. He smiled when he thought of his youngest daughter. She was away in Israel for the year and then after that would be starting college at Barnard. His children ranged from midthirties to eighteen and he had yet to experience an empty nest, courtesy of two very disturbed people who unwittingly enlisted his and Rina's help in raising their child. Gabriel was a good kid, though—not a bother, but he was a presence.

Currently, Rina was teaching the fifteen-year-old how to drive.

I thought I was long past that one, she had told him. *We plan and God laughs.*

The good news was that his baby grandsons, Aaron and Akiva, from his elder daughter, Cindy, were almost three months old. They had been born three weeks early at five pounds, thirteen ounces and six pounds, one ounce. At the end of her pregnancy, Cindy had been carrying around more than sixty pounds of baby weight. But being athletic and working out almost every day, she had dropped the pounds and then some. She was currently on maternity leave from her position as a newbie detective with Hollywood. She planned to go back as soon as she found the right nanny. In the meantime, Rina and his ex-wife, Jan, were willing substitutes. The babies were way more work than Gabe.

Decker smoothed his mustache while studying the phone message.

The tip had been given by the New Mexico State Police. This was the fourth sighting of Garth Hammerling in New Mexico, and Decker was beginning to think that maybe he was on to something. He called up the 505 area code and after a series of holds and call switching, he was connected to CIS—Criminal Investigative Section—in Division 4. The investigator who was assigned to follow up the lead was named Romulus Poe.

"I know the guy who phoned it into the show," Poe told Decker. "He owns a motel in Indian Springs located about forty miles south of Roswell. The man is what you might call an indigenous character. He sees and hears things that elude most of us mere mortals. But that doesn't mean he's totally loco. I've been out here for twelve years. Before that I was ten years in

Las Vegas Metro Homicide. I've seen and heard my fair share of freak. The desert is no place for the faint-hearted."

"What's the guy's name?" Decker asked.

"Elmo Turret."

"What's his story?"

"He claims he saw a guy that looked like the picture of Hammerling shown on *Fugitive.* Elmo said he saw him a few days ago, camping out ten miles south from his motel. I'm just clearing out a drug bust. I spent the afternoon pulling out around an acre of mature MJ plants and I don't mean Michael Jordan. As soon as I'm done with the processing of the local yokels who owned the land, I'll swing by the area on my bike and see if I can't find any veracity to the story."

"Call me one way or the other. You know, this is the fourth spotting I've received from New Mexico."

"Doesn't surprise me. Ever been here?"

"Just Santa Fe."

"That's another country—civilized for the most part. Down here . . . well, what can I say? The Wild West is alive and kicking."

Paperwork took up another hour, and by seven-thirty in the evening, Decker was about to call it quits when his favorite detective, Sergeant Marge Dunn, knocked on the sash to his open door. The woman was five ten with square shoulders and wiry muscle. She was dressed for winter L.A. style, wearing brown cotton slacks and a tan cashmere sweater. Her blond hair—and getting blonder by the years—was pulled back into a ponytail.

"Have a seat," Decker told her.

"I've got a woman outside wanting to talk to you," Marge said. "Actually, she wanted to talk to Captain Strapp but since he left, she settled for the next in line."

"Who is she?"

"Her name is Wendy Hesse and she told me that her business is personal. Rather than push my weight around, I figured it would be easier to send her to you."

Decker peeked at his watch. "Sure, bring her in while I go grab a cup of coffee."

By the time he got back, Marge had seated the mystery woman. Her complexion was an unhealthy shade of putty and her blue eyes, though dry at the moment, had cried many tears. Her hair was cut helmet style—dark brown with white roots. She was a big-boned woman and appeared to be in her late forties. She was dressed in a black sweater and black sweatpants with sneakers on her feet.

Marge said, "Lieutenant Decker, this is Mrs. Hesse."

He put the coffee cup on his desk. "Can I get you something to drink?"

The woman looked at her lap, shook her head, and mumbled something.

"Pardon me?" Decker said.

She snapped her head up. "No . . . thank you."

"So how can I help you?"

Wendy Hesse looked at Marge, who said, "Maybe I'll get some coffee. Are you sure you wouldn't like some water, Mrs. Hesse?"

The woman refused a second offer. After Marge left, Decker said, "How can I help you, Mrs. Hesse?"

"I need to talk to the police." She folded her hands and looked at her lap. "I don't know how to start."

Decker said, "Just tell me what's on your mind."

"My son . . ." Her eyes watered. "They say he . . . that he committed suicide. But I don't . . . I don't believe it."

Decker regarded her in a different context. "You're Gregory Hesse's mother."

She nodded as tears flowed down her cheeks.

"I am so sorry, Mrs. Hesse." He handed her a tissue. "I can't even imagine what you're feeling right now." When she started sobbing openly, Decker stood up and put his hand on her shoulder. "Let me get you some water."

She nodded. "Maybe that's a good . . . idea."

Decker caught Marge at the coffeepot. "The woman is Gregory Hesse's mom—the teen in the paper who committed suicide." Marge went wide-eyed. "Anyone from Homicide at the scene yesterday?"

"I was in court." She paused. "Oliver was there."

"Did he talk to you about it?"

"Not really. It got him down. You could read it in his face. But he didn't say anything about the death being suspicious."

Decker filled up a wax paper cup with water. "Mrs. Hesse has her doubts about suicide. Would you mind sticking around? I'd like another ear."

"Of course."

Both of them went back to his office. To Mrs. Hesse, Decker said, "I've asked Sergeant Dunn here. She partners with Scott Oliver who was at your house yesterday afternoon."

"I'm sorry for your loss, Mrs. Hesse," Marge said.

Tears ran down her cheeks. Mrs. Hesse said, "There were . . . lots of police at the house."

"Detective Oliver was in civilian dress. I don't remember what he was wearing yesterday. He's in his fifties—"

"That one," she said, drying her eyes. "I remember him. Amazing . . . it's still a blur . . . a nightmare."

Decker nodded.

"I keep expecting to . . . wake up." She bit her lip. "It's *killing* me." The tears were falling again faster than she could dry them. "What you can do for me is find out what really happened."

"Okay." Decker paused. "Tell me, what don't you believe about your son's death?"

Wet droplets fell onto her folded hands. "Gregory did not *shoot* himself. He's never used a gun in his life! He hated guns. Our entire family abhors violence of any kind!"

Decker took out a notepad. "Tell me about your boy."

"He *wasn't* suicidal. He wasn't even *depressed*. Gregory had friends, he was a good student. He had lots of interests. He never even remotely hinted at suicide."

"Anything about him change over the last few months?"

"Nothing."

"Maybe a little more moody?" Marge suggested.

"No!" She was resolute.

Decker asked, "Did he sleep more? Did he eat more? Did he eat less?"

Wendy's sigh signaled exasperation. "He was the same boy—thoughtful . . . he could be quiet. But quiet doesn't mean depressed, you know."

"Of course not," Decker told her. "I hate to ask you this, Mrs. Hesse, but how about past drug use?"

"Nothing!"

"Tell me a little about Gregory's interests. What about extracurricular activities?"

She was taken aback. "Uh . . . I know he tried out for the debate team." Silence. "He did very well. They told him to come back next year when there's more room."

Meaning he didn't make it. "What else?" Decker said.

"He was in math club. He excelled in math."

"What did he do on the weekends?"

"He was with his friends; he went to the movies. He studied. He was taking a full load including an AP course. "

"Tell me about his friends."

She crossed her arms in front of her ample bosoms. "Gregory may have not been one of the popular kids." She made air quotes over the word *popular.* "But he certainly wasn't an outcast."

"I'm sure he wasn't. What about his friends?"

"His friends were . . . he got along with every-one . . . Gregory did."

"Can you be more specific? Did he have a best friend?"

"Joey Reinhart. He's been friends with him since grade school."

"Any others?" Marge asked.

"He had friends," Mrs. Hesse kept repeating.

Decker tried a different approach. "If Gregory had to fit into a high school category, what would it be?"

"What do you mean?"

"You mentioned the popular kids. There are other cliques: jocks, skaters, stoners, nerds, rebels, brainiacs, philosophers, hipsters, Goths, vampires, outcasts, artistes . . ." Decker shrugged.

The woman's mouth was set in a thin line. Finally, she said, "Gregory had all sorts of friends. Some of them had some problems."

"What kind of problems?"

"You know."

"Problems to us usually mean, sex, drugs, or alcohol," Marge said.

"No, not that." Wendy kneaded her hands. "Some of his friends were a little slower to mature. One boy, Kevin Stanger . . . they picked on him so bad that he transferred to a private school over the hill."

"He was bullied?" Decker asked. "And by bullied, I mean physical contact."

"All I know is he was transferred."

"When was this?" Marge asked.

"About six months ago." The woman looked down. "But that wasn't Gregory. No sirree. If Gregory were being picked on, I would have known about it. I would have done something. I'll tell you that much."

Precisely the reason why Gregory might not have told her. Decker said, "He never came home with unexplained bumps or bruises?"

"No! Why don't you believe me?"

"I do believe you," Decker said. "But I have to ask certain questions, Mrs. Hesse. You want a competent investigation, right?"

The woman was quiet. Then she said, "You can call me Wendy."

"Whatever you'd prefer," Decker said.

Marge said, "Any girlfriends in his life?"

"I didn't know of any."

"Did he go out on the weekends?"

"Mostly, he and his friends go to each other's houses. Joey's the only one old enough to drive." Wendy's eyes welled up with tears. "Mine never will." Instant sobs. Decker and Marge waited until the hapless woman could find her voice again. "A couple of times"—she wiped her eyes—"when I went to pick him up . . . I saw a few girls." She dabbed her eyes again. "I asked Gregory about them. He said they were Tina's friends."

"Who's Tina?" Marge asked.

"Oh . . . sorry. Tina is Joey's little sister. She and Frank, my younger son . . . they're in the same grade."

"Did Joey and Gregory go to the same school?"

"Bell and Wakefield. In Lauffner Ranch."

"I know it," Decker said.

Bell and Wakefield was the North Valley's exclusive prep school on twenty acres with a state-of-the-art football field and indoor basketball arena, a movie studio, and a computer lab worthy of NASA. It prized sports, dramatics, and academics in that order. Lots of pro athletes and actors lived in the area and B and W was a natural repository for their children. "About fifteen hundred students?"

"I don't know exactly, but it's a big school," Wendy said. "A lot of breathing room to find your special place."

And if you don't find your place, it's a lot of room to get lost, Decker thought.

Wendy said, "Joey's a goofy kind of kid. About five eight and weighs about a hundred pounds. He wears big glasses and his ears stick out. I'm not saying this just to be mean, just to tell you that there were lots of other kids that would have been bullied before Gregory."

"Do you have a picture of him?" Decker said.

Wendy rummaged through her purse and pulled out his grade-school graduation picture. It showed a baby-faced boy with blue eyes and pink chubby cheeks. Puberty was years away, and high school never treated those boys kindly.

"May I keep this?" Decker asked.

Wendy nodded.

He closed his notebook. "What would you like me to do for your son, Wendy?"

"Find out what really happened to my boy." There were tears in her eyes.

Decker said, "The coroner has ruled your son's death a suicide."

Wendy was resolute. "I don't care what the coroner says, my son didn't commit suicide."

"Could it have been an accidental shooting?"

"No," Wendy insisted. "Gregory hated guns."

Marge asked, "So how do you think he died?"

Wendy glanced at the detectives while kneading her hands. She didn't answer the question.

Decker said, "If it wasn't accidental death by his own hand and if it wasn't intentional suicide, that leaves homicide—either accidental or intentional."

Wendy bit her lip and nodded.

"You think someone murdered your boy?"

It took a few moments before Wendy could speak. "Yes."

Decker tried to be as gentle as possible. "Why?"

" 'Cause I *know* he didn't shoot himself."

"So you think the coroner missed something or . . ." Wendy was silent. Decker said, "I have no problem going to the school and talking to some of Gregory's friends and classmates. But the coroner is not going to change her determination unless we find something extraordinary. Something that would directly contradict a suicide. Usually, it's the coroner who comes to us because he or she suspects foul play."

"Even if it was . . . what you say." Wendy wiped her eyes with her fingers. "I don't have . . . a clue . . . to what happened." More tears. "If he did do it . . . I don't know why. No idea whatsoever! I couldn't be that dumb."

"It has nothing to do with brains—"

"Do you have children, sir?"

"I do."

"What about you, Detective?" She had turned to Marge.

"A daughter."

"So what would either of you do if you suddenly came home one day . . . and found your child . . . had committed suicide?"

"I don't know," Decker answered.

Marge's eyes watered. "I can't imagine."

"So tell me," Wendy continued. "How would you feel if you knew there was absolutely no reason for your child to do this? He wasn't depressed, he wasn't moody, he didn't take drugs, he didn't drink, he wasn't a loner, he had friends, and he never ever handled a gun. I don't even know where he got the *gun!*" She burst into sobs. "And no one . . . will . . . tell me . . . *anything!*"

Decker let her cry it out, handing her the box of tissues.

Marge said, "What do you want us to do, Mrs. Hesse?"

"Wen . . . dy." She answered between sobs. "Find out what happened." Her eyes were imploring. "I realize this is probably not a police matter, but I don't know where to turn."

Silence.

"Should I hire a private investigator? I mean, at least maybe he can find out where Gregory got the gun."

"Where is the gun?" Decker asked.

"The police took it," Wendy told him.

"Then it should be in the evidence locker," Marge said. "It's also in the files."

"Let's pull it out and find out where it came from." He turned to Wendy. "Let me start with the gun, and we'll work it from there."

"Thank you!" A new fresh round of tears poured out of Wendy's eyes. "Thank you for believing me . . . or at least thinking about what I said!"

"We're here to help," Marge said.

Decker nodded in agreement. The woman was probably in massive denial. But sometimes, even in these situations, parents really did know their children better than anyone else.

Chapter Three

Sitting on the living room sofa, Decker pop-topped a can of Dad's and basked in the warmth of his wife's presence and the aftertaste of cured meat. "Thanks for picking up my dinner."

"If I knew you were that close to coming home, we would have waited for you at the deli."

"It's better this way." He took Rina's hand. He had showered before he ate, changing from his suit to a sweatshirt and sweatpants. "Where's the kid?"

"Practicing."

"How's he doing?"

"Seems to be okay. Did you know that Terry contacted him?"

"No, but it was bound to happen sooner or later. When was this?"

"About a week ago." Rina recapped the conversation. "It obviously upset him. He wasn't himself over dinner tonight. Whenever he gets uncomfortable, he talks about his upcoming competitions. Paradoxically, competition seems to calm him down. Renting him a piano is a lot cheaper than therapy."

The baby grand was in the garage—the only place where they had enough room. Gabe shared his music studio with Decker's Porsche, workbench, and power tools and Rina's planting and potting station. They had soundproofed the space because the kid practiced at the oddest hours. But since he was homeschooled and was basically done with high school, they let him march to his own drummer. He wasn't even sixteen and had already gotten into Juilliard and early action at Harvard. Even if they were his legal guardians—which they weren't—there was really no guidance left to give him. At this point, they were just providing him with food, a safe shelter, and a little company.

"Tell me about your day," Rina said.

"Pretty routine except for the last half hour." Decker recapped his puzzling conversation with Wendy Hesse.

"That poor woman."

"She must be really hurting if she wants a homicide over suicide."

"Is that what the coroner ruled? Suicide?"

Decker nodded.

"So then . . . she just doesn't want to believe it."

"True. Usually the ominous signs are there but parents look the other way. I honestly believe that Wendy is dumbfounded." He smoothed his mustache. "You know when we first met and you were adamant about sending the boys to Jewish day school, I thought you were nuts. For what we were paying in tuition, we could have sent the boys to Lawrence or Bell and Wakefield, not a school housed in a one-story dilapidated building that doesn't even have a library and a computer lab."

Rina smiled. "Many people would have agreed."

"But I've gotta say, most of the kids we've met are nice. Granted, I'm seeing the worst of the prep school teens, but I don't think those places breed healthy attitudes. On balance, you did the right thing."

"The school, although disorganized and sorely lacking in resources, is a very kind place. Thank you for saying that."

Decker leaned back. "You talk to any of the kids today?"

"Of course, the boys are busy as usual. I did Skype with Hannah this morning. She was just going to bed. She'll probably be up in a couple of hours."

"I miss her." Decker looked sad. "Maybe I'll give Cindy a call. Find out what she's up to."

Rina smiled. "Grandchildren are always the anti-dote to what ails you."

"You want to take a ride over and see them?"

"You should ask Cindy first."

"Yeah, I guess I have to do that." Decker made a phone call and hung up grinning. "She said, come on over."

"Then let's go."

"What about Gabe?"

"I'll tell him we're going," Rina said. "He likes Cindy and Koby, but I have a feeling he'll decline. He wasn't himself today. Maybe it has to do with his mother. Anyway, when he gets like that, he retreats inward."

Decker took in her words. "Should I talk to him?"

"He'll just tell you everything's okay."

"I don't want him to feel like a stranger," Decker said. "But I don't do much to make him feel like a member of the family. I'd feel really guilty if I came home one day and found him in the same condition as Gregory Hesse."

Rina nodded. "I think his music is and always was his salvation."

"Is it enough?"

"I don't know. All I can tell you is he's function-ing well. He takes the bus twice a week to USC for his lessons, he did all his own college applications even though I offered to help, he went for his own interviews and auditions even though I offered to come with him, and he booked his own flights and hotel rooms even though I offered to do it. He's already guaranteed admission into Harvard and Juilliard. It seems to me like he wouldn't be planning his future if he didn't think he had one." Rina paused. "If you want to do something nice for him, take him out driving. That excites him."

"Okay, I'll take him out on Sunday."

"He really admires your Porsche."

"Uh, let's not carry this niceness thing too far. Being emotionally sensitive is one thing. The Porsche is quite another."

The Coffee Bean was about two miles from the Starbucks where Gabe had encountered Dylan and posse, hopefully out of their range of operation. Not that he expected to meet up with anyone else at six in the morning. The place was empty and that was just fine. He had chosen a padded leather seat in the back, after he bought a bagel and a large coffee as well as the *New York Times*. When he lived back east, he read the *Post*. It felt strange reading the intellectual paper when all he wanted to do was read "Weird but True" or "Page Six" to find out who was banging whom.

The café was about fifteen minutes away from his bus stop to USC. Tuesdays and Thursdays were lesson days with Nicholas Mark, and although he wasn't scheduled to meet with his teacher until eleven, he decided to get a jump on the day. He had slept fitfully last night. His mother's voice knocking around in his head . . .

He slathered cream cheese onto his bagel and started skimming through the news, which was even more depressing than his current life. A few minutes later, he felt the presence of eyes and looked up.

A kid in the Jewish school uniform. Not surprising since the place was a two-minute walk from the day school. She must have had mufflers on her feet since he hadn't heard a thing until she was standing over him, clutching her backpack as if it were armor.

Her smile was shy. "Hi."

"Hi," he answered. Upon a second glance, he realized that she was probably older than he had initially thought. She had a mocha complexion, a small, pointed chin, full lips, and big black round eyes topped with black eyebrows carefully arched and shaped. Her hair was equally as dark, very long and tied into a ponytail. She was actually cute, although her body wasn't much—two scoops of ice cream for a chest and not a curve in sight. "Did you need something?"

"Do you mind if I sit down?"

He was the only occupant in the entire place. He shrugged. "No, go ahead."

But she didn't sit. "I heard you play last year at graduation," she told him. "My older sister was in Hannah's class. You were . . ." She clutched her backpack to her chest. "Just . . . fantastic!"

Gabe said, "Thank you very much."

"I mean it was like . . ."

She didn't finish the sentence. Silence ensued. It was awkward.

"Thank you. I appreciate it." Gabe picked up his coffee cup and sipped it, his eyes slipping back to his paper.

"Do you like opera?" she blurted out.

Gabe put down the paper. "As a matter of fact, I do like opera."

"You do?" Her eyes got wide. "Well, that's good. Then at least these won't go to waste." She put down her backpack and started rummaging through it until she found what she was looking for—an envelope. She offered it to him. "Here you go."

He regarded her for a few moments, then took the envelope and opened it up. Tickets to *La Traviata* this Sunday at the Music Center. First row loge. "These are good seats."

"I know. They cost me a lot of my own money. Alyssa Danielli is playing Violetta. She's wonderful, so I'm sure it'll be wonderful."

"Then why aren't you going?"

"I was gonna go with my sister, but she flaked on me. I just couldn't compete with a pool party and the lure of Michael Shoomer."

"So why don't you find someone else to go with?"

"No one my age is going to want to spend their Sunday afternoon at the opera."

"What about your mom?"

"She's busy. She's not interested anyway. The only reason my sister agreed to go is I told her I'd clean her room. So I guess now I don't have to do it." She looked wounded. "You might as well use them. Take your girlfriend."

"I don't have a girlfriend."

"Well, then take a friend."

"I don't have any friends. But . . . I certainly will use a ticket if you're going to throw them away. Are you sure?"

"Positive."

"Then thank you very much." He handed her back the envelope with a single ticket.

"You're welcome." She heaved a big sigh.

Gabe tried to stifle a smile. "Would you like to go together?"

The kid got excited. "Do you have a car?"

"No, I'm only fifteen. But we can take the bus."

She looked horrified. "A bus?"

"Yeah, a bus. That's how you get around if you don't have access to a car." Her complexion darkened, and Gabe pointed to a chair. "Why don't you sit down? I'm getting a pain in my neck looking up at you . . . although it's not that far."

"I know. I'm a runt." She sat down and glanced over her shoulder, speaking softly as if they were conspiring. "Do you know how to get to the Music Center by bus?"

"I do."

"Where do you find a bus?"

"At a bus stop."

She bit her lip. "You must think I'm a doofus."

"No, but you're probably a pampered pooch who's been carted around her entire life."

Instead of taking offense, she nodded. "Carted everywhere except where I really want to go." She sighed. "I love Alyssa Danielli. Her voice is so . . . pure."

Gabe sat back in his chair and gave her face an honest appraisal. He admired passion in any form, but classical music was something he could relate to. "If you want to go to an opera so bad, just go."

"It's not that simple."

"Why not?"

"You don't understand Persian culture."

"Is there something in Persian genes that make them *not* like opera?"

"My father wants me to be a doctor."

"I'm sure there are doctors who are opera fans." He took a bite of his bagel. "You want some coffee or something?"

"I'll get it." She stomped away, but left her backpack behind. A few minutes later she was back with something foamy. A sheen of sweat coated her forehead. "People are starting to come in."

"That's good. It'll keep the place in business."

"I mean it's . . ." She glanced at her watch and sipped her coffee. "Is taking the bus dangerous?"

"I wouldn't go in the wee hours of the morning, but this is a matinee." Gabe rubbed his neck. "If you're going to continue to talk to me, could you please sit down?"

She sat.

He said, "Look . . . whatever your name is. How about if I give you directions by bus? If you're at the bus stop, then we'll go together. If not, I'll buy you a CD and write you a review."

She sighed. "Maybe we can go by cab."

"A cab is like twenty times the money."

"I'll pay for it."

Gabe stared at her. Who *was* she? "I'm not pleading poverty. *I'll* pay for the cab if you definitely go. Otherwise, I'm going to go by bus."

"How about this?" the girl said. "You'll pay for the cab if I go, and if I don't go, I'll pay you back."

Gabe shook his head. "This is getting very complicated."

"*Please?*" she implored.

"Fine." He rolled his eyes. "You'll pay me back for the cab if you crap out . . . which doesn't make any sense because I have to pick you up anyway and by that time, you should know whether or not you're going."

Her big eyes got even wider. "You *can't* pick me up at my house. I'll meet you a few blocks away."

"Aha." Gabe got it. "You're sneaking around your parents."

"Sorta."

"Jeez, it's not like you're going to a rave; it's a freakin' opera." When she didn't say anything, he said, "It's not just the opera; it's going with me to the opera. Because I'm not Jewish."

She stared at him. "You're not *Jewish*?"

"Nope. I'm Catholic."

"Oh God. My dad would kill me just for going with a white boy." She leaned over and spoke softly. "Why were you in a Jewish school if you're not Jewish?"

"It's a long story." He paused. "This isn't a good idea. I don't want to be responsible for getting you into trouble. Would you like your ticket back?"

"No, of course not. If you don't use it, it really will go to waste." She blew out air again. "I mean, it's just going to the opera, right?"

"Yes, it's just going to the opera. It is not a date." He studied her face again. "How old are you?"

"Fourteen."

"You look around ten."

"Thank you very much," she snapped. It was clearly something she heard all the time.

"You look young, but you're very cute." Gabe said it to mollify her, but he actually meant it. "This is what I'm going to do. I'm going to give you my phone number and you call or text me if you can make it." He waited a moment. "You have a cell, right?"

"Of course."

"So Persians can have cell phones—"

"Ha, ha!"

"Take down my cell number. Do you know my name?"

"Gabriel Whitman."

"Excellent." He gave the girl his number. "I'll take your phone number now. But to do that, I first need to know your name."

"Yasmine Nourmand." Pronounced Yaz-meen. She spelled it and then gave him her phone number.

"That's a very exotic name. What is your older sister's name?"

"I have three older sisters."

"The one that was in the class with Hannah."

"That's Sage. My other sisters are Rosemary and Daisy. Yasmine is the Hebrew of Jasmine."

"So Mom had sort of a botanical thing going."

Yasmine smiled and checked her watch. "I have to go. School starts at seven-thirty."

"I remember that. Why were you here so early?"

"Sometimes I come early to listen to my CDs." She pulled out six operas—two Verdi, two Rossini, and two Mozart. "I mean, I really love my parents. And I love my sisters. They're gorgeous and wonderful and everything. And I enjoy the regular pop stuff, too. But sometimes when I listen to my music—that no one else seems to like—I like being alone."

Her eyes were far away.

"It's my dream to see a real-life opera. And to hear someone as good as Alyssa Danielli." She hefted her backpack. "Thanks for offering to come with me."

"It's my pleasure."

"And thanks for not making fun of me."

"Well, I kinda did."

"Yeah, you kinda did." She gave him a wave and was off.

He returned his eyes to the paper, knowing full well that this was a mistake. But in talking to her, he suddenly realized how lonely he was.

She had awakened a sleeping lion.

Girls.

Chapter Four

Autopsy reports involving self-inflicted gunshot wounds were always grisly. The damage done by an up-close-and-personal weapon was horrendous. Details were even harder to read when the victims were young like Gregory Hesse. As Marge scanned the lengthy police file as well as what the coroner's examiner had to say, she didn't see anything out of the ordinary. All the signs of suicide were there: single bullet in the head, close-up burn mark on the temple, the position of the body with regard to the gun, stippling on the boy's right hand. She got up from her desk and knocked on Decker's open door. "Did you want to see Gregory Hesse's file?"

"Yeah, that would be great." He motioned her inside. Marge wore a light knit brown sweater and black slacks—much more comfortable than Decker's gray suit. Today he was wearing a thin black turtleneck so at least he didn't have to wear a tie. The captain had given his attire the once-over, asking if he was going Hollywood. "Anything I should be aware of?"

Marge sat down and laid the paperwork on his desk. "Most of it was plain depressing."

"What about the gun?"

"The files say it was a Ruger LCP .380."

"A mouse gun," Decker said.

"Mouse gun, ladies' gun—whatever it was, it did the trick. Oliver told me it was an older-model Ruger."

"How old?"

"I don't think he said. He's pulling it out of the evidence locker sometime today." She paused. "If everything seems consistent with a suicide, what's our next step?"

"Well, I can make a phone call to Mrs. Hesse and tell her there's nothing for us to pursue. Or I can make a phone call and tell her that I'll talk to some of Gregory's friends and teachers and try to find some clues as to what happened."

Marge nodded.

Decker said, "What's on your mind?"

"I know that she lives in the community we serve. So we are her employees in a very broad sense. But is that really our job—a psychological autopsy? Not that I mind doing it, but I don't want to get into areas that we're not familiar with."

"Valid point, so let me put it this way. When we do an investigation, we try to find the motive behind every crime. Technically suicide is a crime."

"I suppose every crime starts with a weapon," Marge said. "I'll see where Oliver is on that."

"Could you also get me a couple of phone numbers?" He flipped through his notes. "For Joey Reinhart and Kevin Stanger. You probably can get those by calling up Bell and Wakefield. I don't want to contact Wendy Hesse until we have something to say."

"The school might be more cooperative if I added a personal touch." Marge checked her watch—eleven. "I can go there right now."

"Sure. And while you're there, try to get a feel for the place."

Oliver knocked on the door and came in. "I just got some information on the Ruger used in the suicide. The gun was stolen from Dr. Olivia Garden who, according to our computers, is a sixty-five-year-old dermatologist practicing in Sylmar."

Decker pointed to the chair next to Marge, and Oliver sat down. Scott, always the dandy, was appointed today in a black shirt and tie, gray trousers, and a herringbone jacket. His shoes were black buffed leather loafers. "Did you contact the doctor?"

"I put a call into her secretary. Doctor was with a patient. Her lunch hour is from twelve-thirty to two. I'll just pop in and try to catch her then. Maybe Gregory Hesse was her patient. You know teenagers and acne. Could be he lifted it from her desk."

"The gun was stolen six years ago," Marge said. "Gregory would have been eight or nine."

"Right," Oliver said. "So it probably passed through a few hands since then."

"Was just her gun stolen or was it part of a larger burglary?"

"I don't know. I just plugged in the serial number and there it was."

"Where did the theft take place?"

"From her office," Oliver said.

"Her *office*. Interesting." Decker thought a moment. "Maybe she had problems with previous drug break-ins and felt she needed protection."

"When I speak to her, I'll ask her about it."

"Okay. Also find out who knew about the gun and who had access to it."

"Got it." He stood up and looked at Marge. "Want to come with me?"

"I'll go with you if you come with me to Bell and Wakefield. The Loo wants some phone numbers. Those kinds of things are easier to get if we show up in person."

Decker said, "And while you're at it, get Gregory Hesse's class schedule. At some later date, we may want to talk to his teachers."

"Sure, I'll come with you," Oliver said to Marge. He regarded Decker. "Is this Gregory Hess thing like a full-fledged investigation? I mean all signs point to the kid killing himself. Case closed."

"A fifteen-year-old boy shoots himself with a mouse gun stolen six years ago from a doctor's office. I'm a little curious. For now, let's say case still open."

The beep from his cell distracted Gabe's concentration . . . which was okay with him because he really wasn't playing very well.

Some days you hit it, some days you didn't.

He'd forgotten to turn off his phone. Why he kept it was still a mystery to him. Not many people called nowadays: the Deckers, his piano teacher who was usually switching times on him, and his father engaging him in thirty-second conversations. For the amount of minutes Gabe used per month, it didn't even pay to keep the line going except that it was more expensive to cancel the service than to keep it current.

It was a text from a local number that Gabe didn't recognize: *i'm coming with u on sunday.*

It was from the Persian girl. Yasmine. The smile that spread across his face was involuntary. He had been thinking about her the last couple of days. Not on-purpose thinking. That's the kind of thinking when you longed to keep the image fresh in your brain—like the last time he saw his mother. It wasn't like that . . . just that Yasmine had popped into his head from time to time.

His thumbs pecked across the keyboard of his phone.

g8. where do u want to meet?

She texted him back an address of where to meet her with the cab.

it's 3 blocks from my house. what time?

The show started at three. A taxi wouldn't take nearly as long as a bus, but he still wanted to allow a little breathing room because he was a stickler on punc-tuality.

is 1 ok?

a little early for me to get out. how about 2?

cutting it too close. 1:30 max.

ok.

A pause.

B there 1:30.

He wrote, *looking 4ward. Bye.*

bye.

He put down the phone. Then it beeped again.

Thx.

He smiled again. *ur welcome.*

This time he turned off the phone and went back to his piano. He stowed the Mozart piano sonata no. 11 in A major and instead chose Chopin—the polonaise in C-sharp minor, op. 26, no. 1, first movement—allegro appassionato.

His mood of the moment was very appassionato.

The banners hanging across the two-story buildings announced that Bell and Wakefield was currently celebrating thirty years of excellence. It was built when Marge had just come on as a rookie detective in the Foothill Division with Decker. The school's architecture had held up well because the style was classical: California mission with large leaded-glass windows, wood-trimmed doors, stucco walls, and red tiled roofs. The campus was set on acres of rolling lawns shaded by sycamores, eucalyptus, and California oak. Facilities included a library, a computer lab, and a faculty building along with a football field, a bank of tennis and basketball courts, plus an outdoor swimming pool. Cars in the student and guest parking included subcompacts, compacts, and lots of four-wheel drives from Ravs to Range Rovers. Faculty had their own dedicated lot.

Marge and Oliver arrived on campus at 11:30. The Administrative Building was the largest building on campus in size as well as height, and it hummed with activity. The walls were festooned with material—term papers that had received A+ grades, high-quality artwork, news articles, colored flyers, announcements, photographs, and one giant overstuffed complaint box. The Admission Offices took up the first floor. The largest of the rooms resembled a bank with a line of students standing on one side of the counter and the school employees sitting on the other side. Behind them was an open space of desks with computers. Lots of people were tapping on keyboards.

The two detectives waited in line and when they got up to the counter, Marge flashed her badge, asking a startled woman if she could speak to someone from the administration on a personal matter. Five minutes later, they were escorted into the office of the boys' vice principal. Dr. Martin Punsche, they were told, would be with them shortly. His office was small—a desk with a computer, four chairs, a bookshelf, and not much else. It did have a window with a view of the lawns.

Punsche appeared with an outstretched hand, welcoming them to Bell and Wakefield. He was a man in his fifties, broad shouldered and bald with a broken nose. Put a white shirt on his body and a whistle around his neck and he could have been the football coach. Instead he wore a blue shirt, gold tie, and gray slacks.

"Maggie told me it was a personal matter," Punsche said. "I hope it's not trouble. The school has been going through some difficult times. Have a seat."

The detectives sat down. "Difficult times?" Marge asked.

"You must know that one of our students met a terrible fate a couple of days ago."

"Gregory Hesse," Oliver said. "That's actually why we're here."

"I figured as much. Terrible, terrible thing. We've already held a school assembly about it. We've been encouraging our students to talk about it. I've also scheduled several psychologists and doctors to come and talk about suicide prevention. Our student presidents, Stance O'Brien and Cameron Cole, have set up a student hotline. Around a dozen of our seniors have volunteered to meet with the freshmen for an informal rap session during lunch. I'm so proud of how our students have mobilized."

Marge stared at him. The poor kid had just blown his head off, and the dude was a booster for school spirit. Did he ever turn it off?

Punsche placed his hands atop his desk. "So . . . how can I help you?"

Oliver straightened his tie. "We're still tying up a few loose ends with the case."

"What kind of loose ends?"

"Things that don't add up just yet."

Marge said, "They may add up later, but right now we're investigating a few things at Wendy Hesse's behest."

Oliver shrugged. "For starters, we need a few phone numbers."

"You mean phone numbers of our students?" When Marge nodded, Punsche said, "You know I can't just give out numbers without asking the parents."

"We're interested in Joey Reinhart, Gregory Hesse's best friend," Marge said. "We can get the number from Wendy Hesse—she's the one who told us about Joey— but the lieutenant didn't want to bother her. You can understand that."

Punsche stroked his hairless chin. "Why did Wendy Hesse contact you?"

"Like my partner said, some things are not quite adding up. We take all crime seriously, and suicide is a crime."

"It's a crime in only the most technical sense."

"That's the LAPD," Oliver said. "We're very technical."

Marge said, "We also found out some interesting things about another friend of Gregory's. A boy named Kevin Stanger. He transferred from Bell and Wakefield around six months ago at the beginning of the sophomore year. I'm assuming that you'd still have his address and phone number."

"Kevin Stanger." Again, he stroked his chin. "I'm sorry. I can't put a face to the name."

Marge said, "Maybe you don't know him, so I'll clue you in to what I heard. Kevin Stanger transferred because he was bullied."

Punsche shook his head. "If he were bullied here, I would have heard about it."

"You didn't hear about it," Oliver said. "But that doesn't mean it didn't happen."

"Look, I don't know everything, but I do know a lot. If we knew that a child was being bullied, we would deal with the situation quickly and efficiently. We have no patience for that kind of nonsense."

"So bullying doesn't go on here?"

"There are cliques. Although the school excels in academics, sports, and theater arts, it's still a high school filled with teenagers. There are popular kids and I'm sure they're not the most gracious to everyone. There are bound to be kids who feel like outcasts. But that's a far cry from bullying."

Marge tried a different approach. "I'm sure you've got an excellent feel for your students. Right now, all we're looking for is a couple of phone numbers. Heck, all we want is to bring a little, bitty piece of comfort to Wendy by nailing down a few details. Help us with that."

Punsche said, "I suppose I can get you the phone numbers. Kevin Stanger may take a few minutes because he's not current and is no longer in the computer."

"That's okay," Oliver said. "We can wait."

"If you can get us Gregory's class schedule, that would be helpful," Marge added.

"Surely you didn't come all this way just to get a few numbers and a class schedule," Punsche said.

Marge said, "Actually we did. We were in the neighborhood anyway. But while we're here, if there's anything else you can tell us about Gregory that might be helpful, please feel free to talk."

Oliver said, "Things like what he did, who'd he hang out with, what clubs he was in . . . what made him tick."

"This is embarrassing but I'll say it anyway." Punsche's cheeks pinkened. "I didn't really know the boy.

I never had any cause to become . . . involved with him. Usually, I deal with problems and problem boys. As far as I knew, Gregory fit in nicely."

"Is that opinion based on something concrete or the absence of problems?"

The VP hedged. "I'm sure I would have gotten to know him better. But when all this went down, I was . . . unaware that he was troubled."

Oliver said, "Since you didn't know him well, maybe you can direct us to someone who did."

Punsche seemed bothered. "Try some of his teachers. I'll get you that class schedule, and then if I were you, I'd just go down the list."

Chapter Five

I'd shoot myself if I had to be in high school for nine hours a day, five days a week." Oliver was looking over the class schedule. "Whatever happened to creative boredom?"

"That's why Hollywood is mostly remakes of old stuff." Marge was behind the wheel. They had finished up with Bell and Wakefield by one and were headed toward Dr. Olivia Garden's dermatology practice in Sylmar. "No ingenuity. And I'm not even talking redoing the classics. It's like sixties sitcoms or *Charlie's Angels.* Lowbrow stuff."

"There I disagree." Oliver looked wistful. "*Charlie's Angels* had redeeming virtues."

Marge smiled. "I told Lee Wang to take the Ruger to ballistics and see if it's been used in other crimes."

"How do you think Hesse got hold of it?"

"Beats me." Marge's cell rang. "Can you get that for me?"

"You could use Bluetooth."

"So you could hear all my personal stuff? No, thank you."

"Picky, picky." Oliver rooted through her purse and picked it up. "Detective Oliver."

The voice on the other side was female and hesitant. "I'm returning a call from Sergeant Dunn."

"She's driving right now. Who am I talking to?"

"This is Nora Stanger."

"Ah, thank you for calling back, Mrs. Stanger. I'm Sergeant Dunn's partner, Detective Scott Oliver. We're going over some details of Gregory Hesse's tragic suicide and wondered if we could talk to you. I understand your son, Kevin, was a friend of his?"

"The boys hadn't seen each other in a while."

"Yes, I know Kevin transferred out of Bell and Wakefield. I was hoping that your experience could shed some light on what happened. Gregory's mother, Wendy Hesse, is suffering, and any answers we could give her would be helpful."

The voice over the line was baleful. "That poor woman."

"She's really in the dark about what happened. And we don't know a lot about Bell and Wakefield. The administration, of course, is protective of the school. Maybe you can fill us in. My partner and I have an open schedule. What would work for you?"

"I . . . I have to talk to Kevin. At this age, I can't make decisions for him."

"You have Sergeant Dunn's number. Let me give you mine." Oliver rattled off some digits. "Le me know when it's convenient for you to meet us. And thanks for calling back."

"You're welcome." Nora cut the line.

Oliver stowed Marge's phone back in her purse. "She has to ask Kevin."

Marge nodded.

"What did you think about Punsche?"

"Glad-hander and a bullshit artist," Marge said. "But I believe him when he said that he wasn't aware about Kevin Stanger's problems."

"He must have known that the kid transferred."

"Maybe he knew about the transfer, but maybe not why. If the kid was bullied, I do think the school would have reacted."

"Maybe." Oliver thought a moment. "I wonder how much Nora Stanger knows about her son's problems."

"Enough to pull him out of the school," Marge said. "Kevin's the one we really want to talk to. He's the one who can name names."

Dr. Olivia Garden, M.D., and Dr. Gary Pellman, M.D., ASDP, was a medical corporation. The office was in a one-story strip mall that shared a parking lot with a doughnut shop, a sandwich shop, and a Laundromat. Marge found street parking and fed the meters.

Once inside the office, Oliver knocked on the sliding glass partition. The woman behind the door was in her sixties, with short gray hair, a round face, and brown eyes. She wore no makeup but her skin was baby smooth—a walking advertisement for the practice. She had on a white coat, and a stethoscope dangled from her neck.

"The office is officially closed until two, but maybe I can help you."

"We're looking for Dr. Garden," Marge said.

"You found her." After Marge presented her badge, the doctor said, "Come around the side." She opened the door. "Let's go into my office. I'm just finishing lunch."

"We're sorry to interrupt," Marge said.

"No problem." She ushered them inside her personal domain. "Pull up a chair." She sat behind her desk and took a bite out of a half sandwich. "So what's this about?"

Oliver said, "About six years ago, you reported your gun stolen—a .380 Ruger."

"You found it?"

"Yes, we did. It was recently used in the suicide of a fifteen-year-old—"

Olivia Garden gasped. "The one in the papers?"

"Yes. His name was Gregory Hesse. Did you happen to know him or his family?"

"No." The doctor shook her head. "Oh my, my, my. How'd that poor boy get my gun?"

"That's why we're here," Oliver said. "We have a couple of questions about the burglary."

Marge pulled out a notebook. "We understand that the gun was taken from your office."

"Yes, it was—a long time ago. . . ."

"Was it only the gun taken or was that theft part of a larger burglary?"

"No, I believe it was only the gun."

Oliver said, "Why did you have a gun in your office?"

A pause. The doctor said, "As I recall, there had been a rash of medical office break-ins in the area. The police never arrested anyone, but we held some neighborhood watch meetings and we all thought that it was some hype looking for drugs. Anyway, the tipping point for me was when a nurse who was working late was knocked over the head and had to go to the hospital. She turned out to be all right, but I was shaken up. My husband suggested I get a gun because I often work late."

Oliver said, "So how long did you have the gun before it was stolen?"

"Not too long at all. I'd like to say around six months."

"Did you get another gun?"

"I did not." She took another bite of her sandwich. "After the theft, I felt that I didn't want to contribute to the vast arsenal of black market weapons. I figured I was better off with a baseball bat. But luckily, it never came to anything. The burglaries stopped, and we figured the thief went on to greener pastures."

"Did you realize right away that your gun had been stolen?" Marge asked.

"Good question. I kept it in a lockbox in my bottom drawer and I didn't open up the box very often. It could have been stolen months before I discovered it."

"Who knew you had a gun?" Oliver asked.

"No one besides my family. I never did tell my employees. I didn't want to frighten anyone."

"What about your children?"

"My sons are thirty-nine and forty-four. They've been out of the house for years. I certainly wouldn't have told them about a gun. They would have worried about me. We're not a gun family. It's just at that time, I felt vulnerable."

Oliver said, "Is it possible that one of your employees might have stolen it?" When she looked skeptical, he said, "Did you have any problems with someone who worked for you?"

She shook her head no. "I've had the same people for years. I think the last time I actually had to let go of someone was a decade ago. It wasn't someone I knew. It was a stranger. I'm sure of it."

Marge said, "I would say that was probably true if the gun had been part of a larger burglary. But how would it be that a thief found the weapon, but took nothing else?"

She didn't answer and finished her sandwich. "What are you going to do with the gun?"

"Right now, it's regarded as evidence."

"You can keep it. I don't want it anymore, especially after what you just told me." She munched a carrot and looked at the clock. "I have to make a few phone calls before the office reopens. I hope you don't mind."

The two detectives stood up. Marge said, "Thanks for making the time. I must say, Dr. Garden, that your skin is beautiful. Do you have a special secret?"

"I won't tell you my guarded secrets." The woman smiled broadly. "But I'll give you a hint to one of my secret weapons. It starts with B and ends with X. And if you can't figure that out, you're probably a Luddite."

She said she bought the gun for protection and six months later found it had been stolen," Marge said. She and Oliver were in Decker's office. It was around four in the afternoon. "She's positive that no one else knew about the weapon other than her family."

Oliver asked, "Did Lee hear back from ballistics?"

"If he has, he hasn't called me with anything," Decker answered.

"I can't believe a stolen gun would have been floating around for six years without it being used for something criminal."

Marge said, "The bigger question is, how did it get into Gregory Hesse's hands?"

"And we're no closer to a solution on that one. Mrs. Stanger hasn't called back. I don't know if she will. She seemed reluctant to talk." Oliver regarded Decker. "Maybe if someone with more authority called, she'd relent."

"How close were her son and Gregory?"

"Don't know," Marge said.

"But we do know that Gregory and Joey Reinhart were best friends. Maybe we concentrate on him."

Marge said, "We left messages on the house machine and Joey's cell. No call back."

"When did you leave a message?"

"About two hours ago."

"Give me his address." Decker stood up. "It'll stop by on my way home."

Decker always had reservations about working on Friday night. And with this case, there was no immediate urgency—just a desire to help out a distraught woman. There was no real justification to be parked across the street from Joey Reinhart's house when he should be home inaugurating the Sabbath. He rationalized it by telling himself that it was only six in the evening. He had promised Rina that he'd be no later than seven. He was just about to get out of the car when a scrawny teen came out of the house, jiggling car keys. He was hunched over and wore a windbreaker and jeans. He opened the driver's door of a blue Ford Escort, got inside, and began to inch out of the driveway.

One of the kid's taillights was out.

Perfect.

Decker turned on the ignition and followed him several blocks until the kid turned onto the main street.

A minute later, Decker pulled out the red light and stuck it onto the roof of his car. The kid dutifully pulled curbside. When Decker approached the Escort, the kid rolled down the window, regarding Decker with fear.

"May I take a look at your license?"

The boy's hands were shaking as he handed over his wallet. "What did I do?"

Decker took the license and gave him back the wallet.

Joey Harmon Reinhart. Five eleven, one fifty (*when pigs fly*, Decker thought), brown eyes, brown hair. His date of birth put him at sixteen and three months. Decker gave the kid back his license and motioned him out of the car and onto the sidewalk.

The kid complied. He was so nervous, his knees almost buckled.

"Your left taillight is out."

"I didn't know. I'll get it fixed right away."

Decker studied him. "You know, Joey, if someone pulls you over in an unmarked car, don't get out. Stay inside your car with the doors locked and ask for ID. I don't care how belligerent the guy on the other side of the window gets. Any real officer won't take offense. Getting out before you know what's going on is dumb."

The poor kid just nodded.

Decker took out his wallet and showed him his badge and registration. "Even this could be fake. So the next step is to use your cell and call my name into LAPD. Because I could be anyone, right?"

The kid nodded like a bobblehead.

"Who does it say I am?"

The kid read the registration. "Lieutenant Peter Decker."

"So then you call up LAPD and get my badge number."

"You want me to do that now?"

Decker smiled. "Don't bother. I am a police lieutenant." He regarded the license. "Where are you going?"

"Just hanging out with some of my friends."

Decker gave him back the license. "I'll let you go with a warning, but get that fixed."

"Yes, sir. Right away. I mean, first thing tomorrow. I think all the garages are closed—"

"Just get it fixed." Decker took in the kid's fearful eyes. "You know, Joey, I recognize your name."

"You do?"

"Yeah, you were a friend of Gregory Hesse's, right?" The boy didn't answer. "One of my detectives left a message on your cell about Gregory Hesse. You haven't called him back. Neither has your mom or dad. Any reason for that?"

The kid started shaking in earnest. Even in the dark, Decker could see the ashen complexion. The last thing he wanted was for some teenager to whine to his parents about police brutality.

"Don't worry about it," Decker said. "I'll call your parents again."

"No, no, don't do that!" the boy implored. "I was gonna call, but it was already like Friday night and I figured no one was in."

"The police do work on the weekends."

"Yeah, of course. I know. That's stupid." He hit his head. "Greg was my best bud. We can talk about it. Not now. It's not a good time, I mean place. I mean, place or time."

Decker said. "Give me a time that's good for you and your parents."

"I'd rather leave my parents out of it."

"Any reason why?"

"You know how it is . . . they know stuff, but they don't know everything."

Decker regarded the teen's face. "Joey, do you believe that Greg committed suicide?"

The boy licked his lips. "I . . . I don't know."

"Was Greg upset lately?"

"Not upset. Different."

"Can you define different?"

"Distracted. Something was on his mind."

"Any ideas?"

"Nothing that I can put my finger on."

Decker said, "How about we talk on Sunday? That way it doesn't interfere with your schoolwork. Do you want to come to the station house?"

"That would work. Can we make it at eleven? No . . . sorry." He banged his head. "I'm so messed up. That's Greg's memorial. It's gonna last a while. You want to meet on Saturday?"

"That won't work for me. How about later Sunday afternoon, four or five?"

"Five would be okay."

Decker handed the boy his card. "If you get hung up, call this number. Where's the memorial?"

"First Presbyterian on Tanner Road."

"I'll stop by." Decker scribbled something down on his notepad. "Here." He handed the boy a piece of paper. "This is for the taillight if you get pulled over again. It says I let you go with a warning and you're going to get it fixed over the weekend."

"Thank you, sir." The teen looked at Decker, but didn't say anything.

"What's on your mind?"

"Um . . . did you really just happen to know my name or were you, like, following me or something?"

"Your taillight is broken, Joey." Decker smiled. "Don't look a gift horse in the mouth."

Chapter Six

From the backseat of a cab that reeked of tobacco, Gabe texted her at 1:23 in the afternoon.

I'm here.

A minute later, Yasmine texted back: *running a few minutes L8. B there soon.*

A few minutes stretched to five minutes. Compulsive and punctual, Gabe was particularly antsy when waiting.

As a young child, he was always waiting: for his mom to finish up at her school, for her to finish her homework, for her to cook for him, for her to read to him, for her to tuck him into bed. Mom was always busy, busy, busy.

The five minutes turned to ten, then to fifteen. At 1:45, he texted Yasmine again.

It's getting L8.

sorry. B right there.

It was only in retrospect that he realized how hard his mother had been working. Every spare minute of her time was taken up with her education or making ends meet. He never knew when she actually slept because she was always up before he was and went to bed after him. When he was a preschooler, they lived in a shithole studio apartment in Chicago with minimal heating in the winter. He distinctly remembered being smothered under a pile of blankets while he slept. He hated the weight. It made him feel like somebody was on top of him. But as soon as he took off one or two blankets, he was freezing. He could vaguely remember the warmth of his mother's body, sliding into their shared bed, all of it in a fog of childhood and sleepiness.

It wasn't until he was around five that Chris came into the picture.

No matter how he now felt about his dad, Gabe felt gratitude for Chris's intervention. As soon as he came on the scene, they moved into a two-bedroom apartment and life became livable. They not only had more food, they had better food—chicken, fruit and vegetables, and even cookies—a far cry from his previous diet of milk, white bread, peanut butter, and macaroni.

In the back of his mind, he remembered eating a lot of noodles before then. Sometimes he'd eat noodles for days. Most of the time, Mom joined him, but there were times where she fed him and just watched him eat. He realized even at the age of two or three that Mom wasn't eating with him. He remembered thinking that maybe she was hungry and he should share. But he was so hungry himself. And before he knew it, he had eaten up his entire bowl and drank all of his milk. And his mom would kiss his head and tell him he was a good boy. And those nights, he never saw her eat anything except drink coffee.

He sighed.

After disappearing from his life for almost an entire year, she had reached out to him. And he had blown her off. He suddenly felt ashamed, and when he felt guilty, he became moody.

Where the hell was the little girl? This was a bad idea. He became even tenser.

After Chris appeared, they never went hungry again. They had heat, they had air-conditioning, and he had the greatest luxury of them all—a piano.

Chris had taken him to Paris six weeks ago for New Year's. Being with his dad was always like being with a powder keg with a very long lit fuse. It would eventually go off, but you never knew when. Gabe had been polite and quiet and for once, his dad decided to behave himself. The two of them actually had a pleasant time.

Not that they were around each other all that much. Chris usually slept all morning while he was out taking in the city, long walks by himself, snapping iconic architecture on his camera. They'd usually meet in the afternoon and take in a museum and then they'd go to dinner and/or a concert. Then Gabe would go back to his room while his father trawled for women.

Trying them out one by one by one. The age of consent was younger in France, and Chris took advantage of the more liberal law, screwing girls that would have landed his ass in jail in the States. All in all, his dad went through around fifteen girls in ten days. Sampling the merchandise was how he put in. There was a tacit understanding that Gabe could take what he wanted, but that would have only led to complications. So he sequestered himself in his hotel room every night and looked at the varieties of porn offered on the French Internet.

In the end, Chris had offered only one girl a job. She was a beautiful but drug-addicted nineteen-year-old. He had bought her a coach ticket on the cheapest airline he could find while Gabe, Chris, and Chris's current girlfriend, Talia, flew back first class on Air France.

"What are the chances she'll actually come work for you?" Gabe asked him.

"Fifty-fifty."

She showed up two weeks later. Such spoke to the power of Chris's charm.

When Gabe's watch read two, he became pissed. He had already racked up twenty dollars in waiting charges and she was nowhere in sight. He told the cabdriver to hold on for another moment and got out of the taxi, texting while pacing the sidewalk.

Where are u!!!!

Sorry.

Fuck! They were going to be late. He hated being late. It set his teeth on edge. Finally, at 2:20, he saw her running down the block. If he wasn't so furious, he would have laughed because she was comical. Red faced, she was running on heels, wearing a mini black cocktail dress that was tight on her nonexistent hips, and a black sweater with an old-fashioned furry collar. Her hair was pinned up in a kind of formal ball gown style. She was holding a beaded evening bag. His dress? A denim shirt over a black cotton tee, khakis, and vans.

She waved to him.

He didn't wave back.

When she got to the cab, she said, "I'm so sorry—"

"It's really late. Let's get out of here."

She went in first, and then he slid in beside her and slammed the door shut.

Hard.

"Go, go, go," he barked to the driver—a Russian who spoke with a thick accent. "Take the 405 to the 101 east that turns into the 134. Take that to the 5 south until you hit the 110 south. Get off at 1st."

"Hokay."

"We need to get there in a half hour."

"That is impossible."

"Do it and I'll make it worth your effort."

"You the boss."

The driver punched the accelerator and pitched them backward. Yasmine let out a slight gasp, but he ignored her. He sat back in the bench seat, fuming inwardly, his folded arms across his chest.

"I'm sorry," Yasmine told him.

He didn't answer. Then he said, "What took you so long?"

"I told my mom I gave back the tickets. So I had to wait until my mom and sisters left for shopping and Michael Shoomer's party. Then I had to get ready."

Get ready for what?

He glanced at her. She was wearing a ton of makeup, stockings, and fucking pearls—like it was a coming-out party. Even those girls look so dorky. She looked like she was playing dress-up with her mother's clothing. He glanced away.

Nervously, she fingered her necklace. "I'm sorry."

"Don't matter to me," Gabe told her. "*I've* seen opera. Although I hate to be seated late. Everyone looks at you and you're climbing over people. It's so rude to the performers."

She was red faced and still panting. Her eyes swept over his body and she was quiet. When she spoke, her voice was filled with self-loathing. "I'm totally over-dressed."

Gabe said nothing and continued to stew. She turned and sat peering out the side window of the cab.

Traffic was light. They were making decent time.

Finally Gabe said, "Opera attracts a lot of different people. People dress anywhere from jackets and ties to jeans. Don't worry about it."

She continued to stare out the window.

They rode another five minutes in silence. Gabe suddenly softened. What was the point of being nasty? That was his father's domain. He said, "You look nice."

She started to say something, but changed her mind.

Gabe said, "Really, Yasmine. You look very nice."

She faced him for the first time. Her eyeliner was slightly smudged. "I'm really sorry I'm so late. My family is always late. I should have warned you. If you wanted me to come at one, you shoulda said twelve. I thought going to the opera was a real fancy thing."

"Sometimes it is." Gabe said to the taxi driver, "Can't you go any faster?"

"I already go sixty-five."

"Go seventy-five. There's no one in front of you."

"You pay for my ticket?"

"Yes, I'll pay for your ticket."

"You the boss."

Again the cab shot forward. Gabe checked his watch. They had about a half hour to go and were about a half hour away. "Nothing in L.A. is formal, especially a matinee."

"Now I know. I've never been to the opera. I've never even seen any kind of live stage performance."

"Your parents don't believe in culture?"

"They have culture, just not American culture. In Iran, I'm sure my father was very cultured. He didn't learn English until he was thirty. Why would he go to the theater here? All the nuances would be lost on him."

"Point well-taken. That was rude. Sorry."

She fidgeted with the beads on her evening bag. "I look ridiculous."

He tried out a smile. "No one's going to be looking at you because we'll be stumbling through the dark when we come in."

"Sorry I made you miss everything."

"We won't miss *everything*. We'll just have to wait until there's a natural interlude before they'll seat late-comers. It's no big deal to me. I've seen *La Traviata* before."

"You have?"

"Yeah, I saw it about four years ago at the Met."

Her made-up eyes got wide. "You did?"

"Yeah. I used to live in New York."

"Oh golly." She sat back and sighed, closing her eyes. "That's my dream."

"To live in New York?"

"No, to go to the Met." She sat up. "Who sang Violetta?"

"I've got to think. It was a while ago . . . I think I saw Celine Army."

"She's great!" She faced him, her eyes not quite meeting his. "But Alyssa Danielli is better."

"I don't know about better. They're different."

"Well, I like Danielli's voice better. It's sweeter."

"I'll go with you on that one." He regarded her made-up face with her smeared eyeliner. "How does someone who's never heard a live concert come to have such a discerning ear?"

She shrugged. "I'm an alien."

Gabe held back a smile. "Liszt used to introduce Chopin by saying that he was from another planet, so maybe that's not so bad."

"Maybe." Yasmine pulled out a mirror and lipstick from her purse. When she saw her face, she became horrified. "Oh, my God! I look like a freak!"

"You look fine—"

"I'm totally embarrassing . . . like I came off a binge in Intervention." She pulled out a premoistened lotion wipe from her purse and started blotting her eyes. All that did was make it worse. Her lower lip began to tremble. "God, I'm a mess."

She began to attack her face with the towelette, taking off gobs of gook. With each swipe, she smeared more and more makeup. Tears began to trickle down her cheek.

Gabe rolled his eyes. "Stop, stop, stop." He took the wipe from her. "Just calm down. You look fine. Hold still." Carefully, he started removing the paint from her skin until it was gone. "There you go."

With trepidation, she looked in the mirror and said nothing.

"I don't know why you'd want to cover your face in all this shit," Gabe told her. "You're much cuter without it."

"I told you Persians dress up for occasions. Besides, now I look around ten."

"But a very cute ten."

She finally smiled and then carefully applied some lip gloss. "Thanks for bearing with me."

Gabe shrugged. "You know, as long as you're making changes, you should take your hair down. No one our age wears their hair like that unless they're in a bridal party."

She made a sour face and started pulling bobby pins out of her hair.

"Need help?" he asked.

"I think you've done quite enough, thank you—"

"You're gonna tear your hair if you keep yanking on it like that." He reached toward her, but she backed away. He rolled his eyes. "Hold still. I'm trying to help you, okay?"

She suddenly stopped, and her shoulders sagged in defeat. "Do whatever you want."

Never say that to a guy. He stifled a smile. "You've got a lot of hair."

"I can see you know nothing about Persian girls. We all have lots of hair and much of it in unwanted places."

He let out an unexpected laugh. "Ever think about stand-up?"

"Glad I'm amusing."

"Hold still." He closed the distance between them as he carefully picked bobby pins out of her hair, one by one by one. His face was inches from her. He could taste her breath. He inhaled her perfume. Her dress was a scoop neck that had exposed her collarbones.

After he took out all the clips, he pretended to smooth out her hair, letting his fingers dance over her bony protrusions. He raked his fingers through the long strands—downy soft, black and wavy. He pulled out a few loose tresses from the back of her sweater, feeling the nape of her neck.

And there it was: that all-too-familiar jolt below his waistline. Not that his pants were tight, but he was tall and, lucky him, he was proportional. All she had to do was look down to see it. Thankfully, she was too naive to notice. It was going to go to waste, but it did feel good to get a buzz from something other than porno.

"There you go." He laid the strands over her shoulders and sat back. "Now you look hot."

"Yeah, right!" Yasmine turned away. It was hard for her to look at his face without blushing. He was the most gorgeous boy she had ever seen in her entire life.

Gabe checked his watch and became irritated again. Which was good but it was hard to be aroused and angry at the same time. He tapped his foot as the taxi sped to its destination. He checked his watch as they approached the Music Center. By the time the taxi pulled over, they had five minutes to go.

They were at the Ahmanson Theatre side of the block instead of the Dorothy Chandler Pavilion where the opera was. Rather than redirect the cabbie, it was quicker to run it.

Gabe peeled out five twenties for a sixty-two-dollar bill. "Thanks." He threw open the door. "Let's go, let's go, let's go."

He began to run across the pavement, assuming she was with him. But a moment later, when he looked over his shoulder, she was twenty paces behind. Her dress was too tight to allow unrestricted movement and her heels too high for her to run with any speed. He stopped and grabbed her hand, dragging her along, hearing the *click, click, click* of her heels.

"How much did you tip that guy?" she asked.

"I dunno. Who cares?"

"I'm splitting the bill with you so I care."

"I said I'd pay for it, if you came . . . even though you were forty-five minutes late."

She was panting. "I said I'll pay half—"

"Forget it!" He pulled her forward. "Let's go, let's go!"

They made it to the entry at 3:04.

The lights were giving their final on and off blink, indicating that the show was about to start. Over the speakers, he could hear the orchestra tuning.

He started bounding up the steps, taking two at a time with Yasmine in tow, but her weight was dragging him down. He turned around and saw the problem. Her mouth was agape. She was gawking upward. "Look at the size of those chandeliers!"

"Yeah, they'll still be here at intermission." He yanked her forward. "*C'mon!*"

They made it inside just as the lights were dimming. He ran past the usher telling her he knew where their seats were.

Stepping over people.

Excuse me, excuse me, excuse me, excuse me.

Finally, he found the seats.

"Turn off your phone," he told her.

"Right."

Gabe slumped backward in his chair and exhaled out loud. He glanced at Yasmine who was unfazed by their in-the-nick-of-time arrival and seemingly unscathed by his churlish behavior. As soon as the orchestra launched into the overture, she sat at attention with her knees pressed together, her hands gripping her beaded purse, her body pitched slightly forward as if there was something to see besides a velvet curtain.

Unbelievable!

After several breaths, he rolled his shoulders and started to relax. They were in the first row of the loge so he had the luxury of a little more legroom for his six-foot frame. He sat back, spread his legs apart, and dropped his hands into his lap.

By accident, his knee touched hers. He pulled his legs together.

She glanced at his face and gave him an ear-to-ear grin, mouthing a silent *thank you* before returning her eyes to the stage.

He raised his eyebrows, a small smile of his own settling across his lips. He made himself comfortable in the seat, slouching back with his arms folded across his chest. Slowly his legs fell open until once again his knee found hers.

This time he kept it right where it was.

Chapter Seven

Since the station house was quiet, Decker was planning to rip through some of last week's paperwork, but he couldn't concentrate; his mind was still on Gregory Hesse's memorial service. A giant blowup of the boy's face had been strung across the altar, young eyes without a hint of the disaster to come. To a packed church, the minister delivered wrenching prose about a life cut short by the deepest secrets of the heart. He had to stop several times to compose himself. Then friends and family spoke, dredging up memories about a child too young for the past tense.

The service ended at twelve, and the reception lasted another hour. Decker did note that there were a lot of kids in attendance. After waiting in line to offer condolences to the parents, Decker figured he made the right move by coming to the service because Wendy Hesse squeezed his hand.

Please don't forget about my son.

"Knock, knock." Rina was at his door, holding a paper bag. "Room service."

"Sit down." He grinned. "What'd you bring me?"

"Cold roast sandwich on rye with horseradish and mustard. I have a meeting at school in twenty minutes. In the meantime, I thought I'd do what I do best and that's feed you."

"You do a lot of things extremely well, including feeding me."

She sat down. "And you will be home by seven, right?"

"Yes, I'll be there." Koby and Cindy were coming over with the babies for dinner. "Are you sure you don't want to go out?"

"If we went out, none of us would be able to eat. So I cooked. Even if none of us eat, it's still more cost-efficient than going out."

"No one cooks as good as you do. What are you making?"

She gave him the menu: roasted veal breast stuffed with rice pilaf and dried fruit, green beans, whipped yams, and peach pie for dessert. His mouth was watering even as he ate his sandwich. "Try to be on time."

"I will not try, I will be on time. Look around this place. I'm the only one crazy enough to be here Sunday afternoon. Where's Gabe?"

"He went to the opera. He said he'll be home by dinner."

"The boy is an enigma, but he knows a good meal."

"How'd the memorial service go?"

Decker gave her a recap. "Actually I'm here to talk to Gregory's best friend. He's a little odd. Or maybe I made him nervous when I pulled him over."

"Y'think?" When Decker made a face, Rina said, "What struck you as odd?"

"He's holding back."

"That's not odd, that's cautious."

"Since when have you been hired as his defense attorney?" The intercom beeped, the receptionist informing Decker that Joey Reinhart was on line two. "Hi, Joey, this is Lieutenant Decker."

"Uh, I could make it a little earlier."

"Sure. What time?"

"I'm actually right outside the station house."

"Go inside and I'll come get you." Decker put the receiver back in the cradle and stood up. "My interview showed up early."

"I've got to go anyway." She stood up and gave him a peck on the lips. "Today we're discussing whether to install a vending machine or to set up a snack bar and sell our own food to the kids."

"What's the issue?"

"Well, if we let a vending machine company provide the food, there could be potential problems with kashrut. But the pro is that they handle everything and just send us a check. Plus we don't have to have someone manage it. If we sell our own snacks, we make more money and kashrut isn't a problem. But then we have liabilities issues and health department issues and we have to find someone to run the snack bar. Yes, it seems trivial, but these kinds of niceties go a long way with the kids."

"I get it. Ever since we put in a professional coffee/cappuccino machine to go along with our candy dispenser, everyone's been much happier."

"So there you go." Rina smiled. "Just goes to show you. Never underestimate the power of caffeine and sugar."

Even layered in a bulky, hooded sweatshirt and baggy jeans, the kid was all limbs and bones. Decker took the boy into an interview room, setting him up with a glass of water and a candy bar. The kid said, "I got the taillight fixed."

"Great."

"Thanks for not giving me a ticket."

"No problem. Glad you got it taken care of." Decker pulled out a portable tape recorder. "Do you mind if we record the conversation? It's standard procedure. No one has a perfect memory."

"Sure, go ahead."

Decker gave the introduction, the name of the person he was talking to, the time and the date. "Thanks for coming in."

"Sure." Joey interlaced his long fingers and shrugged. "What's there to say?"

"Gregory's mom is completely in the dark about what happened. It caught her off guard."

"Tell me about it."

"You didn't see it coming, either?"

The boy looked doleful. "No."

Decker said, "Tell me about Gregory Hesse. What was he like?"

Joey's eyes darkened. "It's hard to describe a person that you've known forever. Greg was Greg."

"What did you two do together?"

Another shrug. "We hung out . . . went to movies, played video games. We always got along. We're both kinda nerdy . . . like you can't tell. I'm more the typical math/science guy. Greg was great in math also, but he liked English. Reading and writing came easy to him.

He used to help me with my essays." Joey bit his lip. "He was a smart dude."

"You have other friends in common?"

"Yeah, we have group—Mikey, Brandon, Josh, Beezel. If you're going to survive at B and W, you need buddies."

"What happens if you don't have buddies?"

"You're screwed. B and W is not a nice place. But if you don't come across as desperate, you can get by and get a good education."

"What happened with Kevin Stanger?"

"Oh man, poor Kev." He shook his head. "Survival of the fittest, you know. Kev couldn't hack it."

"Why not?"

"You know, not all nerds are smart. That was Kevin's problem. He was dorky without having any brains to back him up. It made him a target."

"Guys were beating on him?"

"Nah, it's more subtle. They just crowd you, man. Like you're walking along and suddenly there're a dozen of them walking next to you, flicking the back of your head or groping you or asking for money, which you give them. But even afterward, they don't let up. With Kevin, it went on day after day after day."

"He didn't go to the administration with his problems?"

"You do that, it gets worse. Best thing to do is ride it out and hope they find some other target. Crowding is especially anxiety provoking because inside you're thinking that any moment, it's gonna turn violent."

"That's what they call it? Crowding?"

"Yeah, a group of guys and girls just get in your face."

"How many?" Decker asked.

"Anywhere from four or five to upward. And since they're not really hurting you, who are you going to whine to? It's just all about mastery—like who's the boss."

"Who are they?"

"Just jerk-offs," Joey said. "It's stupid for me to name names because once you become a target, it's like the word gets out and you're fair game for everyone. I get by just fine. No offense, but I'm not going to screw myself over."

"They wouldn't know the source, Joey. We could keep it private."

"Find someone else. It wouldn't help you anyway, because Greg didn't have a problem. He could work it." Joey appeared lost in thought. "We both do tutoring—which is also why I'm not naming names. I have to pay for my car, and gas is expensive. Tutoring brings in good money."

"I understand. Tell me about Greg and his tutoring."

"I wouldn't swear to it, but I think Greg was doing some heavy tutoring."

"As in writing papers for some seniors?"

"Nah, he couldn't get away with that. It was more like . . . filling up the space. Senior theses are a minimum of thirty pages. That's a lot of writing for most people."

Decker nodded.

"There's nothing evil with that. I mean most of the kids at B and W have been getting tutored for years: from professional teachers, SAT tutors, college kids. It's well known that if you do a term paper at school, like forty million people have already looked it over before you turn it in. B and W has strict grading policies. You're expected to perform at a college level—which never made sense to me. Why do you need high school if you're already at a college level? But you know how it is. The competition is fierce."

Decker scratched his head. His own kids were past the rat race, but he remembered all too well the stress associated with getting into top-tiered universities. Gabe was the only teen Decker knew who wasn't nervous about college. So basically it took a musical genius to go through the process without anxiety.

"If Greg was doing well, Joey, why do you think he took a gun to his head?"

Joey's eyes watered. "It's a mystery."

"You told me he was acting different lately."

The kid paused. "Just that the past couple of months, he became obsessed with his video camera. At first, it was okay, but then it gets annoying to have a camera in your face while you're eating a hot dog."

"What was Greg recording?"

"He claimed he was just documenting the lives of typical teenagers."

Decker thought a moment. "When Greg started filming, did he start distancing himself from you and your group? Did he start hanging with different friends?"

"Not that I could tell. I mean he didn't start hanging with the bohemians."

"Who are the bohemians?"

"Ah, you know the type—artsy-fartsy, weird dress, and soooooo intellectual. They give you this crap about how formal education is worthless and the real education is on the streets. Which means they're stupid. I mean, give me an effing break! Anyone who goes to B and W is a spoiled brat. I mean all those so-called tough guys wouldn't last a day on the streets."

"Who are the tough guys?" When Joey waved him off, Decker said, "Did you ask Greg why he started videotaping?"

"He said it was fun . . . that it took the tedium out of high school." Joey didn't speak for a moment. "I don't know why, but I got the feeling that maybe the hobby had to do with a girl."

"Did you ask Greg about it?"

"I did. He denied it, said if he had a girlfriend I'd be the first to know so he could lord it over me."

"Girls can lead you in all sorts of directions," Decker said. "Is your theory a guess or are you thinking of someone specific?"

"I've gone through the roster of possibilities in my head. I can't come up with anyone."

"What about your sister?" Decker said.

"My sister?" He made a face. "You mean Tina?"

"His mother once picked him up from your house. She said there were girls there and when she asked Gregory about it, he said they were friends of your sister."

"Tina's like a kid." When Decker didn't say anything, Joey said, "Nah . . . impossible. And even if they did flirt—which I never saw—she certainly wouldn't be the reason why Greg did what he did. She couldn't possibly inspire that much passion."

"What about her friends?"

"I can't see it." Joey shook his head. "If you want me to ask her, I will."

Decker thought a moment. He really didn't have any good reason to start questioning a bunch of thirteen-year-old girls. "Whatever you're comfortable with." He focused in on Joey's eyes. "So again, what do you think is the reason behind the suicide?"

"I dunno, Lieutenant, and that's a fact."

"Do you think Greg could have gotten into drugs?"

"I don't think so."

"Did you guys light up together?"

Joey turned bright red. "Occasionally on weekends, and nothing heavy. Maybe a joint between, like, four of us."

Decker nodded. "Could Greg have gotten in deeper?"

"Greg never acted like he was out of control with anything." He regarded Decker's face. "Don't you test the blood for drugs in an autopsy?"

"Absolutely, but it takes a couple of weeks. Let's go back to Greg and the possibility of a girl. I'm curious as to why you'd throw that out as a possibility."

His eyes were doing a dance. "He smelled better." A sip of water. "You know how it is when it gets a little chilly and the heat's cranked up. A bunch of dudes get together and eat and hang out and sometimes . . ." He turned red again. "You know you watch some stuff that you can't watch when your parents are around. It gets a little rank."

"I get it," Decker told him.

"Greg had always carried some extra pounds. He sweated a lot. The past month or so, I think he started showering more often." He averted his eyes. "And when a dude starts showering that often, it means to me that there's some girl involved. Plus . . ." A long pause. "How do I say this without sounding like a perv? We watched stuff. I think Greg finally discovered he had a dick, if you know what I'm saying."

"Understood. Was Greg addicted to porno?"

"We're all addicted to porno. We're teenaged boys."

Decker thought a moment. "Could he have been filming material that he shouldn't have been filming? Maybe secretly filming the girls' gym lockers?"

Joey gave him a wide-eyed look. "If he did, he never showed anything to me."

"How do you think Greg might have reacted if he got caught doing something like that?"

"Well, for starts, the school would have kicked him out."

Decker nodded, thinking: What would have happened if a quiet, bookish kid had been caught secretly filming a popular girl in the nude? What kind of number could she have done on him: embarrassed him, humiliated him, blackmailed him, or worst of all, threatened to go to the principal? And if the kid would have been faced with torment and expulsion . . . who knew what he might have done.

Joey's mind was still on the question. "I think he would have showed me something like that. Not that it's nice, but it's the way dudes are."

"Did you ever see what was on Gregory's camera?"

"Sometimes he'd show us a playback, but I don't have any idea of the totality."

"Does his mother have the video camera?"

"I would think so."

"Okay, Joey. This gives me a little bit of a start."

The boy nodded. "Can I ask you a question?"

"Sure."

"Why are you doing this?" Joey looked pained. "I mean if Greg was doing something bad, why dig it up?"

"That is a very good point. Originally, his mom asked me to help her understand her son's motives for doing something so terrible. But if it is something distasteful, I'm going to be doing some serious editing."

"Yeah, I think that would be a good idea. Not that I think he was doing something bad."

Decker regarded the kid's face. He looked sincere. "Do you think your pals would mind if I talked to them?"

"Nah, they wouldn't mind. I don't know what they'd tell you. I probably knew Greg better than any of them."

Decker gave him a pad of paper and a pen. "Could you write down names and phone numbers for me?"

"Sure."

While he was writing, Decker was figuring out his next move. Get the camera, get the kid's computer, and look around the room. Joey was right about one thing. How much did Wendy Hesse want to know? After Joey handed him back the pad, Decker said, "I do have one other important question. Do you have any idea where Greg could have gotten hold of a gun?"

"Not that specific gun, no." Joey exhaled. "But I can tell you this much. It isn't hard to get weapons at B and W. You can get guns, you can get booze, you can get dope, you can get porn, and you can get good grades and test scores."

"That easy, huh?" Decker said.

"That easy," Joey answered. "All you have to do is pay for it."

Chapter Eight

During the final duet—"Gran Dio, morir si giovane"—Gabe's eyes wandered to Yasmine, whose face was buried in her hands. Her eyes were visible through splayed fingers, tears streaming down. The entire time he had been concentrating on pitch, voice timbre, sound mixture, and volume. But the little girl next to him was sobbing because Violetta was about to succumb to tuberculosis.

So who was really getting the most out of the afternoon?

As she blinked, a new batch of tears poured out of her eyes. In a protective motion, Gabe put his arm around her shoulder and she simply melted, fat saline drops soaking his shirt. When Violetta finally died and the curtain came down, she sat up, took a tissue from her bag, and wiped her face. Curtain calls took another five minutes, and then the house lights went up.

It was five-thirty by the time they actually made it out of the building. The sky held the afterglow of a dazzling sunset—pinks, oranges, and purples. The ground was wet, and the air was chilly.

Yasmine hugged her body. Her voice was still shaky. "How do we get a taxi?"

"We don't." Gabe checked his watch. "By the time we call it in and the guy gets here, it's easier to take the bus."

"How long will it take to get home?"

"About an hour plus."

"I told my mom I'd be home by six."

"That's not going to happen even with a cab. We've got to hustle. The bus is due in five minutes, and it's a half-hour wait if we miss it." He took her hand and pulled her along. They arrived a minute before the bus pulled up. She was jumping up and down, massaging her arms. "Cold?" he asked.

"I'm always cold."

"It's cold outside." He rubbed her shoulders with his hands.

When the bus came, she said, "I'm sorry I got emotional. I hope I didn't embarrass you."

"It's theater. You're supposed to be moved. We performers live for people like you."

They boarded the bus, and he paid for the tickets. The inside was stale smelling, but at least it was warm. Gabe found two empty seats toward the back. He gave her the window seat and took the aisle—better for his legs and his body would shield her in case some gang-bangers decided to board. In L.A., rapid transit didn't really exist. Buses were the primary transportation of those too poor or too young to have cars. She took out her phone and began to talk in a foreign language—presumably Farsi. A few minutes later, she hung up.

"Everything okay?"

"My friend said she'd cover for me. I'm supposed to be at her house anyway."

"Nice friend. Why didn't you just take her to the opera?"

"She would have come with me, but she would have hated it. It's not fun to go with a person who's looking at her watch all the time."

"Gotcha."

"Thanks so much for doing this for me."

"Honestly, the pleasure was mine. I've never heard Danielli live. She was great."

Yasmine brought her hand to her heart. "Oh my God, it was like being transported." She took in a deep breath and let it out. "This might be terrible, but I didn't think the guy who played Alfredo did her justice."

He raised his eyebrows. "Yeah, he hit a few clunkers."

"Like right at the end . . . oh my God, wasn't he embarrassed? I mean how can you sing like that when you're singing with Alyssa Danielli?"

Gabe regarded her face. "You really do have a great ear. Is your family musical?"

"My mom used to sing."

"Opera?"

"No, just like sing at parties and stuff. She doesn't do it anymore."

"Why not?"

"Because she's married. I mean, she still sings, but just not professionally." Yasmine looked deep in thought. "She has a lovely voice."

Gabe nodded. "And your parents didn't give you *any* music lessons?"

"Oh sure. We were all given piano lessons. It didn't take. I'm terrible."

"How long did you play for?"

"Technically, I'm still playing, but I'm hopeless. I don't want to talk about it. Especially not with you."

They rode for a few minutes in silence. Gabe took a Balance Bar out of his pocket and as soon as he did, Yasmine's eyes glanced to his snack. Wordlessly, he offered it to her.

"Do you have another one?" she asked.

"Take it."

"We'll share."

"Take it."

She took it and broke it in half.

Gabe kept his hands in his lap. "I'm really fine."

"Then why did you take it out if you didn't want to eat it?"

"Force of habit. Sometimes I need a sugar rush." He regarded her face. "You look tired. Did you have anything to eat today besides the Diet Coke at intermission?"

"I had coffee." When Gabe rolled his eyes, she said, "I didn't have time." Carefully, she took a nibble at the bar.

Gabe waited a moment, then said, "Do you like piano music?"

"Of course I like piano music. I like the way you play it, just not massacred—which is the way I play it."

He smiled. "The reason I ask is that SC is having a concert next Saturday afternoon." He paused. "Wait. Are you Shomer Shabbat?"

"We go to shul in the morning, but we drive and stuff." She looked at him. "For a Catholic, you know some pretty obscure expressions."

"You live with the Deckers, you pick up a few things."

"Anyway . . ." She averted her eyes and bit her lip. "What were you saying?"

"Oh, yeah. Anyway, the pianist is a guy I know from competitions. Paul Chin. He's a student at SC, and we have the same piano teacher. He's pretty good." A beat. "I'm definitely going. If you want to come with me, I'll be happy to take you."

"I would love to come. What time?"

"Same time, three o'clock." She didn't talk, her eyes calculating something unknown. He said, "Why don't you just tell your parents?"

"They wouldn't let me go."

"Yasmine, it's not a date—"

"I know that."

"You obviously have a love of classical music and it's a shame to stifle it."

"My parents are old-fashioned. Especially my dad. He doesn't allow me to go out, period, even with Persian Jewish boys." A pause. "I know it's not a date and you're just being nice, but . . ." She sighed.

Gabe said, "Well, the offer is open. If you change your mind, just show up at the bus stop."

She nodded, looking thoroughly dejected.

"Finish your bar."

"I'm not hungry." She offered it back.

"Eat it. Don't be one of those ridiculous anorexic girls."

"I'm not anorexic."

"Then prove me wrong and eat."

She took another lackluster nibble.

"Hey, don't fret." He gently nudged her arm. "You'll have plenty of time to hear concerts when you get to college. Besides, it's probably better not to sneak around your parents."

She didn't answer. Then she said, "What is the pianist playing?"

"It's all Saint-Saëns. I think the orchestra's doing some golden oldies like 'Danse Macabre' and 'Bacchanale.'" He thought a moment. "When I was a little kid, I saw *Samson and Delilah*. My father took me. I inherited my ear from him. Anyway, it wasn't like a Met opera, it was one of these experimental things that the New York avant-garde just love to do. So when the company did the 'Bacchanale,' they started stripping until they were nude and started simulating you know what." He grinned. "Man, I don't think I heard a note of music."

She giggled. "How old were you?"

"Around nine."

"What did your father do?"

"I dunno. I was too embarrassed to look at him."

She giggled again. "So you got your talent from your dad?"

"Yeah, only I'm better than he is and we both know it. It's funny. My father is an absolute tyrant. I've never,

ever talked back to him except in music. It's the one area where I can tell my dad that he's full of shit in that language and he'll just laugh or agree with me. It's weird."

"You're probably living his dream."

"Nah, my father likes what he does just fine."

"What does he do?"

It took a few moments for him to speak. "He owns brothels." Yasmine's face was blank. Gabe said, "Brothels. You know. Whorehouses."

"Whorehouses?"

"You don't know what a whorehouse is?"

Her complexion darkened. "I know what a whore is. I didn't know there was a special house for them."

Gabe said, "Eat your Balance Bar."

She took another bite. "Like how does that work? Do all the whores just decide to live together?"

"Change the subject."

"No, I'm curious."

"A brothel is a place where whores work." A pause. "So instead of having to go out on the street and hustle for guys, they just stay in one place and the guys come to them."

"To have sex?"

"That's the idea."

"So your dad owns like a big motel or something?"

"Yeah, something like that."

"Wow." Her eyes got big. "Is that even *legal*?"

"In certain parts of Nevada, it is."

"And the whores pay him rent?"

"It's a little more complicated than that." He tapped his toe. "Yasmine, you can ask me any question you want, but I'd appreciate if you kept this between us. It's a little embarrassing."

She shrugged. "My dad owns all sorts of properties. I'm sure he rents to some unsavory characters."

Gabe laughed. "Okay."

"But I don't think he owns any whorehouses."

"I'm sure he doesn't. Don't ask him about it."

"No, that wouldn't be a good idea."

"It would be a very bad idea." He pointed to the rest of the Balance Bar. "Eat."

Yasmine took a small bite. "So what's the piano music?"

"Piano music?"

"For the concert on Saturday."

"Oh yeah." The conversation was meandering all over the place. "Paul's playing a piano concerto called 'Africa Fantasie.' It's not particularly hard but I happen to like it a lot. And I like to show support."

"I've never heard it."

"It's a good one. Several versions are on YouTube."

"So . . . like what time are you going?"

Gabe regarded her. "The bus leaves at one. That puts you into SC at around two-fifteen, two-thirty."

She nodded. "How much are the tickets?"

"Not much. Like fifteen, twenty bucks. I'll buy you one. If you show up, fine. If you don't, that's fine, too. No pressure. But if you do want to come, you can't be late. I'm not waiting around."

"Understood." She sat back and closed her eyes. "This day was magical . . . just magical."

"I'm glad you enjoyed it," Gabe said. "You should probably buy your friend something for covering for you."

"Ariella?" Yasmine smiled. "I've covered for her like a zillion times. This doesn't even make a dent in the list. Now that girl is a real sneak."

"So you're the good girl?"

She shrugged.

"Nothing to be ashamed of," Gabe said. "You'll do fine."

"I'm sure somewhere out there is a perfect twenty-four-year-old Persian Jew just waiting until I grow up." She looked at him. "Persian girls tend to marry older guys. I mean, not always, but that's the tradition. My oldest sister is engaged to a thirty-one-year-old. She's twenty-three."

Gabe nodded. "Interesting."

They rode the remaining time in silence, Yasmine nodding off until she slumped to the side and slept with her head on his shoulder. Her face was turned upward, her full lips slighted parted. He could feel her breath warm against his neck. Her hair tickled his face.

He was tired as well, but he couldn't tear himself away from watching her sleep.

A real cutie. Too bad.

A few minutes before their bus stop, he gently shook her awake. She inhaled a deep breath and let it out, sat up, and rubbed her eyes. "I fell asleep?"

"It happens." He got up and pulled the string. A moment later, the bus lurched to a stop. "Let's go."

It was a moonless night—cold and dark.

"I owe you money for the cab."

"You don't owe me anything."

"I insist."

"I won't take it. C'mon. I'll walk you home . . . or a few houses away from home, I guess."

"I'm supposed to be at Ariella's."

"Where does she live?"

"Just right around the corner, so I'm fine."

"I'll walk you to the house. She's covering for you anyway, so she must know about me, right?"

"Sort of."

"That sounds ominous."

"More like mysterious." Yasmine started walking . . . very slowly. She didn't want the night to end. "Thanks again."

"You're welcome."

They strolled for a few moments in silence, the only sound made by her clacking heels.

"No, *really* thanks." Yasmine stopped. "It was the most wonderful, special day of my life. I'll never, ever forget it." She stood on tiptoe and kissed his cheek, running away and disappearing up a sidewalk, her heels clapping against the pavement until he could hear a door open and close.

Then all was still.

Gabe stood for just a few seconds, then turned around and started home, his cheek still burning with the feel of her lips.

Chapter Nine

From a detective's standpoint, suicide was a strange crime. There was a victim, but the perpetrator wore many faces: depression, psychosis, humiliation, overwhelming debt, rage, self-loathing, or that tragic combination of teenage angst paired with a firearm. Reconstructing Gregory Hesse's mind at the moment of impact was impossible. All Decker was looking for was a hint of why.

The week following Hesse's memorial had been busy, the station house humming with crimes of every stripe. Most of his detectives were in the field, attempting to gather enough evidence to bring in bad guys who were at current, walking the public streets. Marge and Oliver seemed to be in and out of court, testifying on cases that took over a year to bring to trial. Thursday afternoon, Decker received a call from Romulus Poe of the New Mexico State Police.

"It appears that your serial killer, Garth Hammerling, was in fact around my area. I've been trying to retrace his movements, but I've got gaps. The last I heard, he had bought a bunch of camping equipment and was headed for the National Forest in northern New Mexico. The area is the southern tip of the Rockies and it's easy to disappear there. Around this time, it's also real easy to get lost and freeze to death. You'd have to be a real good survivalist to make it through the winter, especially the one we're having now."

Decker said, "I don't know anything about Hammerling's survival skills. I know he's done some camping in the past."

"Camping in the Rockies in wintertime isn't Yosemite in summer with power hookups and porta-potties. It's rigorous and it's dangerous."

"Good thing for Hammerling that he knows how to kill," Decker said.

"Maybe he's good with drunken women. A mountain lion is another beast altogether. And let me tell you, in the winter, they're hungry. I myself live off the grid—been doing it for decades. But even I wouldn't camp up north in wintertime."

Decker said, "If you flew over the area in a helicopter, could you see anything?"

"The area is filled with pines so even in the summer you can't see much from up top except green. At this time of year, it's all white, and after a few minutes you get snow blindness. I suppose if you got extremely lucky, you might see some smoke or something. Best to wait until he comes down to civilization. If we don't hear from him, we can start looking when the thaw comes in March and we'd be just as likely to find a body as a live person. I'll apprise the park rangers and let you know if we get any action. If he was smart, he'd realize that it's cold outside and shimmy back down to warmer temperatures."

"Okay. Just don't drop your guard. He is a very dangerous guy."

"Understood. If I get a bead on him, you'll be the first to know."

"Thank you, Sergeant Poe, we'll keep in touch." Decker hung up the phone just as Marge Dunn was coming into his office. She said, "My schedule just cleared up. Anything you need?"

The clock read ten after three. "I'm sure I can come up with something." He checked off items on his to-do list and was left with Gregory Hesse. "Could you run an errand for me?"

"Pick up your dry cleaning or wash your car?"

"Everything I have is wash and ruin, and my car is hopeless." Decker pointed to a chair and Marge sat down. Today she was dressed in brown slacks and a pink sweater. Color looked good on her. "I'm still looking into a motive behind Gregory Hesse's suicide."

"How's that going?"

"I'm still waiting for the tox report. I keep thinking that maybe the kid was high on something, because every one of his buddies seems to be in the dark as to why." He gave her a recap of his conversations, especially the one last Sunday with Joey Reinhart. "Why don't you go to Wendy Hesse's house and pick up Greg's laptop and his camcorder. Videotaping seemed to be Greg's passion. Also ask Mrs. Hesse if you can look around his room. Greg's best friend, Joey Reinhart, implied that maybe there was a girl in Greg's life."

"And if we find her?"

"Ask her about the relationship and if it went south. Maybe that was the reason behind the act."

"We don't want to make anyone feel guilty," Marge said.

"No, of course not. For Greg to do this, he was clearly disturbed. Most guys can get over girls pretty quickly. Even if their brains are still sad, their gonads are still heat-seeking missiles. But there are those rare sensitive types that can't see a future beyond a broken heart. Did we find anything new with the gun?"

"We ran it through ballistics. Now we have to pull up cases where we have shells from a .380 Ruger. It's going to take time."

"Think the gun has been sitting around doing nothing for five years?"

"It could have been doing something but we may not know about it. The obsession with a camera is intriguing. Maybe he filmed something he shouldn't have."

"I was thinking about the same thing." He handed her an address. "I hope Wendy Hesse is still cooperative. I haven't talked to her since the memorial service."

"She hasn't called you up?"

"No, and I've called her several times. All I've gotten is the machine. So maybe she changed her mind about poking into Greg's personal life."

"So why stir up things?"

"You know how it is with an investigation. The damn thing takes on a life of its own."

Gabe hadn't heard from her since Sunday evening. She had texted to say her final thanks, and he had texted back, anytime, which he had meant. Then his phone had gone cold.

During the week, he thought about contacting her, but what was the point? She'd either show up on Saturday or she wouldn't, and the way things were going, *wouldn't* looked like the likely option. It was affecting him and his playing. Even his teacher noticed.

Especially his teacher noticed.

You're distracted. Then Nick graced him with one of his famous withering looks. *Gabriel, you're a good professional-quality pianist. You'll always be a good professional pianist. But if you want to be great, you're going to have to be one hundred percent focused on what you're doing. In this business, good isn't going to cut it.*

For Chrissakes, he was fifteen. Most dudes his age were smoking dope and sniffing girls. What did the man *want* from him? Instead, Gabe told Nick that he was right and he'd try harder.

It's not your hands, Gabe, it's your brain. Get your head wrapped around the music.

He had meant to take the advice to heart. He really had meant to do it. Plus, Nick had given him some composing assignments that ordinarily he really liked. But instead of making progress in his chosen field, he was alone in the house, sitting on his bed at four in the afternoon, surfing Facebook.

Chopin would just have to fucking wait.

Distracted.

His Facebook account was still active, but his pictures were old. There were several snapshots of him and his buddies when he had buddies. There were a couple of him and his mom when he had a mom. There was one old picture of his dad who happened to be the only one still in his life. He hadn't answered anyone's mail or posted any comments in over a year. Wistfully he surfed the pages of his old buddies, looking at updated photographs. His friends had grown taller and broader, and some of the more swarthy ones had sizable clumps of facial hair. His own cheeks and chin had sprouted stubble, but it was hard to see because it was growing in blond.

Anyway he wasn't really interested so much in his old friends—just his new one.

For the fifth time in an hour, he pulled up Yasmine's profile. She had accepted his invitation to be her friend, but that was as far as their contact had gone.

He stared at the pictures of her (gorgeous), her three sisters (gorgeous), her mother (the original gorgeous), and her dad who was bald and square faced and looked to be in his late sixties. Yasmine resembled her sisters (who in turn resembled the mother) except that she was still childish whereas the other three were closer to being women. He got a clear idea how she'd mature, would love to take a bite out of her two years from now. Even as is, he wouldn't mind a nibble. He continued to gape at her face, wishing she'd never approached him. He had even gone to Coffee Bean several times in the past week at six in the morning, hoping to catch her, but she didn't show.

As a last resort, he thought about hanging around her school, acting surprised when he saw her. He had a legitimate excuse. Rina was a teacher there. But he nixed the idea because it was clearly stalking.

So he stared at the same dozen pictures that he had stared at a few minutes before.

His computer broke in with an IM.

Are you there?

The screen name was different from the last time, but he suspected who it was.

Mom?

A long pause.

How are you?

He felt his eyes blur and his throat close up.

I'm fine. His brain was awhirl. She never told him about her pregnancy—the reason why she had abandoned him. He decided to jump the gun and let her know that he knew. *How's my sister doing?*

Another break from the text. It was taking her a while to answer. What time was it in India? It had to be in the wee hours of the morning.

She's fine. Did Chris tell you?

Gabe wrote: *Yes, he told me. But Decker figured it out also. We've all known for a while. What's her name?*

He waited for her to respond.

Juleen.

I like it. Someday I'd love to meet her.

I would love that, too. Maybe sooner than later?

His heart felt very heavy. The moment was awkward.

We'll see how it shakes out. Give her a kiss for me. And don't worry too much about Chris. I've seen him a few times. I think he's moved on to other things.

Another pause.

I love you, Gabriel. I love you and miss you very much.

A very, very heavy heart. He wasn't angry anymore. His rage at her desertion had been replaced with engulfing sadness. The piano seemed to be calling his name.

I miss you, too. I've got to go practice, Mom. Don't worry about me. I'm really fine.

He shut off the computer before she could respond and walked over to the garage where the Deckers had set up a piano studio for him. They were wonderful people—just the best. But they weren't his flesh and blood.

Focus, Gabe, focus.

The subtleties of Chopin never sounded so good.

After giving the door a firm knock and receiving no answer, Marge stuck her business card in the space between the door and the frame. She was just about to turn around when the door opened and the card fell onto the ground.

Wendy Hesse looked bleary eyed, dressed in blue sweats, with socks but no shoes on her feet.

Marge bent down to pick up the card. "I'm so sorry, Mrs. Hesse, did I wake you?"

Her expression suggested confusion. "What time is it?"

"Four o'clock."

Wendy rubbed her eyes. "I was watching TV and I must have fallen asleep." Several seconds ticked by. "Four o'clock?"

"Yes, ma'am."

"I've got to pick up my kids from school." She put her hand over her mouth. "Is it Friday?"

"Thursday."

"Oh . . ." She regarded Marge's face. "You look very familiar."

"Detective Dunn, LAPD." She handed the woman her card. "I was wondering if I could come in."

"Of course."

Marge crossed the threshold. It was a cool February day in the Valley, but the house was as hot as a foundry.

It had been a long time since the interior had experienced fresh air. The place was tidy especially considering the circumstances. Wendy Hesse sat down on a red sofa, and Marge sat next to her.

"Do you need anything?" Marge asked her.

"No, I'm . . ." She tucked an errant strand of hair behind her ears. "People have been kind. Some are a little shy about approaching me, but for the most part, it's been . . . Thank God for friends." She needed her hands. "It's Thursday?"

"Yes."

"Almost two weeks."

"Have you gone into his room yet?" When Wendy shook her head no, Marge said, "Would it be possible for me to look around his room? We're still searching for a reason . . . all of us. It would be helpful if I could take Gregory's laptop to headquarters and probe its contents."

Wendy looked nervous. "Maybe I should ask my husband about this."

"Sure." Marge waited a beat. "Have you looked at Gregory's laptop?"

She shook her head no.

"Do you know his screen name and password?"

"I know his screen name. I used to know his password, but I think he's changed it."

"Should we go to his room and see if your password works?" Wendy bit her thumbnail. Marge said,

"Or I can bring his laptop out of the room if you're not ready to go in yet."

"I really should talk to my husband about this."

"Whatever you want," Marge told her. "I know that you're interested in finding a reason—"

"I don't know about that anymore." She inhaled and let it out slowly. "What difference will it make? It won't bring him back." Fat tears rolled down her cheeks. "Maybe it's best to just let it go."

"Whatever you think is best." Marge proffered the woman her card and she took it. "Call if you change your mind."

The woman stood and her sorrowful eyes met Marge's. "Thank you for coming."

"Sure." Marge hesitated, but decided to ask the question anyway. "I understand that videotaping had become Gregory's favorite hobby. Was he interested in making films?"

Wendy said, "Gregory was always the one that recorded family events."

"So he's had the interest for a long time."

Wendy was silent.

"Just curious," Marge said. "Do call if you need anything."

When the woman still didn't talk, Marge turned around and let herself out the door.

Chapter Ten

Rina loved the quiet of Shabbat morning, when the neighborhood was without construction noise and leaf blowers. Through her kitchen window, she could actually hear birds chirping. Last year there had been a nest of finches in one of her bushes. She had heard a racket of squawks several times every day when the parents had returned to feed the young. Food was primal, and with a big family, much of her life revolved around meals.

She had been dressed for shul since eight, but Peter was taking his time. So she sat at her kitchen table, sipping coffee and reading the paper—a rare moment of alone time that proved to be short-lived. Gabe came in, dressed in a black long-sleeved T-shirt, jeans, and sneakers. Behind his wireless specs sat sleepy green eyes.

"Hey," he said.

"You're up early."

"Yeah, I thought I'd catch up on a few things. Get a jump on the day."

"Would you like some breakfast?"

"Yeah, that would probably make sense." The boy took down a mug from the cupboard and made himself a cup of instant coffee. He was comfortable enough to open pantry doors and raid the fridge without asking permission. He fixed himself a bowl of cereal and began shoveling food into his mouth.

Rina said, "We're eating lunch here today if you're interested."

"Thanks, but I'm going out." He looked at her. "A guy I know is playing a piano concerto at SC. I thought I'd show him support."

"That's very nice. Is he good?"

"He's very good." Gabe gave her a sly smile. "But not as good as me."

"That goes without saying." She smiled back. "When's the concert?"

"Three. But to get there on time, I've got to take a one o'clock bus, which means I have to leave here around 12:30."

"Sorry I can't take you."

"That's fine. I don't mind walking. If I didn't walk to bus stops, I'd get absolutely no exercise."

"We've got a treadmill."

"Yeah, my life's already too much of that."

"Poor Gabe," Rina said. "It's hard being a genius."

He let out a laugh. "I like when you do that. It means that you're not pitying me."

"You, my boy, are anything but an object of pity. In fact, you're overloaded with assets. You should lend a few out to those less fortunate. What time are you coming home?"

"I don't know. Maybe Paul and I will go out to dinner. I suppose it depends on how well he performs."

"Call and leave a message on the machine. Not that I have to worry about a big independent guy like you, but I'm a mother and I'll fret if I don't know where you are."

"That's okay. It's nice to get a little mothering every now and then."

The room went quiet. Rina studied his face. "She contacted you again?"

"Yeah." Gabe plunked the spoon in his cereal and pushed the bowl away. "I found out that my sister's name is Juleen."

"Pretty name." Silence. "What else did she say?"

"Nothing much. I told her that Chris knows about the baby and she shouldn't worry too much about him."

"Is that true?"

"Mostly. I mean he still likes her. He's told me that he'd take her back, baby and all. But he certainly isn't chasing her down. I think he likes being a martyr for a change. After all the misery he put her through, he's happy with the role of the aggrieved spouse."

"I've got an aunt and uncle; they're about ninety now. For forty years, they lived in two separate houses and got together only on Shabbat. People used to ask, are they separated, are they divorced? Nope. Just didn't want to live together all the time. For them, it worked."

"As long as they're okay, I'm okay." He wiped his glasses on his T-shirt. "I think she wants me to come to India."

"That would be an interesting trip."

"Yeah, maybe in the future." *When I'm fucking ready, which isn't now.* Gabe put his glasses back on. "I should get started. What'd you make for lunch?"

"Corned beef and turkey."

"Oh man!" He made a face. "Please save me some."

"I will take some aside and hide it in the refrigerator where no one will find it." Rina kissed the top of his head. "Thank you for the compliment."

Gabe stood up and spontaneously gave her a small hug, then pulled away self-consciously. His face was warm, and he knew he was blushing. "Thanks, Rina. Not only did I land in the home of two of the nicest people in the world, you cook better than anyone I know."

"You'd better believe it."

He gave a small laugh and headed for the garage, the one place where he felt totally at ease—his piano, his music, his solace. Once in a while, when no one was home, he sat in the driver's seat of Peter's Porsche, his hand gripping the clutch, his eyes looking out the windshield and imagining an open road that led to anyone's guess.

Arriving at the bus stop at ten to one, but Yasmine was nowhere in sight.

Oh well.

He sat down on the bench and opened his composition book, playing his piece in his head, correcting and editing until the bus pulled up at five after. He stood and when the doors swung open, he stepped up, his brain still focused on his music. In the background, he heard a scream.

"Waaaaaiiiittt."

He held up his hand to the driver, stepped down, and saw her running toward the bus. She was a block away with her hair flying like a stallion's mane. His heart leapt out of his chest. To the driver, he said, "Could you hold on a minute? My friend's coming."

"I got a schedule and a route to do."

Gabe took out a ten. "Please?"

The driver pushed the money away. "I still got a schedule. I'm gonna count to ten."

Stepping back out, he waved her on. On the count of eight, she had made it, completely winded and doubled over. Gabe paid for their tickets, the door closed behind them, and the bus jerked forward. She pitched backward and Gabe caught her before she fell. Her face was bathed in sweat. It didn't help that she was wearing a quilted pink puffy jacket. At least her attire—jeans and flats—was more appropriate than last time.

She was panting . . . gripping her side. Gabe led her to an open row and gave her the window seat. He sat next to her and for the first five minutes, all he did was listen to her wheeze.

"You okay?" he finally said.

She nodded.

He started to say something, but just laughed instead.

"I . . . had . . . to change . . . from shul."

"You look very nice, Yasmine," Gabe said. "Maybe you want to take off your jacket?"

She nodded, and he helped her pull it off. Underneath she was wearing a pink scoop-necked sweater that exposed those lovely collarbones. She said, "I brought . . . food." She held up a purse slightly smaller than a shopping bag. "Hungry?"

He was. His half bowl of cereal had been digested hours before. "What do you have?"

"Cookies . . . and fruit." She was still holding her side.

"You have a cramp?"

She nodded and pulled out an apple. "Okay?"

"Sure." He took it and she fished out another one for herself.

"Sorry . . . I'm late."

He took a bite. The apple was big, juicy, and tart. "No prob."

"At least I made it."

"Barely." Another chomp. His thigh was touching hers. "Who's covering for you today?"

"Ariella."

"Again?"

She nodded and nibbled her apple.

"You better hope she stays your friend. She's got dirt on you."

Yasmine gave him a thousand-watt smile. "Oh my God . . ." Still breathing audibly but slower. "It's like she is so keyed up about all this."

"What?"

"That I'm sneaking around my parents to meet up with you."

He smiled. "Like I'm *evil boy*?"

"More like *forbidden boy*. At least I hope you're not evil. I think the only thing that would excite Ariella more is if you were a vampire."

Gabe laughed as he inched closer to her. "Sorry to disappoint."

She was talking to him, her speech going a mile a minute. "She's a little nuts!"

And closer still.

"I keep telling her it's not a date, that you're just being nice . . ."

Until he could smell her sweat . . .

". . . that we just have common interests . . ."

Sweat mixed with her perfume.

". . . that it's nothing romantic and it's just a concert and . . ."

He turned and faced her.

". . . no big deal . . ."

Eye to eye, he lifted her chin with his index finger and gently brushed his lips against hers. When she didn't resist, he did it again. Did it a third time, making it last longer, nibbling her juicy lower lip, tasting the salt on her skin. She was sweet, sweaty, soft, and fragrant.

Man oh man!

He sat back in his seat, putting his hands behind his head, closing his eyes, his erection jammed between his

leg and his jeans. "I'm sorry, Yasmine, I got distracted."
He turned to face her. "What were you saying?"

She didn't answer him. Instead, she sat stock-still
with sweat pouring off her forehead and hands in
her lap, her eyes on her hands. She was still holding
her apple. Her mouth was slightly open, and she was
breathing rapidly.

He knew he had blindsided her. Not nice, but at
least she knew where he stood. Gently, he nudged her
arm. She looked up, and he raised his eyebrows. She
looked down again.

Maybe he had misread her. Maybe he had wanted to
misread her. Even if he had, surely she couldn't be that
freaked out by a couple of chaste pecks on the lips even
if it was her "first" kiss.

Slowly she unfolded her hands. The fingers on her
right hand spider-walking across her thigh onto his
until her hand rested about four inches away from the
danger zone.

His brain screamed: *higher, baby.* Instead he took
her hand, brought it to his lips, and then placed their
entwined fingers back on his thigh, a comfortable distance from his boner. His body relaxed and so did she.

They rode in silence for a while, every so often ex-
changing glances while holding hands. Finally, she
dropped her apple in her purse and then let out an

audible sigh. "I give up!" In a swift motion, she threw her arms around his neck, weaving her fingers in his hair, and mashed her lips against his.

Whoa!

Sweet!

Time passed muy rapido. Hot and sweaty and dizzy with arousal, he kept reminding himself that she was innocent and they were in public. But he couldn't help himself. They kissed and kissed and kissed, and it took all his willpower to keep his hands from slipping under her sweater. Her mouth was soft and warm, her breath smelled like apples, her perfume was something floral, and her sweat was musty. He was practically swooning. He became so enrapt that he almost missed their stop, jumping up from her embrace at the last moment to pull the cord. The bus lurched and they pitched forward. He felt heat coursing through his face and knew he was beet red. This time, he was breathing hard. "We get off here."

She nodded and picked up her purse, and they stepped off the bus, avoiding the disapproving looks of some of the older ladies. As soon as the bus pulled away, he threw his arms around her body, lifting her way off the ground until she wrapped her legs around his waist. He carried her for a block or so, the two of them kissing as he walked. Over and over and over until he felt like he was going to explode. He put her back onto her feet. "Oh God," he told her. "I need to calm down."

She giggled. He held her hand and they strolled in silence.

"Are you okay?" she asked a minute later.

"No," he said. "I'm a little light-headed."

"Want a cookie?"

He grabbed her by the waist and spun her around. "I want you." He put her down, took her face in his hands, and planted a wet kiss on her mouth. He looked at his watch and his eyes went wide. "God, we've got about ten minutes to get across campus." He took her hand and they started speed-walking.

"Did you buy a ticket for me?"

"Of course I bought a ticket for you. I was hoping you would come." Pulling her along. "It would have helped if you had told me that you *might* come."

"I didn't know until the last minute."

"Well, you could have at least texted me a maybe. I didn't hear a peep from you."

"Well, that's because I didn't hear a peep from you."

"What are you talking about?" Gabe said. "I asked you to be my friend on Facebook."

"And I accepted."

"But you didn't write back."

"The boy writes first."

Gabe rolled his eyes. "Since when is that the rule?"

"I dunno. But it is the rule."

"You know I came to Coffee Bean looking for you."

"You did not."

"I did so." Gabe was offended. "I came on Tuesday and Thursday."

Yasmine said, "I came on Monday and Wednesday."

"Ooh, psych!" He took her hand and started running. "If you would have texted me, I would have met you. I mean I can't exactly call you."

"Why on earth would I assume that you'd want to meet me?"

"Why wouldn't you assume it? I asked you to the concert."

"I thought you were just being nice. You said it wasn't a date."

He stopped and grinned. "I lied."

They arrived just as the lights were dimming . . . again. The first half of the concert was fine, but he was constantly aware of Yasmine's presence, her hand in his, setting off motion below his waist. It wasn't until Paul took the stage that Gabe was finally able to relax and lose himself in the music. When the concert was finally over and the lights came up, Gabe was calmer.

"He did a good job."

"You approve?"

"I do." He turned to her. "What'd you think?"

"I really enjoyed the piece. I think I like Saint-Saëns. He composes with a common theme or voice or whatever you call it. He's not all over the place like some composers."

"Good call." Gabe eyed her face and was dying to kiss her, but he didn't want to get aroused. It would be a big faux pas to greet Paul with a woody. "I gotta go show my face. Do you mind?"

"Not at all."

He led her backstage where Paul was talking to a few of his classmates and a young woman named Anna Benton who Gabe knew well from previous piano competitions. Anna was eighteen with long blond hair, bright blue eyes, and legs that wouldn't quit. As usual, she was blabbing a mile a minute to whoever was listening. Paul and Gabe exchanged a guy hug.

"Excellente!"

"Yeah, it worked out."

"Did a great job."

Paul nodded. "Not bad. Thanks for coming."

"Anytime." Yasmine was hiding behind his back. Gabe pushed her forward. "This is my friend, Yasmine."

"Hi, there," Paul said.

"You were terrific," Yasmine whispered.

Anna butted in and gave Gabe a bear hug along with a kiss on the mouth. "Well, hello there, Whitman, have you been living in a cave?"

"It hasn't been that long—"

"You weren't at Atlanta, you weren't at Paris, you weren't at Brussels . . . were you at Chicago? No, you weren't at Chicago either."

"I had a few issues last year," Gabe said. "I'm coming to Budapest."

"For Liszt in Junior competition?"

"Yes, Liszt; no to Junior. I'm Adult now."

"You're fifteen? Fuck!" She glared at him. "When the fuck did you turn fifteen?"

"Like seven months ag—"

"Fuck!" Anna said. "Shit! You had to choose Budapest to turn fifteen? Fuck!"

"First you yell at me for not coming, and then when I say I'm coming—"

"Yeah, you're going against me. Fuck!"

"Maybe I'll choke."

"Why would you choke? You never choke. You're the antichoke. And now that you're working with Nicholas Mark, you must be really good."

"He is really good," Paul told her.

"Well, that's just terrific! Just terrific! Fuck!"

"I love you, too, Anna." Again, Yasmine was ducking behind him. Gabe edged her out until she was standing by his side. "This is my friend, Yasmine."

"Hi." She gave Yasmine a once-over and returned her eyes to Gabe. "It's not that I don't love you, Gabriel. I do love you. But I hate you. Fuck!"

Paul said, "You have time for dinner, Whitman?"

Gabe looked at Yasmine who seemed terribly out of place. He knew the feeling. "Nah, I've got some shit I've gotta do for Nick."

"Nick the prick."

"Not as big a prick as you are," Anna said to Gabe.

"Nick is fine except when he isn't." To Paul, Gabe said. "I'll be on campus on Tuesday. Can you meet for lunch?"

"I think that would work."

Gabe said, "I'll text you." He looked at Anna. "Bye, darling."

"Just shut the fuck up!"

"I love you, too."

They hugged, and Gabe led Yasmine into daylight. They walked a few minutes in silence. Then Yasmine said, "I think she didn't like me."

"Who?"

"Your friend Anna."

"Anna always swears."

"No, she was giving me the stink-eye."

"No, she wasn't. She was probably scoping you out. She's a lesbian."

"She's a *lesbian*?"

"Yep."

"How can that be? She's beautiful!"

"Why can't lesbians be beautiful?"

"I mean they can but . . . what a waste!"

"You're sounding like the guys. I like Anna, but she's a handful. I was never attracted to her even before I knew she was gay."

But Yasmine's mind was elsewhere. "If I were that beautiful, I'd . . ."

Gabe waited for her to continue.

How could she explain it to him? She loved her culture. She truly, truly, truly loved being Persian. But sometimes, it was hard to be a minority, really a minority within a minority because most of the Jewish kids she knew were white. She knew what their parents said about the Persians: that they were clannish, that they were aloof, that they were always cheap, that they were cheaters, that they were untrustworthy. It was all a stereotype. Besides if you had to run away from your country with just the clothes on your back, you might be a little cautious also. Her father was a wonderful, honest man. Her mom wasn't aloof, but she was shy. It was terribly hard having to justify who you are in your mind. Sometimes, it would be nice to just fit. "Nothing. Never mind."

Gabe kissed her gently on the mouth. "You know what's really sexy?"

"What?"

He grinned. "When a girl shows up *on time*." He grabbed her hand and started running to the bus stop. They made it right as the bus was pulling up. Yasmine started toward the back like the first time, but Gabe pulled her arm.

"Go in here. Take the window seat."

"Okay—"

"Put your head down."

"What?"

"Just do it. Don't talk." He swung around until most of his body was blocking hers. Two stops later, a group of four gangbangers came up from the back, pushing and shoving each other. When they got to the exit doors, one of them spied Yasmine and his eyes went wide.

Gabe took out his crucifix and spoke to the cholo in Spanish—not that he was fluent, but he could make himself understood. The guy answered back, his voice somber. A moment later, the bangers were gone. Gabe turned around, slumped in his seat, and blew out air. "I keep forgetting what area we're in."

Yasmine said, "What was that all about?"

"It was about someone as pretty as you being dog meat to these guys."

"What did you say to him?"

"I told him I was a priest and that your brother was just shot. That you and I were going to the hospital to deliver him last rites. He sends his sympathies."

Yasmine stared at him. "He believed that you were a priest?"

"Apparently." Gabe kissed his crucifix and tucked it back into his shirt. "It was my grandmother's who gave it to my father who gave it to my mother who gave it to me."

"When did you learn to speak Spanish?"

"I've been taking lessons from the lieutenant. I don't speak like a native, but I suppose that made me more convincing."

"I can't believe they believed that you were a priest."

"It's all attitude, Yasmine. Anytime I'm in a tight spot, I channel my dad and usually I do just fine."

"Isn't there anything you can't do?"

"I can't draw a straight line and I can't speak Farsi." He threw his arm around her shoulders. "Nothing I can do about the first one, but maybe you can help with the second."

"Why do you want to learn Farsi?"

"So when you talk to Ariella or your parents, I can eavesdrop." He smiled, then said, "Seriously, I like languages."

"I'll teach you Farsi. What do I get in return?"

Gabe wanted to grin, but kept himself in check. "I'm sure . . . if I give it some thought . . . I can teach you a thing or two."

"Like piano?" She shook her head. "Forget it. It's a lost cause."

Man, she was naive, didn't even recognize a come-on. But she sure could kiss. He said, "Maybe not piano, but like the cliché goes, I bet we could make some beautiful music together."

She blushed and turned her head to look out the window. He'd grown up with fast-tracked girls. This one was definitely a throwback to another age. "If I flirt with you, don't get all nervous. I like you, but I know how to behave, okay?"

She nodded. A slow smile spread across her mouth. "Don't behave *too* good."

Gabe grinned and threw his arm around her delicate shoulders. "Your words are music to my ears."

Chapter Eleven

An uneventful weekend gave way to a hellish week, as if everyone saved their felonious activities for working hours. By four-thirty Tuesday afternoon, Decker was finally ready for a lunch break when Marge came into the office, a black purse slouched over her shoulder, keys in hand. She said, "Off to see Kevin Stanger."

"Who?"

"The bullied boy who transferred out of Bell and Wakefield. Why I'm bothering is another question. First of all, the tox came back on Gregory Hesse. None of the regular drugs were in his system. He did have a .05 BAL, which for a kid his size is probably a few beers."

"Maybe he was steeling himself to do the deed."

"Could be," Marge said. "But the fact remains that he shot himself and he wasn't doped up to the point where he didn't know what he was doing."

"We all agree it was suicide. The question is why?"

"A question we may never answer because it seems that Wendy Hesse had a change of heart. She hasn't called back since my visit last Thursday. Has she called you?"

Decker shook his head no. "Maybe we shouldn't bother with Kevin Stanger."

"The kid agreed to talk to us, Pete. The police would look like idiots if I said never mind."

"I'm not too busy right now. Want company?"

"You sure? I know you're busy."

Decker picked up his jacket. "I've got to get out of here. I've been here since six and have yet to see daylight."

"You'd better hurry. The sun is going down fast."

"Yeah, even an inanimate star knows when to call it quits."

By his stature alone, Kevin Stanger didn't look like the type of kid that could be easily bullied. He was around five ten, one fifty, with a fair amount of muscle across his back. His face told a different story. It was round and weak chinned with cheeks spangled with acne. He wore braces. His hair was unruly, and his brown eyes were hooded under thick brows. Even before hello, his expression exhibited a defeatist attitude.

The boy led them into the living room and seated them on the sofa. Then he glanced out the glass picture window and sat down, his leg shaking a mile a minute. He said, "We have to make it quick. My mom'll be home at six."

Marge's watch read ten after five. She said, "You told me your mom was okay with this."

"Well, kinda. She didn't say no." Kevin wore a sweatshirt and a pair of pajama pants. His face was flushed. "I wasn't feeling well so I decided to skip my last two classes. I mean, I told one of the school's VPs, Mrs. Holloway. She said I could go home if it was okay with my mom. So I pretended to call my mom and then told Mrs. Holloway it was okay with mom. I mean, I don't know that it's not okay with my mom because I didn't call her. 'Cause I wanted to talk to you guys and I didn't want to ask. Sometimes it's easier to leave parents out of it."

Decker nodded and said, "What can you tell me about Greg?"

"He was a good guy."

"Nobody seemed to have had a problem with him," Marge said.

"Yeah, I thought Greg held his own." He scratched his head. "Maybe not. If he was going through hard times, I wish he told me. He never said anything."

"Could you talk about what you went through?" Decker asked.

"It's hard to talk about."

"Do the best you can," Marge told him.

"I thought I could ride it out, but after a year of it, I had enough. My mom wanted to go to the administration, but I put my foot down. We still live in the area."

"What'd they do to you?"

"It's not the physical stuff." Kevin looked up. "I mean they knock you around and everything, but that wasn't the bad part. It was the constant harassment."

"Joey Reinhart called it crowding." Decker took out his notepad.

"Yeah, they'd crowd you in school—the girls were worse than the guys because the girls would do things and when you'd, like, respond, they laughed at you, you know."

Marge took out a notebook. "If it's not too much for you, could you go into detail?"

"Well, they'd like grope you and try to get you . . . you know, aroused and then if you did react, they'd laugh and call you names . . ." He buried his red face in his hands. "Even so, I thought I could handle that. It's when they started crowding you out of school, it became a little scary. No one was around to help, you know?"

"What'd they do?"

"They'd surround you . . . like a pack of wolves. The last straw was when one of them pulled a gun on me and stuck it into my balls. I . . ." Kevin bit his lip. "I pissed in my pants. I knew after that I was never going back."

"Who was the kid?" Decker asked.

"I don't even remember."

"Yes, you do."

Kevin said, "I remember which dudes crowded me, but I don't remember who stuck the gun in my crotch. I blocked it out."

"Who was in the group?" Decker said.

"Like names?"

"Like names."

"You know if you started to question them, I'd deny it."

Decker said, "I suppose if I were gung-ho enough, I could go into the school and start pulling out guys and start questioning them, because what you've described is aggravated assault. But I'm not going to do that because the incident happened months ago and you're not going to be reliable. But I do want some names for my files. So give me names."

Kevin said, "It's like a whole stratified thing with the don at the top doing orders and his capos, like, carrying them out."

"Kevin," Decker said. "Who was there when the gun was pulled?"

Kevin looked at the ceiling. "I remember Kyle Kerkin was there."

"Who else?" Marge said. "Give us some names."

"Stance O'Brien, Nate Asaroff, JJ Little, Jarrod Lovelace—that's the core group of capos. The don is a guy named Dylan Lashay. But he wasn't there that day."

"The don?" Marge said. "Capos. Do these boys fashion themselves after the Mafia?"

"Yeah." Kevin nodded. "The B and W Mafia."

"Great," Decker said. "Tell me about Dylan Lashay, the leader."

"I think he got in early decision to Yale."

"Well, that's just super," Decker said.

"Ironic, isn't it?" Kevin said. "He's got all the stats, you know. The high SAT, all the extracurriculars. He's captain of model UN, captain of the football team, he directs all the school plays, he's got all the girls; and if life isn't fair enough, he's really rich. His stepdad is, like, head of an oil company. He's got everything that every kid wants, so he has to find different ways to get his kicks."

"Does the school know about him and his posse?"

Kevin rolled his eyes. "Dylan's the poster boy for B and W."

"So why do you think the group singled you out?" Marge asked him.

"I dunno. I mean, I tried to keep a low profile . . . we all did—Greg and Joey and Mikey and Brandon and Josh and Beezel. But I was the one with the target on my butt." He appeared thoughtful. "Greg tutored some of the guys. I think that bought him a pass."

"Did he tutor Dylan?"

"Dylan was pretty smart. I wouldn't think he'd need much tutoring. Anyway, this is all beside the point."

"Why's that?" Marge asked.

"Because that's not why I called you guys back." A pause. "Is it okay that I called you, you guys?"

"It's fine, Kevin," Marge said. "What do you want to tell us?"

"Greg kept in touch . . . he'd call me every couple of weeks to find out how I was doing. Anyway, about two months ago, he called me up, like, all excited."

Marge said, "About what?"

Kevin leaned forward. "This is the deal. Last year, Greg and I were in Journalism with Mr. Hinton. He was kind of a boring teacher, but he's also administrative head of the school paper. Mr. Hinton was really hot on investigative journalism. He told us a great detail about the Nixon years and Woodward and Bernstein and a guy named Sore Throat and . . . Do you know what I'm talking about?"

"We do," Marge said. "It's Deep Throat."

"Oh yeah, that's right. Anyway, Mr. Hinton bored me to tears, but that whole thing got Greg very excited. I thought he was gonna work on the paper. But when I asked him about it at the beginning of the year, he said he wasn't interested. Then I transferred out because tenth grade was becoming a repeat of ninth grade, only worse. So I was real surprised when Greg called me up and said that he had some news that was going to turn B and W on top of its head."

"Go on," Decker encouraged him.

"So I asked him what the news was, and Greg said he couldn't tell me. And then he said not to tell anyone, not even Joey Reinhart who is his best friend. And the only reason he told me is because I'm not in the school anymore."

Marge and Decker waited for Kevin to continue. After a few moments of silence, the boy got to the point. He said, "The next time I talked to Greg, I asked about the *big story* again. And he said he still couldn't talk about it. But he definitely sounded less excited than the first time, like things weren't going so well. And I asked him if he was okay, and he said he was great. But something was off. So I tried to press him, but he kept insisting that he was great, only he was working hard and a lot more tired than usual."

He stopped talking.

"That's it."

"He never told you any more?" Marge asked.

"Nope. I don't know anything more than what I just told you. But I thought I'd tell you because you never know what's important. So . . . that's it."

Decker said, "He didn't give you *any* idea as to what he was working on?"

"Nope. I'd tell you if I knew."

Marge said, "Do you know if he was working on the story with anyone else?"

"It never got that far." The boy looked at his watch. "My mom's gonna be home soon. I'd appreciate it if you, like . . ."

Decker stood. Both he and Marge gave Kevin their cards. "If you think of anything else, feel free to call."

"I will." Kevin stood up and opened the door. "It's not so hard to understand . . . what Greg did. There were times back in B and W when I thought about doing the exact same thing. All I can say is I'm happy that I didn't have a gun close by."

They decided to meet on Tuesdays and Thursdays at six in the morning since Gabe had to wake up early anyway to catch the bus to SC.

Monday for him was torture. They texted each other about a billion times.

Tuesday turned out to be just as torturous but in a different way. They met for coffee and they talked, which was nice and all that, but they couldn't be physical except maybe hold hands under the table and give each other's leg a quick squeeze. So the space between them, although inches in reality, felt like miles. After she left for school, Gabe felt frustrated and aroused and had to sit on the damn bus for an hour plus with all the other L.A. castoffs.

His lessons went well. Nick commented on it . . . that he was playing with more passion. He also told Gabe that it was time for him to start playing gigs.

I arranged for someone to come hear you. You've got to start soon. You're not that young anymore.

A has-been by fifteen.

Who's the guy?

A very well-known agent. He deals with all the summer chamber music festivals. That's as good a start as any to get your feet wet. He'll be here on Thursday. I want you at the university by eight in the morning, well fed and well rested. Got it?

Got it.

He came home at six in the afternoon, hungry and pissed. There was nothing in the fridge. Rina came into the kitchen and saw him foraging in the cupboards.

"There's not a whole lot to eat," she told him.

"I can see that."

Rina said, "I'm meeting Peter at the deli. Want to come?"

"I'm tired," Gabe told her.

"I'll bring you something home."

"I'm tired but I'm hungry." Gabe thought a moment. "Can I drive?"

"If you're not too tired, yes."

"Can we take the Porsche?"

"No."

Gabe made a face. "Okay. I'll come. I'm starved."

"Let's go." She picked up her purse and extracted the keys. "When was the last time you ate?"

"Like ten in the morning."

"The last time the lieutenant ate was at six in the morning," Rina told him. "Dealing with two hungry males is not my idea of a good time."

"I'll try to behave myself."

"I hold no great hope for either of you." She tossed him the keys. "But . . . at least you're both good-looking."

Chapter Twelve

The key to hungry males was getting them fed as quickly as possible. So Rina was really in a bind when they walked inside the deli and Sohala Nourmand waved to her. Should she go over and make pleasantries for a few minutes, or should she wave back and risk being thought of as unfriendly?

Of course, Rina had to come to the table and say hello. Sage had been in Hannah's class, and the two of them were friends. Plus, Daisy and Yasmine were students at the high school.

"Don't do it," Decker growled out a whisper. "I'm starved."

"Just for a moment." She tossed him a look that said, *Be nice or there will be consequences.* Then she went over to Sohala with a smile on her face.

Gabe had turned away, burying his face in a hand, hoping to keep his panic under control. Peter mistook his alarm as crankiness because he was grumpy himself. He threw his arm around the boy's shoulders. "Just be very sure that you're in love before you get married."

Rina looked around. Peter and Gabe were in tow, her husband barely concealing his petulance. That was okay. Bakshar, the pater of the Nourmand clan, didn't look too happy, either.

Rina gave Sohala a kiss on her cheek. "You look beautiful as always."

"And you are gorgeous as well," Sohala answered.

There were four Nourmand girls, each one as pretty as the next. Bakshar was considerably older than Sohala, always with a stern expression on his face. It couldn't be easy raising four daughters. Rina turned to Rosemary, the oldest, noticing the rock on her finger. "So when's the big day?"

"August second."

Sohala said, "When Aaron finishes his residency." Rosemary gave her a stern look that her mother ignored. "In dermatology."

Rina smiled and said, "Congratulations, Rosie."

"Thank you."

Sage asked, "So how's Hannah?"

"Loving Israel."

"Of course."

"And what are you doing?"

"I'm in Pierce College."

"That's great."

Sage shrugged. "It's school." She looked up at Gabe. "Congratulations to you."

Gabe had been hiding behind Peter. "Me?"

"You got into Harvard, no?"

Yasmine gave him a quick glance that he didn't dare interpret before returning her eyes to her soup. Gabe knew he was blushing. "Uh, how'd you know about that?"

"Hannah posted it on Facebook."

The teen looked pleadingly at Rina, who said, "I'll have her take it down."

"Why?" Sohala said. "It's nothing to be ashamed of. You should be very proud."

With his heart going a mile a minute, Gabe was desperately trying to maintain composure. He shuffled his feet, feeling like a dork. "Uh . . . I kinda got in by cheating."

Why the fuck did he say that?

"Cheating?" Bakshar said.

"Uh, not really cheating, cheating." His face was hot. "I mean my scores were good, but I got in because I play the piano."

The father perked up. "Yasmine play piano."

"No, Daddy," Daisy, the sixteen-year-old, said. "He *really* plays the piano."

Yasmine's face darkened. *Poor girl,* Rina thought. Sohala and her girls were a happy lot, usually smiling . . . except for the youngest. Yasmine carried the weight of the world on her shoulders.

Sage said, "Daddy, he played for graduation, remember?"

"Ah . . . yes." The father looked at Gabe with new-found respect. "You were very good."

"Thank you," Gabe said. *Can I go home and die now?*

Rosemary said, "Yasmini, when you go to college, you should send them a CD of your voice." She looked at Gabe. "The admissions board likes stuff like that, right?"

His eyes scanned Yasmine's face for an explanation, but her focus was still on her soup. "Sure," he answered. "Yeah, they like it a lot."

"Yasmini has a beautiful voice," Rosemary explained.

Sage said, "At least someone got Mommy's talent."

Daisy said, "Yeah, you can always tell when Yasmine is home. You can hear her down the block. What's that new aria you're always singing?"

Gabe regarded his love interest with new eyes. "You sing opera?"

"No," she said without looking up.

"What's the name of the aria again?" Daisy asked. "The latest one. She sings a lot of them. She's got this whole repertoire and goes from one to the other to the other to the other."

Yasmine had turned a strange color of red and brown—like finely polished mahogany. She kept her eyes on the table. Sohala patted her daughter's arm. "I like it when she sings."

Rosemary said, "You really should send in a CD, Yasmini. Who your age sings opera? It's different. It'll attract attention."

"Yasmine doesn't need singing to get into college," the father said with finality. "She's got brains. She's going to be a doctor."

Decker had had enough chitchat. "Rina, we need to sit down or we won't get a table."

Sohala said, "You want to join us?"

Gabe's heart went into overdrive.

Rina said, "Thank you, but I'm afraid I have to tend to the boys or we'll all be in trouble. Nice seeing you all. Enjoy your meal."

Sage said, "Tell Hannah I say hello. Is she coming in for Passover?"

"Absolutely," Rina said.

"I'll give her a call."

Decker took his wife's arm. "Have a good dinner." He led her to the single unoccupied table. The rest of the place had filled up with diners. Menus were already on the table, and Gabe conveniently hid his face, pretending to peruse his options. His stomach was rumbling from hunger, but he had to calm down before he could digest anything.

"I understand that you have to be nice," Decker said to Rina. "But you don't need to carry on a lengthy dialogue when you know I'm starving."

"Are you getting an appetizer?" Rina asked him.

"So just ignore me," he said.

"How about soup?"

"I'm getting chopped liver," Decker grumped.

"I'll get cabbage soup. We can share." She turned to Gabe. "Do you want an appetizer?"

I wanna get out of here. The menu was still in front of his face. "I'll have meatballs."

"Maybe I'll get meatballs, too," Decker said.

"That sounds like a great idea," Rina said.

"Aren't you perky?"

"Someone has to be," Rina told him. "And don't give me those looks. At least I said no when she asked us to sit with them."

"Under penalty of death."

Rina said, "Peter, I understand your position. But truly, you need to eat before you say another word, okay?"

"Got it."

"You, too," Rina said to Gabe. "You're looking very pale." The waitress came over and brought pickles and bread. "Let's wash."

Decker sneered, got up from the table, and ritually washed his hands. Then he said the blessing over the bread before diving into the basket. Everyone ordered and five minutes later, the appetizers came, which the boys wolfed down. Gabe didn't taste much. In truth, he didn't even know what he was eating.

To Gabe, Rina said, "Sorry about Hannah posting your private life."

"It's okay." He was more rattled than he'd been before any competition. "I just don't like the attention. I mean I don't dislike attention . . . I wouldn't perform if I disliked attention. So sometimes I like attention. But some attention is better than other attention . . ." He knew he was rambling. *Make a point, Gabe.* "I'm auditioning for an agent on Thursday."

"Really," Decker said.

"That's exciting," Rina said.

"Yeah, my teacher set me up with this hotshot guy who staffs all the summer chamber music festivals.

I'm hoping to pull a few slots on some of the lesser vetted programs. I think it would be fun."

"So that means you'll get paid to perform?" Decker said.

"Yeah, I guess," Gabe said.

"Good deal."

The sandwiches came. At that point, the Nourmand family got up from their table. Sohala waved good-bye and Rina waved back.

A smile formed on Decker's lips. To Gabe, he said, "She likes you, you know."

The boy felt his face go hot. "What?"

Decker turned to Rina. "Which one of the girls was the wise guy who was making her little sister miserable?"

"Daisy," Rina said. "She's a junior, and she is a wise guy."

"Yeah, she likes you." Decker wagged a finger at him. "Don't fall for it."

"You're in a mood," Rina said. "Stop teasing him."

"I'm not teasing him. I'm telling him the truth." He looked at Gabe. "The father would cut your head off. Then he'd probably go after me and cut my head off."

"Stop it," Rina said.

"He's a dour guy."

"Bakshar is in his late sixties with four daughters and now he has to pay for a big wedding. How would you be?"

"Dour." Decker chomped on his sandwich, then chomped again. "Good."

Rina looked at Gabe. His sandwich was hardly eaten. "You're not hungry anymore?"

"I think I filled up on meatballs." He looked at Decker who had polished off his dinner. "You want some of mine, Peter?"

"If you're not going to eat it."

"Take it."

"See, that's why you're skinny and I'm fat." Decker caught Gabe looking at his watch. "You need to go?"

"I have to prepare for the audition."

Decker put his sandwich down and called for the check. He looked at the teen with sudden concern. "Gabe, do you feel comfortable working at such a young age?"

"In this business, I'm not so young."

"But in real life, you are." Decker suddenly realized he was looking at a child—very talented, very smart, but still a little boy. "I'm serious, Gabe. I know you've been . . . led in this direction your entire life. But make sure it's what you want. Keep an open mind."

Gabe nodded.

"I mean it, son. Only you can live your life."

He smiled. "I think that's the first time that anyone has ever told me to consider options other than music."

"See, I'm an original," Decker said.

Gabe picked up his half-eaten sandwich and took a bite. He suddenly regained his appetite.

Decker said, "You want your sandwich back?"

"Nah, this is fine." He felt okay. "I actually like what I do. I can't see myself doing anything else."

"That's what I like to hear." Decker had just finished paying the bill when his cell phone went off. "It's Marge. I should take this."

"Absolutely."

"Can I call you back?" Decker said. "I'm just finishing dinner."

Marge said, "All right."

She sounded grave. "Two minutes." He hung up.

Rina got up and so did Gabe. She kissed her husband's cheek. "We'll meet you at home."

"Maybe."

"One of those calls?"

"I think so."

"Good luck." She tossed the keys to Gabe. "Yes, you can drive."

Decker accompanied them to Rina's Volvo and watched Gabe back out of a tight spot and pull away in one swift motion. Like most boys, he had a good sense of spatial relations. Hannah was constantly bumping into things—poles, bushes, mailboxes. Was that being sexist? Maybe, but he was too set in his ways to be upset about it.

Decker called his favorite sergeant back. "What's going on?"

Marge said, "Just got a call from one of the patrol officers. There's been another suicide."

That got his attention. "One of Gregory's friends?"

"I don't know yes or no, but she was a teenager. Myra Gelb—an eleventh grader at Bell and Wakefield."

"Good Lord." Decker put the key in the ignition. "What's the address?"

Marge gave him the numerals. "This is just . . . horrible."

He turned on the ignition and put the car in drive. The phone hooked up to Bluetooth. "I'm on my way. Did you call the coroner's office?"

"Everyone's on his way."

"How'd she do it?"

"Single gunshot to the head?"

"Like Gregory Hesse?"

"Eerily like Gregory Hesse."

Chapter Thirteen

Two cruisers were nose to nose, blocking the street to through traffic. An ambulance stood about fifty feet away. Decker trotted over to the scene, nodding at the two officers stationed outside the yellow tape before ducking under the ribbon. The apartment building was made from plaster and wood, each unit having a balcony and a view of the street below. The Gelb family lived on the second floor of a four-story building.

He walked through the unlocked door, finding the paramedics treating a dazed woman sacked out on the sofa. She wore gray slacks and a red blouse, the right sleeve rolled up to accommodate a blood pressure cuff. Next to her stood a young man in his twenties, dressed in jeans and a UCLA sweatshirt, holding her hand.

The living room led to a dining room and then into a kitchen. Decker found Marge leaning against the counter, her notepad open but she wasn't writing anything.

She spoke softly. "It happened in her bedroom."

"How many bedrooms?"

"Two. One for the daughter, one for the son. He goes to UCLA but he lives at home. The mother sleeps in the living room on a pull-out bed." Marge's eyes were just shy of wet. "I'll show you where it happened if you want."

"Who's guarding the death scene?"

"Hosea Nederlander. He's waiting for the CIs."

"Let's hold off on viewing the body for a moment. I want to get a feel for the family first."

Quietly, they returned to the living room. The paramedics, speaking in low tones, were conversing among themselves. The mother was in her late forties, eyes red-rimmed but dry. She sat stiffly as one of the men continued to check on vitals.

A paramedic named Lanie spoke to the young man. "Her pressure is still sky high. She really needs to come down with us."

"I'm not going anywhere," the woman insisted. Her eyes suddenly fixed on Marge and Decker. "Are you the police?"

"Yes, we are." Decker introduced himself.

Lanie said, "She should go to the hospital."

"I don't want to go!"

"Mom—"

"No. I can't leave her alone! I can't do that!"

"I'll stay here and take care of things," the son said. "But I can't do anything if I have to worry about you."

"I'm not going!" The woman's complexion was one shade short of ghost.

Marge said, "Would you like some water, ma'am?"

The son said, "That's a good idea."

Marge went into the kitchen. Decker said, "Do you have a doctor that I could call?"

The son said, "Mom, do you still use Dr. Radcliff?"

The woman didn't answer.

"Brian Radcliff," the son said. "I don't know his number."

"I'll get it," Decker said. "I could have him meet your mother at the hospital."

"I'm not going!"

The son's eyes were desperate. "Please call him."

Decker said, "Maybe he can come here."

Marge returned with a glass of water. She slowly brought it to the mother's lips. Decker made the phone call, then walked back to the living room. "He'll be here in about ten minutes."

"Thank you," the son said.

Decker said to Marge, "Stay with her, okay?"

"Absolutely."

To the boy, Decker said, "Can I talk to you for a few minutes?"

The young man followed Decker into the kitchen. "First of all, I am so sorry for your sister's death."

"Thank you." He swiped at his eyes, brimming with tears.

"I'm sorry, sir, but I didn't catch your name."

"Eric Gelb."

"The victim is your younger sister?"

Eric nodded.

"And your mother's name?"

"Udonis."

"Gelb?"

The boy nodded.

"Divorced, widowed?"

"Divorced."

"And your father?"

"Dead."

"I'm sorry."

He shrugged.

"Were you here when it happened . . . with your sister?"

"No."

"Was your mother here?"

"At work."

"So you came home or she came home . . ."

"I found her . . . Myra." He clamped his hand over his mouth. "She was already . . ."

Decker nodded. "And then what did you do?"

"I called my mom but didn't tell her what happened. Then I called the police." Tears streamed down his cheeks. "The police got here before my mom. They stopped her from going into the room. When they— the police—told her that my sister had passed on, Mom fainted. So I called the paramedics."

"So this all happened about a half hour ago?"

"Maybe an hour. I have no sense of time."

Decker nodded. "Are you up to answering a few more questions?"

Eric nodded.

"First of all, how old are you?"

"Twenty-four."

"Okay. And you're at UCLA?"

He nodded. "Second-year law."

"Okay. Is it just you and your sister?"

"Yes."

"So you two were pretty close or . . ."

"There's an age gap. I'm not home a lot. But when we saw each other, we got along."

"Are you from the same mother and father?"

"Yeah. My parents separated, then reconciled and had my sister. But eventually they got divorced when I was eighteen."

"So Myra was ten?"

"Yeah. Right after that, my dad came down with cancer. He died two years ago. My dad and I weren't very close—no animosity, but nothing in common. Myra and Dad were very close. The divorce hit Myra very hard. My dad's death was devastating to her."

"Depression?"

"Major. She was put on medication."

"Is she still on medication?"

"I think so."

"Did the medication help her?"

"I wouldn't know. She was also seeing a psychiatrist."

"Do you know the name?"

"My mom knows."

"Had your sister ever made any suicide attempts in the past?"

"Yes. Right after my father's death. She seemed to be getting better . . ." He threw up his hands.

Decker said, "She went to Bell and Wakefield?"

Eric nodded. "Scholarship. We both were scholarship students."

"How was that for you?"

"For me?"

Decker nodded.

"It was okay. I got a good education."

"Socially?"

"Not the warmest place, but I had my friends. I didn't have problems."

"What about your sister?"

Eric blew out air. "I don't know. She never complained. I know that she has a few friends."

"Do you know their names?"

"First names only. Heddy . . . Ramona . . ." He shrugged. "That's as much as I can recall."

"Has anything about your sister changed over the last couple of months?"

"Not that I noticed. But I wasn't home a lot."

"Did you see a deepening of her depression?"

"No . . . not really."

"Do you know if your sister had any outside activities?"

"She painted and drew," Eric said. "She was a great artist. I think she did some cartooning for the school paper."

"Anything else?"

He exhaled. "She might have had other interests, but I don't know. I'm not here most of the time. It was just a fluke that I . . ." His eyes watered. "I'm either at school or in the library. I also have an internship after school and on the weekends. Mostly, I just sleep here. I told my mother to switch beds with me—I don't need my room anymore—but she's stubborn. I guess you can see that."

Decker heard voices from the other room. Marge peeked her head in. "The doctor's here."

"Good." To Eric, Decker said, "Thank you very much for answering the questions. Again, I'm very sorry."

Eric nodded and they returned to the living room.

Radcliff was in his fifties with gray hair. He was dressed in a sweater over an oxford shirt and jeans. He patted Eric's shoulder. "We decided to meet up at the hospital."

"Thank you very much," Eric told him.

Marge got off her cell. "We've got two CIs downstairs. Maybe we should wait until Mrs. Gelb leaves for the hospital."

Decker agreed as Udonis Gelb was helped onto a wheelchair. Dr. Radcliff said, "I'll let you know what's going on, Eric. Can I have your cell number?"

He gave it to him. "Thank you, Doctor."

As soon as the mother left, the two coroner's investigators—Jamaica Carmichael and Austin Bodine—came into the apartment.

Decker said to Eric, "I have to check out what happened. Lots of people coming in and out. You don't have to stay."

"I promised my mother."

"You can wait in the living room."

Eric nodded.

Marge led the CIs to the death scene. Decker took out his notebook. An average-looking bedroom—blue walls, white furniture, and a white silky cover splattered with blood. The gun—a .22 Taurus revolver—still rested atop the duvet, but the body was on the floor, crumpled at the foot of the bed. Her face lay sideways in a pool of congealing blood, a blackened hole dripping blood down her cheek and skull, clotting into her short, dark hair. Her right hand had a lot of stippling from powder burns. She'd been dressed in a gray T-shirt and dark jeans. Her feet were bare.

Decker said, "Did you take any trajectory measurements?"

"I took measurements from the gun to her hand and from the gun to her head, but she was on the floor when I came in. I've been looking around the room. I haven't found a bullet."

Coroner investigator Austin Bodine carefully turned the head. "You didn't find any bullet because it's still inside. No exit wound."

Marge checked her notes. "To me, it appears that she was sitting on the edge of the bed when she did it. The gun shot back onto the bed, but she slid down to the floor. The comforter is satiny material . . . slippery."

Decker said, "Are you sure it's just one shot?"

"So far just the one to the head." Jamaica carefully turned the body onto its side. "Everything else appears intact."

Bodine bagged the hands. "You want to check her clothes before we take her?"

Marge said, "Yeah." Meticulously, the two detectives went through the clothing looking for foreign objects—hair, fiber, anything to suggest the presence of another person in the room. Blood had splattered everywhere. It looked like a self-inflicted gunshot to the head, not unlike Gregory Hesse. But at least in this case, there were some answers as to the why.

When Marge and Decker had finished with the clothes, the CIs began the arduous process of wrapping and transferring the body, sliding the remains of Myra Gelb onto a steel gurney and wheeling her out the door. Eric sat on the sofa while all this was happening, head down, with his hands in his lap. It took a while for the young man to speak even after the investigators had left. Finally Eric said, "What now?"

"My partner and I would like to go over the room thoroughly. Open drawers, go through the closet, look under the bed . . . Do you have any objection to that?"

"No."

Marge said, "Do you have any idea where Myra got the gun?"

Eric looked up and stared at her. "That's a very good question."

"Could it be your mother's?" Decker said.

"Not likely. She never said anything about it to me."

"We'll ask her," Marge said. "We're going to take the gun with us to make sure that everything matches."

"Okay." Eric was very pale. "What happens after you go through the room?"

Decker handed Eric a card. "Once we clear the area, you can call up this woman. She and her son will come into the room and dispose of what needs to be cleaned up."

"God, I never thought of that." His head sank in his hands. "I guess you just don't call up the cleaning lady." Tears trickled down his cheeks.

"It has to be done by a professional. There are other people who do this, but we've found that this woman is very sensitive."

Eric took the card. "Thank you, Sergeant . . . Lieutenant."

"She's the sergeant, I'm the lieutenant." Decker and Marge gave Eric their cards. "Call us if you need anything."

"What about the body?"

"After the autopsy, someone will call you to pick it up." Decker gave him another card. "This is a contact at Forest Lawn. I don't know if you have a cemetery, but at least here's a name. I also have the name of someone who does cremations, if you want that. Once the body is released, the professionals will do the rest."

Eric took the cards. "Thanks for the direction." He looked up. "I'm totally lost."

"We understand," Marge said. "We're going back to the room if that's okay with you. In the meantime, do you have someone you want us to call?"

"No one I want to be with," Eric told them. "I wouldn't wish this on my worst enemy."

Chapter Fourteen

The bedroom was functional: Myra's belongings were meager. She was neat. Her desk drawers and her clothing drawers were organized and sparse. It was one of the few times that Decker ever remembered a female closet with room to spare. Myra had six dresses, almost identical in style—short sleeves, V-necks in solid colors. She had four skirts, and a half-dozen each of sweaters, tees, and jeans. Her shoes were sneakers, a set of black pumps, and flip-flops.

Not much in the way of ornamentation—nothing frilly like stuffed animals, glass figurines, or heart jewelry. Nor was there anything rebellions; no Goth accoutrements, no combat boots, no chains, no signs of cigarettes or pot. She didn't appear to be into athletics, she didn't appear to be into drama. There was nothing to put your finger on and say: Hey, this was Myra. She was a psychologically impoverished girl.

Her books must have provided her with some escapism: the Harry Potter series in hardback, the Twilight series in hardback, and Gossip Girls in paperbacks. She had no CDs, but she did have an iPod and a cell phone. With a gloved hand, Decker checked her most recent calls. Most were from Mom, but there were several from Heddy, Ramona, and Lisa. Eric had called her cell once in the last few weeks. There were also several numbers with no names ascribed to them. Decker wrote down the digits.

He asked Marge, "Do you have a Bell and Wakefield yearbook?"

"I can get one."

"I'd like to have faces to go with the names. In the cases of Heddy, Ramona, and Lisa, I'd like to have last names." He went through some of Myra's texts: *c u soon, pick u up at 5.*

It would take way too long to go over all her texts. Decker returned the phone to the nightstand. "I'd love to keep it, but I suppose I have to ask permission." He regarded Marge. "Two kids from the same school kill themselves within a month and a half of each other. Both of them were . . . outsiders. What do you think?"

"That it's often the outsiders who commit suicide. Plus, one was male; the other was female, different ages, different grades."

"And the female had a history of depression," Decker said.

"But . . ." Marge said. "It's still two kids from the same school within a very small period of time. I'm thinking maybe some kind of suicide club or suicide pact or . . . Did they even know each other?"

"I'm wondering about the gun. Where did it come from?" The room fell quiet. Decker finally said, "I don't see a computer."

"Maybe there's a shared computer," Marge suggested. "I can ask Eric about it."

"If we want to break into Myra's personal life, we're going to have to ask Mrs. Gelb for permission." Decker raked his hair with his hands. "And unlike Wendy Hesse, she hasn't asked for our help." He returned his eyes to the closet. In the corner were two cardboard moving boxes. He pulled one out and opened it up. "Lookie here, Margie."

Hundreds of drawings—pen and ink, pencil, crayon, pastels, watercolors—on random pieces of white paper, scratch paper with advertisements on the other side, a dozen sketch pads, and lots of napkins, newspapers, and Post-its: anything made of pulp.

"At last," Decker said. "We've found the real Myra Gelb."

"She was good." Marge picked up some material on the top and regarded it with a critical eye. "Very good, as a matter of fact."

There were faces, there were landscapes, there were still lifes and lots of cartoons and caricatures. They began to sort through the material one by one by one. An hour later, Decker was looking at a detailed pen-and-ink drawing of a big jock-type guy grunting on the toilet. The caption was *Dylan's artistic output.* He showed the drawing to Marge.

"Dylan Lashay?" When Decker shrugged, she said, "Whoever he is, Myra wasn't a fan. I'll get a yearbook tomorrow."

By midnight, Marge stood up and stretched. She'd been in the apartment for almost six hours, the last four of them spent in the bedroom. She heard footsteps. Eric knocked on the doorpost, and Marge and Decker came out of the room.

"What's up?" she said.

"I just got a call from Dr. Radcliff. They've admitted my mom. I need to go to the hospital. I'd really like to close this up for tonight."

"Not a problem," Decker said. "We're going to rope off the room with tape. Please don't go in or out of it."

"I guarantee you that won't be an issue."

"We'll come back tomorrow. Thanks for letting us stay so late."

"No problem." Eric paused. "What are you looking for?"

"I know your sister was depressed. But she was on medication and seeing a psychiatrist. She was also functioning. She certainly was drawing a lot." Decker paused. "Do you think your mother would mind if I took these boxes to the station house and looked them over?"

"What's inside?"

"Your sister's artwork."

"My mom's going to want them back."

"Of course," Decker said. "But this way, I can look through them and not be in your way."

"I guess it would be okay." Eric exhaled. "Sure, take them."

Marge took one box, and Decker took the other. They were bulky but not heavy. Eric locked up the door, and the four of them walked to the elevator. When they got to the ground floor, Eric went out first.

"Give our deepest sympathies to your mom," Marge said.

"I will."

Decker hefted one of the boxes. "This may be a little awkward, Eric, but I'm going to ask it anyway.

We couldn't find your sister's computer. Did she have one?"

Eric nodded. "She had a Mac. That's weird."

Marge lifted her box. "Maybe we'll find it tomorrow."

"That's really strange. It's usually right out in the open."

"Could someone have taken it?"

"I don't know who. But if it's not there . . ." A beat. "I'm stumped."

Decker said, "Sometimes people give stuff away before they act."

Eric shook his head. "She only had a few friends. Ask them."

"Okay." Decker picked up his box. "Again, I'm sorry for your loss."

But Eric didn't appear to hear. "Do you think she might have left like a note on it or something?"

"Can't say for sure," Decker said. "But if we don't look, we'll never know."

Even though Yasmine had told him that the boy writes first, Gabe always waited until she texted him. That way he knew that she had total privacy. His phone gave off a beep at 12:30 in the morning. He had been in his bed with the lights off, resting, thinking about her and getting very aroused.

r u up?

He felt his heart sing in his chest.

w8ing 4 u. Without waiting for a reply, he texted: *that was a close one 2nite.*

omg, i was going 2 have a heart attack.

u were cool. i was a real dork.

no, i was a dork. at least u talked.

if u call mumbling, talking. Then Gabe wrote: *ur sister's a brat.*

daisy is daisy. it's hard being in 11th grade.

Gabe smiled. Yasmine was probably one of those nice people who always saw the good in everyone. *i'm just protective of u.*

☺ *thx.*

Gabe texted: *btw, someone's been keeping secrets from me.*

someone should talk!!! She texted another line. *harvard!!!!* Another pause. *HARVARD!!!!*

He texted back: *Maybe.*

Maybe????? r u nuts?

there r other options.

Like?

Tell u 18r.

A long pause. Then she wrote: *r u going 2 college in the fall?*

He wrote: *yeah.*

☹

maybe i'll stay here.

seriously, gabe, if u get n2 harvard, u go 2 harvard.

maybe. A beat. *i want to hear u sing.*

no.

c'mon.

no.

chick-en.

sticks and stones . . .

how long have u been singing opera?

i don't sing opera.

Gabe smiled. *liar.*

m not.

ok. u don't sing opera. so what aria were u singing in the house over and over and over according to Daisy.

nothing.

c'mon yasmine enuf. i want 2know.

u'll laugh.

Gabe texted back: *?????*

Yasmine responded: *promise u won't laugh.*

of course i won't laugh.

der holle rache.

"Der Hölle Rache"—the revenge aria from Mozart's *The Magic Flute* sung by the Queen of the Night. It was an iconic piece of music, one of the first arias that children hear when introduced to opera. Yet it was one of the hardest bits of music to sing because of the coloratura required.

Not too shabby. Feeling mischievous, Gabe texted back. *lol.*

shut up!

seriously, that's really impressive.

not the way i sing it.

i don't believe u.

u should.

so ur a coloratura soprano.

so they say.

who's they? ur voice coach? u must have a teacher if u can sing der holle rache.

i do. my dad thinks i take piano lessons but i really take voice lessons.

The truth comes out. Gabe wrote: *ah. now things r making sense. ur mother is n on this?*

yeah.

anyl else besides me know?

just u n ariella.

ah, ariella, the keeper of the secrets. i hope she's a gd friend.

she is.

Sneaking around seemed to be the Nourmand family pastime. Not unlike Gabe's own family. He texted: *i* can't picture all that coloratura coming from such a small chest.

ur horrible. now i'll **never** *sing 4u.*

i didn't mean it like that. But of course, he did. He loved teasing her.

i h8 u, Yasmine wrote.

Gabe texted: *2 bad cuz I'm madly crazy 4 u.*

A long pause. Then Yasmine wrote: *maybe i don't h8 u.*

Gabe wrote: *let's kiss n make up.*

kiss n make out u mean.

that, 2. A pause. *i'm serious. when can i hear u sing?*

never.

Gabe wrote: *come over this saturday. the deckers are going out 2 lunch 4 shabbos. They'll leave at 10 so come at 11. i'll play accompaniment 4u.*

i can't. i've got 2 go to shul. i already missed last saturday bcuz of u.

plzzzz?

gabe, I can't.

☹

i'll c what I can do. no promises.

Plzzzz, plzzzz, plzzzz???

i'll c.

u know i don't want 2 get u n trouble. i just miss u.

i miss u,2.

She added: *a lot.*

Gabe wrote: *plz come, yasmine. i want to c u cuz I really like u, but i also really want 2 hear u sing. if u don't come, it'll be an entire week w/out c-ing u.*

A long pause. *rn't we on 4 thurs?*

i can't. have 2 meet with this agent and b at SC by 8.

agent?

yeah, musicians need agents 2 get jobs.

did he get u a job?

maybe. there're openings 4 a pianist at some chamber music festivals in wyoming, texas n oklahoma. mozart piano quartet. i have to play it for him so i need 2 b perfect.

u only play perfect.

c, that's y i like u so much. can u make fri morning?

no, i have a math test.

so come sat, plzzzzzzzzzzzz.

A long pause. *ok. i'll come sat. i'll think of something.*

Thx,thx,thx. Then he wrote, *u know i really m crazy 4 u.*

She responded: *i feel the same way.*

Gabe texted: *a thousand kisses.*

a million kisses.

it's 18. u have school. go to bed.

Yasmine wrote: *i will. it's just that i'm soooooo happy when i talk 2 u.*

i know. it's so hard to let go. But it's after 1. u need 2 go 2 bed, i'll see u on sat.

okay.

gnite n sweet dreams.

they'll b sweet if i dream of u.

Gabe wrote: *ur intoxicating. i can't stop thinking about u. i can't w8 4 sat., gnite, my luv, gnite, gnite.*

Yasmine wrote: *gnite, my angel gabriel, gnite, gnite.*

His phone went dead.

His heart was thumping in his chest. He closed his eyes and let his brain and other things take over, imagining the feel of her lips, the taste of her skin.

It didn't take long.

The second time didn't take long, either.

It seemed sacrilegious to do it after talking to her. She was so gorgeous, and pure and angelic. But he couldn't help it.

He was a dude. He was fifteen. He was Chris Donatti's son.

It was what it was.

Chapter Fifteen

Wednesday morning—the day after Myra Gelb put a gun to her head—Bell and Wakefield had canceled all classes. The daily grind of AP calculus and advanced composition had been replaced with special programs on the hour every hour starting at eight in the morning. Scheduled were three all-school assemblies held in the massive auditorium as well as smaller class seminars. The topics ranged from bullying to establishing healthy peer relationships to teenage depression and suicide, all the information printed on packets embossed with the B and W lion logo in crimson. The cover page featured school photos of both Gregory Hesse and Myra Gelb with an *in memoriam* and the dates of their truncated lives printed underneath the photos.

Waiting in Dr. Martin Punsche's office, Marge and Oliver sat on hard-back chairs and perused the pages of the paper packet. It was now ten in the morning and they had been there for fifteen minutes. Oliver was getting antsy. Today he wore a brown suede jacket over a black shirt and black pants. His penny loafers were shined to maximum reflection. Marge was dressed in one of her favorite cashmere sweaters. Good knit-wear was like wearing a blanket—roomy and soft. These particular sweaters fell below the waistband of her pants, camouflaging the imperfections. She had bought the same garment in six colors. Today, it was baby blue day.

Oliver hit his hand on the papers. "You think any of this psych crap helps?"

"Who knows?" Marge said. "Teenagers are on another planet. Only fate and pain stop them from self-destruction, and sometimes even those are not enough."

Oliver studied the pictures of the deceased teens. "So there was like a month between the two deaths."

Marge nodded. "Six weeks. If they were two random suicides, that's bad enough. But you can't help but wonder if something weird is going on inside the school—like a suicide club or gun games."

"Gun games are a white male thing. Maybe Gregory Hesse. Not Myra Gelb. Do the two victims have *anything* in common besides going to the same school?"

Marge thought a moment. "They're not exactly outcasts, but they certainly weren't part of the 'in' crowd like the B and W Mafia, nothing more than a bunch of stupid rich kids playing criminal idiots. But that doesn't mean that the boys can't do damage."

"Yeah, teenagers with guns aren't good news for anyone," Oliver said. "So Myra was suffering from depression?"

"According to her brother, yes. We have no indication that Gregory was also afflicted. The two of them don't seem to have friends in common. Also, with fifteen hundred kids in the school, it's likely that the two of them didn't know each other, especially since she was a grade older."

"What about teachers in common?"

"Don't know," Marge said. "To tell you the truth, after Wendy Hesse stonewalled our mini-investigation, we stopped with the psychological autopsy on Gregory Hesse. But now with *two* suicides, and Kevin Stanger's bullying and reports about mini Mafia gangs, it may be worth dissecting. There are always cliques, but this may go beyond."

At that moment, Martin Punsche flew in like a tornado, attired in a white shirt and dark pants. His face had gathered a heavy etching of lines since the detectives had last seen him. The VP checked his watch. "I know that I'm late. Couldn't be helped. It's been . . . hellish. There's no other word for it. Hellish. This is totally unprecedented."

"You've never had suicides at B and W before?" Oliver asked.

"Two in the past eight years, and we thought that was extraordinary. We screen for the psychologically robust. Of course, you can't predict things like death and illness that crop up during the four years that the kids are here, but we try to deal with those things right away. We knew that Myra had some issues. We require all parents to report what medications their children are on for legal reasons. Her mother told us that Myra had gone on antidepressants. But she seemed to be doing fine."

"What is your definition of doing fine?" Oliver asked.

"Her grades were excellent and she had friends. Her teachers didn't report anything odd."

Marge said, "Would you like to sit down, sir?"

Punsche realized he was pacing in a tiny space. He collapsed into his cushioned desk chair. "I've only got a minute before the next seminar. What can I do you for?"

"Last time we spoke, you said that you didn't know Gregory Hesse very well," Oliver reminded him.

"Yes, that was true. Since that time I did speak to a couple of his teachers. Gregory didn't seem to have any problems, either. He was an excellent student, no behavioral and social issues. He actually did some tutoring that I wasn't aware of. I'm completely in the dark." Punsche stared at the detectives. "I'm not even sure why you two are here. It's great to have the police interested in the welfare of our young people, but I'm not sure this is really a police matter."

Oliver said, "We want to make sure that these deaths aren't part of a larger issue at the school . . . that the two cases aren't related."

Punsche ran his hand over his bald head. "I don't see how. Myra and Gregory weren't even in the same grade."

"That doesn't mean they didn't know each other."

Marge said, "Maybe the two of them were in some common class."

"Usually eleventh grade and tenth grade are pretty separate, but there are some electives that can be taken in any year in any grade. Let me see . . ." He booted up his computer. "I'll pull up Myra's class list and Gregory's class list . . ."

"We still have that list of Gregory's classes." Marge pulled out a piece of paper. "We understand that he was particularly interested in investigative journalism."

Dr. Punsche shrugged. "I wouldn't know."

Oliver said, "Was Gregory working on the school paper?"

"I don't know."

"What about Myra?" Marge asked. "She was a very good artist and cartoonist."

"I wouldn't know about that, either. The journalism teacher and newspaper adviser is Saul Hinton. Feel free to talk to him. He's in room . . ." He clicked a few keys on the computer and pressed the print button. "What was I saying?"

"Saul Hinton's room number."

"Twenty-six or twenty-seven." Punsche pulled the list from the printer and handed it to Marge. "Here you go—Myra Gelb's classes."

She briefly compared it to Gregory Hesse's class schedule. The lists didn't appear to intersect, and neither was currently taking any journalism class.

"Anything else?" Punsche made a show of looking at his watch. "I do need to go."

Oliver said, "A few more little things. What do you know about Dylan Lashay?"

Punsche was taken aback. "What does Dylan have to do with any of this?"

Marge said, "We understand that he's the leader of a group of boys who . . . well, they fashion themselves after the Mafia, complete with Dylan being the don and having a bunch of capos."

"*What?*" Punsche made a disbelieving face. "I've never heard of anything so ridiculous. Dylan is one of our star students—academic, athletic, and a terrific actor. He was accepted early decision to Yale."

"Okay," Marge said. "And that contradicts what we just told you because . . ."

"Well, that's just preposterous! Dylan doesn't have to play games to be a leader. He *is* a leader."

Oliver said, "We've heard he has an unhealthy passion for guns."

"I don't know *what* you're talking about!" Punsche said. "And furthermore, it is not my habit to talk about specific students to the police."

"Except to say that he got into Yale," Marge said.

"I think our business is done here." Punsche got up from his chair. "Even though you've crossed some boundaries, I still invite you to talk to Mr. Hinton or any one of our staff here at B and W. We have nothing hidden here although I don't know what Mr. Hinton or anyone on our staff could offer you."

"I appreciate your openness," Marge said. She could mentally hear Oliver snickering. "You never know what will turn up, so thanks for giving us free range with your teachers."

"I didn't say *that!*" Punsche shook his head as if he were dealing with two errant students. "Look, Detectives, I won't presume to tell you how to run your investigation, but I will offer you a word or two of friendly advice. The school has undergone two terrible tragedies, two self-inflicted deaths. It makes no sense for you to go poking into other people's affairs."

"By other people do you mean Dylan Lashay?" Oliver said.

Punsche said. "The Lashays are wonderful people, and Dylan is no exception. They are very involved in the local community and charity, which includes support for the local police."

Oliver grinned. "Good to know whose feet we'll be stepping on."

Marge nudged her partner. "We all have a job to do, sir. And I'm sure you respect the fact that we take our work seriously. Thank you for your help."

Oliver wasn't done. "I'm not quite sure I'd call your advice friendly, Dr. Punsche."

Marge pinched him hard as Oliver threw her a dirty look. Punsche didn't notice the interaction. "I'm just laying it out for you. What you do with it is your business."

Saul Hinton was in his forties, tall and lanky with a sloping nose and a bad comb-over of gray unruly hair. With his spindly arms and elongated torso, he moved like one of those inflatable balloon tube men placed as come-ons in front of car lots.

The classroom was empty. The front wall had a blackboard, a whiteboard, and a mounted forty-inch flatscreen. Pinned up on the cork board was the most recent edition of the school newspaper—*B and W Tattler*—again emblazoned with the lion mascot. Hinton offered them a seat at any of the twenty built-in desktops, each one containing several Ethernet ports for laptops.

"Actually those are already out of date," Hinton told the detectives. "The whole school went wireless six years ago. The ports are used only for backup."

"What happens if the kid doesn't have his own laptop?" Oliver asked.

"The school provides it for him or her," Hinton replied.

"What's the tuition?" Marge asked.

"Forty thousand a year. About twenty percent of our student body is on scholarship," Hinton said. "The administration does what it needs to do to keep the quality up and balance the budget. Unfortunately we have to turn down a lot of otherwise great students to do so." He sat on the edge of his desk. "What can I do you for? I wouldn't think these deaths, as tragic as they are, are police business."

Oliver said, "Technically, suicides are crimes."

"And that's ridiculous."

Marge said, "Mainly, sir, we've here because we want to be sure that the suicides aren't some part of a larger problem at Bell and Wakefield."

Hinton looked at her with focused brown eyes. "What larger problem?"

"Do you remember a student named Kevin Stanger?"

"Of course. He transferred out at the start of tenth grade."

Oliver said, "Do you know why?"

"Do you?"

"He was having some social issues," Marge told him. "Is that what you heard?"

"Something like that."

Oliver said, "Then you're one step ahead of the VP. Dr. Punsche claimed he had no idea why Stanger transferred."

Hinton was quiet.

"Or maybe he lied."

Again, Hinton didn't talk—a tactic of police interrogation as well as journalism. Marge said, "What do you know about crowding?"

"Was that what Kevin talked about?" Hinton asked.

Answering a question with a question. Oliver changed the subject. "Kevin told us that he and Greg Hesse kept up contact even after Kevin left. He also mentioned that Hesse had taken an interest in investigative journalism when he took your ninth-grade course."

"Yes, that's true. Greg was intrigued by Watergate."

"Did Watergate inspire Greg to do some kind of investigation on his own?"

"Not that I know of and certainly nothing under my auspices."

Marge said, "Kevin Stanger seemed to think that Gregory was involved in something secretive. Hesse was attached to his camcorder. Furthermore, he claimed he was onto something that would turn Bell and Wakefield upside down."

"Would you know what Stanger is talking about?" Oliver said.

Slowly Hinton shook his head. "No, I really don't." Another pause. "Anything else you can tell me . . . maybe something will strike a chord."

Marge said. "That's all Stanger knows. We were just wondering if this had something to do with the school paper."

"Gregory wasn't on staff for the paper."

"Did he ever write a guest column maybe?"

Hinton bit his bottom lip, stood up, and went to his desk, booting up his computer. "Hold on a moment." It took him around five minutes of searching. "He actually did write a column . . . just one and at the beginning of the year." His eyes scanned over the screen and then he pressed the printer button. "I remember this now. It was advice on how to survive ninth grade. Humorous but informative."

He pulled the sheet from the printer and gave it to Oliver.

"It's coming back to me. Greg was a very good writer. But he never signed up to join the paper. I don't know why."

Marge said, "Were there conflicts with other students?"

"I don't recall that."

"Who's the student editor of the paper?"

"We have a junior editor and a senior editor."

Marge took out her notebook. "Could I have the names?"

"I can give you the names because you could find that out easily enough. But no one is going to give you permission to talk to these kids without their parents."

"Point taken," Marge said.

"Junior editor is Heddy Kramer; the senior editor is Kyle Kerkin."

"Kyle Kerkin," Marge said. "He's a friend of Dylan Lashay, isn't he?"

Hinton paused. "Why are you asking me irrelevant questions?"

"Lashay's name keeps popping up when we talk about the suicides," Oliver said.

Marge switched topics before Hinton could respond. "Heddy Kramer was a good friend of Myra Gelb. We know that from Myra's brother, Eric." She held up a finger. "You know, Myra was an excellent artist. And with one of her good friends editing the *Tattler* . . . Do you know if Myra ever did work on the paper as a staff artist?"

"She wasn't on staff, but she did some freelance. Cartooning, I believe."

Oliver said, "Maybe Myra met Gregory through the paper."

Hinton shook his head. "I wouldn't think so. Neither was a regular contributor."

Oliver said. "Myra Gelb didn't like Dylan Lashay much. She drew a few derogatory caricatures of him."

Hinton glared at him. "You know, the police, like journalists, should be impartial when conducting an interview. It's clear to me that you two have an agenda.

I don't know what your investigation has to do with Dylan Lashay and frankly, I don't care. I think we're done."

"Exactly what Dr. Punsche said when he didn't like our questions," Oliver said.

Marge got up. "Thank you for your time and help."

"I hope I didn't help you at all," Hinton said.

Oliver smiled. "Sometimes it's what you don't say that helps us more than what you do say."

Chapter Sixteen

Decker said, "Myra Gelb's gun came back as stolen."

Oliver said, "Why am I not surprised."

He and Marge were in the Loo's office. She was standing, he was sitting across from Decker's desk. It was three in the afternoon.

Marge said, "How long ago?"

"A year."

"Who was it pilfered from?"

"Lisbeth and Ramon Holly." Decker handed Oliver the address and phone number. "They live in the area. Give them a call and find out the details."

"I'll set something up." He walked out of the office.

To Marge, Decker said, "So what's going on?"

"We've got bits and pieces about the two kids but nothing that you can sink your teeth into. Plus, I don't think the school likes us that much. Not nearly as much as they like Dylan Lashay." She recapped the morning to the boss. "Myra and Greg did some freelance work on the paper, but we still don't have anything to tie them together."

"Is Heddy Kramer the Heddy from Myra's contact list on her phone?" Decker asked.

"Yes. She's also the junior editor." Marge shrugged. "Maybe she was a contact point between the two kids. The journalism teacher doesn't remember them knowing each other, but he wasn't helpful, especially after we mentioned Dylan Lashay's name."

"Dylan the Mafia don."

"His parents must have made the school an offer they couldn't refuse."

Decker smiled.

Marge said, "It's possible that Myra and Greg met through the paper. Maybe they started talking about some unsavory things that were going on in the school. Neither one was an outcast, but they certainly weren't in the popular crowd." A pause. "Or maybe a suicide is just a suicide."

"What intrigues me is that both guns were stolen. Gregory Hesse is puzzling enough. Why would Myra Gelb have a stolen gun?"

"Beats me," Marge said. "I can interview Heddy Kramer if you want?"

Decker thought a moment. "Myra's memorial service is tomorrow at eleven. Let's wait until that's over before you talk to Heddy or any of Myra's other friends. The shock needs to wear off before they can talk coherently."

"I'll try to set something up for next week."

Oliver came back. "No one's home at the Hollys. I left a message."

Marge said, "Myra's funeral is tomorrow afternoon. I'm going to set up an interview with the friends early next week."

"Try to talk to the Hollys sooner than that," Decker said. "If you can't get them on Friday, do it over the weekend."

Marge turned to Oliver. "I'm okay this weekend. What about you?"

Oliver said, "You know my number, sweetheart. Call me anytime."

At 6:30 in the morning, Gabe sat at the bus stop, head in hand, cursing the hour and the singing birds whose current cacophony was giving him a headache. He knew that the upcoming audition was important to his future, but his mind was elsewhere, and his focus was scattered. If he was going to get up this early, at least he should be spending time with Yasmine. They saw each other on

Monday, Tuesday, and Thursday mornings (they had up the count by one more day) and it pissed him off that he had to miss seeing her even though he knew that Nick had worked hard to set this thing up. He continued to mope over the situation, in his own world, so he vaguely noticed a figure walking by. He didn't even hear the voice until she was right on top of him.

"Chris?"

Gabe looked up.

The girl was truly gorgeous: long blond hair and silky blue eyes, tall and leggy. Her boobs were big and perfect, probably from surgery even though she was young. Surgery or not, it didn't matter. She was the perfect ten.

His thoughts had been concentrated on Yasmine, so it took him a while to realize that she was addressing him. He started to say that she had made a mistake, but then it clicked who she was.

"Do you remember me?" She flashed a blinding white smile.

" 'Course," he said. "You were one of the girls with Dylan."

She sat down next to him on the bench. "Dylan's an asshole."

That was definitely true. Gabe said, "If he's an asshole, why do you hang with him?"

She cocked her head to the side. "He has some . . . hidden attributes."

Flirtatious little wench. Gabe laughed. "Good for Dylan."

"I'm sorry if he was a jerk to you," she said.

"He was irrelevant to me."

"He was impressed with you. I could tell."

Gabe shrugged it off.

"You sure know a lot about guns."

"My dad collects guns." On the sly. The man still technically had a record. Not that any law had ever stopped any felon from owning guns. "Frankly, I'd rather he collect cars or guitars—something less lethal."

"Is your father really a pimp?"

"Yes."

"Wow, that's pretty . . . weird."

"I ain't gonna lie. It is weird when I think about it. So I don't think about it." He turned to her. "What are you doing out so early?"

"I could ask you the same thing."

"You go first."

She opened her purse and showed him a baggy filled with vegetative matter.

"Ah . . . stuff any good?"

She regarded his face. "We could find out together. I live six blocks from here."

Gabe let out a small laugh. "You have very liberal parents."

"I have workaholic parents who have left for the day."

"Ah . . ." He studied her face and it all came back to him. He knew the type backward and forward. In New York, there was always a party every Friday and Saturday night if you were in the right crowd. And being that he was Chris Donatti's son, he was always in the right crowd. Even though he was a year younger because he had skipped a grade, the guys accepted him. He was labeled as the smart, talented one who knew how to keep his mouth shut when shit went down. And because he was tall and good-looking enough, the older girls also accepted him, too.

It was same old, same old. You go up to a room, take a couple of hits, and within ten minutes the girl was going down on you. But that wasn't what he wanted now. Well, not the going down part. He would have loved a blow job, but not from this weirdo stranger, as stunning as she was. He could hear his father's voice calling him an idiot. And maybe he was an idiot. Because it scared him sometimes, that he was so obsessed with a skinny little virgin with small boobs and a very big personality. He couldn't shake Yasmine from his mind. He kept picturing her naked, which proved to be embarrassing because when he did it, he always got aroused.

Just thinking about her for a couple of seconds and he was already semierect. The blonde was looking at his groin. She took the discernible shape in his pants as a sign of interest. "I take it that's a go?"

"I can't." Gabe threw up his hands. "I'm meeting my bandmates. We have an audition at a studio for a major record company at eight in the morning, and they'll kill me if I'm late."

"It's only six-fifty."

"It takes a while to go by bus."

"You don't have a car?" she asked.

"I don't have a license," he said. "I'm fifteen."

She was taken aback. "Really?"

"Really." He shrugged. "I wouldn't lie about that."

She looked him up and down. "Why aren't you in school?"

"I think I told you . . . or maybe I told Dylan. I'm homeschooled. It's great because it gives me lots of flexibility to play with my band. And being that I don't drive and I have to take the bus everywhere, it gives me time to do things."

Her eyes were on his face. She said, "We could walk back to my house and I could drive you to your audition."

"You don't have school?"

"This is what I think of school." She pointed her middle finger up in the air. "Besides, I already got accepted to college."

"Where?"

"Reed . . . or should I say weed." She grinned. "C'mon, Chris. It'll relax you."

She wasn't a girl who'd take no easily. His brain was reeling on how to get out of this without pissing her off. "I'm a little amped about this audition. It's just not the right time."

She leaned in closer and began to massage his neck. Her touch was cold. "You sure you wouldn't like a little good-luck toke? It'll probably relax you."

"Maybe, but I'm . . ." He tried to look sincere. To truly get her off his back, he probably should kiss her or something, but it didn't seem right. "You really are gorgeous. I'm probably a huge moron right now, but I know myself when I get like this. Another time, okay?"

"Your loss."

"Believe me, I know."

She took her hand from his neck. "What do you play?"

He could have said keyboards, but he didn't feel like telling her anything about himself. Since he wasn't carrying a guitar or a bass, he said, "Drums."

Again, that smile. "I like a guy who can carry a steady beat."

"You know what they say. Drummers do it with a bang." Thank God the bus was in sight. "Hey, I don't even know your name."

"Cameron."

Gabe made a show of pulling out his phone and entering her name in his contact list. "And your number?"

She gave it to him. When she asked for his number, he mixed up the digits. That way if he ever ran into her again, he could claim that she typed them in wrong if she actually tried to call him.

"Do you have a last name?" she asked.

"Donatti." He spelled it for her. If she googled the name, she'd get references to his dad and see that he was telling the truth. She'd probably figure that he was Donatti junior. Gabe didn't ask for her last name, and she didn't offer it up.

The bus pulled to the curb. "Good talking to you, Cameron," he said. "Another time?"

Cameron tilted her head, but her eyes had turned stormy. "You can always dream, little boy."

"I suppose I deserved that." He stood up.

Her eyes went up and down his body. "I might be forgiving . . . it all depends. Ball's in your court, Chris." A pause. "I'm assuming you're good with balls?"

He forced out a laugh and pointed to her purse. "Think of me when you try it out." He climbed the two steps up to the driver and gave him the money.

He was thrilled when the bus pulled away.

Immediately, he erased her name from his contact list and sat back on the bench seat, feeling his heartbeat slow until it was back to normal. A few minutes later, his phone sprang to life.

r u there?

His smile was immediate. *on the bus to sc.*

gd luck on the audition. i know u'll do g8.

thx. i'm pretty confident. gd luck on ur bio test.

thx. i'm not as confident as u r, but who is?

Gabe laughed. *r u saying i'm arrogant?*

i'm saying that ur 2 perfect 2 ever worry.

If she only knew! He texted: *if i'm perfect, it's cuz i hang with the goddess of perfection.*

ur the best. ☺

Gabe wrote: *i really missed u this morning, Yasmine.*

missed u soooo much. A pause. *i dreamed . . . dreamt about u last nite.*

i hope it was a good one.

we were kissing.

then it was a very good one.

it was so real, gabe. i could taste ur mouth. i didn't ever want it 2 end.

Seven in the morning and her words were making him hornier than a springbok. Embarrassed, he crossed his legs and texted her: *what u do 2 me, little girl. it's obscene.*

lol. Another pause. *seriously, i miss u so much, gabriel. i'm so pathetic.*

not as pathetic as i am. i think about u all the time. being away from u sucks.

yeah, it really does. i can't w8 4 sat. how long will the deckers b away?

they leave 4 shul between 9 and 10. they'll probably b gone for 4 hours so hopefully we'll have lots of time 2gether and alone.

Yey! i can't w8!!!!

He wrote: *maybe we can act out ur dream.*

She wrote: *only if we can do it over and over and over.*

Gabe felt faint. *omg, ur **killing** me.*

looks like u'll need some mouth 2 mouth resuscitation. ☺

ur waaaaay 2 sexy 4 ur own gd. i can't w8 for sat. come at 10:30 2 b safe.

i'll b there at 10:30 . . . on time.

Gabe smiled. *right.*

no, really.

A pause between her texts. Then she wrote: *dang, i have 2 go. daisy is banging on my door 2 leave 4 school. if i don't go, she'll leave w/out me.*

dang ur sister. go on. i'll text u when i can.

i'll do the same. will u miss me 2day?

ur a cuckoo bird. of course, i'll miss u. i miss u every second ur not with me.

i can b a cuckoo bird just so long as im ur cuckoo bird.

u r definitely my cuckoo bird. a million hugs n kisses, yasmine. have a g8t day.

a million hugs n kisses back 4 ever n ever, gabriel. u know u own my ♥.

His cell went inert and he stared at the blank window hoping for one more time. When nothing came, he kissed his phone and returned it to his back pocket. He sat back and closed his eyes. He simply ached with longing. Nothing else mattered. Not his crazy parents, not the Deckers, not his teacher or this audition or any audition, none of his upcoming competitions or even his future as a pianist.

Just Yasmine.

Only Yasmine.

Chapter Seventeen

G abe thought he played pretty well and by the look on the agent's face, his assessment wasn't too far off. Jeff Robinson was in his thirties, a typical L.A. guy with the dark suit and T-shirt with the high-tops on his feet. He had brown hair that grazed his shoulders and jumpy eyes. He twitched a lot and used his hands when he spoke.

He said, "I think you have a real winner here, Nick. He's young and plays with that youthful energetic brio, his reading skills are excellent, he's got a strong command of the instrument, and equally as important, he's got stagecraft. He's fun to look at. I'm in the business of entertainment and ladies, being ladies, have an eye. In private events, they use the musicians like flower arrangements; and the better looking they are, the more they sell."

"The kid is more than decoration, Jeff."

"Absolutely. And if he continues to develop, I could do big things with him. I can do a lot with him now."

"I don't want him overexposed."

Talking about him like he was a old-time photograph.

"I agree, he needs seasoning. But if he continues to progress, by the time he gets out of Juilliard, he should be ready to tackle something other than chamber music in small venues." He turned to Gabe. "You're starting school in the fall."

Gabe said, "Definitely somewhere."

"What does that mean?" Robinson asked.

Gabe felt his face go hot. "Um, I got into Harvard—"

"Harvard?" Robinson stared at him. "You can't seriously be thinking of going to Harvard."

Nick said, "Jeff, let me handle this."

"You got into Juilliard?"

Gabe nodded.

"So you go to Juilliard. Harvard is a waste of time. Why would you even consider it?"

"Jeff—"

"I want to hear what the kid has to say."

Gabe took a deep breath. "I just thought it would be good for me personally as well as musically to maybe go to a regular university."

"So go to Juilliard and take some courses at Columbia. Students do that all the time."

"I haven't heard from Columbia yet," Gabe said. "I'll probably get in—"

"No, no, no. You've got it backward. You don't go to Columbia. You go to Juilliard and take courses at Columbia." A pause. "You heard from Harvard but you didn't hear from Columbia?"

"I applied early to Harvard."

"Don't tell me that's binding."

"No, Harvard isn't binding."

Jeff breathed a sigh of relief. "Gabe, let me tell you something. You don't have a lot of time. If you don't make something click between twenty to twenty-five, it ain't gonna happen for you."

"Jeff—"

"I'm not saying you can't be a musician, but solo piano with big orchestras on major venues . . . forget it."

"Will you let me handle it, Jeff?"

"Nick, I'm running a business. If the kid isn't serious, I'm not going to waste my time grooming him."

"I am serious," Gabe said.

"You can't be serious if you're thinking about Harvard. And don't tell me Yo-Yo Ma went there. You're no Yo-Yo Ma." He stared at the kid. "I got at least a hundred kids out there who'd love to be in your shoes with talent like yours and a face like yours and a teacher like Nicholas Mark. And you want to blow it all by taking four years out of your musical life and go on some kind of personal quest to find yourself?"

"I didn't say that—"

"Jeff—"

"Why should I believe you're serious, Gabe?" The guy was literally in his face. "Convince me."

Gabe said, "Because I don't want to be a musician, I *have* to be a musician. It isn't volitional. I have no choice. When I sit down and play, it's like I'm . . . whole. It's my communication, okay, like talking." He shook his head. "Music is the only thing that I speak fluently. Anything else is a foreign language."

Robinson said, "So if that's really the case, why would you consider putting yourself in a place where you can't communicate? I didn't even know that Harvard had a performance tract."

"They don't—"

"Jesus, kid! Harvard? At least go to Princeton where they have a performance tract. How can you seriously think of going to a school without a performance option? And I'm supposed to believe you're serious?"

Gabe said, "I figured I'd do maybe a joint program with New England Conservatory—"

"Which is a fine place, Gabriel. I'm not knocking NEC. But it isn't Juilliard, and Boston isn't New York."

"Jeff, he's very young."

"Not so young."

Nick said, "Young enough to take a year off to study."

"A year yes, but not four years." To Gabe he said, "If you want a university, USC is better than Harvard. At least you can study with Nick."

"Jeff, have I ever steered you wrong?"

"Nick—"

"Have I?" Silence. "For the last time, let me handle this. You just concentrate on getting him some bookings."

Gabe blurted out, "I'm not out to screw myself up, okay. If it's a bad idea to go to Boston, I won't go. And I know I'm not Yo-Yo Ma, but I figured if he went, it must be okay. But if you think it's stupid, I'll pass on Harvard, okay."

Robinson sighed. "Look, Gabe. These are the facts on the ground. You have adult skills, but you're still a kid. I know that. Nick knows that. In a perfect world, Nick and I could nurture you, but that isn't going to happen. You're going into an adult business with an emphasis on business. Got it?"

"I understand."

"I don't think you do, and that's not your fault. We're not talking about a recital or a competition or a schooled jury giving you marks. We're talking ordinary people.

Some will have decent ears, most will have appreciation for music, and there will even be some who are tone-deaf. But they'll all be paying hard-earned money to see you *perform*. You've got to go out there every single time and put out. And you've got to know that every time you put your hands on a keyboard, you're going to be critiqued. If you work hard, if you learn a sizable repertoire, if you practice, practice, practice, I have no doubt that you'll be good enough to make a go at it. I've been at this for a while. I can tell after a few pieces who has it and who doesn't. You've got the potential, and you certainly have the stagecraft. And you may rise to the vaunted top of being good enough for a solo career. You'll get your raves, but, buddy, there are times when you're going to be slammed. I'm your advocate out there. I'm the one who's going to be reading the reviews and underlining the salient remarks. If I think the review is bullshit, I won't even show it to you. But if I think you're fucking up, I'm going to tell you and I expect you to change. I don't represent losers, understand?"

"I have no problem with that." Gabe shrugged. "Without being haughty, I know I'm terrific. But I also know how to take criticism. Just ask Nick."

"He's got an ego, but he's also not stubborn," Nick said.

"That's good," Robinson said. "That's exactly what I want to hear."

"Satisfied?" Nick said.

"For the time being."

"Can we talk about what you potentially have for him this summer?"

"Depends how much he wants to work."

"He wants to work."

Jeff turned to him. "Do you want to work?"

"Absolutely. That's what I'm here for." Gabe stood up. "I'll be right back."

"Where are you going?" Jeff demanded.

"Can I take a piss?"

Jeff waved him away.

Gabe went into the hallway and blew out air. Jeff was difficult but up-front. Compared to Chris, he was a grounder. Gabe took out his mobile and punched in his father's number. Chris changed his cells like cigarettes so Gabe was always surprised when the line actually kicked in. He was even more surprised when Chris answered the phone.

Donatti answered, "You okay?"

"Yeah, I'm okay."

"What do you want?"

"I just auditioned for this agent."

"What agent?"

"His name is Jeff Robinson, and he books everything from Carnegie Hall to expensive private salon events. Nick is trying to get me slots in some of the summer chamber music festivals."

"How's it going?"

"Well, I think Jeff's going to place me somewhere. He's still got some openings in smaller cities in the middle of the country. Nick wants me to do about six of them. I think it'll be fun."

"It's a good start. There must be some contracts involved."

"Yeah, I got a bunch of papers. You're still my legal guardian, right?"

"Unless you know something that I don't, I'm still your father. Send me the contracts. I'll have my lawyers look them over."

"Okay. Thanks."

"Need anything else?"

"No, I'm okay."

"Who's the girl?"

Gabe was stunned into silence. Then he managed, "What?"

"Don't give me that stupid teenager *what?* You bought something for one hundred and twenty-eight bucks at Sterling Silver Jewelry Exchange. You don't wear jewelry except my mother's cross. And you're not gay so you didn't buy something for a guy. So who's the girl?"

Gabe tried to come up with a decent lie, but his mind was a blank. He was just too tired for invention. Besides, he couldn't bullshit his father on anything. "Just someone."

"I know she's *someone*, Gabriel. I didn't assume she was a fucking apparition. Start with a name."

"Yasmine."

"You like her?"

"Yeah."

"A lot?"

"Yeah."

"Don't knock her up."

"We're not having sex."

"Then you're an idiot."

Gabe got irked. "You know, *you* waited over a year before you had sex with Mom."

"Who said I wasn't an idiot. Look where it got me. And since when have I been your fucking role model?"

At this point, Gabe felt his best option was to say nothing.

"How old is she?"

"Fourteen."

"Jesus, no wonder you're not screwing her. She's one step above a toddler. Has she even gone through puberty?"

"I've never asked."

"You can't fucking *tell?*"

Again, Gabe was silent.

"So you like them young," Donatti said. "None of my business."

"First of all, in case you're not aware of my age, I'm only a year older than she is. Second, I don't like them young per se, Dad, I just happen to like *her.*"

"No need to get defensive. You wouldn't believe the shit I cater to."

"I'm just saying it's not weird, okay?"

"If you wind up in jail, I got your back."

"That's not funny." Especially because they were sneaking around. "I'll talk to you later."

"Don't you dare hang up on me."

"Fine. You hang up on me."

"Whoa there, stallion, I'm on your side." His father laughed out loud. "Gabriel, I'm glad you found someone who can keep your interest. And she must be okay because you don't suffer fools. Just make sure that she doesn't interfere with your music. That's a deal breaker."

"She gets me. Besides, she's an opera buff. That's how we met."

"Good to hear. Just watch yourself. You think you've got it under control, but take it from me. You're all hormones."

It wasn't like that at all. Well, maybe a little. "Duly noted, okay."

"Send me the contracts. I'll have my lawyers contact your agent. And don't worry. I won't piss him off."

"He's kinda hard-nosed, Chris. If anything, he'll piss you off."

"Fine with me. I like a good pissing contest." His father hung up.

Not a bad conversation actually. For years, Gabe had felt that the only reason Chris tolerated him was because of Mom, that he and his mother came as a package. Now Mom was out of the picture and he and Chris had talked more in the past six months than they had in previous fourteen years. Sometimes his dad even sounded like he gave a shit.

He knew he should get back to Nick and Jeff, but talking to his father made him feel even more anxious. He texted Yasmine. *r u busy?*

He didn't hear anything for a moment. He put his phone back in his pocket and headed back to the auditorium, but then it beeped.

everything ok?

can I call u?

i'll call u.

He waited a minute. Finally, his phone rang. "Hi."

"What's wrong?"

"Nothing." A pause. "I just wanted to hear your voice."

"Where are you?"

"I'm still at SC."

"How'd the audition go?"

"It went really well. How'd your test go?"

"It was hard! Everyone thought so."

"I'm sure you did great."

"I hope so." A beat. "Are you okay?"

"Yeah. Everything's fine."

"Really?"

"Yeah. I've got to get back soon. My teacher and this agent . . . are like discussing my future."

"What do you mean?"

"They're discussing like where I should play, when I should solo, what I should play, where I should go to college." He heard a toilet flush and smiled. "Are you in the bathroom?"

"Where else can I talk?"

He laughed. "Thanks for calling me back. Just hearing your voice makes me happy. I'll catch you later."

"Why are your teacher and an agent discussing where you should go to college?"

"'Cause the agent thinks that going to a regular college is a waste of time for my career."

"Harvard isn't a regular college."

"It isn't Juilliard. It doesn't even have a performance department."

"Do you even need a music department? You're probably better than anyone they could hire for faculty."

"See, that's why I need you. My ego can't function without your compliments."

"I just say what's true. Dumb question but I take it you got into Juilliard?"

"Yeah, and nothing you say is dumb."

"Tell my bio teacher that. Do you want to go to Juilliard?"

"I dunno. Probably. It makes the most sense."

"More than Harvard?"

"I dunno. I thought it might be fun to go to a regular university—someplace that wasn't obsessed with music. I could also go to SC, you know. Nick is here, not in Boston."

"What do you *really* want, Gabe? That's the only thing that's important."

"I dunno. I'm so used to being led by the nose, I never thought about it." He heard a bell in the background. "You have to go?"

"I can be a few minutes late." She paused. "I know how you feel. It's like my dad has determined my future. In his mind, he's already sitting at my graduation from medical school. I mean, I might want to be a doctor, but it might be nice to have a choice."

"I have no doubt that you could rule the world if you wanted to."

"You're the best," she told him. "I really, really miss you."

"I miss you, too. Did you *really* have a dream about kissing me?"

"Yes." Her voice became breathy. "And I kept wanting it to last, but I woke up and couldn't get it back. It was really frustrating."

"I guess we'll have to make the dream a reality."

"What a great idea." Another bell rang. "That's the tardy bell. I've got to go."

"Thanks for calling me, Yasmine. I have to go back in and play some Chopin anyway. That's cool. I like Chopin. But not as much as I like you, cuckoo bird."

There was a pause. He could feel her smile. She said, "You know I adore you."

"I adore you, too," Gabe told her. "Kisses."

"Kisses." She hung up.

Every time he stopped talking to her, he felt low. He hated it. He wanted not to care so much, but all he could think about was how much he liked her. How happy he was whenever they were together. He loved their early mornings together, sitting in the corner at Coffee Bean, holding hands under the table, stealing kisses when no one was looking. The way she talked about opera or school or her sisters or whatever while squeezing his leg. The way she allowed him to put his hand underneath her skirt, his fingers walking up her bare thigh until he almost reached the golden spot. And then she'd giggle and swat his hand away. And then he'd do it all over again.

He was tired, he was confused, he was frustrated, and he was lonely. Most of all, he was horny.

All hormones.

Chris was right.

Damn him.

Chapter Eighteen

An overcast sky teased the L.A. basin with the promise of rain. Instead all the city got was bleak weather—dirty fog and damp air. The low sixties bordered on coat weather, but a good cable-knit sweater would do in a pinch. The only reason Marge wore her leather jacket was for fashion. She had purchased it last year at the Camarillo Outlets—a favorite meeting spot for her and her boyfriend, Will, who worked in Santa Barbara. Theirs was a long-distance relationship that worked well.

Lisbeth and Ramon Holly's house was her last stop before she and Oliver were kicked loose. The address put them at a sixties ranch house in a neighborhood of modest homes on small lots and no sidewalks. Lawns were dotted with mature trees, most of them bare except for the pines and cedars that stretched to the pewter skies. Although it was two months past the holidays, some of the houses still had multicolored Christmas lights twinkling in the dusk. It was straight up five in the afternoon and the sun had set. A distinct chill hovered. It was just plain dreary.

The door was opened by a tall, tweener girl with olive skin, long dark hair, and a stick body. She was garbed in skinny jeans and a spangled sweatshirt and was on a cell phone. A woman in her thirties, presumably Lisbeth Holly, stepped into the foreground and welcomed them inside. She stood around five foot ten, with pale skin and long straggly blond hair, and she also had a stick body including her chest. Her face was filled with wrinkles, and her earlobes held about four pierces a pop. She had a rose tattooed on her right wrist and a butterfly on the back of her neck. She also wore skinny jeans and a sleeveless red sweater.

Lisbeth introduced herself and offered each of the detectives a bony hand. She took their cards, and the group walked into a small living room with pink floral furniture and a once-white carpet that had aged to mottled gray. Her daughter, Sydney, remained on the cell and barely gave them a glance. She finally disappeared down a hallway.

Bemused, the woman shook her head. "One of these days they'll figure out a way to implant the dang things right into their brains. At least that way she couldn't lose it. I don't know what it is with kids today. They lose everything. I always took care of everything I owned. 'Course I didn't own a lot. You'll never find me fretting about what to wear in the morning. Not like that one."

She cocked a thumb in the direction of the hallway

"Anyway, have a seat."

She lit a cigarette. "I hear you found my gun. You mind if I smoke, by the way?"

Marge said, "It's your house."

"Yeah, but people are funny. Sit down, please."

The two detectives chose the floral sofa. Lisbeth took the matching chair, curling her legs under her.

Oliver said, "It was your gun that was stolen?"

"Yep." A plume of smoke filtered through her nostrils. "I have a few guns, and they're all mine."

"How many do you have?" Marge asked.

"I have a rifle and a revolver for target practice and a 16 mm semiautomatic for protection. In case you haven't guessed, I'm the shooter in the family. I grew up shooting at targets. Ramon, in his community, they grow up shooting people. He's long past that now. He still knows how to use guns, but he doesn't like 'em anymore. Not since his brother was killed."

"When was that?" Marge asked.

"About ten years ago. Ramon idolized his brother. The guy, frankly, was scum, but I don't say anything. We all have that one fantasy that we cling to. Mine is I coulda been a supermodel if she hadn't come along." Again a thumb indicated that she meant her daughter. "It's nonsense, but I use it on my husband when I'm pissed at him."

"And the gun was stolen around a year ago?"

"Yep. My bad. I keep the suckers locked up in a vault like a good citizen. I had just bought the Taurus and the only reason I bought a mouse gun is because the dealer was practically giving it away. It was still on top of my dresser when it was stolen. Damn kids."

Oliver looked at her. "How do you know the thieves were kids?"

"Because of what else was taken. Sydney's phone, her iPod, and a couple of her rings, including the one her grandma gave her for her confirmation. Big blue aquamarine. Sydney's favorite color is blue. It was inscribed so if you ever find it, you'll know who it belongs to. And of course Grandma replaced it right away. You'd think Sydney would take care of it after that. But nooooo."

"It still could have been adults," Marge said. "Phones and iPods are commonly stolen items."

"You're right. But they also took Sydney's CDs. Believe me, no one but kids would want those CDs. And although my gun was stolen, my jewelry wasn't touched. The pieces were hidden in the bottom drawer of my dresser, but you didn't have to look too hard to find them. Whoever did it went through my daughter's drawers but not through mine. And the thief was obviously in my room if he took my gun. He just wasn't interested in my shit. That's why I think it was kids."

"Maybe the thief ran out of time," Oliver suggested.

"Then why go to my daughter's room first? Okay, I get someone taking the phone and the iPod, but then why bother filching her five-and-dime jewelry? The good stuff—if there is any good stuff—is gonna be in the parents' bedroom. Her room was hit first. The parents' room was an afterthought."

Marge smiled. "You should be a detective."

"It's in the blood. I come from a cop family. Indianapolis. My mom worked Grand Theft Auto, my dad worked Burglary. My grandfather was in uniform his entire life. My grandma raised me and my four brothers because my folks were never home. And guess what my brothers are? Cops. When I married Ramon—a former gangbanger—I thought my dad was going to have a heart attack. Turns out, I was right and they were wrong. Nyah, nyah, nyah. They like him now . . .

my parents. They should like him. He stuck with me through three years of rehab." She held up a cigarette. "This is the last piece of my addictive self." Her eyes got misty. "That man saved my life."

She stubbed out her cigarette and lit another.

"Anyway, you don't want to hear my sob story. What else can I help you with?"

Marge said, "Do you have any idea who might have broken into your house?"

"Someone from the neighborhood. Our house wasn't the only one that was hit."

"There were other thefts?" Marge asked.

"Yeah, ours was the third or fourth house. We finally said, enough!"

"What'd you do?"

"The neighborhood got together to talk about it. We all came to the same conclusion that it was kids. Around here, we're all kinda middle-of-the-road people, not poor, thank the Lord, but we aren't Wall Street wonks if you know what I'm saying. Most of us need two incomes to get by. Which means two working parents. And since most of us have school-age kids, that means a lot of empty houses during the day. That's when we were all hit."

She took another puff.

"We had a couple of meetings with the local police about the situation. They stepped up their patrol. Plus, we pooled some spare change and hired a couple of the out-of-work husbands to patrol the streets. Gave the boys some dignity as well as something to do. No problems since."

"Do you have any specific candidate for the thief?" Oliver asked.

"Nah, wish I did. Where'd you find the gun?"

"This is the hard part," Marge said.

"Oh shit! It was used in a crime?"

"It was used in a suicide," Oliver said.

"Oh God, that's gross! Who?" Lisbeth's pale complexion grayed. "Oh no! Not that teenage girl in the paper?" When no one spoke, she covered her hand over her mouth. "Oh fuck! Excuse me. That is . . . just . . . awful!"

"Did you know her?" Oliver said.

"No. What was the name again?"

"Myra Gelb," Marge said.

"No, I didn't know her. How old was she?"

"Sixteen."

"Christ!" She lit up another cigarette before finishing the first one. When she noticed, she stubbed one of them out. Tears were in her eyes. "I'm sorry." Wet droplets rolled down her cheeks. "I'm really just an old softie."

Marge handed her a tissue.

"You can keep the gun." Lisbeth wiped her eyes. "It's bad juju. I don't want it."

Marge said, "Thanks. We'll need you to sign a release—"

"Whatever." She waved her hand in the air. She was still disturbed.

Oliver said, "We'll want to run it through ballistics and see if it was used in any other crime as well."

"Oh my Lord, I sure hope not." A pause. "Did the girl's suicide have anything to do with the one that happened about six weeks ago?"

"Why do you ask?" Oliver said.

"I don't know. Two teen suicides so close together? I'm just wondering. I mean there's no such thing as a suicide epidemic, but you know kids. One gets a stupid idea and that influences another one. They're such sheep."

"Did you know the first victim? His name was Gregory Hesse."

"No . . . I don't know either one. How did the girl get my gun?"

"We're looking into that," Marge said.

"Was she . . . I don't want to say a bad girl because I've been there. Did she, like, hang with the wrong crowd?"

"It doesn't appear that way," Oliver said.

"We're just starting to look into that," Marge said. "And you haven't had trouble with break-ins since about a year ago?"

"That is correct." She took a final drag on her smoke and tamped it out. "You know, that whole thing worked even better than we could have imagined. Before the break-ins, I knew just a few people on my street. Then we had the meetings and got to know one another. By last summer, it was one block party after another. It's nice. Sometimes you don't realize how lonely you are."

Again her eyes watered.

"That poor girl. God only knows how lonely she was."

Chapter Nineteen

Of course, 10:30 Yasmine Time meant 11:00.

When Gabe answered the knock, he tried to hide his disappointment when he saw that she had brought a friend, whom she introduced as Ariella. He had pictured her like the Disney character with a mermaid's body and long red hair. Instead, the girl was around five three and buxom with unruly black hair and flashing brown eyes. She looked around eighteen, while Yasmine looked around twelve.

He invited them in and the three of them stood awkwardly inside the Deckers' tidy living room. Yasmine was wearing a full black skirt and a white top and looked as if she were going to play in a school orchestra, especially because she was gripping sheet music. Ariella was garbed in a tight red sweater dress that showed every curve. Yasmine had described her as a wild woman. Now Gabe knew why. He finally said, "Why don't we go in the back where the piano is."

Ariella said, "I'm not staying, I'm sure much to your relief."

"I didn't say anything."

"Yeah, you didn't see your face when you opened the door." Her laugh was raucous. "I came to tell you that if you hurt my best friend, I'll kill you."

Yasmine giggled. "Stop it!"

Gabe held back a smile. "Your warning shot has been heard. I promise you I would rather die than to hurt a single hair on Yasmine's head."

"Okay. I just wanted to get that out." Ariella was still looking stern when she returned her attention to her friend. "I'll come pick you up at one-thirty."

Gabe said, "That's only two and a half hours!"

Yasmine said, "Don't worry. She's always late, too." She kissed her friend. "Go already."

"Ariella," Gabe called out to her as she walked out the door. "Thank you."

She winked at him and left.

Silence. Gabe closed the door and leaned against it. "You know, I think this is the first time in six weeks that we've known each other that we're actually alone." A blush came to Yasmine's face. "Can I kiss you hello?"

"You have to ask?"

He took the sheet music from her and gently swept his lips against hers. It was instant electricity. He put his arms around her waist and drew her to his body while she threw her arms around his neck. They kissed passionately for a few minutes and then he abruptly drew away. His face was hot and his glasses had fogged up. He never minded specs, but it was annoying at certain times. He wiped his lenses on his T-shirt, trying to contain his obvious arousal, but it was there and that was that. At least she didn't say anything.

"You know, I really do want to hear you sing."

"Later." She stepped forward and planted her lips against his.

Again they kissed. He said, "I think you're trying to put this off."

"You're right."

He broke it off and put his arm around her shoulders. "C'mon before I faint. I'll show you my studio. My piano shares space with the lieutenant's Porsche."

Walking with difficulty, he led her outside and into the makeshift practice room. It was far safer to be with her there than in his bedroom. He handed her the sheet music and sat down at the piano bench. "Do you want to warm up?"

Yasmine smiled. "And here I thought *we* were warming up."

"I am trying to be considerate and you're making me *die*!"

"Okay . . . I'll sing for you." Yasmine sat down next to him and looked into those gorgeous green eyes. "You know, I've never heard you play other than at graduation."

Gabe ran his hands over the keyboard. "You're stalling again."

"No, really. I want to hear you play." She put her hand on his knee. "Please?"

He leaned over and kissed her. "If you keep touching me, I won't be able to do anything."

"Please play for me, Gabriel?"

"Okay." He took in a breath and let it out. "What do you want to hear?"

"I dunno." She thought. "How about . . . like . . . 'Flight of the Bumblebee'?"

Gabe groaned. Without looking at the keyboard, he began to run through the piece. "God, I think I learned that when I was five or something." He stuck out his tongue.

Yasmine stopped him. "So if you don't want that, play something else. You like Chopin, play Chopin."

"Do you want flash or class?"

"How about flash?"

He thought a moment, then from the bang of a C-minor chord, his left hand flew down the keyboard at lightning speed in twists and runs until it was joined by his right hand, the music playing out a story in forte dynamics. He talked while he played. " 'Revolutionary Étude' in C minor. Written after Russia invaded Warsaw. Chopin was Polish, so this is his like paean to his homeland although he was more French than Polish. It's a good piece but it is a little bombastic."

He stopped abruptly. "You know what an étude is, right?"

" 'Course. It's a study piece."

"Yeah. Chopin wrote a bunch of them. That's one of the most famous. I like his 'Opus 10 number 5.' " With his right hand, he launched into a series of triplets in varying dynamics. "It's all on the black keys except for like one white note. Not at all easy to play but fun once you got the fingering down."

He stopped the music and smiled at Yasmine. She was wide-eyed.

"What?"

She just shook her head, speechless.

He shrugged. "How about . . . Let's try 'Grand Waltz Brilliant' in E-flat major? I like it because it's so musically vivid. I mean, every time I play it, I can picture this big ballroom with guys in foppish clothing and girls in antebellum ball gowns twirling around the room. It really takes you back to a different era."

He began the introduction, which was a series of marchlike chords before launching into ¾ time. Again, he spoke as he played. "You can see the dancing in the music. Like you can picture the Viennese Waltz. You know, twirl . . . twirl . . . twirl . . . twirl. All the colors . . . the satin and lace and pomp. It's just such a blend of visual and auditory . . . I dunno . . . it just is like . . . a snapshot in time."

His fingers ran over the keyboard in effortless fashion.

"I just love the lightness of it . . . the grace . . . dancers floating through the air."

He stopped playing and looked at her.

"Tell me when you've had enough of my narrative. Sometimes I go on a little bit."

"You really make the music come alive."

"You make me come alive." He stopped playing, reached atop the piano and gave her a wrapped package. "Here you go."

Yasmine stared at the gift, her eyes turning wet. "For me?"

Gabe made a point of looking around the garage. "No one else here. Guess it's for you by process of elimination. Open it."

With shaking hands, she undid the ribbon and opened the box. It was a blue-faced sterling-silver watch. She whispered a thank-you as tears streamed down her cheeks. Although she was already wearing a gold Movado, she tried to put it on. But her hands were too unsteady.

"It's like a conceptual gift." Gabe grinned. "Maybe if you wear two of them, you'll be on time." She laughed through her tears. "Why don't you put the new one back in the box and it can be your school watch. I think your parents might notice if your gold one was gone."

"My mother would, that's for sure." She stared at her present. "I really love it. It's totally my taste."

"I'm glad."

She was still staring downward. "That was the nicest thing ever." She regarded his face. "I think you're the most marvelous human being in the entire world."

"You do?"

She nodded.

"Thank you." A pause. "Can I feel you up?"

She slapped his shoulder and he laughed.

"Please?"

"You want to feel up my *small* chest?"

"I love your small chest. I love everything about you." He picked her up and sat her on his lap so they were face-to-face. She immediately wrapped her legs around him and he sprung to life. He slipped his hand under her blouse, then under her bra. "Your chest may be small, but it is truly a marvel of nature. Kiss me."

She obliged, the two of them delighting in tasting one another. Kissing for several minutes as she squirmed on his lap until he felt as if he was going to explode. Without warning, Yasmine burst into tears.

Gabe pulled away, shocked. "What's wrong? Did I hurt you?"

She shook her head and sobbed.

"What'd I do?" Gabe said.

"Nothing," she wept.

"Then why are you crying?"

"Because . . . I'll never . . . ever . . . like another boy as much as I like you." Again, she erupted with a fresh set of tears. "I can see it like . . . fifteen years from now," she sniffed out. "You'll be like this rich and famous pianist. And I'll be like this Persian house-wife . . . dressed in Juicy sweats . . . driving my two kids to soccer practice . . . in my black . . . Mercedes!"

She broke out in newfound wails. He hugged her as she cried on his shoulder. "First of all, there's nothing wrong with being a good mom—"

"You're right! I love my mom! I'm such a terrible daughter!"

She started sobbing anew.

Gabe patted her back. "Um . . . is it like . . . you know . . . that time of the month?"

"Probably," she cried out.

At least she'd gone through puberty, he thought. That was a relief.

"I don't wanna sing for you!" she wailed.

"No, no, no." He pulled her off his chest. "You're not getting away with that."

"You're gonna think I sound like a turkey fart."

He held back a smile. "You will not sound like a turkey fart. And even if you did sound like a turkey fart, I wouldn't tell you." He stood up, her legs still wrapped around his waist. He set her down so she was standing upright. He started looking through her music. "Okay. Here we are. Der Hölle Rache." He clucked his tongue. "This is a very challenging aria. You must have been taking lessons for a while."

She nodded.

"You ready to warm up?"

"No."

"C'mon."

"I don't want to warm up."

"You just want to sing this cold?"

"Yes."

"You want to sing F6—that's F above high C—without warming up?"

"Yes."

"Now you really are being a cuckoo bird." She just pouted. Gabe spread out the accompaniment on the piano stand. "Okay." He gave her the D-minor chord and nodded for her to start.

Nothing happened.

He stared at her. "How about you start when you're ready and I'll catch up to you?"

"I don't wanna sing."

"Stop it." He struck the chord in tremolo and waited. She got the first few notes out and then the tears came back.

"You're gonna laugh at me."

"No, I will not laugh at you." He sighed and blew out air. "Can I let you in on a little secret?" When she didn't answer he said, "When a boy likes a girl the way I like you, we're like . . . brainless. All you have to do is like show up and we're happy. So stop worrying. Anything you do is going to be okay. Just sing your little heart out."

"In my small chest."

"You're never going to let me live that down." He glared at her. "I'm sorry, okay?"

"It's okay," Yasmine told him. "It is small. But it won't always be small."

"I know. I've seen your sisters. I just hope I'm still around to see the transformation."

She hit him again.

"I'm going to have bruises."

"Serves you right."

He gave her a D-minor chord again. "Just go, for Chrissakes!"

She finally started. Definitely shaky at first, but by the time she got to the coloratura, she had found her vocal chords. When she finished, he wasn't just amazed, he was astonished.

"Holy moly." He let out a small laugh. "You really have a *voice*."

Instant smile on her face. "You're just saying that to be nice."

"I'm not really nice when it comes to music. I'm very critical. You were . . . good."

She was all light and happiness. "Really?"

"Really." He shook his head. "Man, you're gonna be killer in a few years when your vocal chords lengthen and chest cavity gets bigger and no comment please about your small chest. I mean that in a very positive way."

"I need to work on my breath control."

"Yeah, honestly, you do. But that's what a vocal coach is for." Again, he shook his head. "You really hit your notes. Do you have perfect pitch?"

She nodded.

"If you and I ever bred, we'd produce a flock of little kids who'd walk around with their hands covering their ears because everything in life would sound off-key. Really good job, Yasmine. Just incredible."

She was beaming. "Anything else?"

Gabe said, "No, not really."

"What do you mean by not really?" Yasmine sat beside him. "I'm a big girl. I can take it." When he didn't respond, she said, "What's on your mind? If you don't tell me, I'll be anxious."

"Well . . . you need to figure out what to do with your hands."

"Absolutely. I know I'm a little stiff when I sing."

"Kinda." Gabe cleared his throat. "If I had to say anything critical, the one thing I'd say is . . . you sang the notes . . . but not the words. I mean, opera is theater. You know what you're singing?"

"I know the translation."

He said, "'*Der Hölle Rache kocht in meinem herzen*—the vengeance of Hell boils in my heart!' The Queen of the Night is so consumed with hatred for her rival, Sarastro, that she is willing to sacrifice her own daughter to satisfy her lust for revenge. I mean, I can totally see my dad doing something like that. Like him saying, 'Here, Gabe, whack this guy or I'll disown you.'" He stared at her intense face. "You've gotta channel into someone like that. You've gotta channel pure unadulterated hatred."

Yasmine nodded.

"That doesn't mean you didn't sing beautifully. You did. Almost too beautifully. When I hear the *ha, ha, ha* part, to me, it always sounded kinda like maniacal laughter . . . not like *ha, ha, ha,* happy laughter."

She nodded dutifully, something smoldering in her eyes.

He looked at her. "You're pissed at me."

"No, I'm not."

"Yes, you are. I'd be, too. We have egos. No one likes critiquing."

"No, I'm not." Her eyes filled with water that streamed down her cheeks.

What was I thinking? Gabe said, "I shouldn't have said anything."

"I'm glad you did." She was trying so hard not to lose it. "At least I know you're honest."

"That I am. Sit on my lap." When she complied, he kissed her tears. He said, "I want you to promise me something, okay?"

"What?"

"No matter what happens, you'll continue with your voice training. You have too much talent not to continue on."

"I promise."

"No, Yasmine, I mean *really* promise. You've got to do more than just take some lessons. You've got to realize your talent . . . put yourself out there even if it means ruffling some feathers. I mean I know how hard it is to defy your parents. Hell, I should talk. I'm afraid of my dad. And I wouldn't ever ask you to do it . . . not even for me."

She looked up at him.

"I mean, let's face it. Boys come and boys go, but a voice like that. It's forever. It's a gift from God. More important, you can't see your face. You're so happy when you sing. It's a natural. It's what you are."

She was quiet.

"You've got to promise me that you'll continue with it, okay?"

She shrugged.

"What?"

"You don't understand. Nice Jewish Persian girls don't become opera singers."

"Why not?"

"Because they don't. It's just not done, okay. I'm sorry my sister ever said anything about a stupid CD."

He blew out air. "Yasmine, there's nothing wrong with being a doctor. My mother is a doctor. She sacrificed everything including me to be a doctor. But that was *her* dream. Maybe I'm wrong, but I don't see it as being your *dream*."

"I don't know what my dream is." Her eyes grew wet. "I'm only fourteen. Right now my only dream is to be with you."

Gabe smiled. "You know what? That's my dream, too." He brought her mouth to his and kissed her soundly. Within seconds, their tongues were dancing. He started unbuttoning her blouse as she tugged upward on his T-shirt until both of them were naked from the waist up. The feel of her chest against his sent shivers down his spine.

She was sitting on his erection, constantly shifting positions and that only made it worse. He thought he would have a heart attack.

"Does it hurt?" she asked.

He was licking her breasts. Two dark drops like Hershey's kisses. "What?"

"You know." Shifting again. "Does it hurt?"

He picked his head up and kissed her hard on the mouth. "No, it doesn't hurt. It feels good." He ran his fingers down her spine and moaned. "I mean it'll hurt if I don't do something, but I'll take care of that later."

They kissed and kissed.

"What do you mean?" she asked.

He talked through his kisses. "What do you mean what do I mean?"

"Like are you gonna go to another girl?"

Gabe stopped kissing and stared at her face. "What are you *talking* about?"

"You know . . . to take care of it."

"Oh my God!" He shook his head in disbelief. "Are you serious?" When she didn't answer, he said, "First of all, there is no other girl. Second of all, even if there was another girl who was willing, I don't want her. I only want you. Third of all, what I meant was . . ." He held up his hand and stroked the air.

Yasmine looked at his pantomime and then covered her mouth in embarrassment. "Oh . . . I get it."

"God, Yasmine, I adore you. I truly do." He wiped the lenses of his steamed-up glasses. "But you really need some . . . brothers or something." He took her hand away from her mouth. "Kiss me."

They necked for a few more minutes. Then she said, "Do you want me to do that?"

"Do what?"

"Do to you what you were gonna do to yourself later on."

He stopped kissing and stared at her. "Uh, that would be unbelievably fantastic."

"I don't mean sex, you know."

"I know you don't mean sex. I don't expect sex."

Her eyes got wet yet again. "I don't know what I'm doing."

"No worries. I'm so turned on right now, it won't take any skill at all."

"You won't think I'm a slut?"

"No."

"You won't like me less?"

"I won't like you less if you do it, I won't like you more if you do it. I'll adore you just as much either way." He kissed her. "Honestly, do what you want, okay."

"Do we have time?"

He looked at his watch. It was twenty after twelve. "We have *oodles* of time." Pressing his bare chest against her naked skin. "Oh my God, you are so fine. I just want to eat you up. Kiss me."

She planted a wet one on his mouth. "Okay. I'm yours. Show me what to do."

Wordlessly, he grabbed their discarded clothing and then lifted her up. He walked out of the garage, both of them half-naked with her legs entwined around his waist.

She said, "Are you taking me to your bedroom?"

"Yeah." He paused. "Is that okay?"

"Yeah." She leaned her head against his bare chest. "That's really okay."

Chapter Twenty

Monday morning eight A.M., Marge walked into Decker's office, holding two cups of lidded coffee. She set one on the desktop and took an empty seat. "I just had a troubling conversation with Wendy Hesse."

"At eight in the morning?"

"Seven actually." She popped the lid open, and her face was engulfed in steam. "Someone broke into her house last night."

"That's terrible." He raked his fingers through his hair. "Did she report it?"

"No, she didn't. But she was very upset by what was taken—Gregory's laptop."

Decker picked up his coffee and sipped. "What else was stolen?"

"Nothing but the laptop seemed to be missing. The only reason why Wendy noticed the missing laptop was because she had put it on the dining room table the night before. She had intended to bring it into the station house today."

Decker sipped coffee. "Why?"

"There were some disturbing images on it that she wanted us to see. She said that some of the pictures showed Gregory playing with a gun—pointing it, twirling it, putting it to his head."

"Good Lord. How painful for her to see that."

"She was crying over the phone. Since she doesn't know one gun from another, she wanted us to see if it was the same gun he used to kill himself."

"Why now? Hasn't she been dodging you for over a month?"

"Yeah. I must have called her three or four times before I finally got the hint."

Decker put his coffee down and fished out a notepad. "Did Gregory look upset or was he just fooling around or was he acting out some kind of weird fantasy . . ."

"I didn't ask, Pete. I figured the most sensible thing was a face-to-face interview."

"And those were the only pictures she told you about?"

"Yes. They were probably the ones that upset her the most. She did say that in the pictures, Greg didn't look like himself. He looked drugged."

"When are you meeting with her?"

"Seven-thirty tonight. She's coming into the station."

"Why so late?"

"I've got things to do and she's got things to do. It was the earliest we both could make it. You don't have to stick around. Oliver said he'd be there."

"Be sure to ask about Gregory's camcorder."

"It's on the top of my list," Marge said. "I think we're both wondering who took the pictures. I have no idea if someone was photographing him or if Greg had a camera on his computer or what."

"We should get hold of Myra Gelb's laptop," Decker said. "See if there's anything weird on her computer."

"I phoned up Udonis Gelb yesterday after the memorial service. I got her answering machine and left a message, offering condolences and my number if she needed anything. I also phoned Eric Gelb. Again, I got a machine. I don't want to push either one of them right now. I'll call in a few days and set something up."

"That's fine. But I'm still concerned about her laptop. I don't think it's too intrusive to call and tell them to put Myra's computer in a safe place . . . just in case."

"I can do that, but she has to find it first. We didn't find it in her room, remember?"

"Ah . . . right."

"Two missing laptops . . ." Marge thought a moment. "Two kids were going to the same school where suicides are not very common. And both deaths involved stolen guns and maybe laptops. You have to wonder."

"What about Myra's friends? Get a chance to talk to any of them?"

"I lined something up with Heddy Kramer on Thursday evening, the only evening when her parents don't work late. They're all coming into the station house at six."

"So anything new with Dylan Lashay and the B and W Mafia?"

"Nothing. He doesn't have an adult record. When I asked Juvenile about him, they claimed they've never heard the name. No wants or warrants. Not even a parking ticket. Mr. Eli seems squeaky clean. So maybe he is an upstanding citizen."

"Or another Teflon don," Decker said. "Either he's clean or he's careful. If it's the former, then he's out of the picture. If it's the latter, we'll wait until he screws up."

The original text had come in an hour ago, at six-thirty. Gabe had turned off his phone because he'd been at the piano all day. He'd been coasting for the last week, spending too much of his time thinking about the wrong things. He knew he'd have to do better, especially because he now had some actual paying jobs in his future. This had been his first real day of work, his fingers and brain working as a unit. It felt good. He rewarded his hard work by allowing himself to read the text.

g8 lesson. made a breakthrough.

Gabe smiled. Maybe this would be the impetus to continue on with her voice. He texted back: *u still there, cuckoo?*

He waited and his phone burred a moment later.

hi.

what happened?

at the lesson?

yeah.

my vocal coach said I sounded like a real opera singer 4 the 1st time, that I sang w/real emotion.

congrats.

thx . . . teach.

ur welcome, student. just don't sue me for sexual harassment.

lol. want 2 know how i did it?

of course.

i thought of u w/another girl.

He broke up. *that would never happen but use what u need.*

it better not happen.

better not w/u either. seriously keep up the gd work. knew u could do it . . . u got stuff in u just w8ting 2 come out. that's y u need 2 sing.

thx ☺

i mean it, yasmine. u really need 2 sing. if u don't, u'll get depressed.

i get depressed when i'm not w/u. r we on 2morrow?

b there at 6:30.

it opens at 6.

but ur always 18.

i promise 2 b there at 6 . . . 6:15 L8est.

Gabe smiled. She was hedging her bets. *it's still dark outside at 6. i'll w8 for u on the corner so b there on time!*

ok.

u know, if u make me get up extra early and ur 18, u buy breakfast.

I always offer. u never let me pay.

of course u don't pay. only when ur bad.

u know me, gabe, I can b very bad.

Ugh!!! u wreck me.

think of me tonite when ur alone.

I always think of u especially when I'm alone.

my mom is calling me 2 help w/dinner. gotta go. kisses.

kisses, Gabe texted back, then disconnected the line. His stomach growled. He realized he hadn't eaten since breakfast.

It seemed indeed that music was the stuff of life.

Play on, Gabriel, play on.

Wendy Hesse had dropped some pounds in a month, but the weight had come off too quickly and the excess skin on her face sagged like deflated jowls. Her blue eyes were clear instead of red, and her hair had grown out and was styled, her white roots no longer showing. It was a good sign that she took enough pride in her appearance. She wore a red sweater like the first time she had come into the station house and black pants. Marge had seated her in an interview room, offering her a chair and a cup of coffee. Oliver joined them a minute later.

Wendy looked uncomfortable in her surroundings. "Isn't this where you interrogate the criminals?"

Marge said, "We use the rooms for all kinds of interviews."

"Most of us just have cubicles," Oliver explained. "This is a little more private."

"If you would prefer it, we can go outside and talk in the open."

"Oh good God, no. We need privacy." She regarded Marge's questioning eyes. "I know that you've called me several times and I haven't called back."

"You've had a lot on your mind."

"All of it bad." She reached in her purse and pulled out several photographs, but didn't reveal them, keeping them close to her breast. "Right after it happened, I was going through Gregory's drawers, hoping to find some answers."

She put them on the table and looked away. Marge kept a blank face as she picked up the graphic snapshots. The girl's features were obscured by long hair and a close-up of an erect penis halfway into her mouth. A few of that pose and a couple more of a tongue licking testicles. She passed the photos to Oliver.

Wendy said, "Obviously, there was a lot about my son that I didn't know about."

"Any idea who the girl is?" Marge asked.

"I didn't even know that Gregory had a girlfriend."

Oliver scanned them several times. "I don't want this to come out the wrong way, but are you sure that's even Gregory? There's no face."

Wendy turned to him, dumbfounded. "You know, I'm not sure at all. I just . . . assumed." She exhaled forcibly. "Maybe it's one of his friends. It certainly doesn't look like professional smut."

"No, it's amateur stuff," Oliver said.

Wendy bit a thumbnail. It had been painted red and some of the polish was chipping off. "I guess I was in the dark about my son. I feel stupid."

Oliver said, "I don't want to sound cavalier, Mrs. Hesse, but things like this . . . it's sort of normal for a teenage boy."

Marge said, "And please don't feel stupid. Most fifteen-year-old boys don't confide in their mothers."

"It's just shocking when you think you know some-one and then . . ." She threw up her hands.

"Tell us about the photographs on the computer," Oliver said.

"After I found these, I became curious about what was on Gregory's computer. I hired someone to hack into it because I thought I knew his password, but he changed it. I felt a bit sheepish breaking into his pri-vacy even though he's . . . gone. But I wanted to know more about my son, get a clue as to why he did this. Most of the pictures were just him and his friends." Her eyes got wet. "But then I saw other pictures like the ones I brought to you. I can't imagine Snapfish printing them."

"No, these were probably done with a photo printer hooked up to a home computer," Oliver told her. "Does your son have a photo printer?"

"I didn't see one. Even though he's gone, it really upsets me that he would take such indecent pictures of himself. And what girl in her right mind would let herself be photographed doing something so obscene?"

"It's not all that uncommon—kids being kids," Marge said. "If you can, talk to me about the photos of Greg with a gun."

"Just like I told you over the phone. He had pictures of him pointing it and . . ." Her eyes spilled tears onto her cheeks. "Of him holding it to his . . . head. It got me to thinking that probably what happened was just a terrible mistake."

Marge nodded.

"I don't understand how such a responsible boy could do such foolish things."

The paradox of adolescence. Oliver said, "It's a miracle that more tragedies don't happen to them."

Marge said, "You told me that Greg looked stoned or drunk in the pictures?"

"He had a bizarre expression on his face . . . droopy lids, lopsided smile, and his head was cocked to the side. It didn't look like him. But it was him. That much I can tell you."

Her eyes flitted between Oliver's and Marge's faces.

"That's why I didn't return your calls. I didn't want all this . . . ugly stuff to come out about my son. But once I saw the gun pictures on the laptop . . . I don't know. I just felt I should let you know . . . although I don't know why."

"Your instincts were good," Marge told her. "Especially now that the laptop was stolen."

"How did the thief get into your house?" Oliver asked.

Wendy stared at him. "I don't know."

"Any windows or doors unlocked or opened when you got up this morning?"

"Not that I can remember." She was quiet. "That's very odd. I was so intent on the laptop, I never even thought about how they got in."

"They?" Marge asked.

"They, he, she . . ."

"And you're sure nothing else was taken?" Marge asked.

"All my jewelry was still in the box in my bedroom. So I thought maybe they didn't go into the master. But my purse was still hanging in my closet. All my money was still in my wallet. Plus on the same table as the laptop, I have a pair of silver candlesticks. They weren't touched. I haven't gone through things item by item, but it appears that nothing was taken except the laptop."

Marge said, "Did you happen to find Gregory's camcorder?"

"No—" Abruptly, she paled. "Do you think there might be *those* kinds of movies on it?" When neither Marge nor Oliver answered the question, she shook her head in disgust. "Oh God! It just makes me sick to think about it." She started crying silently. "It hurts me so much that I knew so little about my son. Maybe if I had seen some kind of warning sign, this all would have been preventable."

Oliver said, "There might not have been obvious warning signs, Mrs. Hesse."

Marge said, "If it's okay with you, we'd like to go through your house, including Gregory's room."

"What for?" Wendy asked.

"A crime was committed. We want to see how the burglar got into your house."

"That makes sense. But why Gregory's room?"

Marge deflected the question. "You showed us these pictures. You obviously want to know more about Gregory."

Wendy Hesse sighed. "Initially, I thought I did. "

Oliver said, "I think you'd want to make sure that the laptop doesn't get into the wrong hands . . . some sicko who could post unpleasant things on the Internet."

"Oh my word, I never thought about that," Wendy exclaimed. "Yes, of course. You can come anytime you'd like." She looked at the detectives with newfound respect, blotting her tears with a tissue. "Thank you so much. I'll do whatever I can to help you. I'm sorry I didn't call you back earlier . . . after it happened."

Marge said, "Don't give it a second thought, Mrs. Hesse. Does three tomorrow afternoon work for all of us to come to the house?"

"I have a court case, but I should be done by three," Oliver said.

"I'm okay with three," Wendy said.

"Then we'll see you there. If you get a chance tonight, look for Greg's camcorder." Marge stood up. "And if you find it, hide it in a safe place."

Chapter Twenty-One

Yasmine hated when the hands on her new silver watch with the blue face told her it was quarter after seven. It meant she had to go to school.

It was terrible spending so many long hours without him. No matter how much she tried to put him out of her mind, no matter how often she willed herself to be back to the way it was BG—before Gabe—she was lonely and lost and shaky without him. The past week had been especially painful because of the Passover holiday. The entire family had moved into her aunt's large house in Beverly Hills, and she hadn't seen him in over a week. She was moody and dark, and everyone made fun of her. And all she wanted was Gabe—like she was addicted to him.

She sipped the last dregs of her coffee, waiting for him to come out of the bathroom. Her eyes lifted over the brim of her Styrofoam cup, and she was startled to see a beautiful girl around eighteen staring at her. She was waiting at the order pickup, her hip cocked, her black suede boot grazing the floor, moving back and forth.

Her eyes abruptly narrowed.

Yasmine returned her attention to her coffee, disconcerted. The girl wore a black cashmere sweater, skinny jeans, and, judging by the red sole, what looked like Christian Louboutin fashion boots. Her gold jewelry also looked real. Her face was as white as milk and she had blue, blue eyes with long blond hair that reached halfway down her back. She also had big boobs.

God, how Yasmine wished she'd have boobs already.

She glanced up and the older girl smiled.

White straight teeth on a beautiful face. But her smile was creepy . . . even mean. In the back of her mind, Yasmine wondered if she had offended her somehow, like maybe accidentally cut in front of her last week. Or maybe the girl didn't like Persians. Yasmine was always slightly uncomfortable with beautiful, white girls, especially the ones who weren't Jewish. She wished Gabe would come back. He was so knowledgeable about everything, and when she was with him, she felt secure and large. As soon as he was gone, she retreated into a shell, feeling foreign and very small.

A moment later he returned, much to her relief.

He sat down and threw his arm around her shoulders. "Unfortunately, it's around that time." He looked around and kissed her mouth. "I don't want you to be late."

"Okay." Her eyes lifted upward. The girl was gone. Gabe studied her face. "Are you okay?"

"Yeah, I'm fine."

"You look . . . upset, maybe."

"No, I'm fine." She cleared her throat. "It's always hard going back to school after vacation." She tried to forget about the girl and her mean smile. So she didn't like Persians. That was her problem. "I didn't even ask how your Passover was."

"Me?" Gabe laughed. "Actually I did have Seder with the Deckers on the first night. Then with everyone being home, it was too crowded, so I spent the rest of the week with my crazy aunt, Melissa, who's not much older than I am. She's ditzy and sloppy, but she can be a riot. Still, I was happy to leave. I missed you terribly, Yasmine. This last week without you has been torture."

"I missed you soooooo much." She still felt uneasy. "I'm so glad it's over."

"How was your Passover?" Gabe asked.

"Boring. My aunt had about twenty zillion people over. It was my assignment to cover the table with the romaine lettuce."

Gabe stared at her. "Come again?"

She gave a hint of a smile. "Persian Seders are different from Ashkenazi Seders. Like covering the table in maror—the bitter herbs. Then we actually reenact the whole exodus from Egypt."

"How do you do that?"

"We chase each other around the table and beat each other with onions."

Gabe looked at her. "Doesn't that hurt?"

"No, not onion onions. Scallions. We whip each other with scallions."

"Kin . . . ky!" Gabe grinned. "Invite me over next year."

She slapped him under the table. Then she grew serious. "I've got to go."

He kissed her cheek. "I've got to catch the bus anyway."

Her heart suddenly started beating quickly . . . ominously. She felt weird. "Do you have time to walk with me?"

Gabe broke into a smile. "You want me to walk with you in full daylight?"

"We'll take side streets."

"Aha." He grinned. "So I'm still your dirty little secret."

"Gabe . . ." Now she looked very upset.

He took pity on her. She was in a bind, and he was making it worse. "You know how much I love being with you. Lead the way."

They got up from their booth and left the café, walking for a minute without talking. The day was crisp and the sky was blue. The side streets were residences, the foliage still green by eastern standards; but the sycamores that lined the sidewalks were bare, and many of the lawns had turned brown.

He said, "What's on your mind, Yasmine?"

"Nothing."

"That's not true. Did I upset you with my wisecrack?" When she didn't answer, he said, "I understand your position with your parents. I'm sorry if I made you feel bad."

"It's not that." Her eyes clouded. "I just can't . . ."

"Tell me." He stopped walking and held her shoulders. "You can't *what*?"

She shook her head.

"You can't be with me anymore? Is that it?" He was heartbroken but tried to hide it. "Tell me, Yasmine. It's okay. Whatever it is, I can handle it."

Her eyes were wet. "I'm always trying to hide us. It must make you feel terrible."

"I'd *rather* it be out in the open, but I'm a big boy. I know it's just as hard for you as it is for me."

"I can't understand why put up with it," she blurted out. "With all these beautiful girls around, I just don't understand why you like me."

Gabe waited for more, but it didn't come. "*That's* what's on your mind?" When she nodded, he blew out air, relieved. "You are such a cuckoo bird."

"You are so gorgeous, Gabe. You're gorgeous and talented and smart and funny and you're just perfect." She wiped tears from her eyes. "You could get any girl you wanted."

"But I don't want any girl, I just want you." No one was around. He drew her into a long, lingering kiss. "If you could only see yourself through my eyes, Yasmine. You are so incredibly exotic . . . with these big, big round black eyes, a small perfect nose . . . and your lips . . . oh my God, you have the thickest, most kissable lips ever. You've got this mane of black, wavy hair that I just want to lose myself in. You're just so sexy."

"Even with my small chest?"

Gabe smiled. "Okay. So now I know you're feeling better. You're teasing me." He took her hand. "You're going to be late if we don't move."

She started walking but didn't say anything.

"We have this incredible chemistry, but that's not the only reason I like you." He kissed her hand. "I like you because you've got this wonderful curiosity about everything. You approach everything with this wide-eyed innocence. God, so many girls out there are plowing headfirst into adulthood and you take such delight in being this wondrous girl. Absolutely nothing about you is forced."

He slipped his arm around her waist.

"And of course, you speak music."

"I do speak music," Yasmine said.

"That's a biggie for me. It's hard to find someone my age who speaks music." He stopped walking, pulling her body close to his. "I love you. You know that, right?"

Her eyes watered. "I love you, too."

"I *need* to be alone with you again." He growled out, "*When?*"

She lay her head on his chest. "We're invited out for Shabbat this Saturday."

"What about Sunday?"

"We have a cousin's wedding."

"Exactly how many relatives do you have?" When she didn't answer, he said, "You must have a party every week."

"About." She looped her hands around his neck, entwining her fingers through his hair and kissed him hard. "I'll think of something."

He groaned with lust. "Man, you'd better or I'm going to do something drastic."

She smiled. "The school's a block away. I can take it from here."

"Fine. And no more silly talk about why do I like you, okay? It makes me feel bad."

"Okay." She smiled broadly. "I love you soooooo much."

"I love you, too."

She kissed him, broke away, and started running.

Gabe watched her go. It was nice to see a spring in her step. It was also fun to watch her ass.

The secretary announced that someone was on line three. Decker punched in the blinking light and announced himself.

"Romulus Poe here."

"What's going on, Sergeant Poe?"

"Just wanted to tell you that we've had a few weeks of spring weather . . . beautiful out here—deep blue skies and purple mountains majesty. The waterfalls are particularly spectacular with all the runoff."

"Thanks for the travelogue."

Poe laughed. "If Garth Hammerling was able to make it through the winter in the national forest—and I have my doubts about that—we should be able to start looking for him provided we can slosh through the mud. We got waders but Lord knows, it's slippery out there."

"Any help you could give me would be appreciated."

"Like I said, I have my doubts. Unless your guy was the survivalist type, I'd say he's pretty much in a deep freeze by now."

"Garth's a nurse so he has some emergency medical skills."

"Maybe it'd help him with the cold, but not with a mountain lion. On top of that, our bears just aren't hibernating like they used to. Hungry critters could easily look at your prey as a mighty fine warm-blooded entrée. But there's always that slim chance that we'll find him."

Decker said, "I'll just keep the faith."

"You can do that for both of us, Loo. I could use a little God in my life."

The suicide scene had been ghastly. Since then Gregory Hesse's bed had been removed and the walls, once covered with posters and personal effects, were bare after being scrubbed down, disinfected to remove any remaining biological matter spread by the shotgun blast, and then painted apartment white. The original carpet had been replaced by something brown and flat. The space felt vacant and haunted.

"I don't go in here much." Wendy Hesse's eyes grew wet. She was wringing her hands, her complexion very pale. She wore a green blouse and black double-knit pants. "Not much left." A statement applicable to her life.

Oliver looked around. Original to the room were a couple of nightstands, a desk and a dresser with nothing on top, and a bookshelf. The room had a sliding door closet. He remembered that he had wanted to go through the closet, but there had been so many people from the coroner's office, it had been impractical.

Wendy said, "I wish I hadn't gone through his drawers." A pause. "I think I'll wait in the living room. Would either of you like some water?"

"I'm fine for now, but thank you," Marge said.

Oliver smiled. "I'm all right."

The two detectives put on rubber gloves and went to work. First, they combed the bookshelf, which contained more CDs and DVDs than paper pages. There was a dock for an MP3 player with an iPod in the charge. They pulled out every single book and flipped through the pages hoping something significant would flutter out. They opened every single jewel box. They checked his iPod. Nothing looked even vaguely sinister.

They moved on to his drawers, slowly emptying out the contents and putting them back once they had gone through the items. Everything was organized and neatly folded: first drawer, socks and underwear;

second, pajamas and gym clothes; third, shirts and T-shirts; and fourth, shorts and more gym clothes. The desk drawers held nothing. Neither did any of the nightstands.

The closet contained polo shirts and several white dress shirts, pants, jeans, jackets, coats. Shoes on the floor were carefully aligned. The open shelving held sweaters and sweatshirts. They sorted through the clothes in the closet. They didn't find the camcorder. They didn't find anything.

The top shelf appeared empty. Marge took the chair from the desk. "Make sure I don't break my neck."

"I can do that." Oliver held the legs as Marge climbed atop the seat and peered across the space. "Find anything?"

"No." She stepped off the chair and regarded the shoes. They were all around the same size except for a pair of smaller patent leather loafers—something left over from a bar mitzvah or a confirmation. She bent down, felt inside the formal footwear, and fished out a plastic bag. About an ounce of pot, which she put back in the shoe.

She stood up. "He wasn't as innocent as Mom thought, but it certainly doesn't explain why he did what he did. I don't see the point in bringing this to Mom's attention."

"I agree with you there," Oliver said. "No camcorder."

"No camcorder, no camera." Marge thought a moment. "If Mom found naked printed pictures, I betcha he hid his camera."

"You know we think of camcorders as big hulking things. They're really mini these days. Easy to hide."

Marge said, "I hope he didn't hide them under his mattress."

Oliver said, "If he did, the people who cleaned up would have found them and given them to the mother, don't you think?"

"Yeah, probably." Marge shrugged. "Want to do another round?"

"Why not?"

The next half hour of searching proved fruitless. Oliver said, "Unless there's a secret compartment in the walls or floor, the camera and the camcorder aren't here."

Marge said, "Kevin Stanger told Decker that Greg was supposedly working on something that would turn Bell and Wakefield on its head. First thing that comes to mind is a sex scandal, considering he had pictures of blow jobs on his computer."

"Yes, but Kevin also said that the next time Greg spoke to him, he was less enthusiastic about his secret project."

"Maybe it was a student-teacher sex scandal. But then someone paid off Hesse with a blow job."

"Even if that was the case, did it have anything to do with Gregory Hesse putting a gun to his head? And is any of this police business?"

"It is if we stumble across something illegal going on—like an adult having sex with a minor."

"That's true," Oliver said. "What next?"

"Someone stole Greg's computer," Marge said. "That's really the only tangible crime we have. But I will tell you this. When the Loo and I were at Myra's death scene, we couldn't find her computer. Could be we missed it . . . or maybe not."

Oliver drummed his fingers. "There were a couple of months between Hesse's death and the theft. But the theft happened only two weeks after Myra Gelb's death."

"Yeah, they could be related," Marge said. "Whatever the case, it's time to pay Udonis Gelb a visit."

Chapter Twenty-Two

Two A.M. Thursday morning, Gabe was up, cruising Facebook, staring at Yasmine's profile of course, but also looking at other sites just to prove to himself that he really did once have friends. It was interesting for Gabe to see who was doing who, who had done X or meth or crack or who had even tried skag—pretty ballsy. They posted in code so they couldn't be called on it, but since Gabe read "innuendo," he knew what the dudes were talking about. There were new pictures, the guys looking older and bigger. And while Gabe had grown taller, he was still thin and wiry. His arms and fingers were disproportionately long for his torso due to years of piano playing. He looked like an anorexic ape.

His buds were now displaying a good deal of body art and pierces. Gabe didn't go for pierces, but he wouldn't have minded a couple of tats. What really irked him was that a few of the older guys already had their licenses. He, being so young, was forced to take buses in a town built for convertibles.

With their driver's licenses for the lucky few over seventeen came the cars. And with the cars came the girls—ergo the screwing. He knew he'd never contact any of them again even if he did go back east to Juilliard. Those days were long gone.

He used to sulk about all the sex he was missing. But now that Yasmine was part of his life, he didn't think about the parties too often. They weren't doing all that much, but since he really had the hots for her, everything they did do registered nuclear. As pathetic as it was, he'd rather do small shit with her than big shit with anyone else. He knew he was obsessed with her. And he knew he'd never get her. It was doomed from the start and he was in for a crash. He could take the heartache, but thinking of how it would affect her drove him crazy. He couldn't bear the thought of her being sad.

An IM registered on his computer.

Hi.

Gabe groaned inwardly. He loved his mother, but he truly wished she'd stop bugging him. Her contact left him off balance. *How's my sister?*

A little cranky. She's getting a tooth.

Gabe cracked a small smile, thinking about the baby. He hated that his mother deserted him, but he did like the idea of having a sibling.

Give her a hug and kiss for me.

I will.

Can you send a picture of her?

Of course. A pause. *Can you send me a picture of yourself?*

He wanted to type *like you give a shit,* but deep down he knew that his mother loved him and missed him and probably felt bad about what she had done.

I don't have anything recent. If you give me your cell number, I could take one of myself and send it to you.

Does Chris pay your phone bills?

Yeah, he does so it's probably not a good idea.

Do you have Skype account?

Yeah. Do you want to Skype?

Does Chris have access to your computer?

Not really; if it makes you nervous, we'll pass on Skype.

A long pause.

What's your account name, Gabe?

He gave it to her. Five minutes later, his computer rang. He pressed Answer with Video and for the first time in almost a year, he saw his mother's face. It made him suddenly furious, but he tried to keep his hot anger in check.

"Hey there, beautiful," he told her.

"Hi." Her voice was quivering. Tears were in her eyes.

"I have to keep it down," Gabe said. "It's two in the morning. Tell me about my sister."

"Do you want to see her?" Terry asked him.

"Of course." She got up and he could hear her talking offscreen to someone. A moment later, she sat back down. He continued. "You look well." She really did. Young and beautiful with a cascade of auburn hair and gold eyes. Of course, she was always young and beautiful with a cascade of auburn hair and gold eyes. He was just seeing her from a fresh perspective. His mother was simply a knockout. All his buddies used to salivate whenever she was around, but they wouldn't dare say anything inappropriate. She was Chris's wife. "Are you all right?"

Terry nodded, taking a swipe at her eyes.

"Is he good to you?" Gabe asked. "Does he treat you right?"

Again, Terry nodded.

"I'm glad, Mom. You deserve it." Now her tears were flowing freely. So who was the parent and who was the child? "Please don't cry. I'm doing okay. I've got a first-rate piano teacher and an agent. I'm going to play some summer chamber music festivals. It's really exciting."

"That's wonderful." Her voice was still unsteady.

"Yeah, it's pretty cool." A moment later, a baby filled the screen. She had a round face with a thick mop of black hair. She was drooling. Decker had been right. No way she could have passed this one off as Chris's. Gabe felt his lips turn upward into a big smile. "Hi there, Juleen. I'm your big brother, Gabe."

Juleen stared at the screen, then let go with a startling wail.

He did have a way with the ladies. "Did I scare you? I'm sorry."

"She's cranky because she's teething." Terry shifted her until she was over her shoulder. She patted her back. "Most of the time, she's really easygoing."

"She's darling," Gabe said. "Enjoy her, Mom. Before you know it, she'll be giving you grief just like your other child."

"You never gave me grief." Her face crumbled. "I miss you so *much*, Gabriel."

"Miss you, too." Not.

"You look so . . . old." The tears were back. "I'm so sorry, darling. I'm so, so sorry."

"Don't be," he told her. "You did me a huge favor." Said with too much enthusiasm.

Terry said, "There isn't a day that goes by when I don't think about you."

He rarely thought of her anymore. "It's fine, Mom. I'm happy." He grinned. "See?" He faked a yawn. "I have to get up early tomorrow . . . or rather today." It was true. He was meeting Yasmine in the morning. "I need to sleep."

Terry nodded, trying to smile away the defeat on her face. She was still patting Juleen's back. "It's wonderful to see you, Gabriel. I love you very, very much."

"Same, Mom. Have a good night . . . or good day." He waved and then quickly disconnected the line. He closed down his computer and slipped under the covers. In silence, his thoughts drifted from his mother to Yasmine. Whenever he wasn't doing music, he compulsively thought about her. Usually that was enough to quell his angst. But tonight his mother's sadness kept interfering with his peace of mind.

Two-fifteen . . . two-thirty . . . two-forty-five.

He gave up, stood up, and slipped on a T-shirt and jeans and loafers, heading out to his studio. He was a mess: anxious, lonely, depressed, furious at his abandonment, drowning in love, as well as obsessive/compulsive in thought and deed, and perpetually horny.

On the plus side, he was good-looking and exceptionally talented. People were accepting of anything from a
superstar.

The apartment appeared more spacious without the
unwanted crowd of police and other officials. The living room had been neatened to the point of sterility,
meshing with the antiseptic smell wafting through
the hallway. Udonis Gelb wore a loose-fitting house-
dress and had slippers on her feet. She had taken some
time to shower and make up her face—a little blush, a
little lipstick. She had curly, salt-and-pepper hair and
brown red-rimmed eyes with deep discolored skin that
sagged under her lower lashes. She was holding a piece
of paper—a to-do list from her son, she told them.

"It's my bible. It gives me organization so I don't
have to think."

Marge and Oliver were sitting on the couch, drinking lukewarm coffee. It was a dark and chilly Thursday
morning, menacing skies holding the threat of rain all
week.

"What's on the list?" Oliver asked her. When she
handed him the paper, Scott's eyes skimmed down the
items. Most of the numbered chores were errands—
grocery shopping, bank, laundry, and so on—but one
entry leaped out.

Find Myra's laptop.

He handed the paper back to her. "That'll keep you busy for a while."

"Maybe." Silence. "The hardest part of my day is waking up." She regarded her muumuu and slippers. "I should have put on something more respectable."

"You look fine," Marge told her.

"All things considered, I guess that's true." Udonis picked at her nails. "When I go back to work next week, I'll have to dress like a normal person again."

Oliver said, "I noticed item number fifteen—find Myra's laptop. Have you found it?"

"I haven't looked for it. I haven't been in the room."

Marge asked, "Has anyone been in the room?"

"Eric was here when the cleaning service came. I wasn't home. I don't know if Eric was actually in the room, but he took care of it for me."

"My lieutenant and I were in Myra's room on the day of the incident," Marge said. "Would you mind if Detective Oliver and I had another look at her room?"

She nodded. "Go ahead." Oliver thanked her, and then she said, "You took a couple boxes of her artwork with you."

"Yes, we did," Marge said. "We're still looking at the pictures, but we can give them back if you want them now."

"No, just when you're done." She kneaded her hands. "Why do you need them?"

Marge said, "They help us get to know Myra a little, give us a little peek into who she liked at school and who she didn't like."

"She didn't like too many people. She was critical. Most artists are."

"If you feel up to it, it would be helpful to hear about Myra from you."

The grieving mother sighed. "I appreciate your interest in my daughter, but can I ask you why it's a police matter? It's Gregory Hesse, right?"

Marge said, "Yes, it's true that we want to make sure that there's no overlooked connection between the two of them. Is this something you thought of, Mrs. Gelb? That the two incidents might be related?"

"Call me Udonis. And it crossed my mind. It crossed Wendy Hesse's mind, too. She called me up. We spoke for about an hour. Mostly, we commiserated about be- longing to the club that nobody wants to belong to."

Her eyes blurred, and it took her a minute to find her voice again.

"As far as we could figure out, the kids didn't know each other. Besides, Myra, God bless her soul, was having depression problems for some time." She wiped a tear from her eye. "I was stunned it happened, but upon reflection, I should have been more aware. Once they've tried it, I don't think you're ever quite safe."

"There have been other attempts?" Marge asked the question even though she knew the answer from Eric.

"Yes. About three years ago, she took pills. I put her into therapy and I thought we were long past that." Her eyes were brimming over with water. "I should have been more aware."

Oliver said, "Did she seem particularly depressed before this happened."

"Not more depressed, not less depressed. Just Myra—quiet, studious, thoughtful."

"She cartooned for the paper." Oliver checked his notes. "The *B and W Tattler*. Do you know if she was writing for the paper as well?"

"I wouldn't be surprised. Myra is a good writer."

"Did she ever take any journalism classes?" Marge asked her.

"She took one in the ninth grade. That's when she began to cartoon. She liked the teacher, Mr. Hinton."

"Gregory Hesse also liked Mr. Hinton," Marge mentioned.

Udonis said, "They wouldn't have taken the class together. She was a year older. Did Gregory work on the paper?"

"I don't know exactly how active he was, but he did write at least one article."

Udonis sipped coffee and made a face. "This is terrible! I can't believe I served you this swill." Angrily, she took the cups away and marched off to the kitchen. She came back a moment later. "Do you think this has something to do with the school paper?"

"We don't know," Oliver said.

Marge said, "Gregory's friends told us that he was working on something. Unfortunately, we don't know what it was. Wendy Hesse thought his laptop could give us some clues, but that was stolen last Sunday night."

"*Stolen?*"

"Somebody broke into the apartment and took it," Marge said.

"It was the only thing the thief took," Oliver said.

"Which is why we thought about Myra's laptop," Marge answered. "You don't know where it is, right?"

Udonis nodded.

"When we were in the room, we noticed Myra's phone and her iPod. Do you know if those items are still in her room?"

"They're not," Udonis said. "They're in the kitchen drawer. Eric put them away for safekeeping."

"Eric is very wise," Marge said.

"That is true." Wordlessly, Udonis got up and re-trieved the items, giving them to Marge. "If these will help you, take them. But please give them back."

"Thank you." Marge slipped them inside a paper bag located in her oversized purse. "Do I have your permission to go through your daughter's calls and texts?"

"Yes. You think that the theft of Gregory Hesse's laptop is related to my daughter's missing laptop, don't you?"

"We don't know," Marge said. "The phone might help."

"Udonis, do you have any idea how Myra got hold of a stolen gun?"

"No, Sergeant, I don't know." The woman sighed. "Knowing how Myra was, we'd never keep a gun in the house. Where would she get any kind of a gun—stolen or not?"

"Does the name Dylan Lashay sound familiar?" Oliver asked.

"No . . ." She shook her head. "Who is he?"

"What about Jarrod Lovelace, Stance O'Brien, Kyle Kerkin, JJ Little, or Nate Asaroff?"

"I don't recognize any of those names. Who are these people?"

"Some kids at B and W," Oliver said.

Marge quickly changed the subject before she asked too many questions about the B and W Mafia. She said, "We'll ask around. Maybe someone in Narcotics has a lead. Guns usually go hand in hand with drugs."

Oliver stood. "We'd like to take a look at her room now, if you don't mind."

"No, I don't mind." The woman got up. "I'm going to put on a fresh pot of coffee for myself. It'll be ready in a few minutes."

"I think we're okay for now." Oliver put his hand on her shoulder. "But if you don't mind, after we're done, I'll take a cup."

Udonis nodded. She started to tear up and then abruptly let go with a gut-wrenching cry. She grabbed Oliver's hand and held it, squeezing it until the tips of the detective's fingers were bright red. Her lifeline to sanity—if such a word even existed for her anymore.

Chapter Twenty-Three

Myra's mobile phone routinely held the most fifty recent calls—received, dialed, and missed. It also had saved forty texts. For the most part, the texts and calls could be assigned to six people: Udonis Gelb, Eric Gelb, Heddy Kramer, Ramona Stephen, Debra Locks, and Madison Blakely. All those people were in her contact list. There were six numbers that Marge had to dial to find out the source: two were from the prerecorded service Movie Phone, two were connected to Saul Hinton's voice mail, one was Macy's Department Store, and the last unknown number had been disconnected. That call had been placed well over two months ago.

The texts were more interesting because Marge could read them and they provided a good timeline of

Myra's last couple of days. One specifically of interest was from Heddy Kramer, dated two days before Myra put a gun to her head.

u need 2 b more discreet, people r talking.

Myra had also texted Saul Hinton to tell him that her cartoons were ready for the latest monthly edition of the *B and W Tattler:* that was four days before the incident. The rest of the texts dealt with Myra and her friends talking about school, about tests, about coffee dates, about stuff that seemed like kid talk.

Marge picked up the phone. Her first call was to Udonis Gelb. She answered on the third ring. "Hi, Udonis, it's Sergeant Marge Dunn."

"Hello, Sergeant. What's going on?"

"I'm looking over Myra's calls. I was wondering if you could help me out on a number. It's currently disconnected but maybe you would recognize it." She read off the digits.

Udonis said, "I don't know the number."

"It's okay. I can find it out. Also, do you know Myra's code to get into her voice mail?"

"Last four digits of my cell phone number."

Marge thought she misheard. "Her cell phone number?"

"No, my cell number." Udonis gave her the digits.

"Thank you," Marge answered. "Do you mind if I listen to her voice mail?"

"Fine with me."

"Thank you very much. I'll let you know if I do find something. You take care of yourself." After Udonis Gelb disconnected the line, Marge looked up Wendy Hesse's mobile in her little black book. The call went directly to voice mail. "Hi, Wendy. Sergeant Marge Dunn here. I was wondering what Gregory's cell-phone number was. If you could call me back, I'd really appreciate it. Thanks."

Then she called Myra Gelb's voice mail and entered the code. With pencil poised to paper, she waited. Instead, she heard the same formal lady say: *you have no new messages and no saved messages. For further options press 1.*

Marge hung up, placed the phone on her desk, and folded her arms across her chest.

How likely would it be that a sixteen-year-old girl with tons of texts had no voice messages in her mail-box . . . not even one saved message?

Had Myra erased her messages as her final act of checking out or had someone else erased them for her? And how likely would it be that someone would crack the code of her mother's digits—unless she gave them the number under duress.

u need 2 b more discreet, people r talking.

Duress was always a frightening possibility.

The girl's hair preceded her. Long thick locks of red waves fell past Heddy Kramer's shoulders and back, swallowing up her tiny frame like a matador's cape. She had small features, brown eyes, and a pointy chin. Her mother, Georgette, was a little taller and had short red hair. Marge met them in the lobby and settled them in one of the interview rooms. She poured them each a glass of water. "I can get you coffee or a soda if you prefer."

"Water's fine." Heddy's voice tinkled.

"I would love a cup of coffee," Georgette said.

"Then I'll be right back." Marge left and signaled to Oliver. "They're in room 3. The mother wants a cup of coffee. Can I get you one, Scotty?"

"Did I tell you I loved you this morning?"

"Are you coming in with me?"

"I'm jammed. Deck wants to be there. Knock on his door. You can fill me in later."

A minute later, Decker and Marge returned with the coffees. Marge said, "This is Mrs. Kramer—"

"Georgette," the mother said.

"This is Georgette and her daughter, Heddy," Marge said. "Lieutenant Decker specifically asked to sit in. Thanks so much for making the time to come down."

Decker sat down. "This has to be a difficult time for you, Heddy." The girl's eyes watered. "You were good friends with Myra?"

"Yes."

Georgette added, "They've known each other since fourth grade."

"Mom, I can answer for myself," Heddy said.

"I'm just saying . . ." Georgette said back and decided to sip her coffee.

"Since fourth grade is a long time." Decker pulled out his notepad. "I understand that Myra was suffering from depression."

Heddy nodded. "Especially since her dad died. She was real close to her dad."

"That was about three years ago?"

"About."

Marge said, "I've heard that you're the editor of the paper."

"Junior editor. You have to be a senior to be editor in chief."

"She's already been offered that position for next year," Georgette said.

"Mo . . . om."

Decker smiled to himself, how kids managed to make *Mom* or *Dad* into a two-syllable word. "I think the point Sergeant Dunn was making is that you're pretty involved with the school paper."

Heddy nodded. "Since I was a freshman. I took journalism in ninth grade and was hooked. The teacher, Mr. Hinton, made the class exciting. He liked my writing. He encouraged me to try out for the paper."

"He's the adviser?"

Heddy nodded. "But he really has a soft touch when it comes to editing. Which is exactly what we need— help, but not someone who's, like, bossy."

"Who got Myra involved in the paper?" Marge asked.

"That would be me," Heddy boasted. "She was a terrific cartoonist. Ever since I've known her she's drawn, like, funny caricatures of teachers and everyone." The girl's smile was sad. "Her cartoons could really make you laugh."

Marge said, "We noticed on Myra's phone that she had Mr. Hinton's cell-phone number. She called him, texted him as well."

Heddy said, "I have his cell number, too. That's not weird or anything."

"I didn't mean to imply that it was," Marge said. "Her texts were about her cartoons. All I meant to say is that he seems like an accessible guy."

"Oh, he is. He's just terrific. Mr. Hinton has been voted Bell and Wakefield's best teacher for like five years in a row."

"We've been looking through some of Myra's things, specifically her artwork. She did do a lot of caricatures."

"It's what she liked to do."

Marge said, "She could be biting."

"Myra could be funny sarcastic. It's what I loved about her." The eyes got wet again. "She had a great sense of humor and didn't pull punches."

Decker said, "How did the recipients of her humor feel about it? Specifically the drawings of some of her classmates sitting on the toilet."

Heddy sighed and shook her head. "She only showed those cartoons to the people close to her." A tear ran down her cheek. "I miss her so much."

Georgette was misty eyed as well. "It was a terrible shock and a terrible loss."

Decker said, "Did she seem unusually upset before it happened?"

Heddy's eyes teared. "She seemed . . . maybe a little down after Gregory Hesse committed suicide. You know about that, right?"

"Of course."

She averted her eyes from Decker's face for just a millisecond. "I hope she didn't get any weird ideas from him. She told me she could understand being that depressed." She bit her lip. "I asked her over and over and over . . . was she okay. She kept saying she was . . . brushing it off." Tears rolled down her cheeks. "I should have pushed harder."

"We've been through this before." Georgette's eyes were moist. "You've got to stop blaming yourself—"

"Of course I blame myself!" Heddy was sobbing now.

Marge put her arm around the girl. "There is no way you could have prevented this."

"That's not true!" she cried out. "I should have told her mother."

Georgette said, "You told Mr. Hinton. It was up to him."

"You told Mr. Hinton that Myra was depressed?" Marge said.

She nodded. "I should have told her mother. She had a right to know!"

Decker said, "Heddy, your mother is right. You brought it to the attention of a responsible adult."

"It didn't help!" She dried her tears.

"Sometimes nothing helps, honey, and that's the sad truth." But Marge's mind was awhirl. Why hadn't Hinton mentioned anything when she and Oliver had talked to him? Did he drop the ball somewhere and was feeling guilty? Could that have explained his hostility toward the police? "Could I ask you a few more questions?"

"Of course! Anything."

"I was going through Myra's voice mail. She didn't have any messages—either pending or saved—before she died."

"That's weird. I called her, like, a few hours before and left a message."

"And she never called back?"

"No." Then Heddy asked, "What does that mean?"

"Maybe she erased all her messages before she died," Decker said. "Or someone erased all her messages."

"Like tampered with her phone?"

"I don't know," Marge said. "We just found it odd because her texts were not erased. You sent her a text saying she needed to be more careful—that people were starting to talk. What was that all about?"

"Be careful about what?" Georgette asked.

"It's nothing, Mom."

"Can you tell us about it?" Decker asked.

Heddy again averted her eyes. "Like I said, Myra could be sarcastic."

Decker said, "She sure didn't appear to like Dylan Lashay."

Heddy said, "Why do you say . . . oh, the picture of him on the toilet. No, she didn't like Dylan, which is okay because Dylan likes Dylan enough for the whole world."

"You don't like him, either?"

"He's okay." Heddy licked her lips. "It's not like you think. Myra had a mad crush on him for years. She and about a billion other girls. It was unrequited of course."

"Dylan's a popular guy?"

"BMOC. He treated her just terrible. He can be very cruel."

"How?" Decker asked.

"He started calling her 'heifer.' And would moo whenever she walked by. Then all his friends started doing it. I yelled at him about it."

"What'd he do?"

"He called me names."

"Like?"

Heddy looked at her mom. Georgette said, "I wasn't born yesterday, Heddy. Tell the lieutenant."

"Okay, Mom. You asked for it. He called me a bitch and the c-word and told me the only thing I was good for was giving a beejay standing up."

Georgette gasped. "Oh my God! How disgusting!"

"Then I told him he's outta luck 'cause I didn't liked gherkins."

"*Heddy!*"

"It was nothing, Mom. The point is he laid off Myra for a while." A pause. "She must have finally gotten angry at him. She started drawing those pictures and showing them around. *That's* when I told her to be careful. That she was gonna get herself in trouble. Dylan's not only popular with the kids, but adults like him, too. He can be very charming, and he's real *smart*. But below the surface, he's really creepy."

"Like how?" Decker asked.

"Put it this way. I wouldn't want to be in a room alone with him."

"Got it." After Marge thought a moment, she said, "Is it possible that Myra got so angry with Dylan that she gave up on him and got interested in someone else?"

Heddy shook her head. "If she found someone else, she woulda told me. We were BFFs. We shared everything."

Marge said, "What if she found someone that she thought you wouldn't approve of. Maybe someone younger than her. Lots of girls might be embarrassed about that."

"Do you have someone in mind?" Then Heddy made a face. "You're thinking Gregory *Hesse*?"

"Did she even know Gregory Hesse?" Decker asked.

Heddy thought a long time. "We have once-a-week after-school meetings for the paper. Gregory was there a couple of times. So was Myra. But they didn't talk to each other or anything. At least, I don't think they did."

Marge said, "If they were a secret item, it would certainly explain why she became so sad after Gregory died."

"Gregory's death affected all of us," Heddy said. "But . . ." A pause. "You know? That *is* when she started doing all those real nasty cartoons of Dylan and Stance and JJ and Cam and Darla . . . like really, really nasty stuff. Right after Gregory's death."

Decker said, "Is it possible that she blamed Dylan for Gregory's death?"

"I dunno," Heddy said. "She never talked about it. Just started drawing some graphic things."

"Like what?" Decker asked.

"Close your ears, Mom." She started whispering. "Like Dylan getting it in the rear end or Cameron doing it with a donkey."

"Oh God!" Georgette said.

"Cameron Cole?" Marge asked. "The girls' president of the school council."

"Yep. She and Dylan are on-again, off-again. Currently, they're on. She's popular and beautiful, but a real *mean* girl. It's not enough that *she's* mean to you, she has to get other girls to be mean to you. She tortured Myra because she had Dylan and she knew that Myra has this mad crush on him."

"How did she torture Myra?" Decker asked.

"Just whenever she and Dylan saw Myra, they'd start French kissing. It was pretty gross. She's a real whore and a real bitch."

"Heddy!"

"It's what she is, Mom." A pause. "Personally, I've never had any problems with her." Heddy shrugged. "But then again, I've never had anything that she's wanted."

Chapter Twenty-Four

After Heddy and Georgette Kramer left the station house, Marge recapped the interview for Oliver. She said, "It's possible that Gregory and Myra knew each other, but we haven't found any real connection between them."

Oliver said, "But you told me that Myra was depressed after Gregory died."

"Yes, that's true, but who wouldn't be sad."

"I'm just thinking it may be a case of overidentification."

"A copycat suicide?" Marge paused. "Sure, it could be."

Oliver said, "Where'd Myra get hold of a stolen gun?"

"Maybe the same place that Gregory did." Neither detective spoke. Then Marge said, "We need to talk to

Saul Hinton again. Heddy told him about Myra's depression. He didn't say a word to us about that when we talked to him."

"Yeah, he didn't say much to us, period. I don't think he likes the police."

"For sure, but I wonder if he acted on Heddy's tip. And if he didn't, maybe he's feeling guilty. And if he feels guilty enough, that might make him more loquacious. I want to ask him about where kids in the school might get stolen guns. Do you mind going down to B and W with me again?"

"You want to just pop in?"

"No," Marge said, "we won't get anywhere with that. I'll call up Hinton and try to arrange it for sometime next week."

"Sounds good," Oliver said. "Don't expect much."

Marge said, "I never do and that's why I'm so rarely disappointed."

Yasmine never called him. Their chief form of communication had always been texting. So Gabe was nervous when he picked up his cell. He asked if she was okay and she burst into tears. He started to panic. "Are you in trouble?"

She was sniffing a lot. "No."

"Tell me what's wrong."

"I dunno."

Gabe paused, confused. "Can you give me a hint?"

"I got a cold, I got my period, and I look like a blob." Yasmine's voice broke. "And it's *yucky* outside!" More tears.

Sheets of rain blasted his window: she got that much right. He heard her blow her nose. "I'm sorry."

"And on top of everything, I'm all *alone.*"

Gabe felt his heart skip a beat. "For how long?"

"The entire night. My family's at a cousin's wedding in Santa Barbara."

It was Sunday, four in the afternoon. He had nothing to do except practice and he'd already done that for four hours. "I'm coming over."

"Don't you dare! I'm bloated with a big red nose and I look terrible!"

"See you later." He hung up while she was still protesting, grabbed a coat and an umbrella, and walked into the living room. A fire was roaring in the hearth, and both Rina and the Loo were reading while drinking red wine. It was TV domestic tranquility.

Rina looked up. Gabe was dressed in a bomber jacket and carrying an umbrella. She knew he frequently took long walks, but this was ridiculous. "You can't possibly be thinking about going out."

"Some friends called," Gabe told her. "I'm meeting them at the mall."

"I'll take you," Decker said.

"No really, I can walk." Outside a gush of wind shoved a bucket of rain against the picture window. He smiled. "No biggie."

"Gabriel, that's absurd," Rina said.

Decker said, "Which mall are you going to?"

Gabe paused, trying to think of the closest area to Yasmine's house. He knew that Peter could tell he was winging it. "Parthenia."

"That's at least a mile away," Decker said.

"Who are you meeting?" Rina wondered who the boy even knew. Of late, she'd stopped keeping track of his comings and goings.

"Some guys from the SC music department. One of them lives around here . . . his parents do." He was sounding like a complete doofus. "He lives on campus but he's visiting his parents for the weekend. So we decided to get together."

Man, he was a shitty liar.

"He can't pick you up?" Rina said.

"He's already at the mall," Gabe told her.

The Loo's face was skeptical, but he got up and said, "C'mon. I'll take you." He got his keys and they made a beeline for Rina's Volvo. Once they were inside the car, Decker cranked up the heat. It was cold on top of being nasty.

They rode a few minutes in silence. Gabe stared straight ahead, the windshield wipers slapping rhythmically, straining out a natural A.

Decker said, "Who's the girl?" When the boy didn't answer, he said, "Going out in the pouring rain. Plus, you're wearing contacts."

Gabe felt himself redden. "Someone I know from piano at SC."

"She's in college?"

"Freshman. She's seventeen."

Decker said, "She drives?"

"Yeah. She can take me home."

"Why couldn't she pick you up?" When he didn't answer, Decker said, "I suppose it's none of my business."

"Thank you for taking me."

"You're welcome."

"We're just hanging, Peter. Probably going somewhere for dinner."

"I'm glad you're getting out." Decker stopped at a red light. "You know, Gabe, I really don't know much about you. And I suppose I haven't made much of an effort. I'm sorry about that. I hope you haven't felt neglected, but if you have, I plead guilty."

"You've been terrific." He really meant it. "You guys have been just perfect—the right combination of being there and not being there if that makes any sense. Me and my friend are just hanging. No biggie."

"Second time you said that . . . which makes me think it is a biggie."

"I like her, I guess."

"I hope so."

Gabe smiled, but it was a sad one. "It's hard to get close to someone. I know I'll be leaving soon."

Decker said, "Gabe, I'm not your father, but we've been through some stuff together. You know that if you have something on your mind, you can come to me."

"I appreciate it, but I'm fine. Honestly. I don't drink, I don't do drugs, and should it be necessary, I know how to use condoms." He regarded the Loo. "Please don't tell Rina. It's kinda a guy thing, right?"

Decker nodded. "I'll try to respect your privacy. And I won't tell Rina. But just to reiterate, if you really ever do have a problem, talk to me. Don't try to handle it on your own. You're still only fifteen."

"I know. Chris says the same thing."

Decker was surprised. "You're in regular contact with your dad?"

"I had to call him last week. To be taken on by my agent, I have to sign a contract. Chris has lawyers, and I didn't want to bother you. Also, I think he has to sign for me."

"He's still your father so that's true. How'd the conversation go?"

"Okay. Chris was a terrible father, but I think he likes me better now that Mom's gone. Besides, I don't live with him so I guess I don't get on his nerves." He turned to Decker. "Do you ever talk to him?"

"He calls from time to time to check up on you."

"What do you tell him?"

"That as far as I can tell, you've adapted well. They're two-minute conversations."

"That's about right."

"Within his capacity, he cares about you."

"Maybe."

"And so does your mother."

Gabe looked at him. "Has she contacted you?"

"An occasional message on my computer telling me to take care of you. I'm assuming she's contacted you as well."

"We Skyped about three days ago. I saw her face for the first time in almost a year."

"How'd she look?"

"Mom always looks great."

"How was it for you?"

"Weird. It was like two in the morning. The good news is I got to see my baby sister. She's real cute. It's kinda cool having a sister."

"Have you told Chris that you're in contact with your mom?"

"No. I don't think he'd even care." Decker raised his eyebrow and Gabe caught it. "Yeah, he probably would care. But I see no need to volunteer any information. If he asked, I couldn't lie. I mean, I would if I could get away with it, but I'm a terrible liar."

"Yes, you are. I'm not even sure this piano girl really exists, but I'm willing to take your word for it."

Gabe was silent, but try as he might, he couldn't keep the smile off his lips. Decker decided not to comment. When they reached the mall, he said, "You got my cell number in your phone?"

"I have Rina's but not yours."

A surge of guilt ran through Decker's veins. He really had left the kid to his own wits. "Let me give it to you, and I want your cell, too. I have it written down somewhere at home, but I should have it in my contact list."

"Okay." They exchanged numbers. Gabe said, "Thanks, Peter. I mean that. And I really do feel okay talking to you. It's just that there's not much to talk about. My days are pretty routine and mostly revolve around my practice schedule."

"I don't know how you do it," Decker told him. "Your discipline is otherworldly."

"I love what I do. Not all the time, but most of the time. The main entrance is on the other side."

Decker negotiated the parking lot, raindrops bouncing off the blacktop like hot grease. He pulled up as close as he could to the doors and Gabe tore out of the car.

From inside the mall, Gabe looked out the glass doors and watched the Loo drive away. He waited the requisite amount of time, then flipped up his umbrella, and embraced the rain.

Chapter Twenty-Five

When he knocked on the door, she told him to go away.

"Yasmine, open up."

"Go away," she repeated.

He shook out his umbrella underneath her covered porch and closed it. "Yasmine, I'm soaking wet! For goodness' sake, open the friggin' door!"

She looked out the peephole. He was dripping water from everywhere. She opened the door. "Come in and take off your clothes. I'll throw them in the dryer."

Gabe stepped over the threshold and began to strip. "I'm liking this already."

She scuffled away in bunny slippers. Her eyes were droopy, and her nose was red. She wore oversized red-and-white-striped pajamas. She looked like a candy cane. The house was big, and it took him a minute to find the laundry room. She took his clothes, threw them in the dryer, and pushed a button. The drum started to rumble. She hung up his sodden bomber jacket over the utility sink, and then leaned against the washer, her back to his face. He came up from behind and kissed the nape of her neck. He was naked except for his briefs.

"You're gonna get sick," she told him.

He kept kissing her neck. She smelled hormonal. Something primal coursed through his body and within seconds, he was rock hard. "I don't care."

She broke away and left the room without explanation as he followed into her bedroom. She went under her covers and crossed her arms across her chest. She was angry that he was aroused when she felt so lousy. But then she noticed he was shivering. She sighed, opened her blanket, and he slid under. They sat without talking. "Viene La Sera" came through her stereo speakers . . . the two of them listening to the haunting love duet from *Madame Butterfly*. Gabe put his arm around her.

"You shouldn't be so close to me," Yasmine said.

Gabe dropped his arm. "Do you want me to leave?"

She looked up with wet eyes. "No." A pause. "I'm sorry I'm so grumpy."

"That's okay. I love you even grumpy." Tears spilled over her lower lashes. He hugged her again. This time she didn't resist.

"It's a horrible cold, Gabe. I don't want you to catch it."

"You're worth a thousand colds."

"Not a million colds?"

Gabe laughed. "A million trillion, okay?"

She ran her fingers through his damp locks. "What happened to your glasses?"

"I'm wearing contacts. Rain messes up the lenses."

"I like it." She smiled slyly. "I can see those gorgeous eyes of yours."

"Thank you. And with my gorgeous eyes I can see your gorgeous face." He started kissing the nape of her neck again. When she didn't resist, he moved around to the front, to that sexy notch at the beginning of her throat and then down to her chest. He slowly started to unbutton her pajama top. When it was open, he slid his hand over her two protuberances, which seemed to be growing by the week. He whispered, "I'm sorry you're not feeling well, but you're still very sexy."

"I feel horrible." He took his hand away. She put it back. "It's okay."

His dick was stiff again. He gently pushed her down until she was supine, and he began to kiss her breasts. He knew he caught colds easily. He knew he'd catch hers. He didn't give a shit. "God, you're fantastic."

Lying on her back caused a drip into her throat. She tried to stifle the cough, but ended up hacking away and had to sit up.

They both laughed.

"Well, that was really sexy," she said.

"I don't care." But his cock had retreated. "We can just talk."

"I feel like crap. I don't even know how you can stand to be around me."

"I love you." He began to kiss her shoulder. "Does this bother you?"

"No."

"Do you like it?"

"Yes."

"I like it, too." He kissed her shoulder and her neck and smelled her musky scent and tasted her salt and got hard again. Her stomach was hollow, and she had a dark line running down the middle of her belly. He traced it with his fingertips until he got to the waistband of her pajamas bottoms. His hand rested there for a few seconds. Then his fingers dipped inside, feeling the good thatch of hair.

She pulled out his hand and placed it back on her breast. He went back to kissing her shoulder. She whispered, "Gabe?"

"What?"

"Have you ever done it?" He didn't answer and she persisted. "C'mon. I wanna know. Have you ever done it?"

He ignored her. "No, I've never kissed a shoulder as beautiful as yours."

She pulled away from him and studied his face. "You have! I know you have!" She sat upright, her eyes wide with interest. "What's it like?"

"It wasn't as good as being with you now." She was still staring at him. "Why do we have to talk about it?"

"Because I'm curious."

"Why? It'll only make you feel bad."

"Please?"

He went soft again. Thinking about the past was the surest way to make him deflated and depressed. In anger, he said, "You really want to know?"

"Yes, I really want to know."

He was barely controlling his rage. "Okay. Then here goes. The answer is, yes, I've done it three times . . . or rather with three girls. The first time was like an initiation to high school. Some upper-class girl takes you in her car and does you. Wham bam thank you ma'am. I was a year ahead in school, so I was thirteen. It was weird. The second time was at a party. I ran with a fast crowd and even though I was younger, my buddies were okay with me because I was tall, I was

Chris Donatti's son, and I played the piano and guitar and all sorts of shit that made me free entertainment and a chick magnet. There were always a lot of parties with a lot of booze, drugs, and sex. Everybody would get drunk or stoned. There was a lot of fooling around. Some screwing, but mostly, the girls gave a lot of head."

"Head?"

"Oral sex," he told her and not too nicely. "Blow jobs. That's what girls do when they want to do something but they still want to be virgins. They'd give blow jobs. I got a ton of blow jobs, okay?"

He was quiet. Yasmine asked softly, "What about the other two times?"

He gave her a dirty look, but she seemed unfettered by his discomfort. "The second time was at a party with my friend's older sister. She was sixteen and totally blasted—a real hot mess. It was a miracle she didn't puke on me afterward. The third time was even weirder. It was my friend's sister-in-law. Her husband—my friend's brother—was in, like, Iraq or Afghanistan. I was supposed to meet my friend at his brother's house—why I don't even remember—but he got hung up and couldn't make it. It was in the summer and it was really hot outside. His sister-in-law offered me a beer before I left. So I'm sitting on the couch, drinking a beer, when she starts massaging my leg, bending over and showing her cleavage. We wound up doing it on the couch with our clothes on."

His anger was gone. He was suddenly more dispirited than anything else.

"It was also strange because she wasn't a girl. She was a woman and she liked it."

He regarded Yasmine's face, her red nose, and her inquisitive eyes.

"You know that most girls don't like it at first. They just do it to please their boyfriends."

Yasmine was very quiet.

"You asked, so now you know. Happy?"

"You did it with a married woman?"

He shrugged. "I felt bad, but not that bad. It was a weird community. My friends' moms were always coming on to me. It was a game with them."

"You did it with your friends' moms?"

"Count on your fingers, Yasmine! First time was in a car, second at a party, and third with my friend's sister-in-law. One, two, three! Three, okay! Three!"

"You're mad at me."

"No, I'm not." But his eyes were smoking.

She said, "I'm sorry I made you talk about it. It wasn't any of my business."

"I'm not mad." He was very pissed. "It's just that it wasn't . . ." He grew sulky. "After I did it the third time, the sister-in-law asked me how old I was. I should have told her fifteen 'cause that was my friend's age. But it caught me off guard. So I told her I was four-teen. Then she said, "Fourteen? Man, you *really* don't count." And I know she said that to make her feel less guilty. But it still made me feel very small. And at that point, I said to myself, 'Gabe, you're not your dad. You really need to raise your standards.'"

He looked at Yasmine.

"And then like a few weeks later, my dad beat the crap out of my mom and we wound up in California. And then six weeks later, my mom deserted me and went to India to have a baby. She accidentally got knocked up, which seems to be a pattern with her. This time it was by some rich old Indian doctor and they moved to Uttar Pradesh. Then my father moved permanently to Nevada. And I wound up with total strangers. So there's the whole sordid tale of my life. Happy?"

She touched his shoulder. He was a ball of coiled muscle. "I'm sorry." She kissed his shoulder, and he felt a tear drip onto his skin. Her voice was plaintive. "Please don't be mad at me."

"I'm not mad." He was still pissed but tried to shrug it off. "It was sex, Yasmine. No emotion." He turned to her. "Not like if we did it. I'm not saying we should do it. But I am saying if we did do it, it would be different."

"Different, but not special because you've done it before."

"Of course it would be special!" He tried to hide the irritation in his voice. "It would be the most extra special thing that has ever happened to me."

"But you've done it before."

"But not with someone I love. You know what the sex was, Yasmine? It was like eating a bad meal when you're hungry. The drive is there and you know you're gonna do it. But you feel lousy afterward."

"It's just . . ." She didn't finish.

"What!" he grumped out.

"It's just if we did it, I want it to be something you've never done."

A thought floated into his brain. He quickly tamped it out.

"What?" she asked.

"What?" he asked back.

"What were you just thinking?"

"Nothing."

"That's not true."

Gabe didn't answer.

"Gabriel, whatever your middle name is, Whitman, you are lying. What were you thinking?"

"My middle name is Matthew."

"Mine is Tamar."

"Tamar?"

"It means date in Hebrew."

He started kissing her shoulder again. "I can see that. You're brown and sweet and I want to eat you up."

"Gabriel, what were you thinking?"

"It's not important."

"It's important to me."

He was getting increasingly exasperated. It was a bad idea to come over. "Yasmine, there are things that you tell someone you love because you love them. And there are things you don't tell someone you love because you love them."

She waited, drumming her fingers.

"Like . . . this is theoretical by the way . . . but like if I saw a hot girl, I wouldn't turn to you and say, 'I'd like to do her.' That would hurt your feelings. So I'd keep it to myself."

"Is that what you were thinking a minute ago? That you want to do another girl?"

"I said it was theoretical, okay! Do you know what theoretical means?"

"Yes, I know what theoretical means!" She stroked his cheek. "Please tell me, what were you thinking?"

"You're just asking for it." When she didn't say anything, Gabe shook his head. "You know the saying: some girls are bitches but all guys are dogs. Well, it's true."

"My father is not a dog."

"I've seen your mother. He's a dog."

She hit him.

"We're all dogs, but it's not like we can't be trained."
He paused. "There's this small percentage like my dad
who are simply hopeless. If my dad were a dog, he'd be
a vicious pit bull and have to be put down. And there's
this other small percentage like the airport drug dogs.
You put a steak in their faces, no matter what, they'll
resist. And then there's everyone else in between. Like
if the master is standing over us, we'll ignore the steak.
But if left alone, we'll start sniffing around the area,
then sniffing the steak, then eventually if no one's looking, we'll take a bite."

"But why would you do that if you truly loved the
girl." She was wounded.

Gabe stroked her face. "I would never hurt you. But
how committed can we be to each other when we're
sneaking around? You can't even tell your parents
about us."

"Do you want me to tell my parents?"

"No. Because they'd forbid you to see me. This way,
at least we can pretend it's really okay. Plus we're kinda
young. I mean maybe this will be forever, but we both
know that we've got a lot of things working against
us. Which is why that even though it would the most
special thing for me, I don't think it's the right time to
do it."

A tear ran down her cheek. "You do it with other girls that you don't like, but you won't do it with me?"

"Of course, I'd do it with you. I'm *dying* to do it with you. I'm trying to be . . . *considerate* of your position. Don't you understand what I'm saying?"

"Yes. I'm not stupid."

"I'm not saying you're stupid." He blew out air. "Maybe I should go."

Her eyes moistened. "All I'm saying is that I'd do it for you, because I love you."

"I know." He softened. "And I love you for it."

"Even if it wouldn't be your first time."

"What do you *want,* Yasmine? If I had known the future, I'd take back my virginity in a heartbeat." He exhaled. "You know, three girls doesn't exactly make me a stud."

She turned to him. "I think you're the biggest stud in the whole wide world."

Gabe laughed. "You are such a cuckoo bird!"

"What were you thinking before . . . that you won't tell me? Please. I want to know."

Gabe sighed. "This is a mistake." She waited. "When you said it wouldn't be my first time . . . my first thought was that it wouldn't be my first time . . . *but* . . . it would be your first time and that would be exciting for me." He gave her a tight smile. "Happy?"

She leaned her head on his shoulder. "And that would be special for you?"

"Yasmine, you'd be special whether or not you're a virgin, okay. I love you, okay."

"But that would be special . . . that it would be my first time."

He paused. "I must admit that the thought was arousing, that I'd be your first. And you'd always remember me because of that."

"So you really do want to do it with me?"

"Oh my God!" He slapped his hand on his head. "Yes, I want to do it with you. But it's a very big step, Yasmine. Once you do it, you can't take it back."

She was quiet.

Gabe said, "We're not gonna do it tonight. You're sick, you've got your period, and I'm not prepared anyway." He kissed her cheek. "I don't have protection. So let's forget about it, okay."

"Okay."

Gabe let out a small laugh. "I think . . . I just shot myself in the foot."

Yasmine smiled. "Maybe."

"See how much I love you? I come over not expecting anything except your company and I turn down sex. Could you ask for a better boyfriend?"

"I love the sound of that . . . that you're my boyfriend."

"I hope I'm your boyfriend. I've never had a girl-friend. Will you be my girlfriend?"

She sniffed. "Yes, I will be your girlfriend." She blew her nose. "I love you, Gabriel. I love you and would do anything for you."

"I love you, too." He meant it in a way she could never understand. Intellectually, he knew that there were people out there to whom he mattered, but the knowledge did little to ease his profound loneliness. Until she stepped into his life, he'd been swirling around in very dark thoughts, a step away from a black hole of nothingness. His eyes hooked onto hers. "I'd do anything for you, Yasmine. I'd even die for you."

Her eyes searched his face for clues to his ghoulish mood. He was often hard to read. She knew he didn't like talking about his past, and it had been wrong for her to probe. "Gabe, what prompted you to even *think* that?"

Gabe took her hand. "Just that . . . you mean so much to me. I want you to know that it isn't just sex." He broke into a slow grin. "Although I wouldn't say no should you have an overwhelming desire—"

She hit his shoulder, and then kissed his cheek. "You know, I'd rather die than to have you die. But let's not talk about that. It's a little morbid."

"So . . ." He smiled at her. "What should we talk about, girlfriend?"

"I dunno . . ." She shrugged. "Music is always safe."

"Okay. What are you singing these days beside 'Der Hölle Rache'?"

She started talking about her lessons. Even with a cold, her voice was rhythmic and musical. Her pitch rose as she warmed to her subject, her enthusiasm infectious and just plain cute. After a few minutes of a nonstop soliloquy, she blew her nose and looked at him. "God, I love you. I can't talk to anyone about my singing except you."

Gabe kissed the top of her head. "We are very well matched."

Yasmine smoothed his hair still damp from rain. "Well . . . as long as you're in your underwear, do you want me to do something?"

He gave her a dopey smile. "Are you up to it?"

"I think so." She climbed onto his lap and brushed her lips against his. "Although you know if you keep kissing me, you're gonna get my cold."

He slipped his arms around her waist and bit her lower lip gently. "Hmmm . . . I think"—a soft swipe against her lips—"that the thrill of kissing you"—his tongue grazing hers—"is definitely worth the risk of a few nonlethal microbes."

Chapter Twenty-Six

Los Angeles was subtropical, mild temperatures with wet winters and dry summers. For nearly a week running, the skies cracked open, drowning L.A. and its environs in water and mudslides. Marge was going over the day's assignments with the Loo. They were sitting in Decker's office. It was ten o'clock on Thursday morning in mid-April and the sky was overcast, the clouds dark and heavy.

"Drop in overall crime this week. Even felons don't like getting their feet wet. Burglaries are way down . . . what else?" Marge continued to flip through her notes. "Okay . . . this is regarding the Gregory Hesse/Myra Gelb suicides. Remember a couple of weeks ago, we were scrolling down Myra Gelb's phone calls and there were a few unknown numbers. One of them was disconnected?"

"Sounds familiar."

"We finally got hold of Wendy Hesse. She'd been out of town visiting her sister. The number was Gregory Hesse's cell phone." She closed the notebook. "So obviously Greg and Myra did know each other."

Decker sat up. "How many calls did she make to him?"

"Only one in her most recent calls. It was placed a few days before Greg killed himself. We asked Udonis for a copy of Myra's old phone records. She didn't have anything on hand. After Myra died, she paid off the phone company and canceled the number. She did agree to contact the phone company for Myra's records."

"Great. It's easier for her to do it than for us."

"I talked to her on . . . Tuesday." She reread her handwriting. "I'll call and see if she did it yet. If so, it'll take a couple of weeks for the records to come in. And even if there were a couple of calls between them and they knew each other, it doesn't mean the suicides are related."

Decker said, "I can understand Myra killing herself after Greg died if there was something between them. But why did *Greg* do it?"

"Lord only knows but this might be a clue. Wendy Hesse saw images of Greg on his computer fooling around with a gun. Teenaged boys do stupid stuff. Maybe Gregory accidentally shot himself." She thought a moment. "Would it make Wendy Hesse feel better if the M.E. ruled it an accidental death?"

Decker shrugged. "Maybe a scintilla."

"Maybe we can get the M.E. to consider accidental death." She looked at the Loo. "And maybe it's time to stop treating the deaths like foul play. Without any evidence, we can't draw any conclusions. We're trying to fit a square peg in a round hole."

"There's truth to that. And I'm willing to let it all go as soon as I find out where the kids got the guns."

"Yeah, that's a sticking point," Marge admitted. "Gregory was way too young to steal the gun from Olivia Garden. Myra's gun was from Lisbeth Holly's burglary. That was only a year ago."

"And in that burglary, other things were taken besides the .22."

"Yes. Some of the daughter's jewelry, her phone and iPod, and some CDs."

"Kid stuff."

"Exactly." Marge thought a moment. "One of the missing rings was inscribed with the kid's name—Sydney. If we find the ring, we'll know who it belongs to."

"And none of the mother's jewelry was missing, right?"

"Correct . . . that's why Lisbeth Holly thought it was done by kids. So it's theoretically *possible* that

Myra Gelb could have stolen the gun. But we didn't find anything else belonging to Sydney Holly in her room."

Decker washed his tired face with dry hands. "Is Gregory Hesse's camcorder still missing?"

"Yes. And both Myra's and Greg's laptops."

"Margie, we both know that there's a missing link out there. We just don't know what it is." Decker drummed his fingers. "Okay. We've got two things to figure out. The thefts and where the kids got the guns. My vote is with Dylan Lashay for both things. We know that he and his gang like guns. And Dylan seemed to enjoy torturing Myra. I could see him selling her a gun."

"You realize we have no evidence, Pete."

"I don't like him."

"You never even met the boy."

"I don't trust anyone who invents a Mafia and calls himself a don."

"Yeah, that is wannabe. But I think you also don't like him because he's good-looking, rich, popular, and smart."

"No, I don't like him because he's a bully."

Marge looked him up and down. "You never were a bully in high school?"

"When you're my height and weight at sixteen, you don't have to be a bully. People naturally give you room." That wasn't entirely true though. Decker did push his weight around, stupid kid that he was. He said, "Even if Lashay wasn't the one with the gun, it's still guilt by association."

"Last week, I put in a call to Saul Hinton asking to meet with him again."

"The guy that Heddy Kramer confided in."

"Yeah, he hasn't returned my call. I thought about using his guilt to ask about black market guns and dealers on campus. Maybe he can point us in some direction."

"What guilt are you talking about?"

"About not preventing Myra's suicide."

"How could he prevent it?"

"Well, he could have intervened with her directly, talked to her parents, gotten mental-health professionals involved . . . but maybe Heddy told him and he forgot about it," Marge said. "Maybe he blames himself for Myra's death. And now that we know that there was a phone call between Myra and Greg, I can also ask him about the relationship between the two of them."

"Go for it."

Marge said, "You know, Loo, I could talk to some of Greg's other friends. Joey Reinhart gave me some names. We were going to interview them, then Wendy Hesse suddenly stopped returning my calls and since it was her son that was dead, we let it ride. But now she seems to be cooperative again."

Decker said, "Why don't you and Oliver go down the list of Gregory's friends and see what you two can pull up."

"Great. I'll talk to Saul Hinton and Greg's friends. Anything else?"

"A couple of Advil would be nice."

"Aw, I've given the Loo a headache."

Decker gave her a dismissive wave. "You can go now, wise guy."

Marge reached into her purse and pulled out a couple of aspirin tablets. Then she took his coffee cup from his desk. "It looks like you need a refill."

"I need a brain refill."

"Can't help you there, big man. But if you want a good cappuccino, I'm the bomb."

The boys' overwhelming commonality was their awkwardness. Three of them: Michael Martinetto, Harold "Beezel or Beeze" Frasier, and Joey Reinhart. No swaggering, no smirks, no arrogance, the three shambling teens appeared apprehensive and subdued when Marge escorted them into an interview room. Maybe they were finally coming to grips with the loss of one of their own.

Reinhart was as tall and gawky as Harold Beezel Frasier was short and stout. Beezel had a round face, dark eyes, and a bowl haircut with bangs that hid a bumpy forehead of acne. Mikey Martinetto was about five ten with broad shoulders. He had blond kinky hair and light brown eyes, and he still wore braces. These were kids who would be thankful when they grew into adults.

Oliver came into the room and Marge made the introductions. He handed each of the boys a bottle of water. "Sometimes the tap gets a little nasty after all this rainfall."

The boys nodded and cracked open the H_2O.

"Is it raining now?" Scott asked.

Beezel said, "Drizzling."

Joey said, "Supposed to kick up tomorrow. I hate driving in the rain."

"Not to mention how funky the school smells," Mikey said.

"B and W leaks?" Marge said.

"Yeah, B and W's got some real roof issues," Mikey answered. "Mr. Hinton's classroom really stinks."

"Moldy," Beezel said. "My allergies are going nuts."

"Fisher auditorium is like a sieve," Joey said. "You'd think with all the tuition our parents fork over, the school would take better care of the facilities."

Marge said, "I'm really surprised. I always thought that B and W was . . . kind of a country club in the form of a prep school."

The boys smiled without joy. Beezel said, "Not any country club I'd ever belong to. I keep telling my parents they're getting ripped off."

Oliver said, "It's got a great reputation . . . B and W."

Joey said, "A mile wide and an inch deep."

Beezel said, "It accepts smart kids, so it does well as far as placing them in universities. But smart kids would do well anywhere."

"So why are you there?" Marge asked.

Mikey said, "Public schools in my district are a joke. Besides, the counselors at B and W have the connections to the top-tiered colleges. That's where they have their rep. Getting their students into the elite universities."

"Yeah, that part is pretty good," Joey said. "The counselors know how to pad the application to make us all look good. It's really stupid, though. 'Cause all the private school applications are padded in practically identical ways."

Marge said, "So what do you do to stand out?"

"It's hard," Beezel said. "Even the standardized test scores don't mean much."

Mikey said. "Either you're the president of everything or you've got a particular skill that no one else has—like you've owned your own artisan cheese factory since you were nine."

"Or you've done cancer research," Joey said.

"And you've published a paper on it," Mikey said.

Marge said, "So how does a guy like Dylan Lashay get into Yale?" Three sets of eyes took in her face. The boys suddenly went mute. The seconds ticked on in silence. She said, "What just happened?"

The boys eyed one another. Joey said, "What does Dylan have to do with Greg?"

"We're not assuming he has anything to do with Greg," Oliver said.

Beezel said, "So why bring him up?"

"We were talking about kids getting into good schools," Marge said. "We happen to know that Dylan Lashay got into Yale. I was just wondering if he was an artisan cheese maker or the president of everything."

Mikey smiled. "The president of everything."

"He's also a legacy," Beezel said. "His stepdad is."

Mikey said, "He also happens to be a smart guy."

Marge said, "Not that smart if he needed Greg to edit his papers." Joey's eyes widened. She said, "Isn't that what you told Lieutenant Decker?"

"Not exactly," Joey stammered out.

Beezel came to his rescue. "Greg was an exceptional writer. He edited lots of papers for a lot of people."

"That he did," Mikey said. "It bought him a lot of . . . goodwill."

"Dylan and company left him alone," Oliver said.

Mikey shrugged.

Marge said, "Does he bother you?"

Beezel said, "We've all become pretty adept at staying out of his way."

Mikey said, "Excuse me, but what does this have to do with Greg's suicide?"

"You know what I'm going to do?" Oliver said. "I'm going to tell you exactly why we've asked you here and take all the guesswork out of the equation. We'd like to close out Gregory Hesse's file."

"Why does Greg have a police file?" Joey asked.

"Every unnatural death has a police file," Marge said. "Greg's file would have been closed a long time ago, but we've hit a few snags. First thing is the stolen gun that Greg used in his suicide. He didn't seem like the type to break into houses and loot firearms, so where did he get the gun?"

"Is there a side of Greg that we're missing?" Oliver said. "Is he a closet klepto?"

Mikey said, "I can't see that."

"So it would surprise you if he stole the gun."

"Yeah, it would shock me. But so did his suicide. So I guess I didn't know him as well as I thought I did."

"Amen to that," Joey said.

Oliver said, "Greg had to get the gun from *somewhere*."

Marge said, "That's why we brought up Dylan Lashay. Kevin Stanger mentioned that Dylan or one of his buddies had once pulled a gun on him. So if Stanger is telling the truth, we know that his gang has had access to weapons in the past."

Oliver said, "We were wondering if Kevin Stanger's case was a onetime deal or if Mr. Yalie has a predilection for firearms."

Joey said, "I already told the lieutenant, I have no idea where Greg got the gun."

"I don't know where Greg got the gun, either," Beezel said.

The conversation died for a moment.

Mikey shook his head. "C'mon, guys, what's the hang-up? Everyone in the entire school knows that Dylan likes guns." When Beezel and Joey glared at him, he said, "Like it's a secret? He did his senior thesis on the history of firearms."

Oliver said, "Does he deal in firearms?"

He just shrugged. "Can't say yes, but there are rumors."

"Unsubstantiated at this time," Beezel said.

"Except by Kevin Stanger," Marge said.

"Who could be exaggerating," Beezel said.

"What kind of rumors?" Marge asked Mikey.

The teen said, "This is theoretical and definitely not *firsthand* . . . but . . . if I wanted to get hold of a gun, there are a few people in the school I might seek out. Because these same people have a reputation of selling a lot of things."

Marge said, "And those people would be . . ."

Mikey said, "I'm not naming names because, like I said, I don't know firsthand."

"Might one of those people be Dylan Lashay?" Oliver asked.

"I've said what I've had to say." Mikey smiled. "Anything else would be mere speculating on my speculations."

"What about his buddies?" Oliver took out a list. "Jarrod Lovelace, Stance O'Brien, Nate Asaroff, or JJ Little? Do they sell things?"

Three noncommittal shrugs.

"Okay," Marge said. "We'll address the topic of guns later. Let's get back to Gregory Hesse's suicide. None of you saw any signs that this was a possibility?"

"Nothing," Mikey said. "But Joey knew him better than anyone."

Joey said, "I already told the lieutenant that his death came out of the blue."

"You also told the lieutenant that you thought there might have been a girl involved in his life before he died," Marge said.

"I said *maybe*," Joey said.

Mikey held up a finger. "You know, I never thought of that, but it kinda makes sense."

"Why?" Oliver asked.

"He started taking better care of himself."

Joey said, "That's exactly what I told the lieutenant. That he started showering."

"But you have no idea who the girl was," Oliver said.

"I don't even know if there was a girl," Joey said. "I certainly don't know a name."

Marge said, "What about Myra Gelb?" When three sets of eyes stared at her, she went on, "They knew each other. They called each other frequently." A lie at the moment but when the phone records came in, maybe it would be the truth. She waited for one of them to speak.

"News to me," Beezel said.

Joey said, "Greg never said anything about knowing Myra. Why? Do you think the two suicides are related?"

"You're telling me you never thought about it?" Oliver said.

"No, not at all," Joey answered. "I mean, why would I? They didn't hang out with each other or anything."

Mikey said, "Both of them worked on the paper." Oliver and Marge turned to him and waited for the boy to elaborate. "I mean, I'm on the paper, too. So are about a hundred other kids. It's one of those silver stars that you put on your college application."

"Kevin Stanger told us that Greg was working on something big before he died," Marge said.

"News to me," Joey said.

Marge turned to Mikey, who seemed to be the most cooperative of the boys. "Do you think it might have had something to do with the paper? Did Greg ever tell you he was working on something top secret?"

Mikey appeared to give the question some deep thought. "No. I would remember Greg saying something like that."

Beezel said, "He never said anything to me about a top-secret project. But I will say this. Greg *loved* his camcorder and seemed to record anything in his path. Maybe he accidentally hit upon something that he felt was newsworthy."

"Just what I told the lieutenant," Joey said.

Beezel said, "He got kind of obnoxious with it . . . it made any real conversation hard 'cause he was always recording it for posterity or something."

"It was real obnoxious," Mikey said. "I used to tell him I was going to smash it over his head if he didn't get out of my face." He looked up at the ceiling, his eyes watering. "I didn't know . . ."

The room fell silent.

"Mikey, did you ever see Myra and Greg working together?" Oliver said.

The boy slumped in his chair. "Myra didn't write for the *Tattler*. She did some cartooning. Greg wrote some articles—at least one was published." He threw his hands in the air. "I never noticed them together, but I wasn't paying attention."

Oliver said, "I told you we had a few snags to clear up before we can clear the file. The first issue was the stolen gun, but we're concerned about a few other things: Greg's camcorder is missing."

Joey was taken aback. "Stolen?"

"It appears that way," Marge said.

"Who'd want Greg's camcorder?"

"Maybe it was like Beezel said," Marge suggested. "Maybe he accidentally filmed something scandalous."

"If he did, he never showed it to me," Joey said. "All we ever saw were clips of us nerds farting around. Nothing even remotely scandalous."

"Mrs. Hesse found things on Greg's computer," Oliver said.

"Porno?" Mikey asked. The boys looked at each other and smiled. "And that's weird because . . ."

Oliver said, "It's not weird at all if they were standard skin flicks. But she found amateur porno on Greg's laptop: a girl giving oral sex."

"Oral sex to *Greg?*" Beezel was incredulous.

"We're not sure," Oliver said. "No faces to match the genitals."

Joey said, "If it was Greg, he never said anything about scoring."

"Would he have said something about scoring?" Oliver asked.

"Yeah." Joey let go with a single laugh. "I mean, who wouldn't?"

"Maybe he cared about the girl and didn't want to embarrass her," Marge suggested.

"If he cared about the girl, why would he film it?" Mikey asked.

"Maybe the images were for his eyes only," Oliver said.

"That's what guys always tell girls. And then they wind up showing it all around," Joey said. "It's bragging rights."

"But he didn't show you anything, did he?" Oliver said.

Silence. Then Beezel said, "Uh . . . I'm not saying this to be weird or anything, but if you showed us the images, we could maybe identify somebody."

"Like I said, there were no faces, so what would be the point." Oliver looked up from his pad. "Not only is the camcorder missing, his computer was also stolen."

Three surprised faces. Mikey said, "Are you *sure?*"

"Positive," Marge said. "About three weeks ago, Mrs. Hesse left his computer on the dining room table before she went to bed and it wasn't there in the morning."

Oliver said, "She was going to bring it into the police station not because of the oral sex, but because it showed Greg playing with a gun. She wanted us to see if it was the same gun he used to kill himself."

"Shit!" Joey said. "That's really weird."

"It's really *creepy!*" Mikey said.

"What do you mean by playing with a gun?" Beezel asked.

"She told us he was twirling it, pointing it at the camera," Marge said. "She also told us that Greg's eyelids were droopy—like he was drugged or drunk."

"Man oh man," Mikey said. "This is getting more bizarre by the moment."

"This is definitely not the Gregory Hesse that we all knew," Joey said.

Beezel said, "I don't mean to tell you how to do your job, but . . . is it possible that Mrs. Hesse changed her mind about the computer and just told you it was stolen to prevent further . . . I don't know . . . embarrassment about her son."

Marge said, "Mrs. Hesse had stopped returning our phone calls. When Greg's computer was stolen, it freaked her out that someone broke into her house and took the computer. That's why she called us. So yes, I do believe that the computer was stolen."

"Maybe the anonymous sex girl stole the computer," Joey suggested. "Maybe she didn't want her identity revealed to the police."

Oliver said, "How would the girl or anyone know that Mrs. Hesse was getting ready to show it to the police?"

Marge asked, "And how would the girl know that Mrs. Hesse had discovered the porno images on her son's computer?"

Beezel said, "Maybe the sex girl had a remote access to his computer."

"Remote access?" Oliver asked.

"Good thinking," Joey said. "It means that maybe she could control his computer from an off-site location."

"It's not weird," Mikey said. "You buy a program that allows select people to access your computer by a remote."

"Why in the world would you do that?" Marge said.

Joey said, "Because if your computer breaks, your tech support guy can access your computer by remote, meaning he can diagnose the problem and clean it up without you having to physically drop it off. It, like, saves a bunch of time."

"It's done all the time," Mikey said. "The thing is, in order for the tech to gain access to the computer, the user has to sign the tech guy on with a password. But c'mon, if you know your way around a hard drive, you probably can bypass the user's permission and access the computer whenever you want."

"That would be illegal, of course," Oliver said.

"Of course," Mikey said. "But c'mon. If you've got motivation to do something, you're gonna do it—legal or not."

Chapter Twenty-Seven

Sitting in his office with Marge and Oliver, Decker raked his hair and sipped cold coffee. It was three-thirty in the afternoon. In a couple of hours, Cindy, Koby, and his twin grandsons would be at the house for Sabbath dinner. He could feel his mind slipping into off-duty mode. To prevent him from zoning out altogether, he flipped through his notes. "So what's with this remote control computer access? What does it have to do with Greg's stolen computer?"

Marge was picking the pilling off her sweater. "Maybe someone realized that Greg's computer was in use and his personal things were being watched. Someone got scared that things would come out."

Oliver said, "Specifically, the girl who was giving Greg a blow job. It could be she wasn't ready for X-rated distribution."

Decker was skeptical. "You actually think that a girl broke into Hesse's house and took the computer before Wendy could give it to the police?"

Marge said, "Or perhaps it was taken by a certain future Yalie and his posse nicknamed the B and W Mafia. Maybe one of the guys realized that there were images on the computer of Greg playing with a stolen gun."

Oliver said, "The same stolen gun sold to Greg by Yalie who was now worried about being implicated in something more serious than stolen weapons. Something like negligent homicide, which doesn't look good on any transcript except maybe Corcoran or Pelican Bay."

"The problem is," Marge said, "that until someone names names, we've got nothing."

Decker wasn't quite ready to give up. "What about Saul Hinton? Could you lean on him a little?"

"That was our next step." Oliver smoothed his silver tie. "We called him this morning, asking him to meet with us next week, but he hasn't called us back."

Decker said, "Call him again. Tell him you want to talk about Myra Gelb. If he forgot to follow up on what Heddy told him about Myra's depression, that'll get his heart racing. Maybe he'll spill something on Dylan."

Oliver checked his watch. "You know, school's letting out right around this time." He turned to his partner. "How about we use the old 'we were on our way home anyway' thing."

"No guarantee he'll talk to us, but . . ." Marge slipped the strap of her purse over her shoulder. "I'm supposed to meet up with Willy at eight in Ventura. I got time."

Oliver stood up. "Let's go."

Marge said, "We'll fill you in if we find out anything." The two of them walked out together. "Do you have any plans tonight, Scott?"

"Actually I'm going to dinner with my son and daughter-in-law."

"That's lovely."

"Yeah, it's fun." He let go with a smile and she asked what was funny. "It's especially fun for them. I always pay."

A flash of the badge and B and W's campus security guard gave ground without a fuss. They walked past the Administration Building and promptly got lost looking for Saul Hinton's classroom. They asked a fireplug of a boy in a letter jacket where to find room 26 and he walked them to the correct classroom. Erasing a whiteboard, Hinton had his back to the door when they came in. Marge cleared her throat and he turned around, frowning with immediate recognition.

But his speech was civil. "I did get your message, Detectives." He continued erasing the board. "I just haven't had a moment to call you back."

Marge said, "I know, sir. We're sorry to intrude if this is a bad time. We were just on our way home."

"Where is home?" Hinton asked.

"About a half mile from here," Marge answered.

"So you live in the district where you work."

"I do. So does Detective Oliver."

"I suppose that's admirable." Hinton put down the eraser. "What can I do for you?"

Oliver said, "Do you mind if we sit down?"

"So this is going to take a while?"

Oliver shrugged. "I'm just old and tired."

A small bit of red came to Hinton's cheeks. "Of course. Sit anywhere. No need to even ask."

Marge said, "Are you all right, sir?"

"I'm fine." Hinton chose a student's desk chair. "What do you want to ask me?"

"The gun that Myra Gelb used to kill herself . . . it was stolen."

"I heard something about that."

"It was taken in a year-old burglary along with some CDs and an iPod. We all think that kids did it." Marge waited for a reaction and she got it—a deep blush. "There are rumors, sir, about certain seniors who like guns. And the same certain seniors were people that Myra did not like."

"She used to draw cartoons of them," Oliver said. "The only reason we're not mentioning names is that we want to see if you mention the same ones first."

"If you do know someone at the school who might be dealing in stolen weapons, now's the time to tell us. Remember, please, that two stolen guns were used in two separate suicides."

The thin man with the long arms seemed to fold up over himself. "We're all probably thinking about the same people. I won't mention names because anything I'd tell you would be speculation and I don't speculate."

"Even if it could save another depressed teenager's life?"

Hinton looked away. "I can't help you. Take it up with the administration. They're the only ones allowed to open school lockers and they won't do it without probable cause or a court order."

"So we have to wait until another child commits suicide to get what we need?"

"First Amendment rights supersede the nebulous possibility of something that may happen in the future." Hinton spoke but his heart wasn't into it.

"First Amendment rights don't apply to the kids in this school," Marge said. "I know that the parents and kids sign contracts that allow the administration to go into school lockers without asking their permission."

"With probable cause."

"If you implied that a certain person might be dealing, that would be probable cause," Oliver said. "Think about Gregory Hesse or Myra Gelb. If you could have done something to stop their suicides, you would have done it, right?"

Hinton became very pale and Marge grew worried. Perhaps the accusation came too fast and too pointed. "You're white, sir. Are you okay?"

He dropped his head between his knees. "I feel a little dizzy."

Oliver stood up. "I'll get you some water."

Hinton said, "There's a bottle of orange juice in my backpack. I think my blood sugar is low."

Marge retrieved it and gave it to the teacher. He drank greedily. A minute later, he could sit up, but his complexion remained wan. "If I tell you names and the administration opens lockers based on my accusations and it turns out to be wrong, I could get fired. Worse still, I could get sued. I would probably lose everything and be blackballed from teaching. There are certain kids in B and W who are products of very litigious parents."

The detectives nodded.

"All that being said . . . if I knew someone was dealing in weapons as a certainty, I would have told the administration a long time ago. It would be morally outrageous for me not to say something." His eyes grew wet. "If I could have prevented past deaths, I would have stepped up to the plate. I'm sorry I can't do more."

Marge spoke softly. "Your sincerity is evident. I hope you're not speaking from personal experience."

Hinton was quiet. "You talked to Heddy Kramer, didn't you?"

"We did."

"So she told you."

"She did."

No one spoke. Then Hinton said, "I did talk to Myra. She said she was saddened, but personally she was okay. We spoke for about twenty minutes. She seemed angry more than anything else."

"Did she say who she was angry at?" Oliver asked.

"No names. Really it seemed she was angry at life. So after she left, I called her mother . . . left a message for her to call me back, that I had some concerns about Myra." He licked his lips. "No one called me back. And then I promptly forgot about it. Now I'm thinking that Myra might have intercepted the message and erased it. I should have made a follow-up call." A pause. "I blew it."

Time to offer him a life preserver. Marge said, "You know that if someone is determined to kill himself—"

"Yes, I know," Hinton interrupted. "It doesn't alleviate the pain or the guilt. It's eating me alive. I'm going to have to find my own expiation. Otherwise . . ." He threw his hands in the air. He finished his juice. Color had returned to his cheeks. "I'll tell you what. I'll keep my ears open. If I discover something concrete, you'll be the first to know about it. I promise you I'll call . . . even though it violates every moral code I've ever established for myself."

"To tell the police about a kid who's dealing in stolen firearms?" Oliver said.

"I'm fifty-nine, Detective."

Marge was astonished. "You look much younger."

"Nonetheless, I am of that age," Hinton told her. "I grew up in the sixties. Old hippie habits die very hard."

The babies wore wristbands, the only way that Decker could tell them apart physically. Aaron, the oldest by four minutes, was calmer by nature than Akiva, but neither boy was very fussy. They were huge: off the charts in height and weight. They ate round the clock: Cindy called them organic milking machines. In addition to nursing them, she had brought a half-dozen eight-ounce bottles of expressed breast milk. By the end of dinner, the boys had depleted everything.

"Thank you for feeding me and by extension, your grandsons," Cindy said. "And as always, we were fed extremely well."

"The curried lamb was delicious," Koby said. "I think I ate an entire sheep by myself. Everything tasted so good, so I overate."

"You and me both, son," Decker said. "You'd think I'd learn by now."

"Would you like a care package, kids?" Rina asked.

"I should say no, but I won't say no," Koby said.

Cindy laughed. "Homemade food has been a scarcity in our fridge since the babies were born."

Rina smiled. "I'll pack you a few meals' worth of grub. We certainly don't need all the leftovers."

Cindy looked at Gabe who had been clearing the table. She cocked a thumb in his direction. "You can pack Mr. Piano Player up some food while you're at it."

"You know, I do eat." Gabe put down a dirty plate. "I'm at that lucky stage where none of it sticks."

Cindy walked over to Gabe and threw her arm around his shoulders. "If I pat your tummy, will your lack of fat rub off on me?"

Gabe gave her a kiss on the cheek. "You look great. Your sons are very lucky to have such a wonderful mother." Said a little too strong.

"Thank you, Prince Charming." Gabe smiled, and Cindy took Aaron from Rina. She patted Koby's flat stomach. "Some lucky people are just naturally blessed with a good constitution."

Decker hefted Akiva and patted his paunch. "Others are born with a good constitution but have resorted to gluttony." He turned to his grandson. "How about you, buddy? Is all that yummy milk going into a hollow leg?"

The baby responded by spitting up on Decker's shirt.

Cindy laughed. "I'm sorry, Dad."

To the baby, he said, "That'll teach me to hold you without a burp cloth."

Koby took Akiva from his grandfather's hands. "Thank you very much for dinner. I think we're wearing out the doormat."

"He means the welcome mat," Cindy said. "As often as we come here, we're probably wearing out both."

Rina returned with a grocery bag filled with plastic containers of food. She kissed Cindy, then she kissed Aaron. "Take care of your mom, little boy. She's a good woman."

Koby, holding Akiva, said, "Thanks for everything, Rina."

Rina kissed his cheek and then kissed Akiva. "Be kind to your parents. They're good folk."

"Listen to her," Koby said to his son.

"Come anytime and I mean that." But as soon as the door closed behind the Kutiel family, Rina let out a sigh of relief. "Oh my Lord, I'm getting old."

Decker whispered in a plaintive voice, "Do you need any help?"

"Oh please, don't give me that 'have pity on me' voice." Rina laughed. "It's fine, Peter. I'm fine. Go read the paper."

"No, I don't want to stick you with all the work."

Gabe said, "Why don't you both relax? I'll finish up everything. I didn't work all day."

"By the way, what do you do all day?" Decker asked him.

"Peter!" Rina said.

Gabe laughed. "It's a good question."

Decker said, "It's a serious question. I want to make sure you're not bored."

"Nah, I'm not bored." Lonely was another story. He answered them with sincerity. "I practice an awful lot. I take it much more seriously now that I'm actually performing for money. Or I will be this summer. When I'm not practicing, I listen to the music that I'm practicing. It's almost as important as practicing. Plus I've started composing. When I'm not doing music, I read . . . I take a lot of long walks." He shrugged. "I keep busy. Certainly I'll be busy enough next year, so I'm kinda enjoying having unstructured time."

"Do you keep in contact with any of your old friends?"

"No." A pause. "That part of my life is over and done."

Said with an angry note in his voice, Decker noticed. "Have you talked to your mom lately?"

He shrugged again. "I'm fine, guys. I'd let you know if there was a problem and there's no problem. So seriously, go rest. I've got KP covered." He adjusted the earbuds of his iPod, then went into the kitchen and closed the door. A moment later, they could both hear the faucet running.

"Serious kid." Decker sat down on the couch. "I hope at some point fun fits into his schedule."

"I think he might be seeing someone," Rina said.

Decker said, "Did he tell you that?"

"No, but he leaves the house very early every weekday morning. I think he's catching someone before she goes to school."

"Good call." Decker thought a moment. "It can't be much of a relationship if all they do is meet before high school."

Rina patted his cheek. "That's why God invented weekends."

"That's true enough. We really don't know what he does once we leave the house," Decker said. "Should we be worried?"

"You know, I thought about being worried." Rina folded her arms across her chest. "But he's never given us any reason to worry."

Decker picked up the paper and settled into the couch. "If you're not worried, I'm not worried. He's leaving for somewhere in the fall. How much trouble could he get into in six months?"

"If he were inclined, he could get into a lot of trouble," Rina said.

"Well, I choose to think positively. You know what they say. Hope for the best, then learn how to duck when the stuff hits the fan."

Chapter Twenty-Eight

The knock was timid. When Gabe opened the door, Yasmine was breathless. "I can't stay more than maybe an hour. I promised my family I'd make it to shul."

She was dressed in a short tight black number with a faux fur jacket, complete with stockings, makeup, and jewelry. Every hair was in place. Clearly he wasn't getting any today.

"So come in for as long as you can," Gabe told her. "You want some coffee? You look lovely by the way."

"Thank you." She stepped into the Deckers' living room. "You always know what to say. How can one boy be that charming? Do you practice in the mirror?"

"Every day along with my piano. Sometimes I combine it by practicing the piano in front of a mirror."

Yasmine's ultraserious face managed a small smile.

Gabe said, "Honestly, I just made a fresh pot of coffee. The Deckers don't use the coffeepot on Saturday. They drink instant. It sucks."

"I'm okay." She perched herself on the edge of the sofa cushion, her back ramrod straight.

"Suit yourself." He got up and went into the kitchen.

She raised her voice to be heard. "I really need to go soon, Gabe. It'll take me twenty minutes to walk to shul."

"Yeah, yeah." Gabe came back carrying two cups. "Two sweeteners and a dollop of nonfat milk, right."

"What am I going to do with you?" Yasmine sighed. "You are perfect."

"Thank you. Wanna fool around?" When she blanched, he said, "I'm just kidding." Not really. "We'll just talk. Rather, you can talk and I'll stare at your beauty."

A blush rose in her cheeks. She took the coffee cup and sipped. She was still wearing her jacket. Beads of perspiration had gathered on her face.

He said, "Why don't you take off your coat?"

"Because I can't stay long."

"I know that, Yasmine. It doesn't mean you have to be uncomfortable while you are here."

She put down the cup. He helped her off with her jacket, and then drew her onto the sofa, hugging her tightly. "Just relax, okay? I won't jump your bones."

"I am relaxed."

"No, you're not." He kissed her soundly on the lips, receiving a healthy dose of red lipstick. "I know relaxed very well and it doesn't say Yasmine. What's wrong, my love?"

"I think my mom is getting a little suspicious."

"Doesn't surprise me, being as you leave home every day at six in the morning without explanation."

"You're taking it as a joke." She was upset. "If she finds out, she'll tell my dad. He'll *kill* me."

"He won't kill *you*, he'll kill *me*, which is okay. I'd rather die than to be without you." He kissed her again. "Can we make out? I've already ruined your lipstick."

"Do you ever stop?"

"Not when you're around." Gabe sat up and sighed. "Okay. I'll let you drink coffee in peace." He gave her back the coffee cup. "Oh. Guess what. I've got something for you. Well, it's not exactly for you. It's sort of for the both of us. Close your eyes."

She looked at him suspiciously.

"No, really. It's not what you think. Close your eyes."

Reluctantly, she obeyed. "This better not be a trick. Like you'd better not be naked when I open my eyes."

"Now there's a thought."

She opened her eyes. "Ga . . . abe."

She had turned his name into two syllables. He definitely wasn't getting any. "Close your eyes, Yasmine. Just cooperate, okay?"

She let out a mock sigh and did what he asked of her. He whipped off his T-shirt. "Okay. Open up."

She saw his bare chest and grew irritated. "Gabe, I don't have time—" She stopped talking, and her eyes got wide. She brought her hands to her mouth.

Gabe grinned. "Do you like it?"

Wordlessly, she touched the blue ink on his right arm below the swell of his shoulder. He had gotten a tattoo of two armlets: the first one was interwoven flowers that framed her name in script; the second band consisted of treble clef notes. She was speechless.

"Did you notice that it's a jasmine vine?" Gabe told her. "A little literal, but I think it came out nice." She still couldn't talk. "Do you like the band below it?"

She was still mute.

"Read the notes, cuckoo bird."

She did. It was the coloratura for "Der Hölle Rache." Her eyes grew moist. "Why . . . did you do that?"

"Why?" Gabe put his shirt back on. "Because I love you, that's why." Tears began to stream down her cheeks. "Don't do that. You'll smear your makeup."

She wiped her tears with her fingers, then leaned her head against his shoulder. "I can't believe you *did* that."

Gabe said, "So now you know . . . that no matter what happens between us . . . I will never ever forget you. You are permanently inked into me."

"I can't bear the thought of never seeing you again." She broke into a fresh batch of tears. "I will never, ever love anyone as much as I love you."

"And I will never love anyone as much as I love you." Gabe felt heaviness in his heart. Whenever they were together, he was elated. The moment she left, a black depression crowded his soul. The last year had been one of unbearable loneliness. His attachments had fallen away one by one by one. Yasmine had been the only bright spot in his dismal life. Eventually her parents would find out about them, and she'd be ripped from him. He tried not to think about it, hoping to steal as much time together as they could before he was set adrift in a sea of desolation.

Yasmine lifted the sleeve of his T-shirt. She touched the blue art and then kissed his arm. "Don't you have to be eighteen to be tattooed?"

"You ever see those places?" Gabe laughed. "They asked me if I was eighteen and I said yes. That was that."

"Did it hurt?"

"Not as much as psychic pain." He lifted her face and brought her lips to his. "I don't want to get you in trouble. Go fix up your makeup and get outta here."

She hugged his arm. "You know I don't want to go now."

She lay down on the couch and pulled him on top. Within moments they were kissing passionately. He became dizzy with lust. "I think you'd better go or something's gonna happen."

Yasmine took his face in her hands. "You did something special for me. I want to do something special for you."

"You already have just by being you."

"It's not enough." She stared into his emerald eyes. "I want to do it, Gabriel."

His heart skipped a beat. He said, "You know it isn't quid pro quo. I got the tats 'cause I wanted to get the tats. Not to get something from you."

"I know that." She kissed the tip of his nose. "Which is why I want to give myself to you."

He swallowed dryly. "When?"

"Now."

"*Now?*" Gabe sat up and pulled her next to him. "I thought you had to go."

She sighed. "We both know that my parents are gonna find out. We've got right now. We may not have tomorrow."

"I . . ." He was nervous. "I just don't want you to do something you'll regret."

"It's my decision, and I won't regret it. And even if I do, who hasn't done something they regretted?" She put her arms behind his neck. "Help me up."

He pulled her up until they were both standing. He was already hard.

"Help me undo my dress."

He moved in back of her and unzipped her dress, revealing her soft, bronze sculpted shoulders. He loved her shoulders. He could have kissed them for hours. She stepped out of her dress, and he unhooked her bra. He reached around and felt her small, defined breasts and a shiver went through his body.

She turned around and, now half nude wearing black panty hose and heels, boldly stared at him. As he lifted her up, she threw her legs around his waist. He took her into the bedroom, laid her atop the mattress, and then pulled off her shoes, stockings, and panties. Drinking in her nakedness, enthralled by every square inch of her being.

He quickly stripped and lay atop her, propping himself up on his elbows, his dick just millimeters away from the spot.

"Are you sure?" he whispered.

"Positive." Again, she wrapped her legs around his waist. "Do it."

He closed his eyes, losing himself in elation as he entered another universe. Her flesh around him—warm, wet, tight. He tried to hold the moment, to savor and relish it, but it kept slipping away, faster and faster and faster, until he knew it was over all too soon. With untold willpower, he forced himself to pull out and climaxed on her stomach, her blood mixed with his seed. It was only then that he could focus on her, witnessing the anguish on her tearless face.

He got up and washed himself off and brought back a warm washcloth, wiping the evidence away. Afterward, he tugged the bedcovers over both of them and took her into his arms. She remained rigid, unyielding to his touch.

He was nervous. He didn't want her to hate him. "You okay?"

She shrugged. A tear fell down her cheek.

He kissed her cheek. "We don't ever have to do it again, Yasmine."

"A little late for that."

He was quiet. The tears were in full force by now. He whispered, "I love you, Yasmine. I'd do anything in the world for you. What can I do for you now?"

"Just hold me."

"Of course." He wrapped her in his arms until he could feel her body melting against his. His cock started to stiffen and she tried to pull away, but he held her in his embrace. "It's just a reflex, Yasmine. I'm not gonna do anything."

"It *hurt!*"

"I'm sorry—"

"A *lot!*"

"I'm sorry it hurt, but I'm not sorry we did it."

"I *never, ever* want to do it again."

"That's fine. I'll love you no matter what."

She was quiet for a few minutes, finding untold comfort in his embrace. Then she broke off the hug and sat up. "I mean, do *you* want to do it again?"

"Me?" Gabe sat up, his eyes sweeping over her naked breasts. "I'm a guy. Of course I want to do it again. And again and again and again. I'd be happy if we did it until it fell off."

She managed a half smile. "It didn't hurt you?"

"My mind was in another sphere. I don't remember anything except complete, unmitigated pleasure."

"I got blood on your sheets. Won't the Deckers be suspicious of something?"

"I'll change and wash them after you leave. I do my own laundry all the time."

She blew out air. "My parents are gonna kill me."

"They'll never find out unless you tell them."

"Not about that. Of course I won't tell them. They're gonna be mad that I'm late for shul."

"I'll help you get dressed."

But she didn't move. She said, "Do you think it'll hurt as much the second time?"

Gabe's heartbeat quickened. "I suppose we won't know unless we try."

"I should really leave," she said.

Gabe kissed her shoulder. "Do whatever you want."

"Stop being so understanding."

"Ah, you're finally catching on to my tricks."

She plopped back down on the bed and spread her legs. Her face was scrunched up into a tense ball. "Okay, do it!"

"Are you—"

"Do it!" she ordered him.

He lay between her legs, this time his eyes open, watching her wince as he entered her. Each movement brought on another taut grimace. Abruptly, he sat up, his legs extended, his cock pointing to noon. "I have an idea." He patted his lap. "You get on top."

She looked at his dick with displeasure. But ever the sport, she straddled his lap while guiding it inside her. She got about halfway down before she made a face.

"Hurt?" he asked.

"Yeah."

Gabe placed his hands on her hips. "Take a deep, deep breath." When she did, he shoved her hips downward and he thrust his hips upward. She let out a little yelp of pain. No surprise there. She was dry and tight. "You okay?"

"Not really." She blew out air. "It's tolerable as long as you don't move."

"So I won't move." He was completely inside her. "Wrap your legs around my waist and just kiss me."

"You won't move?"

"No, I won't move. I promise. Kiss me."

Warily, she brought her mouth to his, her body coiled steal. As promised, he didn't move and within a few minutes, they fell into a familiar routine with their limbs entwined and their mouths enmeshed. His fingertips slowly skipping down her delicious spine while her fingers danced through his hair. She took off his glasses and flung them onto the bed.

And as her body began to loosen up, he felt her becoming wetter and warmer. Her softening flesh made him even harder. Squirming on his lap while she kissed him deeply. Doing all the work for him.

He opened his eyes and was close enough to see her looking back at him. He smiled and so did she. He mouthed "I love you," and she mouthed it back.

And that's how he had always dreamed it would be: staring into the eyes of a girl that he worshipped, face-to-face, chest-to-chest, his body pressed against her, melding together as one. The more they kissed, the more she moved. He felt his breath quicken and knew it wouldn't be much longer. He whispered, "You gotta get off!"

"My period's due tomorrow," she whispered back. "It's probably okay."

"Yasmine—"

"I love you, Gabriel. It's okay."

"Oh God . . ." His body shook with ecstasy, his arms draped around her back as his fingers clutched her shoulders until every drop of his being was squeezed out. Afterward, breathless and spent, he stroked her head while she kissed his tattooed arms, holding her in an embrace, his eyes filled with tears of pleasure and sadness. Because he knew right then and there that no matter what his life may bring, no matter what intimacies lay in his path, there would never be another coupling as perfect as the one he had just experienced.

Chapter Twenty-Nine

Tuesday morning, Gabe's phone buzzed at 5:22, eight minutes before his own phone alarm was supposed to go off. He fumbled for his glasses and then put on the nightstand light and read the text.

Yasmine had written: *had terrible insomnia.*

He wrote back: *what's wrong?*

got my period last night. i feel horrible.

Yasmine wasn't just making small talk. Though they hadn't talked about it, they both knew that until her period came, an accident, however remote, was a possibility. Of course, the overwhelming emotion was relief. The surprise was that he also felt a tinge of disappointment.

so sorry. anything I can do 4 u?

no. always this way.

feel better. i love u. dream of me when u go back 2 sleep.

There was a long pause. He thought she signed off. But then his phone vibrated.

gabe, what r we gonna do?

He wrote back: *what do u mean?*

m obsessed wth u. it's not normal.

m obsessed with u 2. that's what happens when ur in luv.

so what r we gonna do?

Gabe wrote: *what do u wanna do?*

i dunno.

so why do anything?

Another long pause.

She texted back: *it's different now.*

Another text from her: *u know what i mean.*

He understood exactly what she meant. *do u regret it?*

yes n no.

She sent another text: *i don't want things to be different. i still want u to luv me.*

Her words broke his heart. He could feel the tears in her eyes. *of course, i luv u, yasmine. i will always luv u. 2 me, nothing's changed except i luv u even more if that's even possible.*

A long pause. *what if i don't want 2 do it again?*

He sighed again. *He* wanted to do it again. Over the last two days, it was the only thing he thought about. He wanted her physically and totally—inside out and upside down. But he knew that the sex wouldn't be sustainable. She was way too much a good girl and way too young. He knew he could force the issue, but that wasn't him.

No matter. He'd take her on any terms she'd give him.

whatever u want, yasmine. do it or not do it, i will luv u always. A pause. Then he texted: *i would still die 4 u.*

stop saying that. it gives me the creeps.

just proving a point.

i luv u soooooooooooooo much.

He could feel her smile. *i luv u so much with even more oooooooooooooooooooooooo.*

☺

Gabe wrote: *feeling better?*

a lot!

She sent a follow-up text.

now all i have 2 worry about is my mom finding out.

A third text.

maybe we should skip 2day . . . not b so obvious.

Gabe wrote: *now m really depressed!*

Then he wrote: *cn we make out electronically?*

how do we do that?

i dunno. how about ♥ ♥ ♥ ♥ ♥ ♥ ♥ ♥

lol.

go back 2 sleep, yasmine. feel better. I luv u.

i luv u 2. i will always luv u . . . 4ever n ever.

4ever n ever, Gabe texted back, then shut off his phone.

He turned off the light and lay back in his dark room, staring at nothing. With his glasses on, he could make out shapes and shadows. One part of him was glad to have the extra hour of sleep. The other part missed her terribly. He was thankful that they had done it even if they never did it again. At least he'd have the memory—the ultimate sensation of their bodies melding into one. The image still sent shivers down his spine. Not to mention what it did below the waistline.

The clarity would last for a while, but he knew it would eventually fade, just like his mother's love. It's not that his mom didn't love him; Gabe knew she did. It's just that without her physical presence and all that went with it, the love was abstract and therefore mean- ingless to him. It provided no light when he was dark and despondent.

Yasmine was his beacon, but how much longer would that last?

Forever and ever.

Until her mom finds out.

After she hung up the phone, Marge got up and knocked on Decker's open door.

He looked up. "Come on in."

"I called Kevin Stanger." Marge spoke as she leaned against the door frame. "I was hoping he would name names with regard to the gun. But he doesn't want to talk to us. Furthermore, his mother won't let us talk to him."

Decker beckoned her in with a crooked finger. "Can you come in? You're giving me a crick in my neck."

She sat across from his desk. "I can't pry anything more out of these boys. Without names, we're sunk. I'm open to suggestions."

"Too bad, because I've run out of them," Decker said. "As much as I hate to admit it, it may be time to close the books on Gregory Hesse and Myra Gelb."

"Don't fret," Marge said. "We still have Gregory Hesse's stolen computer as an open file. If we get evidence against Dylan or any of his gang, we can always reopen either suicide. Then you can say I told you so."

Decker said, "I'm aghast that you'd think I'd be out for revenge."

"You know what they say," Marge told him. "Revenge is a dish best eaten cold."

"Hmm . . ." Decker mused. "I have a feeling that if I ate cold revenge, all I'd come away with would be a massive case of reflux."

With a jaunty step in his walk and his portfolio case tucked under his arm, Gabe felt spiffy in a patch-pocket, brown corduroy coat, white button-down shirt, black jeans, and three-inch snake boots. He especially liked the added height that put him at six three—one inch shorter than his father's size in stocking feet. He was nicely dressed, casual enough, but not sloppy. He reached up to adjust his glasses.

Then it dawned on him: he shouldn't be wearing glasses.

The audition today was an important one—people from some prestigious recording label in New York—and Nick told him to look his best. He reversed directions and jogged back home just as dawn was breaking. Yasmine had to be up by now, but she probably hadn't left the house. He thought about texting her, but then he thought since she was always late, he'd wait for her to text him.

For *once,* he'd be the late one. He knew she'd tease him about it. It made him smile.

They hadn't seen each other for two days and the anticipation of meeting with her drove him wild with excitement. Although they had been texting words of love and lust, it paled in comparison to a live person: touching her cheek and stroking her hair, his lips against hers, their tongues intertwined, his hand sneaking up under her skirt.

Shit, he was getting hard again.

Made it hard to run.

The detour and the switch from glasses to contacts took about fifteen minutes. When he was on the road again, he texted her.

gonna be a little 18. don't say a word or i'll spank u.

He waited for his phone to jump. When a minute passed and she didn't respond, Gabe texted.

r u there?

Another minute ticked by.

Weird.

Maybe her phone was acting up. Funny because it was fine last night.

His heart began to beat rapidly. As usual he was probably overreacting as he did to everything. No matter, he said to himself. He was just a few minutes away from their trysting place, better known as Coffee Bean.

Maybe he'd actually beat her there even with his being twenty minutes late.

And sure enough when he got there, she was nowhere to be found. The place had just opened, and he was the only patron around. It was still early. But after five minutes passed and she still didn't show, he began to get a strange perception. He even checked both bathrooms, feeling like a pervert.

Nothing.

His gut kept telling him something wasn't right.

"Hey, Gabe."

He turned around. The counter was being manned by Joe today. He and Yasmine had come here so often, the staff knew them by name. "Hey, Joe. Have you seen Yasmine this morning?"

"No."

"You're sure?"

"Positive."

It was approaching six-thirty. A few patrons had come and gone. By now, she usually deigned to make an appearance.

He stepped outside and looked down the empty streets.

He felt an ominous throbbing in his chest. In his heart of hearts, he knew what had happened. Her mother had found out about them. She had taken away her phone.

Shit!

At first, he felt very sorry for himself, but then his thoughts quickly turned to Yasmine.

She was going to get reamed.

It was time to man up.

He had to call her parents, tell them that everything was his fault. He had lied to her, he had duped her, he had seduced her, he had forced himself upon her . . .

Maybe that was too much. He didn't want them to think he was a rapist.

He knew he probably wouldn't even get that far. No doubt, her mother would hang up as soon as he introduced himself.

Still, he had to make the effort. Take one for the team.

Then he realized he didn't know her landline.

The smart thing to do was just to go over to the house.

Her mother would slam the door in his face, but at least he'd make a valiant stab at being noble. But before he made his final appearance, he decided to give Yasmine one last call.

Final appearance. The thought was beyond depressing. All the vitality had suddenly drained from his body. With shaking hands, he punched in her phone number.

He heard the line connect and then he heard the phone ring.

The ringing sounded like it was underneath his feet.

He looked down.

One of the bushes was ringing?

Beyond weird.

When her phone went to her voice message, the ringing stopped.

His eye caught a flash of silver.

He bent down.

It *was* a phone.

Her phone.

Not only her phone but also the silver watch he had given her.

Confused and panicked, he picked up the items and stowed them in his pocket.

Did her mother catch up with her just as she was about to come inside? Did she drag her away? Did Yasmine lose her phone in the process?

He could understand her dropping the phone in the middle of the fray, but why would she lose her watch?

Standing on the sidewalk, he frantically searched in all directions for a sign of what had happened to her just as the sun rose from the horizon.

Yasmine, where the fuck are you?

Maybe he should just go over to her house and . . .

Why the hell her watch?

Be logical, idiot, he said to himself.

He thought for a few moments and kept coming to the same conclusion. She had left him her phone and her watch as a sign . . . hoping he'd find them. Her watch especially, something so cherished that she'd never let go of it voluntarily.

She was in deep trouble.

But how could a girl like Yasmine get into deep trouble?

A mugger?

A pervert?

A kidnapper?

His mind was whirling a mile a minute as his heart thumped in his chest.

And then his brain hit upon something, a micro flashback as to what brought him to Coffee Bean in the first place.

Crazy, gun-toting, asshole Dylan and his loony band of followers . . . the way Dylan had acted like he owned the fucking Starbucks, him going nose to nose with him.

But surely Yasmine wouldn't do anything to offend him. She certainly wouldn't face off against him.

But he couldn't get them out of his mind . . . especially the whacko blonde that Dylan had been with . . . the look on her face the day they saw each other at the bus stop . . . the pot in her purse . . . the anger in her eyes when he had turned down getting stoned with her at her house.

What was her name?

Cam . . . Cameron. Gabe never did get her last name. She was scary-ass loco, the type of girl who'd seek revenge . . .

His throat suddenly seized up . . . what if . . .

Shit!

Think, you moron! Think!

With his heart palpitations going full force, he dropped his music folder and his instincts took over. He took off running now in boots not made for track and field.

Didn't matter. He was galloping full force in the direction of the bus stop.

Chapter Thirty

The group was a block away from the bus stop, walking through Greendale Park and its vast copses of trees and shrubbery. There looked to be around five of them—more or less: Gabe's thinking was still muddled. Putting on a final burst of speed, he flung himself into the tight crowd, throwing his arms around Dylan and another dude with long hair and acne, both of them shorter than he was, especially since he was wearing three-inch heels. Their faces registered utter shock.

"Hey, what's going on?" Gabe asked.

Dylan recovered quickly, creating space between the two of them, pulling the tiny figure he was gripping out of reach. Gabe may have been frazzled, but he was coherent enough to notice the barrel of a .22 S/W revolver pushed into her spine.

"This is what's going on." Dylan yanked Yasmine's hair, turning her head around so that Gabe could see her terrified face. They locked eyes and hers were wet, pleading with him to do *something*. Then something hard appeared on the back of his own head.

He heard the telltale click.

And when that happened, an eerie calm suddenly washed over his body, just like the way he felt when he had attacked the mugger a year ago . . . or when his dad used to shoot at him to get him used to the sound of whizzing bullets. His brain instantly transported into a zone he rarely visited—that of his father's son. His heartbeat slowed as he regarded the situation with newfound clarity.

Dylan had jerked Yasmine's head forward so that Gabe could no longer see her face. He said, "You had fun with my girl. So now it's time for payback." He pushed the gun deeper into her spine. She let out a garbled yelp. "You can come along if you want." A sickening smile. "You can hold her arms down while we gangbang her."

Gabe shrugged carelessly, his mind working faster than his mouth. Thinking before he spoke, listening to his father's voice in his head.

I got a lot of enemies, Gabe. You gotta be careful. If you ever do get in a jam and can't reach me, start thinking of a plan. And once you've got a plan, don't ever, ever think about the consequences. Just act.

He picked up his pace, forcing the guy who held the gun to his head to walk a little faster. The others fell into step.

"Honestly, Dylan, I don't know what you're talking about. I never did anything with your girl." Gabe's eyes swept over the crew. Six instead of five. Four dudes, two girls—Cameron and a brunette. "I don't even know which one your girl is."

Cameron says something. "You are such a liar—"

"The blonde?" Gabe walked faster. "The one who called you an asshole?"

Dylan momentarily flinched.

"Look," Gabe said. "I didn't know she was yours. And I certainly didn't fuck her. I've seen your babe twice. Once when I first met you and once at a bus stop." Gabe pointed straight ahead. "That bus stop as a matter of fact."

Where the fucking bus wasn't due until twenty minutes.

Think of a plan, and then act on it.

"It was like six-thirty in the morning." Gabe tried to keep his voice even. "I was waiting for the bus. She had bought some shit and invited me over to her house to have a smoke. Apparently her parents leave very early for work."

Who do you attack first? The one with the piece on Yasmine's back or the one whose gun was pointed at your gray matter?

Dylan said, "She said you doped her up and raped her."

"Give me a break, dude, do I look like a guy who needs to rape for pussy?"

"He's a fucking liar, Dylan," Cameron screamed out. "You saw the marks."

"What marks?"

"Where you tied me up—"

"You *believe* that shit, Dylan?" Gabe laughed. "C'mon, you're a smart dude. I didn't go to her house, not because I was dissing her or anything. I didn't go because I had a record audition at eight in the morning with a major R and D guy from a big label—"

"You raped me, you asshole!"

"—chance of a lifetime, dude—"

"You fucking tied me up and raped—"

"—and no *pussy* is worth missing an opportunity like that." Gabe could tell Dylan was digesting the contrary information. "You can believe what you want, bro, but I've never *touched* her. I earn my pussy honestly, dude. Rape is for losers."

Dylan's eyes were wavering now. Gabe was almost at a jog.

"Besides, anything I need, my dad gives free of charge. Why would I rape if I can have as much pussy as I want any time, any way?"

"Yeah, I forgot." Dylan was sneering now. Maybe it was not so good to bring up Dad. "You're the one whose father is a pimp."

Gabe affected a casual shrug. "It's true. His name is Christopher Donatti. One of your posse must have an Internet connection on his phone. Look him up."

You probably go for the gun at your head. By now, the dude's arm might be getting tired from holding it up that long.

Besides, he was no help to Yasmine if he was dead.

"I'm serious," Gabe goaded him. "Look him up." He spelled the last name. The sun was rising in the sky and it was getting close to seven, the appointed hour of the bus's arrival. The park was still empty, but it wouldn't be long before people came to walk their dogs and do other shit. Dylan had to realize that as well, so Gabe knew he had very little time. They were walking through a maze of trees, still somewhat hidden.

One of the dudes with short spiked hair and a weak chin had pulled out an iPhone. Out loud he said, "Christopher Whitman Donatti."

"That's the man."

He read, "Adopted son of the late Mafioso boss Joey Donatti, head of the Charino gang in New York and Chicago—"

"Guess who took his place when Joey died," Gabe said.

Weak Chin's voice stammered for a second before he read on. "Served six months in Piedmont Penitentiary for the murder of Cheryl Diggs when he was eighteen, released six months later when new information was brought to light."

"That is true."

"Arrested twice in connection with the deaths of Leon Graciano and Paul 'the Pick' Lorelli. First charge he was acquitted, last charge ended in a mistrial due to the death of a state witness and lack of evidence."

Thank you, Dad, for being a psycho.

Dylan's eyes were flitting from object to object. The dude was definitely on something, but he could still understand the enormity of what Weak Chin was telling him. Gabe could see Dylan faltering, hesitant about going up against the son of a real, live bad guy.

"Donatti now owns publishing houses and numerous real estate concerns in New York and Nevada." Weak Chin swallowed and said, "Doesn't say anything about owning whorehouses."

Gabe's sigh was exasperated. "Are you a real dumb fuck or are you just playing the part? My dad's a fuck-ing *felon*, dude. He can't own things like that. All his casinos and whorehouses are in my mom's name. Teresa McLaughlin Donatti. She's in there somewhere, right?"

The kid didn't answer.

"And guess what. My name really isn't Chris. It's Gabriel. Gabriel Matthew Whitman. And I know I'm in there, too, because I've googled my dad like a million times. Now are there any other questions I can answer about my family?"

No one said anything, and now was the time.

Abruptly he stopped walking and ducked, causing the guy behind him to overstep and trip, the gun in his hand now safely over Gabe's head. In a swift fluid motion, Gabe grabbed the dude's hand and in a single twisting motion, wrested a Luger 9 mm semi from his grip. He looked up just in time to see the barrel of Dylan's piece aimed at his chest. He heard a scream and thought it might be his own. Yasmine had whipped around once the gun was off her back, her elbow knock-ing into Dylan's hand a fraction of a second before the gun exploded.

A bullet whizzing past his body.

Which didn't faze him much except that it was a loud motherfucker.

The noise and kickback caused Dylan to jump backward, giving Gabe just enough leeway space. Within a beat, he was in perfect position, behind Dylan with the semi in his right hand pushed into the nape of his neck, digging deep into the skin, pointed upward into his cranium. With the boots, Gabe was a good four inches taller than Dylan. "You move, dude, you're a fucking corpse."

Before Dylan could process, Gabe grabbed the .22 with his left hand, then immediately switched guns, feeling more comfortable with the .22 on Dylan and the 9 mm in his free left hand. It simply had more rounds, in case he had to use it. Out of the corner of his eye, he saw the guy with long hair and acne guy reach into his pocket. With his left hand, Gabe shot at him, the bullet narrowly missing his arm. The .22 in his right hand was still on Dylan's neck.

To the dude with long hair, Gabe said, "Did I give you fucking permission to *move*?"

The guy was shaking, nursing his arm.

Maybe he grazed him. Good if he did.

Gabe screamed, "Answer me, motherfucker!" He fired off another shot in the vicinity of the asshole's head. His voice was soft this time. "Did I give you permission to fucking move?"

"No," he whispered.

Gabe was calm. "If anyone moves, he's future fertilizer." He looked at Cameron. "That includes the ladies. Do we understand each other?"

No one spoke. Gabe suddenly became aware of a piercing throb in his right side. Someone must have punched him in his ribs. His eyes and the gun in his left hand traveled from face to face to face, constantly moving so no one was ever out of the picture. Then he realized the reason he was here in the first place. To Yasmine, he said, "Get the fuck out of here."

She didn't budge, either refusing to leave him alone or paralyzed by fear.

"Go, Yasmine! Run!"

Instead she shook her head, stubbornly remaining rooted to the spot.

Fucking lunatic! She really was a cuckoo bird, as crazy as he was, with some misplaced notion of going down with him. Gabe kept his right hand on Dylan's neck and continued to move the gun in his left hand from person to person.

If she wouldn't leave, at least work with her then. He said, "What time is it, Yasmine?"

"I don't have a watch."

"Right. Take my phone out of my pocket." Gun going from person to person to person.

She did as told—deftly and swiftly. "Twelve to seven."

Ten minutes to go. Good thing he had taken the time to put in his contacts. Otherwise all they'd have to do is pull off his glasses and he couldn't see a fucking thing.

"Yasmine, grab the girls' purses."

"You're robbing us?" asked the dude with the weak chin and short hair.

Gabe peeled off a bullet in his direction. "If I hear your voice again, it'll be the last thing on earth that you'll ever hear. Got it?"

No response.

To Yasmine, he said, "Take their purses." At the sound of his voice, she sprang into action. Once she had them in her possession, he said, "Okay, dump their shit in the bushes . . . just throw everything all over the place. Toss it, throw it, kick it. Whatever."

She did what he told her to do.

When she was done, he asked, "What time is it?"

"Eight to," she answered.

"Okay, okay. Now go into the dudes' backpacks and throw their shit all over the place like with the purses. Got it?"

"Got it."

Yasmine was absolutely perfect. Act first, question later. She dumped out three iPhones and a BlackBerry, four wallets, two crack pipes, several sheets of cigarette rolling paper, several dime bags of weed, a couple of bags of crystal meth, a bag of crack and several bags of E, powders and other pills Gabe couldn't identify by sight, plus books and schoolwork. She took out the cash and the credit cards from the wallets and dumped them randomly, giving Gabe just enough time to see the bus at the curb.

Immediately, he grabbed Yasmine's arm with his left hand, the two of them jogging backward, his right-hand gun aimed at the gang.

"Enjoy your scavenger hunt," he hissed.

Then he turned them both around and stuck the guns in his jacket, the two of them running like the wind until they were at the curb, Gabe pounding on the closing doors of the bus until they opened, and he and Yasmine stepped inside. As soon as they were relatively safe, Gabe discovered his heartbeat, feeling adrenaline pouring into his body. He was shaking harder than Yasmine, who had the presence of mind to pay for the both of them.

They made their way to the back and found two empty seats. Wordlessly, she handed Gabe his phone. He was shaking so hard, he almost dropped it after he punched in the numbers.

The first time the call went to voice mail.

He depressed the green button and tried again.

Please answer. Please answer. Please, please answer.

And when the line connected, Gabe had trouble getting the words from his throat. "Peter . . ." He was panting. "Peter, I'm in trouble."

It took a moment for Decker to recognize the breathless voice. "Gabe?"

"Yeah, sorry. It's Gabe."

Decker's brain went to high alert, but his voice remained even. "Where are you?"

"I'm on the . . ." Gabe was wiped out and winded. "I'm on a bus . . . on . . . God, I don't even know where I am. Hold on . . . let me read a street sign." He gave Decker the road and read off an address. "Can you please come get us?"

Us?

"I'm on my way." Decker had just started to pull into the station house driveway. He put the car in reverse and drove out of the parking lot. "Are you in physical danger right now?"

"Maybe."

Decker placed the red light on the roof of the car and turned on the siren. "How imminent?"

"I dunno. I think we're okay right now." He heard the siren in the background. Never had a G-sharp slide sounded so good. "Where should we meet up?"

"You stay on the bus and I'll catch up to you. I'm about five minutes away. Stay on the phone, okay?"

"Yeah. I'm still here."

Decker could hear muted conversation—clipped words and a lot of breathing. Even with the siren and lights, it took him a little longer to reach the bus because of morning traffic. He said, "I'm right behind you." He turned off the siren. "Get off at the next stop."

"Okay."

The big behemoth chugged away for several blocks until it pulled up to a bus bench filled with working people. Decker got out of the unmarked, stood by the passenger door, and waited. Before long two figures emerged, holding hands.

Gabe absolutely towered over her.

When he and the girl got close enough, Decker saw that her eyes were red and swollen, and she looked a *lot* younger than the seventeen-year-old girl that Gabe claimed to have been seeing.

She also looked familiar.

And then Decker placed her: the Persian girl at the deli, not the one who was flirting with Gabe, but the youngest one who looked about ten and supposedly sang opera. And suddenly everything fit together. He opened the back door and the two of them slid inside. She was trembling and burst into tears as soon as she clicked on her seat belt. Gabe was shaking. He looked pale and wan.

"What happened?" Decker asked.

The two kids began talking at the same time. Gabe was breathless: the girl was speaking through sobs and tears.

He said, "I think a group of thugs kidnapped her—"

She wailed out, "They said . . . they were going to . . . *rape* me—"

"I found her phone and her watch on the ground and knew something was wrong—"

"And *kill* me—"

"I caught up to them and they had a gun on her and then some fucker pulled a gun on me."

"They threatened me with . . . *horrible, wretched* things." She was crying so hard, she was hard to understand. "And the girls . . . they were worse than the *boys!*"

Gabe panted out, "I got the gun away from that dude . . . and then I wound up with two guns . . . it's all kinda blurry."

"Gabe saved my *life*—"

"How'd I get two guns again?" Gabe said to himself.

"Hold on, hold on, hold on," Decker said. "One at a time. Do you know who these people were?"

"No!" Yasmine cried out. "I've never seen any of them in my life!"

"The leader is a dude named Dylan," Gabe said.

"Dylan?" Decker repeated. His heart did a little leap.

"Yeah, Dylan. I met him once before about four months ago. He's a real asshole and he loves guns."

"How do you know him?" Decker asked.

"I don't know him, just met him once. It's a long story."

Yasmine became wide-eyed. "You know, I think I saw the blond girl once before."

"You did?" Gabe asked.

"Yeah, at Coffee Bean. She was . . . *staring* at me."

"When was this?" Gabe asked her.

"About two months ago. She was wearing Christian Louboutin boots."

"Why didn't you *tell* me?"

"That a girl was staring at me and giving me the stink-eye?"

"Oh, God," Gabe moaned. "She probably saw us together!"

"I remember thinking, why does she hate me?"

He groaned. "This is all my fault!"

"I thought maybe she didn't like Persians."

"Hold on, kids. One at a time." Decker's heart was racing. "Does Dylan have a last name?"

"Don't know it," Gabe said. "I could describe him. And one of the girls was named Cameron. The blonde.

She's a real whack job. She said I raped her. I swear, Yasmine, I never even touched her."

"I never believed her." She hugged his arm. "I knew it was a lie."

Decker was trying to keep them on track. "Where did all this happen?"

"At Coffee Bean," Yasmine said.

"They kidnapped you from Coffee Bean?" Decker asked.

"Right outside," Yasmine told him, then she turned to Gabe. "I went outside to look for you because you were late, and I thought that was odd."

"I forgot to put in my contacts for the audit— Shit! I have an audition in an hour!"

"You aren't going anywhere," Decker said.

"I left my sheet music at Coffee Bean. My agent's going to kill me if I don't show up!"

"Gabe, you're not going anywhere," Decker said.

"No, you don't understand," Gabe protested. "Jeff will really *kill* me."

"I'll take the heat," Decker told him. The boy clearly wasn't thinking rationally. "So all this happened outside Coffee Bean?"

"I don't know where they took her from." Gabe was panting hard now. "I met up with them at Greendale Park." Each breath was an effort. "You know, Peter, they might still be there because we threw their shit all over the place and they're probably looking for everything we tossed. I figured if we threw their junk around, it would keep them occupied while we ran away."

Decker immediately called Marge.

"What's going on?" she asked.

"Emergency situation. I want you and all units available to converge on Greendale Park. Pick up everyone you find there and detain them until I arrive."

"Everyone?"

"Everyone. I'll sort it out later. Use extreme caution with any teenagers you find. They may have weapons."

"You could probably arrest them, Lieutenant," Yasmine said. "They were all carrying *drugs.*"

Decker said to Marge, "If you find any of them in possession of weapons, drugs, or any illegal contraband, arrest them immediately. But again, I reiterate. Use extreme caution. They're armed."

"I have their guns," Gabe said. "But they may have more."

The B and W Mafia, Decker thought. "Where are the guns you have?"

"Where?" He felt around. "In my pocket." He gave Yasmine her cell and her watch. "Good thing you left them on the ground for me to find. You're so smart."

"I had to do *something*," Yasmine said.

"You're just brilliant."

Decker was still trying to keep them focused. "How many guns do you have, Gabe?"

"Two. You know, I remember one dude trying to pull a gun on me. He had long hair and zits. I shot at him. He could still have a piece."

Decker relayed the information to Marge.

"I'm seconds away," she said, then got off the phone.

Gabe said, "Do you want me to give them to you . . . the guns?"

"Yes, I want them, but I don't want you giving them to me in a moving car. I'll take them from you when we get to the police station." A pause. "Do you even know if they're loaded?"

"They're loaded," Gabe said. "Dylan shot at me."

Again, Decker punched in Marge's cell number. It took a minute and when her phone finally connected, he said, "Do *not* let any of the kids wash their hands until you've tested them all for gunshot residue. Especially a boy named Dylan."

"*Dylan?*" Marge gasped.

"Yeah, Dylan," Decker said.

"Got it," Marge said. "I'm just pulling up." She disconnected the phone.

Decker's brain cells were firing so fast, it was hard to keep a train of thought. They rode a minute in silence. "Gabe, did you discharge any of the weapons?"

"Yeah. The Luger 9 mm semi for sure at least twice, but I don't remember if I shot the .22."

Decker's heart sank. "Did you hurt anyone?"

"No . . . at least, I don't think so."

"Are you sure?"

"I'm not positive of anything."

More minutes ticked on. Marge called back. "We found six teenagers in the process of picking up their belongings. It's a real mess. Call you later."

"Anyone hurt?" Decker asked, but Marge had already hung up. He said, "They picked up six kids."

"That's all of them," Gabe said.

"And you're sure you didn't hurt anyone?"

"I didn't *kill* anyone," Gabe told him. To Yasmine he said, "They were all standing up when we split, right?

Yasmine concurred. "Yeah, they were all standing up. He didn't hurt anyone."

"You're sure?"

"Almost positive."

"Maybe I'll call for an ambulance to the spot just in case," Decker said calmly.

Gabe slumped in the seat. "Maybe you should call one for me. I feel like I'm gonna pass out."

"For real?" Decker asked.

"No, no . . . I'm okay. One of the assholes punched me in the ribs. He mighta broken something." He opened up his jacket and put his hand over the spot.

His shirt was warm, wet, and sticky. He pulled out his hand, and it was coated with blood. Gabe was confused. "I musta cut myself."

"Oh my God!" Yasmine gasped and drew her hands to her face. "Gabe, you've been shot!"

Again, Decker put the siren on his roof. He made an abrupt U-turn and headed for the hospital.

Chapter Thirty-One

The first call to Rina wasn't an easy one to make, but it was a cakewalk compared to the next.

"This better be important," Donatti barked over the phone. "You interrupted me at a very inopportune time."

"It's Gabe," Decker said flatly. "He's okay, but he's been shot. You need to come down to L.A. immediately."

The silence on the other end was agonizing. "How bad?"

"When they wheeled him into ER, he could answer their questions. He never lost consciousness. He's in x-ray now—"

"Anything vital?"

"I don't know."

Donatti asked, "Through and through or is the bullet still in there?"

"I don't know that, either."

Another protracted, agonizing silence. "What happened?"

"I don't know the details, but I'll tell you what he told me," Decker said. "He called me up about a half hour ago, saying he was in trouble. Apparently, his girlfriend was kidnapped by a group of teenage thugs . . . Did you know he had a girlfriend?"

"Yeah, someone named Yasmine."

Even with all the distance, Chris still knew more about Gabe than Decker did. "From what I could glean, he caught up with these thugs and managed to save her, but he got shot in the process—"

"Who shot him?" The voice that broke in was calm.

Decker said, "I don't know, and that's the truth. We've detained some kids, but I don't know if they're even the ones that Gabe's talking about. Yasmine is with me. We'll leave for the station house when Rina shows up at the hospital. I don't want to leave Gabe alone until Rina . . . Wait, the doctor is coming out. I'll put him on the phone." Decker handed the phone to an MD dressed in blue scrubs. "I'm talking to Gabriel Whitman's father. His name is Christopher Donatti."

"Thank you." Into the phone, he said, "Mr. Donatti, this is Doctor Morland. First of all, your son is going to be fine. He's talking and completely responsive. He does have a gunshot wound, but the bullet missed anything vital. I do recommend that we take him into surgery immediately. The x-ray shows a bullet lodged in his ribs. The bone is broken, and the sooner we can get the bullet out, the easier it'll be for him to heal up."

Silence.

"Hello?" Dr. Morland said.

"Yeah, I'm still here," Donatti said. "He's okay?"

"Yes, he'll be fine. Nothing vital was affected."

"The bullet's in his ribs?"

"His ninth rib to be exact."

"It was a twenty-two?"

"Beg your pardon?"

"The bullet," Donatti said. "Something bigger would have shattered the bone and gone through his body."

"Probably." Morland paused. "Do I have your permission to operate?"

"Yes, you can operate."

"Could you send me down a fax stating that you give the hospital permission to do what's necessary for your son's best well-being?"

"Yes, I can do that."

"Would you like to talk to him before he goes in?"

"Why? You think he won't make it?"

Dr. Morland was taken aback. "There's no reason why he wouldn't make it, Mr. Donatti."

"Then I'll talk to him when he's out of surgery. Put Lieutenant Decker back on."

The surgeon made a face and gave Decker his phone. "He doesn't want to talk to his son. He wants to talk to you."

Decker nodded. "What do you need, Chris?"

"Doctor says he's all right. It doesn't sound like I'm needed right away. I'll try to come down tonight. If that doesn't work, I'll see him tomorrow."

Cold, Decker thought. "Whatever works for you, Chris."

"And Rina will wait with him? I don't want him left alone."

"She'll wait with him until you get here. Even over-night." Decker gave him all the essentials—the name and address of the hospital, his cell, Rina's cell.

"I need the hospital fax number to give permission for them to operate."

"I'll get it for you." Decker paused. "I'm sorry, Chris."

"For what? You didn't shoot him."

"Gabe was in my care. I feel responsible."

"His mother and I dumped him on you. Besides, you can't keep watch twenty-four/seven." A pause. "It's the age. Stupid boys playing grown-up with guns." Another pause. "Was I that fucking stupid when you met me?"

"You were clever, but you were also stupid."

"Yeah, I'd like to think I was different, but I probably was a dumb fuck. Only difference was if I would have shot someone, he would have been dead."

When Decker brought Yasmine into the station house, she was clinging to his arm. She had been crying nonstop, threatening to kill herself if Gabe didn't make it. The squad room was packed, barely controlled chaos filled with teenagers, detectives, police officers, and mounting piles of paperwork. Normally, things were quite civilized. Today it actually looked like a TV set. Detective Wynona Pratt—a newcomer to Homicide—was sitting in the middle of the squad room, talking to a young girl with long dark hair. As soon as Yasmine laid eyes on the teen, she started to shake uncontrollably. The brunette was trembling just as hard, crying out to Yasmine, "I'm sorry, I'm sorry, I'm sorry, I'm sorry."

To Wynona, Decker said, "Get her into an interview room immediately."

The big-boned detective made a face. "They're all occupied, Lieutenant."

"Then use my office."

"Gotcha."

Yasmine was squeezing Decker's arm, sobbing. He looked around for help. Wanda Bontemps came to the rescue. "What do you need, Lieutenant?"

"Any other rooms available?"

"No. We can use the ladies' lounge."

"Okay, take her there. But before you ask her anything, I need to call up her parents—"

"*Noooo,*" Yasmine wailed out.

Decker was firm. "Yasmine, your parents have to be notified. I should have done it when I was at the hospital. I just didn't have time."

"My mother will *kill* me."

"I guarantee you when she finds out the circumstances, she'll be overjoyed to see you breathing." To Wanda, Decker said, "This is Detective Bontemps. She'll take good care of you until your mother gets here."

"I think I'm going to be sick." Yasmine gagged.

"I'll take you to the bathroom." To Decker, she said, "I'll call her mom."

"Even better," Decker told her. After Bontemps hustled her away, he spotted Lee Wang and called him over. "Do you have a minute?"

"I'm with one of the boys."

"Which one?"

"Jerome John Little, better know as JJ."

"Where is JJ now?"

"Room four. Willy's with him." Willy was William Brubeck, a vet of over thirty years. "He's seventeen. Do you want me to notify his parents?"

"If he's talking, let him talk. If he asks for his parents, we have no choice. Tell Willy to go for it. I got another job for you." He waved over Marge as he talked to Lee. He handed him an evidence bag. "Run these guns through the system. There are two of them—a Luger 9 mm semiautomatic and a Smith and Wesson .22LR. Find out if they're registered, who owns them, and if any of them are stolen."

"Not a problem."

Marge blew out air. "You said arrest anyone we could and we did just that. One of them, Kyle Kerkin who has long hair, was in possession of a firearm—a .32 Glock. Dylan had crystal meth in his back pocket. When we arrested him on possession, he fell apart. That's when we asked if we could swipe his hands for gunshot residue. He was so unnerved, he said yes. He tested positive."

"Fantastic! How old is Dylan?"

"Eighteen."

The smile on Decker's face was ear to ear. "Even better!"

"The bad news is now that he's had a little time to think, he wants a lawyer."

"Doesn't mean the evidence will get thrown out, especially if he's an adult."

"Absolutely. Besides, he's not going to talk his way out of a possession charge."

"Right now, Dylan's got worse things to deal with . . . like attempted murder."

Marge nodded. Her mood was guarded. "We've got tons of charges to work with, Pete. Two of the boys were in possession of crystal meth and crack cocaine, one boy had a pipe and a bag of what's probably E, the girls had pot and pills, and the blonde also had crystal meth. The brunette—Darla Holbein—is seventeen. Two of the boys—JJ Little and Nate Asaroff—are also seventeen. Cameron Cole and Kyle Kerkin, along with Dylan Lashay, are over eighteen."

"And Kerkin was the one with the Glock?"

"Yes. He had a Glock and he is over eighteen."

"Where's the gun?"

"Drew Messing is running it through the system. He should be done by now."

"Any other guns besides the Glock?"

"Nope."

"Gabe's not positive who shot him."

"Dylan was the only one with residue on his hands."

"You're sure."

"Yep. We swabbed them all."

"Have you talked to any of the kids to get their side of the story?"

"Of course. They say they were just walking along when Gabe and the girl held them up and tried to rob them."

"Gabe shot himself?"

"I don't even know if they realize that Gabe has been shot. We certainly haven't told them anything. They're all sticking to their robbery story."

"Nothing was found on either Gabe or the girl—her name is Yasmine Nourmand."

"They claim that Gabe and the girl were spooked by a Good Samaritan. They ran away, tossing their possessions in the bushes as they fled. They even claim the drugs belonged to Gabe and the girl and they were only holding them for evidence to show the police. Gotta hand it to them. They had their alibis down even before we picked them up."

"Did any of them call the police and report a robbery?"

"Not that I know of."

"Did any of the group call 911?"

"Don't know. All the units I met at the park were responding to my call."

"Gabe called me right away. Doesn't mean anything . . . just that he reached out for help . . . could be someone will say that I gave him direction . . . which I didn't. Still . . ." Decker thought a moment. "You're the lead. I can't get too involved in this one."

"No problem. I thought as much."

"Gabe claims he dropped his sheet music at Coffee Bean before he took off to find the gang. Send someone down there to photograph it and bag it as evidence. It'll lend credence to his story."

"No problem."

Decker said, "Who do you think is the weakest link in the B and W Mafia?"

"They turned out to be a lot more evil than I gave them credit for," Marge said.

"You and me both."

"The weakest link?" Marge paused. "I'd say the seventeen-year-old brunette—Darla Holbein. She broke down immediately."

"Yeah, when I brought Yasmine in, she kept on trying to apologize to her." Decker took out his pad and jotted down some notes. "Which means that if the gang was being robbed by them, why would Darla immediately start apologizing to Yasmine?"

Marge said, "I'll mention it to the D.A."

Decker said, "Who's the next weakest link?"

"A tie between JJ Little who hasn't stopped crying and Kyle Kerkin, who wet himself when we found the gun."

"Kyle Kerkin is over eighteen, right?"

"Yes."

"Perfect. Darla is with Wynona."

"She asked for her parents. They've already been notified and they're on their way," Marge said. "What should we do with Dylan, who's asking for a lawyer?"

"Give him his lawyer. He'll be the last one we'll talk to—after we get all the others to flip on him."

Yasmine raced into a bathroom stall. She didn't even have time to close the door. It took a few minutes before she came out, wiping her mouth on toilet paper. She was trembling uncontrollably.

"I can't stop shaking."

"That's all the adrenaline." Wanda helped her onto a couch in the ladies' lounge. "Let me get you some orange juice."

"I still feel sick." She suddenly panicked. "I wanna go back to the hospital."

"Are you hurt?"

"I wanna see Gabe." She started to cry. "I need to see him. If something happens to him, I'll kill myself!"

Wanda counted to three. "Sweetheart, first let's call your parents—"

"Oh, please don't call my *mom*." She hugged herself in an attempt to stop her trembling. "She'll *kill* me! My father will disown me. You don't under . . . *stand!*"

"So let's start with your mother. She has to know what's going on."

"Can I see the lieutenant?"

"He's busy right now."

"Please let me see him!"

Wanda's heart went out to her. "Yes, you can see him, but first I need to call your mother."

Reluctantly, Yasmine gave her the number.

The call was not an easy one. The woman fluctuated between gasping and screaming, demanding to talk to her daughter who refused to take the phone. After the conversation, Wanda noticed that her own head was throbbing.

Yasmine was still shaking. "Can I talk to the lieutenant now?"

Wanda said, "I'll see if I can find—"

"Oh, please don't leave me *alone.*"

"Okay, let's go out together."

Wanda helped her up and managed to flag down Decker. "She wants to talk to you, Lieutenant."

"That's fine, but take her back to the ladies' lounge. I don't want her seeing anyone else that we brought in." Decker's cell phone rang. "It's Rina; I have to take this."

Yasmine burst into tears. "I wanna see *Gabe*!"

To Rina, Decker said, "What's going on?"

"I think I'm gonna faint," Yasmine cried out.

Wanda eased her into a chair. "I need some juice ASAP!"

Decker ran to the refrigerator while holding the phone. "I'm sorry, I can't hear well. It's pandemonium down here. Can you shout?"

Rina said, "Gabe's stabilized. He's fine. He's going into surgery in about an hour. He keeps on asking about Yasmine. He wants to talk to her. Can I have him call your phone and you can put her on?"

Decker looked around for Yasmine, but she was gone. "I think she went back to the bathroom. I'll have her call Gabe's cell when I see her."

"He can't use his cell phone in a hospital," Rina told him. "That's why I asked if he can call her before he goes into surgery. He keeps calling her cell, but she's not answering."

Decker took the carton of orange juice from the refrigerator. Scott Oliver was waving him over.

Decker put out a finger to wait, then spotted Yasmine, sitting with her head between her legs. "Hold on, Rina, I found her." He gave the carton and a paper cup to Wanda. "Do you have your cell phone, Yasmine?"

Slowly, she lifted her head up and checked her pockets. She pulled it out. "Here."

"Drink," Wanda told her. "Sip slowly."

Yasmine complied. Decker said, "Gabe's going to call you. You need to go with Detective Bontemps back to the ladies' room. I'll be there as soon as I can come."

"When can I see Gabe?" she asked.

"I don't know," Decker told her.

"C'mon, sweetheart." Wanda helped her up.

"I want to see *Gabe!*"

"He's going into surgery, Yasmine. Go to the ladies' lounge with Detective Bontemps, and he'll call you, okay?"

The girl nodded, tears streaming down her check. She squeaked out, "Thank you for all your help."

"You're welcome, honey. I'm sorry I can't do more right now." He nodded to Wanda, who once again led her away.

To Rina, Decker said, "Yasmine has her phone. Tell Gabe he can call her."

"Thank you, Peter."

"Happy to help. I gotta run." He hung up and walked over to Oliver. "Who's your interview?"

"Kyle Kerkin."

"Perfect. He's the one over eighteen with the Glock, right?"

"Right. The Glock belongs to his father, but here's the kicker. Dad reported it stolen eight months ago. So we've got a stolen weapons charge on top of the drug charges. Kyle is barely dog-paddling in the soup."

"See if you can pull him under. Let's find out who he blames when he goes down."

Oliver said, "Kyle wants to talk to you, and he's willing to do it without a lawyer."

"Me?"

"Yeah, he asked for the lieutenant in charge. He's just waiting to pop. We can't blow this opportunity."

"I can't do any interviewing, Scott. I've got an obvious personal involvement."

"He knows Gabe lives with you."

"He does?" Decker was floored. "How?"

"Because Gabe told him that he lived with a police lieutenant."

"He *did? When?*"

"I don't know when, but he's aware that Gabe has a foster dad who's a cop."

"There's some background story that I missed," Decker said. "Okay, let's do this. You do the interviewing, you get his story, and I'll sit in with you."

"Perfect."

"I'll be there in a few minutes."

"Sooner is always better."

Decker went over to Marge's desk. She was hanging up on the phone call. "That was Darla Holbein's mother. She's furious but not at us. Darla will have some explaining to do."

"Marge, I need someone to make up six-packs of the teens to show to Yasmine and Gabe for ID. Who's free?"

"Drew Messing might be free," Marge said. "He just finished with the Glock. It was stolen from Kyle Kerkin's father eight months ago."

"Yeah, Oliver just told me."

"Messing's writing up the report."

"When he's done with that, tell him to start on the photo arrays, okay?"

"Okay. How about if we do Dylan, Kyle, and Cameron first since they're all over eighteen?"

"Good idea," Decker said. "Do you have any recent pictures of them we can use? Maybe something from their yearbook?"

"I can probably get their pictures from Facebook. If not, I'll do an image search."

"Good. We'll worry about the others later. Does Dylan have a last name?"

Marge smiled. "It's Lashay."

Decker would have smiled if he wasn't so busy. "Okay. Take one of Lashay's photo lineup to Yasmine and to Gabe before he goes into surgery."

"When is he going into surgery?"

"In an hour."

"That'll be tight." A pause. "Shouldn't someone interview him?"

"Shit, you're right."

"I'll do it once I've made the photo pack," Marge said. "If Gabe and the girl make a positive ID, I'll pull warrants for Lashay's house and for his school locker. I'll have Drew do the others."

At that moment, a gorgeous, stick-thin woman with tied-up black hair stormed into the squad room, her stilettos clacking against the hard floor. Sohala Nourmand's perfectly made-up face was a cross between fury and pure panic.

Decker said, "She's fine, Mrs. Nour—"

"I want to see my daughter *now*!"

"I'll take you to her—"

Sohala wagged her finger in Decker's face. "I call my husband now. We go call our lawyer. You'll hear from us very soon! Now where is my daughter so I can take her home?"

Decker tried to remain calm. "Neither you or your daughter are going anywhere—"

The woman was furious. "We are leaving now!"

"Mrs. Nourmand, your daughter may be in extreme danger and no matter how angry or scared you are, you are not going to compromise her safety! I think we both can agree on that."

The woman was aghast. "She's in extreme *danger*?"

"I don't know how much you know, but from what I've managed to gather, she was kidnapped at gunpoint." Decker was talking as fast as he could. "My foster son, who was with your daughter at the time, managed to get her away, but he was shot in the process. Gabriel will be undergoing surgery. We're holding some people who may be responsible on attempted murder charges, but there's a good chance at least some of them will make bail and I want to make sure your daughter is away and completely out of the picture if that should happen. So we need to strategize before you yank her out of her safety net and into this big, bad world."

Sohala's mouth had dropped open. Abruptly her eyes rolled in the back of her head and she began to sway. Then her knees buckled.

Decker and Marge caught her before she hit the ground.

Chapter Thirty-Two

Marge said, "Should I call an ambulance?"

"No, no, no," Sohala whispered.

"Get her some water." Decker took her pulse. It was slow but steady. "Would you like me to call your husband for you?"

"No!" Sohala moaned. "He has a weak heart." Sohala's eyes were brimming with tears. "Was my daughter . . . ?"

"No." Decker assured her. "She wasn't physically harmed at all."

"You are positive?" she whispered.

Marge came back with the water. "Let me go make those photo packs before we lose our witnesses to surgery and Mom."

"Good idea," Decker told her.

Sohala sat up and sipped water. It took her a few minutes to find her voice. "Yasmine is okay?"

"She's fine. You can go see her in a moment, but first just hear me out—"

"This is a bad dream. A nightmare . . . Do you say someone was shot?"

"My foster son, yes."

"Dead God . . ." She regarded Decker. "Who is he?"

"His name is Gabriel Whitman," Decker said. "He's the boy who played piano at Hannah's graduation. You met him at the deli about three months ago."

"The tall white boy who goes to Harvard?"

"He got into Harvard. He's living with us until he goes to college."

"He is Jewish?"

"No."

"*No?* Then why he was with my daughter?"

Decker just looked at her. She sat back in her chair and muttered something plaintive in Farsi. She wagged a finger at him. "I knew something was funny with that girl. She is a sneaky one, but this is too much!" She suddenly looked horrified. "And is he okay . . . your boy?"

"He'll be fine, but it's going to hurt for a while."

"I am so sorry." Tears were in her eyes. "I think I'm very confused."

"It's a lot to integrate," Decker said.

"I am supposed to meet my daughter at the dress-maker in an hour. She is getting married."

"To Aaron the doctor."

"Yes. I have to call her. What do I tell her? I think I feel sick!"

"Take your time—"

"This is just too much. I cannot do everything." She was in tears. "I am one person."

"It's a lot to absorb." Decker was trying not to look at his watch.

"So what do you find out about my daughter?"

"Pardon me?"

"What happened to her this morning?" She sounded exasperated.

Decker said, "I'm still trying to put the pieces of this case together, and I'm needed urgently in an inter-view room. Can I talk about your daughter's safety for a moment?"

"Oh God, I am in a panic!"

"Don't panic, we need to stay calm, okay?"

"Okay." She fanned her face with her hand. "But I still panic."

"Mrs. Nourmand, I'd like Yasmine to stay out of the area until I have a better idea of what's going on. Does she have a relative who lives nearby that she can stay with?"

The woman blanched. "It is that bad?"

"I don't know," Decker said. "Right now I'm just taking precautions."

"My sister lives in Beverly Hills."

"Can she stay with your sister for a little while?"

"How long?"

"I don't know. Once I have a clearer picture, maybe I can give you a better idea."

"She can stay with my sister, but what do I tell my husband? It is crazy just for her to move for no reason."

"Then maybe you should think about telling him what's going on."

"But I don't know what is going on. First, I need to know what's going on. You say she was kidnapped with a gun; this is very serious. You make me panic again."

"That's why I'd like your daughter to stay with your sister."

"That is not a problem. I just think what do I tell my husband. I cannot tell him truth right away. He'll get mad at her, he'll get very scared for her. His heart is not so good for a shock."

"I'm sure you can phrase it in a delicate way, ma'am."

Sohala exhaled. "So your boy and my daughter have been . . ."

"I think they've been seeing each other for a while."

"How bad?"

"How bad?"

"You know . . . what do they do?"

"I don't know." Decker shrugged. "How serious can two teenagers be?"

"It cannot be serious, but it can be bad." She was quiet. "My daughter is very naive. I hope he does not take advantage of her."

Decker tried not to bristle. "Gabriel's a good boy."

"He can be good boy, but he is still boy." She shook her head. "This is terrible. Okay. I got it. I tell my husband that Yasmine wants to try out YULA. Last year, she did want to try it out, but I say no. I say it's too far from home. Now I kick myself for not listening. It is all girls. I think after what's going on, that is good idea."

Marge walked over to Decker and handed him two photo arrays—one with Dylan Lashay in the number four position, and another with Cameron Cole in the number three position. "Are these okay?"

"Perfect."

"I'll take a set to Wanda to show Yasmine. Then I'm off to the hospital. I just talked to Rina. They've postponed Gabe's surgery for another couple of hours because they're trying to find a specific surgeon who can remove the bullet without cutting too much muscle. He hasn't even been sedated yet, so I want to talk to him pronto."

"Go."

Marge turned to Mrs. Nourmand. "I'm glad everything worked out with your daughter."

She said, "Thank you for your wishes."

After Marge left, Decker said, "I'll take you to see Yasmine—"

"I really am sorry about the boy." Her eyes watered up. "It is terrible."

"As one parent to another, I appreciate your sympathy."

"What about the boy? After he gets out of the hospital, he stay here?"

"You mean with me?" Decker raised his eyebrows. "I'm concerned for him as well. Once Gabe is well enough, I'll probably send him to his father's."

"Where does his father live?"

"In Nevada."

"That is very good." She regarded Decker. "I have nothing bad against Gabe, but it can't go on." She sighed. "How much already go on? That is the question."

"I didn't even know Gabe was seeing your daughter until I picked them up this morning."

"You pick them up this morning?"

"Gabe called me and said they were in trouble. I came down and got them."

"So I say thank you." She welled up with tears again but tried to hide it. "I want to see her . . . my daughter."

Decker said, "Good idea, Mrs. Nourmand. She knows a lot more about what happened than I do."

Yasmine's trembling finger pointed to position number four. Her eyes moistened. "This one."

Wanda said, "Are you sure?"

Yasmine nodded as tears streamed down her cheeks. Her voice was very small. "I'm positive."

"Could you circle your choice with this pen?" Marge asked her.

Yasmine complied, the circle wobbly because her hands were shaking so forcefully. Marge brought out the second set. "What about this group of girls? Does anyone look familiar?"

Yasmine gasped and pointed to Cameron Cole. "This one! She was *horrible*!"

"I'm so sorry, honey. Can you circle your choice for me again?"

Her voice rose in pitch. "She kept saying I was going to . . . to die."

Marge placed the pen in her hand, and the girl managed another circle around Cameron Cole's face. At that moment, Decker and Sohala Nourmand came through the door. Instantly Yasmine leaped into her mother's waiting arms, clutching her with such force that her hands turned red. Her sobs were deep and frightening. Sohala started crying as well. She said, "You are okay?"

Yasmine nodded, her face buried in her mother's bosom. "Mommy, I'm so sorry. I'm so, so sorry."

Marge said to Decker, "Positive ID for both. I'll get Lee to pull warrants for the home and school. Right now, I'm off to the hospital. Do me a favor and let Oliver know what's going on."

"You bet. Remember to tell the surgeon to save the bullet for forensics." Decker looked at Wanda. "Do you need anything?"

"Do you want me to conduct the interview here?"

"Everything else is occupied."

"There's no video camera."

Decker said, "I'll get you a tape recorder." He hurried out of the room.

Yasmine sobbed. "I wanna go home!"

Wanda said, "Sweetheart, we have to ask you some questions—"

"Please, Mommy! I don't want to talk anymore." She was wailing. "I'm soooo sorry. I just wanna go home."

To Wanda's surprise, Sohala broke off the hug. "Yasmine, you have to tell the police what happened."

"It was *horrible*—"

"So tell them."

Decker returned with the tape recorder. He was glad to leave the hysteria to Wanda, who busied herself in setting up the equipment. Sohala tried to soothe the panicked teen. She took her daughter by the shoulders. "Yasmine, the boy got shot—"

"Oh God!" she cried out. "My poor Gabriel got hurt, and it's all my *fault*!"

"Yasmine, I worry about *you*. Detective Decker thinks you are in danger."

Yasmine looked at her with wide, wet eyes.

Sohala said, "I am going to send you to live with Auntie Sofi. You finish school at YULA."

"*Why?*"

"Because Detective Decker thinks you are in danger. Don't you hear me?"

"But what . . . about Gabe?" Yasmine's voice was barely above a whisper.

"That is not my business or *your* business, Yasmine. But . . . I will tell you anyway because I have a soft heart. Detective Decker sends him to his father in Nevada."

Wanda watched the teen's face crumple. It was absolutely pathetic.

Sohala wagged a finger in front of her daughter's eyes. "You stop crying now and tell police what happened! Afterward, we talk . . . a lot!"

The hot anger in her mother's voice brought Yasmine back to reality. She dried her tears on her shirtsleeve. She said, "What do you want to know?"

Sohala said, "I want to know *everything*!"

Yasmine's voice was tiny. "I'm sorry, Mommy."

Sohala's burning fury melted into pity. "You okay?"

The girl nodded.

"No one touch you?"

"No. I'm okay."

"That's all that matter. Talk to the policewoman. Then we think together about what lies to tell your father so he won't die."

"You're going to tell *Daddy*?"

"I have to tell him something. Why else would you live with Aunt Sofi? But not right away. You want him to have heart attack?"

Her voice was high and thin. "No." She looked down. "Thank you, Mommy."

"I do it for Daddy, I don't do it for you!" A pause. "Well, maybe a little for you." Sohala's eyes went wet. "Talk to the lady now."

When Yasmine nodded, Wanda turned on the tape recorder.

Watching Oliver chat with Kyle Kerkin over the video monitor, Decker saw that the teen was on the thin side with a developed chest and wiry arms. He had a big nose, thin lips, acne, and a face framed by shoulder-length brown hair. Decker didn't see any defiance in his demeanor. His posture was upright, his hands folded on the table. His voice was on the soft side and nasal. He wore a plaid shirt jacket, currently draped over a chair, with a black T-shirt, Levis, and sneakers. He looked up when Decker came into the interview room. He crossed his arms over his chest and slouched in the chair, his right leg bouncing up and down.

Decker sat next to the teen and introduced himself.

"You're Chris's foster father, right?"

Decker was confused. "Chris?"

"Yeah . . . right. The guy today. He said his name was Chris. Then he said it was something else. I don't remember what it was."

Decker didn't clarify anything. "I understand you'd like to talk to me." The kid's leg continued up and down, up and down. "Detective Oliver will talk to you. I'm just here to listen."

"I'm not an idiot, you know," Kyle said. "I know I'm taking a big risk here. I haven't called my parents yet, although they'll know pretty soon. And I know it's stupid to talk to you without a lawyer. The thing is, I'm putting myself on the line. I need this one shot to make this go away."

No one spoke.

Kyle said, "I mean, I know it's not going to go away unless you make it go away."

Still no comment.

His eyes on Decker. "Look, sir, I will do *anything* you want. I'll answer any questions you want. I will tell you everything, and I mean *everything,* as long as you keep me out of this. I mean, I know I might have to be a witness or something because I was there. But I swear to God, I didn't do anything. I mean, yes, I borrowed the gun from my father and gave it to Dylan, but I had nothing to do with this morning. Nothing whatsoever. When I showed up, it was already a fait accompli."

When the kid stopped talking, Decker turned to Oliver. "Have you read Mr. Kerkin his rights?"

Oliver said, "I did. I have the signature card."

Decker said, "We're open to hear anything you want to tell us."

"Like I told you, Kyle," Oliver said, "this is your one chance to give us your side of the story."

"Look." Kyle moved forward. "I watch *The First 48.* I know the drill. You want a confession. I'm not here to make a confession. I didn't do anything. But, yes, I was there. That much I'll say because there's no sense denying the obvious. I know

I'm in deep shit. What I'm telling you is I'll do anything you want. I'll say anything you want. I just
want *out*."

Oliver said, "Why don't you start at the beginning.
What happened this morning?"

"I gotta get some kind of guarantee first. I got into
Wharton." His eyes watered up. "I'm not going to let
some fucking asshole ruin my life."

Too little, too late. Decker said, "Who's the fucking
asshole?"

Kyle was gnashing his teeth, his jaw working over-
time. "Dylan Lashay. He's a real psychopath, and I
don't use the term lightly." A pause. "I guess you're
wondering why I hang with him."

"I'm a little curious," Oliver said.

Kyle made a swipe at his eyes with his shirtsleeve.
"What a fucking mess! I was hoping it wouldn't come
out until I was out of the house." His eyes wavered between Decker and Oliver. He folded his arms across his
chest. "I'm gay."

Decker nodded. "Your parents don't know."

"No, they do *not* know. My older sister died
ten years ago in a car crash. I'm an only child." He
looked up at the ceiling. "It's like all their hopes
and dreams . . . have been put on my shoulders. It's
bad enough they won't get anything like kids outta me.

If I go to jail, my mother's going to commit suicide. She's not a stable woman."

"You still haven't answered why you hang with Dylan," Oliver said.

Kyle looked down. "We had a thing going for a while in eleventh grade. He filmed it. We both thought it was funny, you know." He hit his head. "God, I was an idiot!"

More silence. Kyle continued to gnash his teeth. Decker could hear the enamel against enamel—like fingers on a chalkboard.

The teen said, "When he threatened to expose me, I asked him what he wanted. He said guns." He looked up. "My father's a huge weapons collector. I gave him a gun—a single gun. I know it was stupid, but I didn't want to be outed."

Oliver nodded. "Obviously Dylan wasn't afraid of being exposed."

"I dunno," Kyle said. "I never called his bluff. We both fuck girls, so . . . I dunno if he likes girls or if he swings both ways or if he just uses his cock as a weapon. Frankly, I wasn't looking to analyze him. I was trying to protect myself. So I capitulated with the one gun and told him if he got greedy that I could make him just as miserable as he could make me."

"How's that?" Oliver asked.

"I've been part of the Maf—. . . his gang for a while. I know things." Decker nodded encouragement. "So we had this . . . tacit understanding." Furtive eyes. "Everyone just assumed we were close buds and that was okay. Dylan's a BMOC. At B and W, he was a good person to be associated with." Pleading eyes. "Are you going to help me?"

Oliver said, "So just like that, you and Dylan broke it off?"

Kyle whispered. "To the world, we kinda had a bromance thing going on, but it wasn't sexual any-more." An evasive glance. "After I gave him the gun, it was over."

Decker's brain suddenly started sparking. "Nah, I don't believe you."

Kyle became defensive. "I swear it's true."

Decker said, "When you and Dylan had your affair, he turned over a rock, Kyle. Once a guy is sexually active, it's impossible to go back."

"You're wrong," Kyle said. "It was *over*."

"Over between Dylan and you, but not over with the sex. You found someone to take Dylan's place."

Kyle turned away and didn't answer, the leg bouncing up and down. Decker mouthed Gregory Hesse to Oliver when the boy wasn't looking.

Scott raised an eyebrow, regarding the Loo with admiration. He kept his voice even. "You know we're pulling search warrants, Kyle. How long do you think it will take before we find Gregory Hesse's stolen computer or his missing camcorder?"

The teen turned ashen. He threw back his head and moaned. "It was an *accident.*"

Oliver put his hand on Kyle's knee. "Accidents happen. Tell us about it."

"I don't know, man." Kyle had tears in his eyes. "We were like . . . stoned."

"Tell us what you remember. We're here to listen, not to judge."

"He told us the gun was empty," Kyle pleaded. "It wasn't *supposed* to happen."

"Yeah, that's a raw deal when accidents happen, man. We all know that." Oliver leaned in closer. "Who told you the gun was empty?"

"*Dylan!*" The boy shouted out. "He was filming it on Greg's camcorder." Water poured from his eyes. "We were just fooling around. You've got to believe me."

"I believe you, man," Oliver said. "I totally believe you."

"It wasn't supposed to *happen.* When the gun went off, I was shocked . . . I was . . . petrified. It was horrible!"

"I'm sure it was," Oliver said.

Kyle's wet eyes went from Oliver to Decker. "Do you know what Dylan did when it happened?"

"What did he do?" Decker said.

"He laughed!" Kyle shook his head. "Brains and shit . . . all over the fucking place and Dylan . . . just . . . fucking . . . *laughed*!"

Chapter Thirty-Three

When Marge walked into the hospital room, Gabe was asleep, a book lying on his lap, spine down and opened. Rina was reading in the chair next to his bed. She gave Marge a small wave. "He's knocked out."

"Sedated?"

"No, just sleeping from pure exhaustion."

"I hate to do this to him." Marge held up two photo arrays. "You know how it is. Time matters."

Rina nodded and gently shook his shoulder. Gabe stirred, inhaled, and then winced.

"I'm up, I'm up." He opened his eyes. "What's going on?"

"I'm sorry to wake you, sweetheart." Rina gave Marge her chair. "This is Sergeant Dunn."

"Hi." He sat up, then grimaced. "I think we've met."

"Probably at Sammy's wedding."

"Yeah, I was there . . . me and five hundred others."

"We invited everyone to my son's wedding," Rina said. "It doesn't pay to make enemies."

"If you ever need enemies, I could loan you a few." Gabe turned to Marge. "What's up?"

"I'd like to show you a couple of photo arrays." She handed him the first one with Dylan Lashay. "See if anyone looks famili—"

"This one." Pointing to number four. "This is Dylan."

"You're sure?"

"The dude shot me. Couldn't be more positive."

"Can you circle your choice and sign your name?"

"I can do that." When he was done, he gave her back the sheet of paper. "Next?" When Marge handed him the girls, Gabe said, "This is Cameron." He took the pen, circled her picture, and signed it. "What else?"

All business. "If you're up to talking about it, I'd like to hear what happened."

"Can I call Yasmine again?" Gabe said out of nowhere.

"She's talking to detectives, Gabe."

"Is her mom with her?"

"Yes."

"Does she hate me . . . her mother?"

Rina said, "Of course she doesn't *hate* you. You saved her daughter's life."

Marge said, "Actually, she expressed concern for your welfare."

"So maybe on balance, it's good I got shot. I got the pity factor working for me."

Rina said, "You don't need the pity factor to be appreciated. I think Sergeant Dunn needs to ask you some questions."

"Are you up to talking about it?" Marge asked.

"Sure," he said. "Something to distract my mind before I go under the knife. Or the laser." He looked at Rina. "Did they find the surgeon yet?"

"They did. He's coming in . . ." She looked at her watch. "In forty minutes." She stood up. "I'm going to catch a breath of fresh air. Do you need anything?"

"I can't friggin' eat until I go into surgery, so I guess the answer is no." His face became angry. "I hurt and I'm starving. This sucks."

"Yes, it does."

"You know, Rina, do you have enough time to get me my glasses? My eyes are killing me."

"Not a problem."

"Thanks." A pause. "And you're going to be here when the surgeon comes in?"

"Of course."

"Thanks for staying with me. I mean, I'm not really your responsibility."

"Gabriel, you most certainly are my responsibility." She kissed his greasy hair. "And I love having you as my responsibility. I wouldn't have it any other way."

"Can you adopt me?" Gabe said.

"I would be happy to adopt you, but your parents wouldn't approve."

"I don't see either of them here to object."

"Your father will be here soon."

"Yeah, when he gets a moment," Gabe said. "But hey, I'm not bitter."

Rina kissed his head again. "I'll get you your glasses."

"Thanks. And my acne medication?"

"Sure."

"Did you call Nick?"

"Yes, I called Nick. He wanted to come down right away, but I told him to hold off until after the surgery."

"What'd he say?"

"That he was horrified."

"How about Jeff Robinson?"

"I didn't speak to him. I'm sure he's horrified as well." Rina gave a wave at the door. "I'll be back in twenty minutes."

Gabe turned to Marge. "What do you want to know?"

Marge took out her notepad. "I wonder if I can set up a tape recorder inside a hospital . . . whether it'll interfere with anything."

"Fine with me."

"Yeah, I suppose if someone has a cow, I can always turn it off." She set up the machine on a tray next to the bed. "So why don't you start from the beginning."

"It's a long story."

"Good. Be as detailed as you can."

Gabe wiped his hands on his hospital gown. "Like how far back should I take it? Like when I first met Dylan?"

"Yes, that's good," Marge said. "Tell me about the first time you met Dylan."

"I only met him one other time until today. I was in Starbucks, minding my own business . . . I think I was reading. This posse of kids comes through the door and I kinda see them out of the corner of my eye."

"When was this?"

"About four to five months ago."

"Okay. Morning or afternoon or evening?"

"Like four in the afternoon." Gabe bit his bottom lip. "I knew right away that they were messed up. They just had that look, like they were spoiling for something. Anyway, they come up to me and I know I'm about to be crowded. You know what crowding is?"

"Kind of."

"It's when a group just totally surrounds you . . . they don't hurt you usually, but its purpose is to show you who's in control."

"Menacing," Marge said.

"Exactly. So they surround me and then Dylan comes up to me and tells me that I'm sitting in his chair . . . like it's his *makom hakavua* or something."

"Excuse me?"

"You know . . . like his designated seat." Gabe looked at her. "That's what Rina calls Peter's Barcalounger."

"I don't speak Hebrew."

"Neither do I, but I've picked up a few things. Anyway, the guy wants my seat."

Marge nodded. "And you're at Starbucks?"

"Yeah. The place was empty! He's playing mind games. Asshole. So he just tells me to move it, and I pretend not to hear him. So he tells me to move it again, and the second time around, he shows me that he's packing."

"He shows you a gun?"

"You betcha, as the lieutenant would say. Now I know that if I accede right away and I see this guy again, I'm screwed. I'm a target. But I'm not about to take him and his gang on. There were three guys."

"So there were three of them?"

"And also two girls—a blonde, Cameron, and a brunette—same girls as this morning. Anyway, they're not gonna do anything to me inside the place, but I know they're gonna jump me the minute I walk outside if I don't do something clever. So instead of backing off, I like pull open the dude's jacket to take a better look at the gun. It was a Beretta 92FS."

"You know guns, Gabriel?"

"I know some guns and I happened to know *that* gun. So I start giving him my opinion on the weapon he's packing, and then we start talking guns. He's still standing up and I'm still sitting in his chair, but in the end I get up and *offer* him my seat. But I'm doing it on *my* terms."

"Okay."

"So the dude invites me to sit down with him and his buddies. Not wanting to be antagonistic, I sit. That's when I found out his name was Dylan. Then he starts asking me how do I know all about guns."

"What'd you tell him?"

"I told him the truth. I told him about my dad, and I told him I was living with a police lieutenant. I did it because both Chris and Peter are impressive dudes and I wanted to scare him a little."

"Go on."

"Then Dylan asks me if I want to hang with them. Like they're so 'cool.' " He rocked his open hands back and forth. "I say thanks but no thanks. And that was that. And I stopped going to that Starbucks because I didn't want to run into any of them again. So I started going to the Coffee Bean near Rina's school. That's where I met Yasmine. She came up to me."

Gabe looked up at the ceiling. His voice got soft.

"She had these tickets to the opera. She loves opera." Gabe's expression became pained. "She was supposed to go with her sister, but her sister crapped out on her. She offered them to me. I took one of them, but I could see she was disappointed. So I asked her if she wanted to come with me." He smiled at Marge. "I think initially she just wanted a ride. But then I told her I didn't drive, so we went by cab. It wasn't even a date or anything. I was just doing her a favor."

He stopped.

"It was a wonderful day." His eyes got far away. "I mean Rina and Peter are like the nicest people in the world, but they have their own lives and that's really good. I don't need a second set of parents. But I do spend a lot of waking hours by myself."

"It must be lonely."

"It has its good points. I practice all the time. As a result, my skill set took a quantum leap. I've expanded my repertoire tenfold. I'm far better than I should be."

"I'm glad something positive came out of it."

"The only positive thing until Yasmine came along. It was just a weird confluence of things that drew me to her. My parents deserted me, and I didn't have any real friends anymore. I certainly didn't want to hang with those idiots in Starbucks. I guess I didn't realize how *lonely* I was until she came into the picture." He paused. "She's such a cutie. Every time I see her, something inside of me just . . . melts." He stopped talking, his eyes moist. "I'm rambling. Sorry."

"Nothing to be sorry for." Marge waited a moment, and then went back to business. "So you're at the table with Dylan and his friends at Starbucks."

"Yes."

"Did he tell you his last name?"

"Nope. Just Dylan."

"And then you talked to him about guns, and your dad and the lieutenant."

"Exactly."

"How'd you excuse yourself?"

"I just said, I gotta go home. Sometimes Rina worries if she doesn't hear from me. It's nice that someone cares enough to notice if I'm alive or dead." His thoughts were far away. He snapped out of it. "I ran into the girl, Cameron, maybe a month or two later. I remember the day was Tuesday because it was the day that I auditioned for Jeff Robinson. He's my agent. I could get you the exact date if you need it."

"Yes, that would be helpful."

"So it's like six-thirtyish in the morning and I was waiting at the bus to go to SC. And this drop-dead gorgeous blonde comes up to me saying, 'Chris, Chris . . .'" He looked at Marge. "I told Dylan that my name was Chris. It seemed convenient at the time."

"Smart."

He shrugged off the compliment. "So the girl says to me, like, 'Do you know who I am?' And I didn't know except that she called me Chris. Then it came back to me. So I said, 'Yeah, you were with Dylan.' And we start talking. I'm like half asleep. And I don't want to tell her anything about me, because I just have this weird feeling about her. So I ask her what she's doing up so early, and she shows me that she just bought some pot."

Marge nodded.

"So she says, 'Come to my house and we'll smoke it together.' Then she tells me that her parents aren't home. And she starts like . . . flirting with me . . . rubbing my *neck* . . . telling me I need to *relax*.

"She's really good-looking, you know. In another world, it would have been a big turn-on. Instead, the girl gave me the willies. I ran with a fast crowd back in New York so I know the type perfectly. She's a druggie and an easy lay, but also a mean girl. I've had enough of crazy people in my life. I wouldn't have done her even if Yasmine wasn't in the picture. But you don't say something like that to a mean girl—especially one who hangs with a guy who likes guns."

"I see your point."

"Yeah, so I'm trying to get out of it without pissing her off. So I tell her I have a band audition, which for the most part was true. And then I make this big point of adding her phone number into my contact list in my cell so she won't feel rejected and pissed off."

"Do you have her number?"

"Nah, I erased it as soon as I got on the bus. I also gave her my number. But I mixed up the digits. She asked me for my last name and I told her Donatti because if she googled the name she could see for herself what a badass my dad is."

"And she told you her name?"

"Cam . . . short for Cameron. I didn't ask her last name."

"Okay. Go on."

"Nothing more to say. I forgot about her—until today."

"Tell me what happened today."

"I was supposed to meet Yasmine at Coffee Bean. That's our regular spot. We've been together every school day morning for a long time. Maybe not *every* morning, but most weekday mornings." He got quiet.

"I lived for those mornings. It turned waking up from a chore to something I cherished. This particular morning I was supposed to meet with some bigwigs from a record company in New York at SC. It took my agent a month to arrange this. Lord only knows what Jeff is thinking now."

"I'm sure his best wishes are with you."

"Nah, that doesn't sound like Jeff. And I doubt that Nick is horrified."

"I'm sure he's concerned about your condition."

"That's true. Neither he nor Jeff wants a lame racehorse. I know, I know. So young yet so cynical."

Marge patted his shoulder. "Tell me about this morning."

"I forgot to put in my contacts when I left the house, so I went back to the house, which made me late in meeting Yasmine. I'm, like, texting her, telling her I'll be late, but she's not answering me. And that's a little weird because she usually does answer me. So I get to Coffee Bean and she's not there. Yasmine is chronically late, but usually not *this* late. And I still can't reach her, so I'm, like, getting a little nervous. So I call her, which I usually don't do because we text. But she doesn't answer, and now I'm getting really nervous.

"In the back of my mind, I'm thinking that her parents found out and she's in real trouble. And I'm feeling awful and nervous. So I leave Coffee Bean and I'm outside the door. I call her again. And then the fucking ground starts ringing. I look down and it's her phone. I also found the watch I gave her. I'm thinking she wanted me to know something was wrong. Why else would she leave it, you know? So now I'm really starting to panic."

Marge nodded.

"I'm thinking maybe her parents dragged her out of the place or she got robbed or mugged or whatever. So I pick up her phone and watch. And I decide to go back to her house to check up on her. I just want to make sure she's okay."

He put his hand over his mouth.

"I'm getting a little ill thinking about it."

"You want to stop for a moment."

"No, let's just get this over with. So I'm thinking, do I go back or do I look for her? . . . It's like all in a space of a minute. And then I just flash on Dylan and Cameron. It was like the most nauseating feeling in the world. I start running for the bus stop because Cameron told me she lived near there. And in the distance I see this group of kids walking together. And I see Cameron's long blond hair. And I'm thinking holy shit! And I start running and running. You know, pure adrenaline. And I catch up to them and bust inside the inner circle. And that's when I see Yasmine. And I also see that Dylan has a gun to her back—a .22 Smith and Wesson."

Gabe blinked several times.

"The bastard looks at me and says something like I raped Cameron so he's going to rape Yasmine. Which is absurd. I never touched the bitch. And then I hear the click and feel the gun at my head."

Again, he put his hand over his mouth.

"Dylan's gun?"

"No, no. Some other dude with long hair. Dylan still has a gun on Yasmine." He swallowed hard and turned to Marge. "If you show me a photo thing like the one with Dylan, I could pick out all of them. I looked at their faces enough."

"I can do that." Marge said. "What happened after someone put a gun to your head?"

"It was weird." Gabe stared into space. "I became supercalm . . . not like my life was flashing before me, but all the panic just . . . evaporated. I was completely focused on how to get Yasmine and me out of this."

"What did you do?"

"First, I guess I tried to stall . . . acting supercool while he accuses me of raping the bitch." He paused, and then pointed a finger in the air. "I remember. I told him that I didn't go home with Cameron because

I had an audition with a record company. Dylan bought it. Deep in his heart, every dude wants to be a rock star. And she's calling me a liar and I'm like ignoring her in the way guys ignore girls who are shit to them. And Dylan can tell that I don't care what he thinks even though I'm like shaking inside. I kept thinking to myself, I have to get the gun away from my head."

"How'd you do it?"

"I stopped suddenly and ducked, throwing the dude behind me off balance. As soon as he pitched forward, I grabbed his wrist and twisted, got the gun away. My dad taught me how to do it. It was simple. And with all that adrenaline inside, it was really easy. That gun was a Luger 9 mm semi."

He stopped talking.

"It gets a little blurry at this point. I think Dylan shot me, but I was so pumped up, I didn't feel it. Somehow I got behind him . . . Dylan . . . I'm taller than him . . . and I put a gun to *his* head. I must have taken his gun away." He looked at Marge. "I wound up with the Luger in my left and the .22 in my right hand, which I kept on Dylan's head."

"You're left-handed?"

"No, right-handed but almost ambidextrous. Oh, now I remember. I wanted the 9 mm in my left because it had more ammo and I was holding the group off with a single weapon. I kept pointing it at them, one by one, telling everyone not to move."

Decker had swiped Gabe's hands, residue on his left. Now was the time to test his truth gene. She said, "Did you discharge any of the weapons, Gabe?"

"The Luger. One of the dudes made a move into his pocket. I fired a shot or two to scare him off . . . near his arm. I mighta grazed it. I remember thinking, just nobody *move* so I can organize my brain." He was breathing hard. "That's all I wanted. For them to keep still with their hands visible while I thought of an escape. Lord knows that I didn't want to shoot anyone, but they had to know I was serious."

Marge said, "How many times did you fire the gun?"

"I really don't remember, Sergeant. I'll say twice, but I'm not sure."

"Okay. So . . . you have the .22 to Dylan's head."

"Yeah . . ." Gabe had his eyes open, but mentally he was replaying the scene. "I have the .22 on Dylan and I'm like . . . threatening the others with the second gun. And I'm thinking how to get out of this. And then I remember Yasmine." He looked at Marge. "I told her to run away but she's . . . like frozen. She just won't budge."

"Fear does that."

"Fear does do that." He smiled. "And maybe she didn't want to leave me. 'Cause when I needed her help, she sure as hell moved."

"How did she help you?"

"All this time I'm thinking about the bus. It pulls up at around seven and I figured if we could just make it on the bus . . ."

He paused.

"Looking back, I suppose we coulda just left or called 911. I had the guns. Maybe they wouldn't have chased us. But I didn't know. I made like split-second decisions."

"I understand."

"I figured we just needed to be at a public place. So I asked Yasmine for the time. The bus was coming in fifteen minutes and I figured I had to stall them until it came."

"Okay. So it was about a quarter to seven?"

"Around that time. I told Yasmine to just dump out their shit all over the place . . . the purses, the back-packs, the wallets . . . I wanted something to keep them busy so they wouldn't be tempted to follow us."

"And Yasmine did what you told her to do?"

Gabe snapped his fingers. "Like that. The girl just *moved*. She was incredible."

Marge nodded.

"Finally I see the bus pulling up and we're about a half block away. At that point, I just grab Yasmine and we take off. We barely make it aboard. And then that's when I called Peter . . . the lieutenant." His blood pressure suddenly spiked.

Marge pressed the nurses call button.

Gabe was trembling. "I'm okay . . . really. I just think how . . . *lucky* we were and I become unglued."

Rina walked into the room and saw Gabe shaking. "I'm going to get a nurse."

"I'm okay, I'm okay," Gabe insisted. "Just stay here, okay?"

Marge turned off the tape recorder and stood up. "I think I have what I need for now. Sit down, Rina."

Rina sat and took Gabe's hand. As soon as he felt her touch, his heartbeat slowed. "Tell the nurse it was a mistake. Please? I don't want to be sedated. I hate feeling out of control."

"I'll tell them." Marge packed up. "I'm sure I'll have some more questions, but for now this was very good. Thank you, Gabriel."

"No problem."

"Heal up quickly."

"Sure." He turned to Rina. "Did you get my glasses?"

Rina pulled them out of her purse. Gabe took out his contacts and wrapped them in a tissue and gave them to her. He slipped his glasses on. "Wow. Better already. Do you think I can call Yasmine now?"

"You can try."

He punched in the hospital's outside phone line and called her. The cell rang and rang, and when her voice mail kicked in, he said, "Hi, it's me. Give me a call. I love you." A moment later, he called back and gave her the room number. Then he sighed. "She isn't going to call me. Her mom's gonna take away her phone."

"I'm sure her mother will let her visit you before she sends her to her aunt."

Gabe sat up and winced. "*What?*"

Rina realized that she had spoken out of turn. "I think Peter's concerned for her safety. She's going to live with her aunt for a while."

"Where does her aunt live?" Panic in his voice.

"In the city."

Gabe threw back his head. "God, then I'll *really* never see her again." He was silent but his eyes were windows to his brain. "Maybe after I'm done with my lesson at SC—"

"Gabriel, you know you can't do that."

"I can't help it."

"You'll just get yourself into trouble. You don't want to do that."

"So let them throw me in jail for stalking her. I don't care. I love her. And she loves me." He tried to fold his arms in front of his chest but he was hooked up to an IV. "It's not like I'm a delinquent or a loser. I mean a lot of mothers would love me for their daughter's boyfriend."

"You're wonderful—"

"Jesus, I put my life on the line for her. Isn't that worth something?"

"No one is doubting your heroism—"

"So what's wrong with this picture?"

Rina didn't bother to argue.

Gabe said, "You think I'm an idiot teenager, but I'm not. I am capable of very deep feelings, you know."

"Gabriel, I know your feelings are real. And her feelings are real as well. No one would ever call you idiotic."

"Except my dad."

Rina said nothing and forced out a smile.

Gabe regarded her face. "What's going on, Rina?"

"Pardon?"

"Something's going on. Please tell me!"

Rina sighed. "If Peter thinks that Yasmine is vulnerable, he also thinks that you're vulnerable. I think he wants you out of the picture for a while."

"Oh . . . okay." He paused. "If it's a safety issue, I'll leave Yasmine alone. I'd rather be heartbroken than to have something happen to her, you know. I really do love her."

Rina nodded.

"Rina, you have a strange look on your face. What aren't you telling me?"

"Peter's very concerned for your safety. When you get out of the hospital, he's sending you to live with your father in Nevada until things settle down and he knows what's going on."

Gabe's mouth dropped open. "You're *kidding!*" When Rina remained silent, he said, "Did my father actually *agree* to this?"

Rina nodded.

"Oh *God!*" Gabe's head fell back on the pillow. "Just when I thought it couldn't possibly get any worse!"

"I'm sure it'll only be for a short while before college."

"It's like four *months.* I'd rather face four *hundred* Dylans than spend four months with my dad."

"If it doesn't work, let me know. We can do other things."

"Like what?"

"After things settle down, you can move back in with us. But if things are still up in the air, there's always your aunt. And I'm sure Cindy would be happy to let you live with her. She's very fond of you."

"Yeah, move in with someone taking care of twin infants; that'll really endear me to her."

"We love you, Gabe. We'll do whatever you need. But right now both Peter and your dad think it's a good idea for you to be in Nevada."

"That's just *swell!*"

Rina's eyes started to water. "I'm sorry, honey. I'll visit anytime you want."

Gabe softened and took her hand. "It's okay . . . I'll be fine."

"Gabriel, it's not forever. You've always got a home with Peter and me."

"Thanks, but that's not gonna help me now." Gabe let out a small, sad laugh. Even that was enough to cause his side to burst with pain. "Do me a favor. Tell the anesthesiologist after surgery not to bother to wake me up."

Chapter Thirty-Four

Decker caught up to Marge as she walked into the station house. "Was Gabe able to make an ID?"

"He was so sure that I believe he could have done it with his eyes closed." She paused. "That makes no sense."

The Loo smiled. "When is he going into surgery?"

She checked her watch. "In an hour. Maybe a little less by now."

"Good. Lee Wang is on his way to the hospital with the remaining four photo arrays, Yasmine picked out two more people—Darla Holbein and Kyle Kerkin. She couldn't make a positive on JJ Little or Nate Asaroff. Maybe Gabe can pinpoint them."

"Let's hope," Marge said.

"This is the deal." Decker looked around to make sure none of the detained teens were within earshot.

"Oliver and I just finished up with Kyle Kerkin. He finally lawyered up, but not before he had a bad case of logorrhea. The good news is we have a connection between Dylan Lashay, Kyle Kerkin, and Gregory Hesse, but it wasn't exactly like I thought."

Marge took out her notepad. "I'm listening."

"The short answer is Kyle Kerkin is gay. He was in the closet when he and Dylan Lashay had a short-lived affair. Dylan broke it off and threatened to out him unless Kyle gave him guns from his father's collection. So Kyle gave Dylan a single gun and that seemed to mollify him and Kyle remained in the closet. I'm not sure but I think Kyle Kerkin and Gregory Hesse were set up by Dylan Lashay."

"Set up as in framed?" Marge asked.

"No, set up as in Dylan the matchmaker. For his services, Gregory Hesse probably edited all Dylan's papers and Kyle gave him a gun. A good arrangement for everyone."

"So Gregory Hesse was gay?" Marge appeared skeptical.

"According to Kyle, yes."

"What about that girl in the snapshots giving Greg a blow job?"

Decker said, "You didn't see a face, right?"

"Right."

"Kyle Kerkin has shoulder-length dark hair."

"Aha. Okay, now I'm feeling it."

"This is the gruesome part. According to Kyle, Gregory Hesse shot himself in front of Kyle and Dylan Lashay, who was filming Greg playing around with his gun."

"God! That is sickening!"

"Repulsive." Decker shuddered. "Kyle claims that the shooting was an accident. The gun wasn't supposed to be loaded. Kerkin could be telling the truth, or he could be spinning total lies."

Marge said, "Who gave Gregory Hesse the gun?"

"Kerkin claimed that Dylan provided the gun. It could be that Kyle is using Dylan as his way out."

"Even so, if it did happen, thank God that Mrs. Hesse never found the camcorder." She looked at Decker. "Does Kyle have the camcorder?"

"Kyle claims Dylan took it when the two of them left Greg's house."

"You know that's really odd," Marge said. "We didn't find any bloody footprints or anything to suggest that other people were there when Greg shot himself."

"Maybe the two of them were far enough away that they didn't get any blowback. Or maybe the entire story is bullshit. Kyle only talked to us because he was still under the idiotic notion that he could weasel his way out of charges. When he asked us if he was still under arrest and we said yes, that's when he asked for a lawyer."

"He really thought you were going to let him go?"

Decker said, "These particular kids have mastered the art of glib. They know how to behave in front of adults. And as of his eighteenth birthday, Kyle has joined the ranks of adulthood."

"Kyle was packing when we picked him up," Marge said. "He's toast."

"Yeah, it looks like we have plenty of stuff against all of them, ranging from kidnapping and attempted murder to gun and drug charges. It would be great if we locate Gregory Hesse's camcorder."

Marge said, "I'll go pull warrants. If the camcorder is around, I'll find it."

"Oliver has already called up Cruz Romero for the warrants on Dylan Lashay, Cameron Cole, Kyle Kerkin, and Darla Holbein: both house and school. If Gabe is able to ID JJ Little and Nate Asaroff, we'll get warrants on them, too. As much as I'd love to be there to toss the houses, I can't. You'll have to supervise."

"I'll take care of it," Marge said. "When I get the warrants, I'll go to Bell and Wakefield first: do all the lockers at the same time. I'll send Willy to Dylan's house, Drew to Kyle's, and Wanda to Cameron Cole's house. When I'm finished with B and W, I'll go to the houses and supervise the others."

"Perfect," Decker said. "We're looking for guns, drugs, and any stolen items—especially things associated with Gregory Hesse."

Marge said, "Did you find any connection between Myra Gelb and the B and W Mafia?"

"She hasn't come up yet, but we've just started."

"So what do you think Gregory Hesse's 'big story' was—if anything?"

"No idea." Decker heard his name and turned around. Wynona Pratt gave them a wave. She wore a thin green sweater under a green glen plaid jacket, brown trousers, and boots. She looked as if she were about to go hunting, and in a way, that's exactly what she was doing. "Darla Holbein is with her parents in your office. They'd like to see you right away."

"They asked for me by name?"

"They're in your office and figured out you're the big cheese. What would you like me to say to them? Do I tell them about Gabriel or . . ."

"I'll come in, introduce myself, and explain the situation. Then if they still want to talk to me, it's their choice."

"How about like right now?" Wynona said. "The Holbeins are deeply religious. They keep telling their daughter that she needs to tell the truth, that it's the moral and Christian thing to do."

"And they haven't asked for a lawyer?"

"Loo, they have a lawyer with them—a man from their church. He has talked to Darla and apparently feels comfortable enough for Darla to talk to us. Her parents keep saying that this is Darla's last chance to come clean before God. The lawyer keeps saying that Darla is lucky because she's still a minor. I think everyone's hoping the D.A. will go easy on her."

"At her age, she probably won't catch much of a break. It all depends what she has to say. I'll be there in a minute."

Oliver broke into the huddle. "I just got off the phone with Dylan's stepfather—Roy Lashay. He and his wife are on their way to see Dylan with a lawyer in tow."

"Where is Lashay?" Marge asked.

"He was transferred to Van Nuys about an hour ago," Oliver said. "I've called the district attorney's office to give them a heads-up. But one of us is going to have to be there before he's arraigned."

"So many charges, so little time," Decker said.

"When will that be?" Marge asked.

Oliver said, "A couple of hours at the earliest."

"What about the warrants?" Decker asked.

"I'm off to see the judge," Oliver said.

Marge said, "After you've gotten them, wanna go to Bell and Wakefield to search some lockers?"

"Yeah, I can do that." Oliver regarded Decker. "A word of warning, Rabbi. Roy Lashay is fuming. He's claiming that Dylan was attacked by the girl and Gabe—who he kept calling Chris."

Marge looked at Decker. "I told you that the robbery was the agreed-upon story when we arrested them."

Decker said, "Seems that not everyone is sticking to the script."

Oliver said, "Lashay was very aggressive. He said his lawyer was going to get everything thrown out because you and everyone else who works for you are obviously biased. He also called up Dylan's biological father, who's apparently this kingshit civil lawyer. Lashay also promised that we're going to get sued civilly as well as criminally and by the time he's done, none of us will own a cent."

Decker raised an eyebrow. "It's an obvious plan of attack and one that's not totally without merit. I am vulnerable."

Marge said, "Who is Dylan's criminal defense attorney?"

Oliver blew out air. "Sanford Book."

"Well, he's pretty top-notch," Decker said.

"And who's Lashay's kingshit lawyer/biological father?" Marge asked.

Oliver paged through his notes. "Maurice Garden. I don't know anything about him, but I don't know too many civil lawyers."

"So why do I think I know him?" Marge said.

Decker said, "Google him. And while you're at it, maybe we can find out why Dylan took his stepfather's last name. There has to be a story there."

"Maurice Garden..." Marge googled his name on her cell phone. "Oh my goodness gracious!" She grabbed Oliver's shoulder. "Scott! The doctor we saw. Olivia Garden!"

Oliver hit his forehead. He turned to Decker. "The gun that Gregory Hesse used to shoot himself was stolen from Olivia Garden's office about six years ago."

Decker felt his heartbeat quicken. "Are she and Maurice related?"

Marge continued her Google search. "He is a civil lawyer... divorced six years ago and remarried... four children. His current wife is named Lily. It doesn't say anything about Maurice's parents."

"Look up Olivia Garden," Decker said.

"Okay here we... Dr. Olivia Garden... went to UCLA Medical School... board certified... married... aha! She has two sons, Maurice and Jonas, both of them lawyers." Marge grinned. "I think we have a love connection, guys."

"Both the divorce and the theft happened around six years ago," Decker said.

Oliver said, "Maybe little Dylan went to Grandma for support."

"And guns," Marge said.

"He would have been around twelve," Decker said.

"Right around puberty," Marge noted. "When all that testosterone kicks in, turning snips and snails and puppy dog tails into snarling pit bulls."

Darla's long hair hid most of her face, but the part that Decker did see was mottled and streaked with tears. Her blue eyes were swollen and red. She favored her father, Dominick, with his round ruddy face and blue eyes. Her mother, Marie, had dark eyes, high cheekbones, and short clipped gray hair. No jewelry, no makeup for Mom. Dad was dressed in a black suit, a pressed white shirt, and blue tie, almost identically to Cecil Quiller, Darla's legal representation.

After introducing himself and explaining the situation, Decker was sure that the lawyer would jump on the bias angle to get his client out of her jam. But it was Marie Holbein who spoke up.

"The boy who was attacked is your foster son?"

Decker said, "Not technically. I don't receive any money from the state. The kid needed a place to live, and my wife and I decided to provide him a home until he was able to go out on his own."

"So you are also a servant of God," Marie said.

Now that was a good sign. Decker said, "Just doing the boy a favor."

The lawyer said, "But you do have a personal involvement with the boy."

Decker said, "Absolutely."

"And you're probably more willing to believe his account of the events than the others."

"Counselor, I've recused myself from the active part of the investigation. That's why you're with Detective Pratt and not with me."

"What do you mean by the active part?" Quiller asked.

Wynona piped in. "He's been acting as a traffic cop. Put this one in room one, get a photo array, pull a warrant. Things like that."

Decker said, "I haven't been actively interviewing any of the teenagers unless someone has specifically wanted to talk to me."

"Has that happened?"

"Yes, that has happened."

Marie held up her hand. "We are not here to absolve Darla on some kind of technicality, Lieutenant. That may work with other parents . . . they think they are protecting their children. In fact, they are making matters worse because what they are doing is morally wrong. Dominick and I do not defend our children at all cost. If we do that, we're not helping Darla."

"And I'm in absolute agreement with my wife," Dominick said.

The two of them were a cop's dream: they were also Darla's worst nightmare.

Marie turned to her daughter, her eyes shining with fervor. "Darla, if you possibly hope to live a moral life, you must clear your conscience before God."

The lawyer spoke up. "I agree with you, Marie, from the standpoint of a practicing Christian. But I do believe that I must also function as a lawyer and do what I can for Darla legally." Quiller turned to Decker. "She's a minor. I want her records sealed. Absolutely no jail time even in a juvenile facility. No probation, no community service. The church will make sure she pays back for her sins. But she walks away from the horrendous fiasco without a blemish."

"Do you want me to function in my official capacity even though I'm involved with Gabriel and he lives with me?" Decker asked.

Quiller said, "If you have the capacity to help Darla out, I will be happy to work with you."

Decker sat down. "Charges are pretty serious. It depends on what she has to say."

"I know what she has to say, because she's already spoken to me. Darla has never been in any kind of trouble."

"When she was arrested, she had crystal methamphetamine in her possession."

Quiller said, "Darla has a substance abuse problem, which we are now aware of. As part of the plea bargain, I guarantee you she will go to rehab. All we want is for her to do community service within the confines of the church. We have a program in Africa. It will be perfect for someone as bright as she is."

"You know that the D.A.'s office is responsible for okaying any plea bargains."

"But you can make recommendations. That's what I'm after. Besides, after you hear what happened, you'll be comfortable with your decision. Darla can tell you many things that would be invaluable."

Decker looked at the tape recorder on the desk. To Wynona he said, "This is working?"

"Yes. I've tested it several times."

"Good." Decker said, "If you want me involved, I'm here to listen."

All eyes focused on the teen. She flipped her hair behind her ears and bit her lower lip. When she did finally speak, her voice was barely audible.

Chapter Thirty-Five

D id Gabe ID . . . he did? . . . and he's sure? . . . Great! Hold on, Lee." Marge turned to Oliver. They were on their way to Bell and Wakefield after picking up the search warrants for Dylan Lashay, Kyle Kerkin, and Cameron Cole. "Gabe just IDed Kyle Kerkin, JJ Little, Darla Holbein, and Nate Asaroff."

Oliver, who was behind the wheel, pumped his fist.

Marge said, "Let's do this. Tell Willy to let both attorneys know that we just got positive IDs on their clients."

As Marge listened on the phone, Oliver said, "What's going on?"

Marge said, "Hold on, Lee, I'm putting you on speaker so Oliver can hear." She punched a button and turned the cell volume on high.

Wang said, "I just got off the phone with Willy who's with JJ Little. The kid is sticking to the robbery story, claiming he was the victim and Gabe was the aggressor. His attorney found out about the personal relationship between Gabe and the lieutenant and he's claiming bias. So Willy is going through the procedure by the book. He's setting up a six-shot photo array with Gabe as part of it."

"Good idea for a couple of reasons," Marge said. "Let's let JJ pick Gabe out, especially since Yasmine couldn't ID the kid. That way JJ can't backtrack at some point and say he wasn't even there."

"That's what we're aiming to do. Put all the aggrieved parties at the scene of the crime and then let the evidence sort it out. Neither JJ nor his attorney knows that Gabe's been shot. When they do find out, they may change their strategy."

"Look, Lee, in order not to appear biased, I want someone to go down to the Deckers' house and check out Gabe's room. Get the Loo's permission to search and invite JJ's attorney to come along."

"Okay, I'll do that. What about the girl?"

"Do Gabe first. If he comes up clean, the girl probably won't be necessary. She's been through enough. I don't want to traumatize her further."

"Does Gabe use drugs?"

"I don't have any idea, but at least we'll be consistent. What about Nate Asaroff?"

"His attorney wants to deal."

"Asaroff is underage?"

"Yes. And as far as I can tell, he was just there."

"What did he have on him when we took him in?"

"A couple of ounces of pot, a couple of pills. He's a good one to flip depending on what he has to tell us."

"Who's with Nate now?"

"Drew Messing."

Marge said, "I'll call Drew as soon as I get off with you."

"What are you doing now?" Wang asked.

Oliver said, "We just pulled warrants on Lashay, Cole, and Kerkin. We're on our way to Bell and Wakefield to check out their lockers."

"Want me to help you out?" Wang asked.

Marge said, "I'd like you to meet us there. You can pick up the search warrant for Dylan Lashay's house and start going through it."

"No problem. What's the school's address?"

Marge gave it to him and hung up. Her next call was to the station house. Within a minute, Andrew Messing was on the line. Marge spoke. "Gabe Whitman just IDed Nate Asaroff. I heard his attorney wants a deal."

"You heard correctly, Sergeant," Messing drawled out. "The Loo put in a call to someone from the D.A.'s office to come down and speak to the parents. The kids are flipping faster than pancakes."

"What does Asaroff's attorney want?"

"All charges against him dropped in exchange for his story. He also pointed out that Nate is a minor. He's two months shy of eighteen."

"We could try him as an adult. As far as the charges, it depends on what he has to say and what the D.A. thinks. Call me back after you've got him on tape."

"Yes, ma'am."

Marge disconnected the cell just as Oliver pulled into the visitors' parking lot. He hunted around for a space. "Here we go." He slid the car into a slot and shut off the motor. "I think Martin Punsche might be a little upset by our drop-in visit."

"He may be miffed."

"I wonder how he'll spin this latest turn of events to B and W's full-tuition-paying parents."

A moment of silence, then Marge snapped her fingers. "I got it."

"Tell me."

"What the kids did wasn't an attempted kidnapping at all." She grinned. "It was a performance *art* project."

"Perfect." Oliver opened the car door. "Too bad Dylan didn't have a camcorder. I'm sure lots of museums would have paid top dollar for the video."

Before coming to Homicide, Decker had worked a number of detective details, specifically six years in Juvenile and Sex Crimes with Marge Dunn. He had interviewed scores of teenaged felons whose emotional state ran the gamut from cocky to scared witless. But in all those years, Decker had never seen a girl as repentant as Darla Holbein. She started the interview with the following statement.

"I deserve to burn in hell."

Marie Holbein, Darla's mother, was unmoved. "If you don't get your act together, Darla, that's exactly what's going to happen. Stop with the dramatics and tell the lieutenant what happened this morning."

The girl mumbled something, and her father told her to speak up.

Darla wiped her eyes. "I just want to really say that I'm truly sorry. If the girl wants to see me and yell at me or hit me or . . . I am willing to do that. I would also be happy to do community service at the charity of her choice. And if she wants me to go to jail, I can do that, too. I'm not afraid of jail, because I can do penance in jail. I am afraid of God."

"Amen," Marie said.

"Amen," echoed Dominick, her father.

"I take full responsibility for my wrongdoing." Her tears were in full force now. "I am very grateful that Jesus has given me this chance to repent and to make things whole again. Our Lord died on the cross for our sins. I just want everyone to know that."

Marie bit her lip as her eyes became wet. "Jesus will forgive you if you do true penance. So start by telling the detectives what happened."

By now, both mother and daughter were crying silently. Darla said, "I slept over Cam's house. We have a project in Government that we've been working on. It was due today. So that's why I slept over her house." She regarded Wynona and then Decker. "When we have a group assignment, we always work together, although I do most of the work. I'm not complaining, just telling you how it is."

Wynona said, "Cameron is a good friend of yours?"

Darla looked at her mother. "We've known each other forever. We met as little kids in church. We went to all the socials together. She's a lot of fun. She's also gorgeous and attracts a lot of male attention."

"Being too pretty is the work of the devil," Marie said. "Look at the trouble it got her into."

"She's popular, yes, but it's more than looks, Mama. She's charismatic. Everyone gravitates to her. It can be fun to be her friend."

She kneaded her hands.

"About six years ago, her parents quit the church." She looked to her mother for confirmation. "About six years, right?"

"Yes. About."

"First her parents quit going to church. Then a few months later, they separated. It was very hard on Cameron. Then her mom got a younger boyfriend, and her dad got a real young girlfriend. Her parents just like . . . freaked. Cameron said they started drinking a lot—right in front of her."

"My daughter never told me," Marie said. "Otherwise I would have called Social Services on them."

Precisely why the girl didn't tell you, Decker thought. "So Cameron was around twelve when all this happened?"

"Yes," Darla said. "We were in seventh grade. At one point, they were all living in the house together—her parents and the boyfriend and the girlfriend. It was really hard on Cam. I think that's when she started smoking pot. I told her to stop, that drugs were the work of the devil, but she didn't listen. Pot was her refuge."

Marie said, "You should have told us immediately. We could have helped her."

Dominick said, "Even if the law wouldn't intervene, the church could have helped."

"I realize that now, Papa, but I was a little kid."

"You still are a child," Quiller pointed out. "If you tell the truth, I'm sure the law will take that into consideration."

"I am telling the truth," Darla said. "It is not only evil to lie, it's too hard." She wiped her eyes. "I figured the best thing I could do for Cameron was to be a friend and try to bring her back into the church."

"Okay," Decker said.

"The home situation lasted around a year and a half. Then right around eighth grade, Cam's parents decided to get back together."

Darla put her hand to her mouth.

"Something major happened, though. Cameron wouldn't tell me, but I'm sure it had to do with her mother's boyfriend. She went from hating him to liking him. They became real . . . close. You'd have to be an idiot not to know what was going on."

The tears began to fall.

"She changed. Cameron had always been an okay student if she worked hard. But she stopped working. She's smart but not smart enough to keep her grades up and do drugs at the same time. She started flirting with the smart boys to get help from them. That's how it started with Dylan. Despite what you think of Dylan, he's really smart."

"I don't doubt that," Decker said.

"He was kind of a nerd when she met him. He was smitten with her. All through ninth grade, he'd follow her around like a puppy dog. She introduced him to sex and drugs. Then somewhere during tenth grade, things reversed. Dylan started, like, working out. He grew taller. He also became real buff."

"Steroids?" Wynona asked.

"Yes. Steroids, too. Dylan became popular with guys as well as the girls. He started cultivating this bad-boy image. He attracted a loyal band of follow-ers. Drugs were a real big part of it. Dylan had money. He bought drugs and started giving them away for free. Then later he started charging for them, not too much at first, just to cover his own expenses. He said he wasn't making any money. Then later on, he started charging more money, especially for crystal meth." She looked away. "Once you're hooked on meth, it's hard to turn back."

Her eyes got wet.

"Cameron knew I didn't have enough money to . . . get what I needed. She gave me some, but she said there were other ways I could earn the money." She looked down. "So I did whatever she told me to do. I really needed the stuff." Her lower lip curled under and her face broke down. "It was all very humiliating."

She started to sob. Her mother put her hand on her head and leaned over and kissed her cheek. "God will love you if you truly repent."

"I do, Mama, I do truly repent. I just need a little help."

Quiller said, "You can see that the girl needs rehab, not jail."

"Jesus loves us all, Darla, saints and sinners," her father told her.

Wiping her eyes on her sleeves, Darla said, "Amen."

"You must confess your sins."

"I will, Papa, I promise I will."

"If you sincerely repent, God will forgive you," Marie reemphasized. "But part of atonement is admitting all your sins. You must tell the detectives what happened this morning."

Amen to that, Decker thought. He said, "We got up to the part where you slept over at Cameron's house because you were working on a project together."

Darla nodded and wiped her eyes. "Cameron was in a bad mood this morning. She met this boy . . ." She looked at Decker. "His name was Chris but then this morning, he said his name was Gabriel and that his father was like the real Mafia." She looked to Decker for confirmation, but he didn't respond.

"Go on," Wynona said.

"Cameron really liked him. He was cute and tall . . . taller than Dylan. She liked that. Dylan's well built, but he's on the shorter side. But the true reason Cameron liked him was because he stood up to Dylan. He knew way more about guns than Dylan did. Dylan thinks he's like an expert on guns." She turned to Decker. "How does your foster son know so much about guns?"

"That's none of your business, Darla," her mother said. "Let's get on with this so we can figure out your future."

Darla sighed. "Anyway, she liked him, but didn't do anything about it. Then one day she met him at a bus stop. She took that as an omen that something was meant to be. Whatever that means I don't know, but that's what she told me. She told me he was in a rock band and he was going to be famous one day. She had invited him to her house to get high, but he turned her down, saying that he had an important audition. It sounded like, you know, BS to me but I didn't say anything." She looked at Decker. "Is he in a rock band?"

Dominick said, "Darla, stop asking questions and just tell the detectives what happened."

The girl blushed. "Anyway, he didn't go to her house, but he asked for her phone number. She took his phone number, too. She expected him to call her, but he never did. She texted him, but it was the wrong number. Cam got real upset. She thought he was shining her on and she's not used to that. Then . . . oh boy . . . she saw him with another girl—some ugly dumb brownie . . . that's how Cam described her. She saw them kiss. They were clearly an item. It made her very mad . . . that he lied to her. More than that, that he liked a brownie over her. It was like instant hatred."

Wynona nodded, encouraging her to go on.

"I kept telling her to forget about it. That he was an obvious idiot, but Cam wouldn't let go. Then she got this 'brilliant' idea. She told Dylan that Chris had raped her and she wanted him to avenge her honor or something stupid like that. Now Dylan's a lot of things, but he isn't an idiot. He didn't believe her. He kinda laughed her off. But she kept at him. He raped me, he raped me, he raped me. Then one day . . . I was there . . . he turned to her and said . . ." She regarded her mother and father. "You might want to cover your ears."

Marie said, "Darla, we know bad words. We just choose not to use them. Go on already."

"Okay." She took a deep breath and let it out. "Dylan said to Cameron, 'What is it, bitch? You fucked him and want me to be all jealous.' And then he waved his hands in the air and oooohhh and laughed. Like he didn't care at all. And maybe he didn't.

"So Cam said, 'Yeah, I fucked him and he's a hell of a lot bigger than you are.'" She turned to Decker. "*That's* what made Dylan mad. So she got him to do what she wanted. The gang decided to crowd the girl. You know, just to scare her. So Cam called Dylan up this morning and said today was the day. I don't know why she picked today, but she did. Probably 'cause she was in a bad mood."

The tears returned.

"So we all met early in front of the place where Cam saw Chris with the girl. And we saw her coming to the front door. She pulled out her phone. And before she could make a call, Dylan came up from behind and put a gun to her back. Cam grabbed the phone and threw it in the bushes. Then we surrounded her and said stupid things."

"What kind of stupid things?" Wynona asked.

Darla's voice was choked with sobs. "It was all a big joke just to scare her. We were going to let her go."

"What kind of stupid things?"

"Dylan told her that he was going to . . . you know." Silence. "That he was going to take her and like . . ." She looked away. "That he was gonna like . . . and then Cam said that it was like . . . something like . . . a gangbang—"

Her mother gasped.

"He wasn't really gonna do it," Darla insisted. "The whole thing was just to scare her."

Wynona said, "To scare her with a gun?"

"It wasn't loaded!" Darla insisted.

"Did he threaten to shoot her?"

"I don't remember what was said." More tears. "Cameron and Dylan were telling her all sorts of stuff. And it was Dylan's idea to bring out the gun. He loves guns."

"And you thought it was okay to threaten her with a gun?" Wynona said.

"No, it's not okay. It's terrible!" She started crying. "I was terrible. But I knew that the gun wasn't loaded, so I wasn't really, like, scared for her."

"It wasn't loaded?"

"I found out later it was loaded when Chris fired the gun. But I swear I didn't know about it until that moment. I would have never . . . you know . . ." She looked at her parents. "I swear I didn't know."

"But you saw Dylan take out a gun."

"Yes."

"What did he do with it?"

"Put it on her back to scare her. But I swear I didn't know it was loaded."

"Okay," Wynona said. "So you crowded the girl and Dylan put a gun on her back. Then what happened."

"We started walking."

"Where were you going?"

Darla said, "To Cameron's house. Her parents leave for work early in the morning."

"What were you planning on doing to the girl at Cameron's house?"

"Just scare her a little."

"How?"

"Just . . . you know . . ."

"No, I don't know. Tell me."

"Just talking trash to her."

"About gang raping her?"

"No one was really going to *hurt* her. I would have never been a part of that."

Wynona said, "So you're crowding the girl, Dylan has a gun at her back, and all of you are on your way to Cameron's house."

She nodded.

"Okay. So . . . what happened next?"

Darla paused. "It happened so fast. We get to Greendale Park . . . then Chris appears outta no- where . . ." The tears reappeared. "Chris and Dylan start talking . . . and Cam says to Dylan that Chris raped her."

"And you know that's a lie."

"Yeah, of course it's a lie."

"Go on."

"So Chris told Dylan that he never touched her. And he and Dylan are going back and forth . . . and all these accusations are flying . . . and then the gun goes off and . . . the next thing I know is Chris is pointing a gun at my face, threatening to shoot all of us. Let me tell you something honestly. Chris was way more scary than Dylan 'cause he actually *fired* the gun. I was *petrified.*" She looked at Wynona and then her lawyer. "The only one who fired a gun was Chris."

"And you're sure about that."

"Positive!"

"And that's when you realized that Dylan's gun was loaded?"

"Exactly."

Wynona said, "Darla, do you know that if something happens and the gun discharges and someone gets hurt, you're responsible for the shooting even if you thought the gun wasn't loaded."

Darla nodded solemnly. "No one got hurt."

"Are you sure?"

"Yes, I'm positive. Like I said, the only one who fired the gun was Chris. And none of us were hurt so . . ."

Wynona said, "Chris's name is actually Gabriel."

"Gabriel . . . Chris . . . whatever."

Wynona looked at Decker who nodded. She said, "Do you know that Gabriel is in the hospital?"

Darla's mother became white. "What's wrong?"

"He was *shot*—"

"*No!*" Darla sputtered out. Her mother gasped. Her father turned ashen. "But that's impossible. When he left, he was *fine!*"

Quiller put up his hands to silence her. "How serious?"

Wynona said, "It's a gunshot wound."

"Is it possible that the boy shot himself?"

Decker said, "Highly improbable. From the gunshot residue on the wound, he was shot from a distance of about two and a half feet."

"It can't *be!*" Darla was trembling. "It's impossible."

Marie asked, "Is he going to live?"

"He's undergoing surgery," Decker said.

"Oh dear God!" She turned to her husband. "We have to pray for him."

"Later." Quiller turned to Wynona. "Who shot him?"

Wynona said, "That's what we're piecing together."

"What have you been told?"

Wynona said, "How much is your client willing to cooperate?"

Quiller said, "If she cooperates, what can you do for her?"

"Provided she's not the shooter—"

Darla said, "I've never shot a gun in my life! You already tested my hands for something."

Quiller said, "She came out clean."

"Maybe she washed her hands," Wynona said.

"I swear I didn't shoot anybody." The girl bordered on hysteria.

Quiller said, "If she cooperates and isn't the shooter, what can you do for her?"

Wynona looked at Decker who nodded. "What do you have in mind?"

"She's a minor, you know."

"She's seventeen, Counselor. We'd have no trouble trying her as an adult for kidnapping and attempted mur—"

"What!" Darla shouted out.

"Calm down, Darla!" Quiller said. "What can you recommend to the D.A.?"

"What do you want?"

Quiller said, "Before she does anything, she needs to undergo immediate rehabilitation for substance abuse. Substitute time in a rehab facility for time in a juvenile facility."

"I don't know if I can make that happen, Counselor."

"Well, that's a prerequisite for her cooperation. Also, if she agrees to turn state's witness, I want all the charges against her dropped. As I said, she'll undergo immediate rehabilitation for substance abuse and then afterward, her church will impose on her five hundred hours of community service."

Wynona said, "I was thinking probation plus two thousand hours of community service might cut it."

"No probation. I don't want her having any record. All charges must be dropped."

Wynona said, "I don't know if I can do that. The charges are serious."

"How about five thousand hours of community service. Mandated by the church."

"I can't answer for the D.A. Plus, the court must have proof that she's actually fulfilling her community obligations."

"How long is five thousand hours in days?" Marie asked.

"It's about three to four years working full-time," Wynona told her.

"That would be fine," Marie said. "The church is involved with several charitable programs in Africa. I will send her there immediately after rehab."

"What about the class trip and graduation?" Darla asked.

Her mother sneered. "You've *got* to be kidding me."

"I'd like to attend commencement. Say good-bye to everyone."

"Are you out of your mind? You can't step foot inside that place. You'll be lucky if Bell and Wakefield agrees to graduate you! When this all comes out, you'll be dirt!"

"If she's a state's witness," Wynona said, "it'll mean that the D.A. is going to want to know where she is at all times. Also, she'll have to come back from Africa if any of the other parties involved go to trial."

"Agreed." Quiller looked at Wynona. "And nothing is guaranteed from our side until it's in writing."

"I think we're okay with that." Decker stifled a smile. "But you know that a guarantee in writing thing works both ways."

Chapter Thirty-Six

This is what Dylan Lashay's school locker did *not* contain: porno, crumpled papers, pens or pencils, broken rulers, old protractors, random scraps of paper, junk food wrappers or rotting fruit, smelly gym socks, or old T-shirts.

This is what the locker did contain: schoolbooks and notepaper, two revolvers, two semiautomatics including an old Raven arms MP-25 commonly known as a Saturday night special, and a Taser. There were also several rocks of crystal methamphetamines, two used crack pipes, four boxes of ammo, two boxes of condoms, a roll of duct tape, fishing twine, two black ski masks, a box of latex gloves, and a box of blue trash can liners.

Marge had brought along a video camera to tape whatever they found, and how well did that work out.

She videoed and narrated as Martin Punsche cut the padlock off. She videoed and narrated as Martin Punsche opened the locker door. Then she videoed and narrated as Oliver, slowly and carefully, took out the locker's contents one piece at a time. When Scott was done, an arsenal had been neatly set out on a series of white towels. Then the two of them began the arduous process of bagging the evidence.

Marge said, "The co-eds of Yale don't know how lucky they are."

Martin Punsche had turned wan during the process, sweating as they pulled out one firearm after another, mumbling as often as not. "I . . . don't know what to say."

"No comment necessary." Marge picked up the SNS and unloaded the chamber.

Oliver said, "This is really scary."

The hallway had been cordoned off. Despite the best efforts of the faculty to keep the students away, there was a crowd of onlookers.

The boys' VP adjusted his tie. "I'm just . . . astounded."

"And when will the principal be back?" Marge asked.

"He's in Europe."

Oliver said, "You should notify him right away. He'll want to know."

"I will as soon as we're done here," Punsche said.

"That's going to take a long time," Oliver told him.

"I realize that but I have to watch the procedure . . . to make sure that nothing's planted." Feeling the heat of Oliver's glare, Punsche said, "No offense."

"None taken," Marge said. "We want everything done correctly. We're going to videotape every single piece as it goes into an evidence bag. And Detective Oliver is correct when he said that it's going to take a while."

So much time that Marge called Decker, explaining to him what they had recovered. "I know you can't do anything that involves you directly, but I don't see why you can't call up the court and get a time on Dylan Lashay's arraignment."

"I'll do that."

"Who's the D.A. in Lashay's case?"

"Nurit Luke."

"She's a shark," Marge said. "Exactly what we'll need. She should come down and look at all the evidence before she presents. Seeing what the kid amassed, I should be there as well."

"I think Nurit is on her way to B and W right now. I'll call the courts. I'm glad I can do something."

"Did Lee talk to you about a search of your house?"

"Yes. I gave him written permission. JJ Little's attorney is going along with him."

"Does Gabe do drugs?"

"So far as I know, he doesn't."

"Tell Lee to call me after he's done with the search."

"I will. What else?"

"I need some detectives to come down here to video and bag everything we took out of Lashay's locker. I can't leave all this deadly stuff unattended while we search other lockers, and if we have to bag and label the stuff ourselves, we'll be here forever."

"Hold on. Let me look around and see who's available." He came back on the line a moment later. "I'm sending Whittiger, Katzenbach, and Marin from Burglary."

"Thanks. That would be perfect."

Twenty minutes later, the three Burglary detectives showed up, allowing Oliver and Marge to concentrate on the two lockers belonging to Cameron Cole and Kyle Kerkin.

"Let's do Kyle first," Marge said.

Oliver did the videotaping this time. Once the locker was open, Marge looked around before she touched anything. There was a slightly off odor emanating from the space. No weapons upon first glance. There were several bags of weed judging by the look and smell. By and large, the contents were school related or junk food related.

"Okay, here we go."

Oliver began narrating as Marge pulled out the material inside. There were books, school papers, and a lot of trash and garbage—old school work, decayed food, and a wrinkled shirt that covered a dozen gay porn magazines. It took them another hour plus to finish off Kyle's locker. Again, everything was neatly laid out on towels, just waiting for the Burglary trio to finish up with Lashay and move on to the next array. At least the contents of Kyle's locker didn't contain anything lethal.

Marge's cell buzzed. "Dunn."

Decker said, "Lashay's arraignment is around six in the evening. But that's an estimate. It might be later."

She looked at her watch. It was already three-thirty. "Thanks."

"I'll keep calling. I'll let you know if there's a change in the docket."

"Did Lee Wang and Little's attorney go through Gabe's room yet?"

"Rina just called me. They're finishing up. The kid made it easy because he's real neat. The hardest part was going through all the junk that my sons left behind."

"Anything damaging?"

"No. But they took Gabe's computer."

"Par for the course. We've just gone through Kyle Kerkin's locker. Drugs and gay porn but no weapons.

We're on to Cameron Cole. I know Lee came back to the station house and brought the search warrants for the houses. Who's on what?"

"Brubeck is on Lashay, Wanda is doing Cameron Cole, and Messing is doing Kyle Kerkin. Holbein and Asaroff are being detained at Juvenile Hall. Both of their attorneys are willing to deal so we're just waiting on the D.A. to sign off. By the way, Little's attorney found out that Gabriel was shot about an hour ago. He's demanding to know who shot him. I think he's figured out that Dylan was the only one with gun residue on his hands. He just wants to hear it from us."

Marge said, "Once Wanda recovers the bullet, we'll know for certain that it's the .22, and Dylan will be toast. But that's not what I'm telling Kerkin's lawyer, because there's always an off chance that Kerkin's Luger or Glock fired *accidentally.* The kid was packing *two* firearms."

"No wonder Kerkin wants to deal."

"He deserves time," Marge said.

"Yes he does, and he'll get it. We've got a lot against Kerkin. His attorney will be grateful for any plea we give him."

"What are you thinking about?"

"We could go with anything from assault and kidnapping to illegal possession of firearms in exchange for testimony and limited jail time. Dylan's a bigger fish. If the bullet is a .22 and you combine it with the residue on Dylan's hand, we've got attempted murder on Dylan. If you add that to what you and Oliver found in his locker, you can stick a fork in him. He's done."

"That's very good."

"One thing in Kyle Kerkin's favor is the info on Gregory Hesse's suicide. Any luck in finding the camcorder?"

"Not yet."

"It'd be nice if Kyle wasn't lying."

"A kid in possession of two illegal firearms might have a veracity problem," Marge said. "Wasn't he the one who held the gun to Gabe's head?"

"Yes, and that is serious. We just have to see how much Kyle can give us and what Chris Donatti can live with."

Marge said, "He's not going to be satisfied with anything less than the death penalty."

Decker didn't answer her. Chris had his own way of dealing with things. Right now the safest place for Kyle Kerkin and Dylan Lashay was jail. He said, "If there are any changes in the arraignment times, I'll let you know."

"Thanks. We're going through Cameron's locker right now. I'll let you know what we come up with."

"Very good. Anything else you need from me, Sergeant?"

Marge said, "I really, really like all this power and deference you're giving me."

"I'm an old man. I'll retire one day."

"When you're gone, old man, I'm gone with you."

The wait, from being wheeled into the OR to returning to the hospital room after being in recovery, was three and a half hours. Gabe was groggy when they transferred him into the bed and immediately fell back asleep. The first time he stirred was at six in the evening. His face distorted in pain when he moved, and Rina rang for the nurse.

"Let's see if we can make you more comfortable," she told him.

He tried to focus on Rina's face. Everything was fuzzy. His insides alternated between electric shocks and dull throbs. He whispered, "Rina?"

"Yes, it's me."

"Can I go home?"

"I think they're planning to keep you here overnight."

"That sucks." It was too much energy to look around. He closed his eyes. "I hate my life!"

"I'm sorry, Gabriel." Rina took his hand, and he didn't resist. "I promise you things will get better."

A few minutes later, a fortysomething black nurse came in, reading Gabe's hospital folder. "Okay, young man, let's see what we can do for you."

"You can shoot me."

The nurse ignored him and injected a small bottle into his IV. "You should start feeling better soon."

Gabe didn't answer. It took too much energy to talk.

Rina sat with him as he dozed in and out of consciousness. Ten minutes later, Wynona Pratt walked into the hospital room. "Everything okay?"

"The surgery went very well," Rina said.

"I heard they did it with fiber optics or . . ."

"The surgeon used the path of the bullet to extract it."

Wynona held up an evidence bag. "Got it."

Gabe opened his eyes and said, "What caliber?"

"Pardon?" Wynona asked him.

"The bullet?"

"It was a .22."

"Dylan's gun," he mumbled. "Tell the Loo."

"I will," Wynona said. "You just concentrate on getting better."

"Anything is up from this vantage point," Gabe said.

Rina smiled. "You've got a wicked sense of humor, my son."

Gabe couldn't even muster a smile. He started to drift off and was awakened again—this time by a male voice. He opened his eyes. Still couldn't make out the facial features, but the guy was too short to be his dad. He didn't know if he felt physically better, but he felt a lot happier. "Nick?" he mumbled. "Is that you?"

"Yes, it is." The ponytailed piano teacher was in his fifties. He came over to Gabe's bedside. "How are you doing?"

The question seemed to stump him. "I dunno." A pause. "I feel kinda . . . high."

"High is okay. You just get better," Nick told him. "This morning's phone call took ten years off my life."

"Both of us," Rina said. "It was . . . shocking."

Gabe reached for his glasses, but winced in pain. Rina put his glasses on for him.

The boy grinned at his teacher. "Nick, Nick, Nick." He giggled. "I fucked up big time, didn't I?"

Nick said, "You are floating, my boy."

"I think so, my man, I think so."

"Demerol," Rina said.

"I'm sorry I fucked up." Gabe let out another giggle. "Jeff must be real pissed!"

"Jeff, like me, is concerned about your welfare, Gabriel."

"I think we're okay, then." Gabe held up his hands and wiggled his fingers. "See. No collateral damage."

Nick kissed the boy's forehead. "Just get better."

"Aw . . ." he said. "You care."

Nick smiled at him. "I do care. I may be a stern taskmaster, but I do have a heart."

"What a guy!" He gave a goofy grin. "Rina is kicking me out of the house. Can I live with you?"

"That is neither accurate nor fair." She kissed his hand again. "No, you cannot live with Nick. We've already made arrangements with your dad."

Nick said, "Anything you need, Gabriel?"

He started to say something, but his eyes stopped his mouth. Yasmine had walked through the door with her mother. She was still wearing her uniform from this morning. Her mother was wearing leggings under a shiny tunic and had on heels. Mom looked pissed off. He grinned at Yasmine. "Hi."

"Hi." There were tears in her eyes. "How do you feel?"

He let out a giggle. "It's tolerable as long as I don't move." A deep blush rose in her cheeks. *Uh-oh,* he thought. *Shouldna said that.* But he couldn't censor his mouth. "Isn't she *beautiful!*" he said to no one in particular. "Isn't she *sexy!*"

Nick extended his hand to Yasmine's mother. "I'm Nicholas Mark, Gabriel's piano teacher."

The smile was tight. "Sohala Nourmand." To Rina: a courteous hello.

Yasmine's voice was small. "This is my mother, Gabe. You met her once before."

"Hi, Mother." Gabe gave her a lopsided grin. "You've got a *beautiful* daughter!"

Sohala said, "Thank you very much for helping her. I will never forget your bravery and kindness."

Gabe continued to stare at Yasmine. "She is so gorgeous! So *sexy!*" He looked at Sohala. "I just *love* her!"

Sohala said, "I hope you get better very soon."

Gabe's eyes returned to Yasmine. "I *love* you." A smile. "I totally . . . *love* you." But instead of being happy, Yasmine started to cry. Gabe felt his own eyes watering up. "Ah . . . don't cry, cuckoo bird. Everything is going to be *terrific!*"

Sohala said, "Please feel better, Gabriel." She held her daughter's hand very tightly. "I am so sorry for your pain. You know it has been a very long day. We must go now."

"So *soon?*" Gabe's voice fell.

"Another minute, Mommy," Yasmine pled. "Please!"

"I'm sorry, but my family is waiting and we have much to explain," Sohala said. "We come back another time."

But Gabe knew there wouldn't be another time.

"Mommy, *please!*" Yasmine begged.

But Sohala was resolute. She continued to grip her daughter's hand. "Say good-bye, Yasmine, now!"

Yasmine swallowed back tears. "I love you, Gabriel."

Gabe had turned somber. "I love you, too, Yasmine." Sohala whisked her away. "Ba-bye," he said to the empty doorway. Wet rills coursed down his cheeks. "Well, that totally sucked."

Rina sighed. "I'm sorry."

"Not as sorry as I am."

Silence. Then Nick said, "I'll come visit you once you're out of the hospital."

Gabe was still staring in space. "I'm moving to Nevada, remember."

Nick turned to Rina. "Realistically, how long will that be?"

"I don't know, Nick. It's up to the lieutenant, and it's also up to Gabe's father."

Nick nodded. "If need be, Gabriel, I'll fly up every couple of weeks and give you a lesson."

Rina said, "That would be fantastic."

"If I'm still alive," Gabe said.

"Stop talking like that," Nick said. "I'm really sorry for what happened, but let's not forget the bigger picture. You're alive, your hands seemed unscathed, and you've still been blessed with enormous talent."

"Lucky me."

Nick patted his head. "I'll see you before you go to Nevada. Take care of yourself, Romeo."

As Nick left the hospital room, Gabe said, "Yeah, don't worry about me. I'll be fine." He looked at Rina. "How much can I pay you to do a Kevorkian?"

She kissed his forehead. It was hot and sweaty. He probably had a fever. "You look a little beat. Why don't you try to sleep?"

"You know when my dad's coming down?"

"No, sorry, I don't know. I'll call if you want."

"Nah." His eyes burned. "Don't bother. He'll come when he comes." He exhaled, and then winced. He squeezed her hand. "A nap doesn't sound so bad. Will you wait here while I sleep?"

"Of course."

"You're the nicest person on earth."

"Ask my kids about me when they were growing up. I'm sure you'd get a different perspective. But thank you for the compliment." She kissed his forehead again. "Take a little rest, okay."

His eyes were already closed when he nodded to her. Alone in his head, there were so many things to think about. It was nice that drugs didn't give him the option of staying awake.

Chapter Thirty-Seven

According to the docket, the arraignments, originally scheduled at around six, were now slated to take place around eight. Marge sat in the commissary at an isolated corner table, eating a Greek salad with little enthusiasm. Twenty minutes later, Nurit Luke joined her, coffee cup in hand. Nurit was five eleven, as thin as a stork. She had on her signature color—hot pink—this time from a jacket worn over black pants. Her accessories were big and chunky. She had flaming red hair, dark eyes, and she wore fire engine red lipstick.

"Where'd you get that?" Nurit was referring to Marge's salad.

"I think they still have a couple left, but I'm done with this if you want it."

"You sure?"

"Positive." Marge handed the plastic container to the lawyer. "Help yourself. I'm going to get some coffee. You want a refill?"

"Thanks. That would be great."

When Marge returned, Nurit was spearing the last bits of wilted lettuce. "I haven't eaten all day."

"Would you like me to get you something else?"

"No, this is perfect." She took the cup of coffee. "Thanks for the offer."

Marge sat and sipped. The brew tasted burnt.

Nurit said, "Want to go over all the charges so we're on the same page?"

"Sounds like a plan."

"The three seventeen-year-olds . . . Hold on." Nurit began rooting around her briefcase. "JJ Little, Darla Holbein, and Nate Asaroff . . . you know we could have tried them as adults."

"They should all do jail time, but we've got bigger fish to fry."

"I get it. I'm just saying . . ." Nurit looked at her notes. "I just spoke to Jack Leandro. They've been released personal recognizance to their parents. The girl, Darla Holbein, is getting off with three thousand hours of community service in her church in Africa and an additional thousand hours in the United States after attending rehab in exchange for testimony against

Cameron Cole. Darla can testify that it was Cameron's idea to initiate the kidnapping. After she's done her service, her records will be sealed and she's free."

Marge nodded.

"For the other two minor boys, I'm pushing for some jail time in a juvenile facility and then three years of probation."

"How much time?"

"Sixty days. They have to finish high school anyway."

"Is Bell and Wakefield offering them a diploma?"

"That's part of the deal: that the three kids will be allowed to receive diplomas as soon as they pass their finals in exchange for a gag order. None of them are allowed to talk about anything. The school just wants them out with minimum disruption."

"And the lawyers have agreed to jail time?"

"Not to the sixty days, no. I'm willing to halve the sentence. They'll go for that. But I'm going to insist on probation plus five thousand hours of community service. After they've given testimony for the State in the trials of the three others—should a trial be necessary— and after they've complete their mandated sentences, their criminal records will be sealed and they can walk away and pretend this never happened."

Marge nodded.

"Too easy if you ask me. Especially for Darla. She may not have initiated the kidnapping, but she didn't try to talk Cameron out of it."

"I know. But she'll be a credible witness against Cameron."

"Like I said, we need her. We don't need nearly as much testimony on Lashay and Kerkin. With the amount of weapons and drugs, they're screwed."

"What are you charging them with?"

"Everything from felony possession of drugs and firearms to kidnapping and attempted murder."

"Yo, Margie!" It was Oliver, his face tense and taut. He was holding an evidence bag. He grabbed a chair and sat down next to the women. "Glad I caught you both."

"How's it going?"

Oliver took in a deep breath and let it out. "Okay from a police point of view. As a person, I'm beat. We went through Cameron Cole's bedroom. In her bottom clothing drawer, we found a bunch of jewelry, including an aquamarine ring that had been inscribed to Sydney."

Marge sat up. "Oh my Lord! You found Sydney Holly's ring."

"What?" Nurit asked.

Oliver said, "Myra Gelb killed herself with a stolen gun taken from Sydney Holly's house. The gun belonged to her mother, but the ring belonged to her."

Marge said, "We now have a tie-in from that burglary to Cameron Cole."

"Who claimed that Dylan Lashay gave her the ring."

"That could be true."

"And if it is, it's probably the only true thing that ever came from her mouth," Oliver said.

Nurit pulled out a notebook. "Let me write this all down."

"That's not the big news," Oliver said. "We found Gregory Hesse's stolen computer and camcorder."

"Where?" Marge was tense.

"Brubeck found them, along with more firearms, in a cubbyhole deep in Dylan Lashay's walk-in closet. The computer has some sex stuff on it, but it's the camcorder that's truly nauseating. I have it in the bag. We need a private space because there's audio on it. My car is parked across the street."

"Mine's downstairs," Nurit said.

The three of them went down to the underground garage. Oliver took up the front seat, the two women sat in back. He put on a latex glove and took the camcorder out of an evidence bag. "It's been fingerprinted." He handed Marge a pair of gloves and then the camcorder. "There's no way to prepare you for this. Just push the play button when you're ready."

"Which one is it?"

Oliver turned around and pushed the button for her. Marge and Nurit stared at the pint-sized screen. Even in miniature size, the images were precise and clear. A smaller-than-life Gregory Hesse was leaning back on his bed, a mop of long brown hair covering his groin area. When the camera zoomed in, there was a close-up of Hesse's penis going in and out of a mouth. There was stubble and acne on the chin.

The voice-over said, "Yeah . . . do it, do it, do it."

"Who is that?" Nurit asked.

"Wait," Oliver said.

There was thirty more seconds of fellatio, then Gregory climaxed. The long-haired figure disappeared from the screen, and Gregory Hesse zipped up his pants. His eyes were waxy. His lids were half closed. He looked stoned no matter what the tox said.

The voice-over said, "You're the man."

In a slurred voice, Gregory Hesse said, "I'm the man."

VO said, "You really want to *be* the man?"

"Yeah . . . I am the man," Hesse said.

"No, you got to *be* the man, dude," VO said. When Gregory Hesse looked confused, VO said, "Now this is being the man."

There was a loud click on the tape. Lots of things can make a click, but Marge sensed where this one was going. It turned her stomach.

The VO said, "Your turn."

A second voice said. "Are you serious?"

VO said, "C'mon, KK, don't wuss out on me."

KK said, "You're crazy!"

"I'm crazy but I'm the man. I've demonstrated that. It's your turn."

A long pause. The camera switched from Gregory Hesse to Kyle Kerkin holding a .22. Kyle said, "Is this thing loaded?"

VO: What do you think?

Kyle: I dunno, asshole, that's why I'm asking you.

VO: C'mon, KK. Show your balls when they're not being licked.

Kyle put the gun to his temple. He was sweating. He pulled the trigger.

Click.

An audible sigh. Kyle handed the gun to Gregory. "Your turn."

The boy looked utterly addled as he held the revolver in his hand. He kept staring at the camera.

VO: You want to be the real man, you've got to be the man, dude.

Hesse: Is this loaded?

VO: You'll find out.

Kyle: C'mon, Dylan. Don't be a prick.

VO/Dylan: What do you think?

A long pause.

VO/Dylan: Of course it's not loaded.

Gregory: I dunno about this.

VO/Dylan: C'mon, dude. Nothing's gonna happen. It'll look real cool on camera.

Gregory: It's not loaded?

VO/Dylan: No, it's not loaded! You honestly think I'd give you a loaded gun?

Silence.

VO/Dylan: C'mon, Greg. It'll look supercool.

Gregory put the gun to his head.

Even though both women knew what to expect, the loud pop caused them both to startle. The screen sprayed a cloud of blood, brain, and bone as a wide-eyed lifeless figure fell backward onto the bed.

Someone screamed out a "Shit!" Then an agitated "Shit! Shit! Shit!"

In the background, someone else was laughing very hard.

VO/Dylan continued to laugh. With a giggle still in his voice, he said, "Oops."

Fade to nothing.

The figure was in the chair next to him, sitting forward, folded hands between his knees. The eyes were usually those of a shark, ice blue and completely without emotion. Today, they were idling in neutral. The minuscule hospital window framed black, contrasting to the space inside, which was brightly lit.

Gabe said, "Hey, roomie, whassup." When his father didn't answer, he said, "Can you get me my glasses?"

Donatti picked them up and placed them over his son's eyes.

Gabe pulled himself into a sitting position, his body throbbing in pain. Chris was dressed in a yellow polo shirt under a brown suede shirt jacket. The man was thirty-five and looked anywhere from twenty to sixty depending on how much he drank. Today he looked younger than his years.

Gabe's eyes focused on his nightstand, specifically a tray filled with comestibles. "What's that?"

"I think it's your dinner." Donatti perused the contents. "You got applesauce, cranberry juice, Jell-O, a couple of slices of white bread—"

Gabe interrupted with a groan. "I got hit in the ribs, not in the stomach."

Donatti reached into his bag and pulled out a fast-food hamburger. "Eat slowly."

Gabe took a bite, which fell into his stomach like a lead pellet. He threw it on his nightstand. "When do I get out of here?"

"After you've taken a piss and a shit."

"Seriously."

"I am serious. That's what the doctor said. He can leave after he's taken a piss and a shit." A pause. "He actually said after you've urinated and had a bowel movement, but I believe in brevity of words."

"How can I take a shit if I haven't eaten all day?"

"So fucking eat."

"Gimme the applesauce." Donatti rolled his eyes and Gabe caught it. It was going to be a very long stay in Nevada. After Chris gave him the applesauce, Gabe said, "Thank you."

"You're welcome."

"When'd you get in?"

"About an hour ago."

"What time is it?"

"You're just full of questions." Chris looked at his watch. "Almost eleven."

"Sorry to inconvenience you."

"No inconvenience." Donatti's voice was bland. "I finished what I had to do before I came here."

"You can go back if you want. I can fly into Elko by myself."

"Gabriel, don't be an asshole. I'm here because I want to be here. If I didn't want to be here, I wouldn't have come. Stop trying to goad me into losing my temper so you can hate me. It won't work."

"I don't hate you."

"Yeah, yeah. By the way, I e-mailed your mother and told her you've been shot."

"You *did*?" Gabe's eyes got wide. "*Why?*"

"I thought she should know."

"Did you tell her I'll be okay?"

"No."

Using his ordeal to get back at his mom. Gabe should have been incredulous, but he wasn't. "Can you e-mail her back and tell her I'm okay?"

"Do it yourself."

"I don't have my computer."

"Then I guess she'll just have to wait."

"You're such a bastard!"

"Tell me something I don't know."

Gabe glanced at his father's face, then looked down. He was too damn sore even to be nervous. "Let me ask you something, Chris. What if the bullet would have, like, gone through my hand and shattered it." He made eye contact with his dad. "I mean, what would you have done?"

"It's not what I would have done, Gabe, it's what you would have done."

"Would you still let me live with you?"

Donatti gave him a hard look. "What in the *hell* are you talking about?"

"I mean, I couldn't be a pianist anymore."

"*And . . .*"

"And I know how important that is to you . . . my career."

"You think that's important to me? That you become a pianist."

"You've always pushed me."

"Yeah, I pushed you. 'Cause you wanted to be pushed. But if you want to give it up, that's your decision. You don't want to go to Juilliard, go to Harvard. You don't want to go to college, come to Nevada and I'll teach you how to run whorehouses. You want to just fuck around and be a total washout, I'll support you. Just do what you want to do and if you don't know what you want to do, that's okay, too."

Neither one spoke for a minute. Gabe was still looking at his lap. "I do want it, you know. Music is my life."

"You have the talent to go all the way, Gabriel. Now it's just a matter of fortitude."

Gabe sighed, which made him wince. His heart was so heavy. He muttered, "I didn't even get a chance to say good-bye to her."

"What?"

"Yasmine. I didn't get to say good-bye. Her mom just yanked her away from me." His father remained stone-faced. "Forget it."

"What would you like me to say?"

"How about, 'That really sucks.'"

Donatti shrugged. "You get shot and you lose your girlfriend in a single day. That really does suck."

Strangely his father's words made him feel better. "I know you think I'm just a stupid kid, but I really, really liked her."

Donatti said, "I believe you. I wish I could make you feel better. If you weren't underage, I'd set you up with my whores. But I can't take the chance. Once you turn eighteen, I'll get you any girl you want—any body type, any hair color, any eye color, any race, any ethnicity, anything you want. Custom-made pussy. In the meantime, you're a good-looking dude. You shouldn't have any problems attracting twat. Once you get to college, you'll be fine."

Gabe stared at his father but didn't say anything.

Donatti shrugged. "Don't look so stunned. You should know me by now. I can't relate to anything I can't fuck. It's not that I don't have feelings. I do. But they're intertwined with sex and that's just the way I'm wired. Yes, it does suck that you lost your girlfriend. But my take on it would be: I'm pissed because I can't have sex with her anymore. So if I can't have sex with her, I'll find someone else. So I'm talking to you like I'd like to be talked to if I were in the situation. And that would be, 'Chris, you can't have A, so here's B.'"

Gabe glanced at his father. Then he said, "Can you pass me the hamburger?"

"Sure."

"Thank you." Gabe ate in silence. Then he realized he was starving, and ate the Jell-O and the bread. He said, "Are you sure you're okay with me living with you?"

"You know you could have moved in with me after your mom left. I thought you were better off with the Deckers. But now you're not. If Decker is saying get out of town, I take him seriously. And that's the end of the story. Just mind your manners and keep out of my way when I'm in a mood and we'll be fine."

"You're nothing if not honest."

"I'm not even honest. I'm a pathological liar."

Gabe laughed. "Yes, you are."

"Watch it. I can say it. You can't. And as long as we're having this heart-to-heart, let me tell you something. In the future, if you ever endanger your life when you don't have to, I'll take you out myself. I don't *ever* want to get that kind of phone call again. If it's a choice between her and you, it's her. No pussy is worth your life. Are we clear on that?"

"I would have done it all over again in a heartbeat."

"Then you're an idiot." A pause. "On the other hand, it's good that you can handle sticky situations. No father wants a pussy for a son." Donatti gave Gabe the cranberry juice. "Drink. If you have to piss to get out of this place, do it sooner than later."

"I could probably piss now."

"Go ahead. You've got to save it in a cup."

"*What? Why?*"

"I don't know *why*, Gabe. That's what the nurse told me. When he gets up to piss, have him save it in a cup. Maybe there is all sorts of important stuff in your piss that they need to look at. Maybe the doctor is a pervert. Just save it in a fucking cup, and I'll ring up the nurse."

"Oh God!" Disgusted didn't even begin to describe how he felt. Slowly he got up on his feet. His head was dizzy, and it took a few moments before he was sure he could walk without passing out. His bandaged chest limited his mobility, but he could move his arms well enough. He wheeled his IV with him into the bathroom, his hospital robe flapping open in the back, exposing his butt in the breeze. His dad just watched, not even bothering to offer any help. He came back several minutes later with a full cup of urine. "This is really demeaning."

The nurse walked into the room and relieved him of his cup. "Good boy."

"So where's my friggin' lollipop?" Gabe grumbled.

The nurse stared at him. Donatti smiled and said, "Thank you very much."

"You're welcome." The nurse took Gabe's arm and helped ease him into bed. "How bad are you feeling?"

Gabe felt contrite. "It hurts."

"I'll see what the doctor wants to give you." She looked at the empty dinner tray. "You ate. That's very good. Would you like something else?"

How about a shot of lead through my temples? "I'm fine for the moment, thanks." After the nurse left, Gabe said, "Chris, get me *out* of here."

"You did your piss. Take a shit."

"This is so degrading."

"Yeah, hospitals suck the big one. What'd you do to your arm?"

Gabe rolled up the sleeve on his hospital robe. "I got a couple of tats." When Donatti smiled and shook his head, he said, "I know. I'm an idiot."

"It's just so *wannabe.*"

"I wanted to do something for her." Gabe blew out air. "Now she's gone."

"And you're stuck with her name inked on your arm," Donatti said.

"Well, I still like it." He sighed. "It's all I have left of her."

"Roll up your sleeve again. What are the notes on the clef below the name?"

" 'Der Hölle Rache.' "

"You tatted opera on your arm?" Donatti stared at him. "Who *are* you?"

"I'm you if you were a nerd."

Donatti laughed spontaneously. "You're growing on me, you know that?"

Gabe said, "If I take a shit, do you promise I can leave?"

"I'll do my best, but I'm not in charge."

"You have a winning way with people."

"It's called a blinding smile and a firearm," Donatti answered. "They probably won't let you leave until tomorrow so why don't you just relax."

"Easy for you to say," Gabe told him. "You're not hooked up to an IV, bandaged like a mummy, and wearing a gown that shows your butt."

Donatti just shrugged. "You just got shot, dude. Live with a bare ass."

"Do you have anything else in the bag?"

"I have grapes, an apple, and an egg salad sandwich. Take whatever you want."

"I'll have some grapes."

Donatti pulled out a clamshell of green seedless. The nurse came back and took Gabe's vitals. Then she injected something in Gabe's IV. "This will help you sleep."

"Thanks." Gabe popped a grape in his mouth. "Sorry if I snapped at you before."

The nurse smiled and turned to Donatti. "You raised him right."

"Thank you," Donatti said. As soon as she left, father and son broke into laughter.

"God, that hurts!" Gabe was holding his side.

"When's my nomination as Father of the Year?" Donatti was still smiling. "So tell me what you were working on before you got plugged."

Gabe started talking music: the default topic between his father and him. He spoke of his lessons, his composing, his upcoming gigs, the pieces he was working on. Before he knew it, he had not only eaten all the grapes, but an hour had passed. Chris always had a way of listening that made you think he was really interested in what you were saying. The man oozed magnetism and charisma. Girls flocked to him because he was not only charming but movie-star handsome. Guys also clamored for Chris's attention, all of them wanting to be his best buddy. Chris didn't have any best buddy. He didn't have any buddies. He had chattel. Gabe could feel his energy flag.

Donatti said, "You look tired."

"Maybe a little." His eyelids felt very heavy. "Must be the drugs. Where are you staying for the night?"

"Here."

"You don't need to do that."

"It's midnight." Donatti yawned, took off his shoes, and plopped his feet encased in socks on the hospital bed. "Even if I had a reservation somewhere else, I'm too lazy to move. It's late and I'm beat. Go to sleep."

Gabe was silent. Then he said, "Maybe I'll try to go to the bathroom."

Donatti threw his head back and closed his eyes. "Go for it."

"Do I have to save that, too?"

"No one said anything about saving your shit. But don't worry about that, son. Even if you flush it down the toilet, there's always life to replenish the stock."

Chapter Thirty-Eight

Despite the emphatic protests of the A.D.A. Nurit Luke, the presiding judge did set bail for Dylan Lashay at five million dollars plus a surrender of his passport. Within three days, the boy was out and about, flaunting his freedom in a brand-new Audi.

Kyle Kerkin's lawyer reached a plea agreement with the D.A.'s office. The teen would be the state's witness against Dylan Lashay in the murder case of Gregory Hesse in exchange for the reduced charges of involuntarily manslaughter, kidnapping, and weapons violation. The plea included an eighteen-month sentence of prison time to be served at CMC (level II) in San Luis Obispo with a chance for early release depending on his behavior.

Cameron Cole was not implicated in Gregory Hesse's murder, but she was charged with attempted murder and kidnapping along with possession of stolen property. She also reached a plea agreement of one year of jail time served in Central California Women's Facility in Chowchilla.

Despite Decker's best efforts, he couldn't find any way to link Dylan Lashay with Myra Gelb's suicide. There was no doubt in Decker's mind that Dylan stole the gun from the Hollys' house. (Charge denied.) Decker was also positive that Dylan sold Myra Gelb the weapon. (Also denied.) But since the booty taken from the Holly house was found in Cameron's possession, not Dylan's, the stolen property was the heated debate of a "he said, she said." And with both of the parties shown to be adroit liars as well as psychopaths, the judge felt it was easier to go with the path of least resistance. Many charges were heaped upon Lashay, but burglary and Myra Gelb's death were not among them.

No personal link was found between Gregory Hesse and Myra Gelb, other than a few phone calls while working on the school paper. Perhaps Myra got the idea of suicide after Gregory's demise. She knew where to find a gun as did almost everyone in B and W. Myra had had problems before, and it could have been that the death of a schoolmate sent her over the edge. Even so, Decker just couldn't shake the idea that if he worked a little harder, if he dug a little deeper, he could have found something: the detective's curse. But there was always the future. No case is ever fully closed.

What really troubled him more than anything was Dylan's freedom while he was awaiting trial. He expressed his concerns to Marge on a hot summer day in August three and a half months after Gabe was shot. The station house's air-conditioning was languid at best, and the two of them were sitting in his office fanning their faces with blank sheets of paper even though Decker had an electric desk fan blowing around tepid air.

"Dylan's been out for months," Marge said. "Why is this still eating at you?"

"It just is."

"You can't allow that, Pete. If you do, he wins." Marge wiped her face with a tissue. Even wearing lightweight linens and cottons, she was still sweating. The heat and smog that hung in the San Fernando Valley's basin at this time of year were twin towers of oppression. "Are you still worried about the kids?"

"Honestly, I think they're fine; however, I will feel better once Lashay is behind bars." Decker paused. "Gabe's certainly okay. Chris will take care of him. I'm not even concerned about Yasmine since her family moved to the city."

"Is it Wendy Hesse then? I know she comes down to the station house and brings you cookies all the time. Do you feel responsible for her?"

"She is what got the ball rolling and, yes, I do want justice for her."

No one spoke. Marge said, "But it's more than that."

"I've seen Lashay hanging around. He drives that red Audi R8. The kid has charges of murder, attempted murder, and kidnapping hanging over his head, not to mention felony weapons and drug charges, and he's not even trying to blend into the woodwork. What is wrong with his parents?"

"I'm sure he's conned them just like he conned everyone else."

"There's denial and then there's stupidity," Decker said.

"I know that. But why are you thinking about it now?" Marge asked.

"Nurit Luke called me yesterday. Dylan's lawyer, Sanford Book, wants to meet with her next week."

"Ah. You think they're going to plea bargain."

"Why else would Book call Nurit?" Decker said. "My guess would be voluntary manslaughter down from premeditated murder."

"That's not going to happen. Not with Dylan laughing like he did on the videotape."

"Yeah, but the camera never ever showed his face." Decker looked pained. "I'm concerned."

"We have Kyle calling the person behind the camera 'Dylan' over the audio."

"Yeah, but without seeing him, you could paint a different scenario."

"Like what?"

"Something stupid. You could say Dylan was in shock and that's why he laughed. Or it wasn't really Dylan with the camera. Or Kyle was trying to implicate Dylan to get back at him for some reason . . . because Dylan broke his heart."

"That's stretching it."

"That's what defense lawyers do. They stretch the truth."

Marge said, "Nurit's a great lawyer. She isn't afraid to go for broke."

"That's what worries me. Suppose she goes for broke and we strike out?"

"Not with those charges."

"I hope you're right." Decker shrugged. "Let it go, right. It isn't up to me."

"Exactly. Let the attorneys battle it out. Even if they plea murder one to voluntary manslaughter, with the other charges of attempted murder, kidnapping, possession of stolen firearms, and drug charges, I would say that Dylan will do heavy time."

He exhaled. "I'm usually pretty optimistic. I just have a bad feeling about this."

Marge was quiet. "Isn't your vacation coming up soon?"

"Two weeks."

"That's great. Where are you going?"

"To that fantastic tropical isle of Manhattan. We're going to New York to help settle Hannah into Barnard and Gabe into Juilliard. Then we're going to visit my folks in Orlando."

Marge smiled. "Florida's nice."

"Not in the summer," Decker groused. "One of these days, Rina and I are going to take a real vacation. And when we do, I might never come back."

When Decker found out that it was New Mexico state police detective Romulus Poe on the line, he thought that, at last, he was in for some good news.

He thought wrong.

Poe said, "No sightings of Garth Hammerling, but we do have a dead girl."

Decker's stomach dropped as Poe described the psychosexual murder scene. He said, "Are you sure it's Hammerling?"

"No, we're not sure. But she has DNA and you have DNA and I thought if my DNA can get together with your DNA, I'll know who I'm looking for."

"I'll send you the profile we have."

Poe was silent for a few seconds. Then he said, "I am so goddamn *pissed* about this. It's like you handed me this guy on a silver platter and I screwed up."

"You didn't screw up, but I know the feeling."

"He was on my radar. I don't know how he slipped out."

"Don't beat yourself up," Decker said. "He slipped from California, he slipped from Nevada. If the cellular evidence matches, it'll be just one more state that'll have a warrant out for his arrest." A pause. "He seems to be making an eastward trajectory. If he keeps going this way, his next stop will be Texas."

"I pray to God that Hammerling is apprehended there," Poe said. "The Lone Star State has the death penalty and she's not afraid to use it."

Deputy D.A. Nurit Luke showed up at the station house in person and unannounced in a hot pink cotton blazer and black linen pants. Her red hair was neatly coiffed, but her makeup could use a refresh. She didn't look happy. When Decker came up to her from behind and tapped her on the shoulder, she jumped.

"Sorry," he said. "Are you looking for me?"

"No apology necessary. I'm discombobulated. And yes, I'm looking for you."

"The meeting didn't go well," Decker stated.

"Can we talk somewhere private?"

"That bad?"

She gave him a forced smile. He escorted her into his office and closed the door. "What's the bad news?"

"Dylan was a no-show."

Decker leaned forward on his chair. "He was scheduled to be there?"

"He was scheduled to be there, he was supposed to be there," Nurit said. "Book was serious about a plea bargain. Book showed, his secretary showed, and Dylan's parents showed. After thirty minutes of waiting, the team went into phone-call mode. He isn't answering his cell, and no one seems to know where he's gone."

"What about his car?"

"It's still in the garage." Nurit fiddled nervously with the straps of her bag.

"Okay," Decker said. "When was the last time anyone saw him?"

"His mother claimed she saw him just a few hours before the meeting."

"I'll send out an APB right away. I'll also have my people start calling up the airlines, the bus lines, train lines, rental cars, and taxi cab and limo services. He couldn't have gotten very far if he left just a few hours before the meeting."

Nurit continued to play with the straps on her purse.

"You don't believe the mother, do you?"

"No."

"Even though the family stands to lose five million dollars?"

"I don't believe her at all."

"You think Dylan is long gone."

"Yes. I think he left as soon as Book wanted to deal—a sign that Dylan would have trouble with a jury trial. That his car is in the garage means it wasn't an impulse flee—something that had been planned a week ago."

"So Dylan could be anywhere."

"Yes."

"Good Lord . . ." First Hammerling, now Lashay. It's enough to give vigilantism a good name. "Okay. We'll start an investigation. The first thing to do is to try to retrace his steps."

"God, I'm pissed."

"I am, too." He paused. "I'm going on vacation this Friday. Marge'll handle this. She's been in charge from the beginning anyway."

"Actually, I called her before I called you. She isn't picking up."

"That's right. She has a court date. She should be out in a couple of hours." He picked up his phone. "If you'll excuse me, I have to make a couple of calls."

"You're calling up the families?"

"Yes, I'm calling up the families. I have to let them know."

"Man, I don't envy you at all."

Decker gave her a sick look and punched in the Nevada area code. He chose Donatti first because he knew the number by heart.

The visit to Olivia Garden's office was a pop-in, and because the doctor wasn't expecting the police, the detectives had to wait until she was between patients. Ten minutes later, the doctor's secretary took them into her personal office. Ten minutes after that, the white-coated physician came inside and shut the door. She sat down behind her desk and wiped her face with her hands. She was all business.

"What can I do for you?"

Marge said, "It's about your grandson, Dylan Lashay."

"As if I didn't know." Her eyes became very sad. "I've been just sick about this. Just . . . sick!"

Oliver said, "Dr. Garden, I understand the love between grandchild and grandparent. It's a deep-rooted relationship that's based on nothing but adoration. I have grandchildren of my own, and I find it's the sole reason to have children. But I must tell you this. If you're hiding Dylan, you are hiding a fugitive. You are breaking the law. You've made a life for yourself. Don't jeopardize it for a man accused of murder, attempted murder, and kidnapping."

"Dear God!" A heavy sigh. "I wish I could help you, Detective. But I haven't seen Dylan in years. When his stepfather adopted him, Dylan cut all of us out of the picture at the insistence of his mother."

"How did your son feel about that?"

"It's complicated," the doctor replied.

Marge said, "When we came and visited you the first time, did you have suspicions that Dylan stole the gun."

"No. I didn't suspect anything!" Olivia was adamant. "Once everything came out, I put two and two together. It made me absolutely sick!"

"Dylan had access to your gun?"

"I suppose he must have." A heavy sigh. "My son isn't really Dylan's father. I found that out later on. At the time of his divorce from Cresta—Dylan's mother— Maurice thought it would be good for Dylan to spend some time at the office. He thought that being near me would be palliative for Dylan's fragile nerves. We were always close, and when the divorce was announced, Dylan *seemed* so vulnerable."

"You think he was faking it?"

"No, I don't think he was faking it at all. Dylan was a quiet child, with his mother always screaming at one thing or another, so who could get a word in edgewise."

"What do you mean that your son wasn't Dylan's father?"

"Cresta had a fidelity problem."

"Who is the biological father?" Oliver asked.

"According to the law, it's Maurice because he was married to Cresta at the time of the conception. According to the paternity test, it was Cresta's plastic surgeon."

"How'd your son find this out?" Oliver asked.

"Maurice became suspicious of the paternity after he found out about Cresta's numerous affairs. It came to a head when Cresta became pregnant with Roy's child, who is now six." A heavy sigh. "The deal was that Roy would adopt Dylan, and Maurice would keep quiet about not being Dylan's biological father. Roy also offered to take over child support. At first, Maurice declined. Dylan was his de facto son whether or not there was a biological connection. But Cresta made a continuing relationship so difficult. After a year or so, Dylan didn't show any interest in Maurice, especially after my son remarried. It was one of those situations that just evolved. When Roy offered again to adopt the boy—something that both Dylan and Maurice's new wife clearly wanted—Maurice caved in."

"How'd you feel about it?" Marge asked.

"Devastated. He was my first grandchild." She wiped a tear from her eye. "My little boy was sweet and funny and so very smart! I thought he would surely become a doctor. If there were warning signs, I didn't see it. No cruelty to animals, no fires . . . he did wet his bed until he was six but that's not unusual for boys. He just seemed like a wonderful, exceptionally bright boy."

"He still is very bright," Marge said. *He'd probably do great in prison,* she thought. *If they ever found him.*

Oliver said, "Do you have any idea where he might be hiding?"

Her eyes watered again. "The truth is I don't know where he is. As I told you, I haven't talked to him in years. But the other truth is that even if I did know where he was, I don't know if I'd tell you."

Marge assessed the doctor and decided that she believed the woman, that she truly didn't know where Dylan was. What Marge felt was beyond pity. Olivia Garden was suffering something that Marge couldn't even imagine.

"Thank you for talking to us." Oliver handed her his card. "If he does call you . . . you know the drill."

"I know the drill."

But neither Marge nor Oliver expected to hear from her again. Marge could have added something very coplike—that it was the doctor's duty to tell them if she found out information. After all, Dylan had caused the death of a young boy with a gun that *he* had stolen from *her* desk. But what purpose would reiteration have served?

So Marge said nothing.

There was pouring salt on the wound. And then there was just plain cruelty.

Chapter Thirty-Nine

Gabe had parked two blocks away from the all-girls' school in a neighborhood of small ranch houses and manicured lawns. Even though it was eight in the morning, there were people on the streets: a few elderly bundled-up women wearing head coverings dragging steel shopping carts, young mothers with pink noses pushing baby strollers, black teens shooting hoops on an asphalt lot that might have been a park in its younger years. He had brought along a stack of books and his iPod to entertain himself while he waited.

The whole thing could turn out to be an exercise in futility because he never heard back from Ariella. She was the supposed messenger between Yasmine and him—the reason why he was caged in his car for who knows how long on a brittle, overcast January day.

He hadn't heard a peep from Yasmine in the last eight months. As far as he could discern, she had walked off the face of the earth. There was no phone number, no computer address to receive e-mails, and her Facebook had been shut down. So Gabe had used the old-fashioned method to contact her. He wrote letters, all of them going unanswered. Ariella was his last-ditch effort to make contact.

I don't see her anymore, Gabe, she had told him. *Her parents moved and she lives in the city. She goes to another school and we lost contact.*

Please, please try for me, he had begged her. *Just tell her I'll be outside her school for the entire day.* He gave her the address of where he would park and the description and license plate of his car—his second-most-prized possession, the Steinway being numero uno.

I don't know if I can get hold of her, Ariella had said.

Just try. With resignation, he said, *Just tell her I'll be here. If she comes, she comes. If not . . . well, then I'll know.*

The entire morning dragged. By midafternoon, he got a sinking feeling. By four, he almost decided to get out and go look for her. But that would defeat the purpose.

If she comes, she comes. If not . . . well, then he'll know.

By five o'clock his stomach hurt. He hadn't eaten all day except for an apple. No big deal really. Fasting wasn't anything new to him. He had dropped twenty pounds in the last eight months.

How's she doing? he had asked Ariella.

I told you, we lost contact. A pause over the phone. *Not great.*

Join the club, he thought to himself.

It was almost dark. He could feel a bottomless pit of sadness gather inside his chest. He'd give it another half hour. By then . . . well, then he'd definitely know.

He leaned back in the seat of his Beemer, his iPod fixed to Brahms, and closed his eyes. It seemed like only a few minutes had passed, but he must have fallen asleep because the knock woke him up. He saw her through the window and his heart started thumping. He opened the lock and she slid inside the passenger seat, closing the door as she sat down.

"I only have about ten minutes." She didn't look at him when she spoke, her eyes on her lap. Her hair had been pulled back in a ponytail, exposing a severe jawline. She was painfully thin even though she was wearing an oversized sweatshirt and a long plaid uniform skirt.

"Thanks for coming." No answer. "How are you?"

A shrug.

"How's school?"

"S'right." Another shrug. "It's okay. No boys."

"You don't like boys?"

"I hate boys."

Gabe rubbed his eyes under his glasses and stuck his hair behind his ears. He had grown it out until it brushed his shoulder blades. It had become his trademark at school. "I hope you don't hate *all* boys. I hope you don't hate *this* boy. Because this boy still loves you very much."

No response. Not even a tear.

He sighed. "Yasmine, just look at me and tell me that it's over. Say that to me. Say, 'Gabe, it's over.' If it's over, it's over. I'll be heartbroken, but at least then I can attempt to move on." A pause. "Anything's better than being in limbo."

She glanced at his face. "You look like a ghost."

He clenched his fists, and then folded his arms across his chest. "Thank you very much, Yasmine; it's good to see you, too."

Silence. Then she whispered, "I don't know why I said that. I'm sorry."

He didn't answer.

She swallowed hard. "It *is* good to see you."

Gabe softened. "I do look like a ghost."

"No, you don't."

"Actually yes, I do. My nickname at school is the Wraith. I'm six one and down to one thirty. To call me skin and bones would be a compliment."

"You look great."

"I look terrible. It's what happens when you're penned up in a practice room for six hours a day *after* a full day of school. Instead of all that pure California sunshine, you get rain and snow in New York. So you wind up with a pasty complexion, zits on your forehead, and bags under your eyes. And that's on a good day."

"Gabe, *please*. I'm sorry."

"No apology necessary. It's true. You should see me in school, floating down the hallway with my greasy hair fluttering behind, my eyes looking very intense and focused . . . like a phantom on drugs. I really do think that most of my classmates expect me to start actively hallucinating by the year's end."

"Please stop." Her eyes got wet. "I'm *really* sorry."

"I think I'm regarded like this modern-day Glenn Gould. I'm not within miles of being as good as Glenn Gould, of course. But my mates in piano think I'm good—a little out there in the quirk department but not without the talent to back it up. And that's not too bad actually. To be considered talented at Juilliard. It's a lot harder than I thought it would be."

She glanced at him and looked back down at his lap. "I'm sure you're still the best."

"It's like this . . ." Gabe uncrossed and crossed his arms again. "All your life you've been told that you're a genius, that you're the best. And then when you're five and you start competing, you realize . . . hey, you really are the best. And then you're ten, and you're still the best, but there are a few others who aren't far behind. And by the time you're sixteen, all the other mediocre competition has dropped out—the ones that were good but not good enough . . . and the ones that were good enough but only played because their parents cracked the whip to their back." He looked at her. "You can't be forced into this. You've got to *want* it."

She nodded with her eyes on her lap.

"And then you get to Juilliard," Gabe told her. "And you suddenly realize that all your classmates want it, too. So you just have to want it *more*. And hence the six-hour-a-day practicing . . . which is okay, really, because I want to make sure that I'm bone weary. That way, when I drop into bed at night, I fall asleep instantly and I don't have any time to think."

Yasmine wouldn't look at him.

"It's not too good to think, you know?"

She didn't say anything. She checked her watch— her old gold Movado—and Gabe caught it. "If you have to go, Yasmine, then go. I don't want you to get into trouble. And I certainly don't want you to be here if you don't want to be here."

But she didn't go. Instead, she spoke. Her voice was a monotone. "After you left for Nevada, my mother and I talked a lot. She said you were a remarkable boy, that you were handsome and smart and gifted and talented. That you would probably go very, very far. And that she could understand why I fell in love with you. And she also said that she could understand why you liked me. Because when I came along, you were very lonely. And I was cute and nice and I had a passion for music like you did. So she could understand what happened."

At last, a tear fell from her eye.

"But then she told me that now you're in college. And that you're not so lonely anymore. And that you're meeting other kids who are like you . . . who like music the way you do And since you're so handsome and smart and talented, many, many girls are going to like you. And you're going to like them back. And it's not your fault. You're a teenaged boy. And that's what teenaged boys do. They like girls."

She wiped her eyes.

"She also said that teenaged boys are way too young to *love* girls. That they think they love girls, but what they really love is sex with girls. And it's not your fault if you have sex with girls. Because that's what teenaged boys want to do. They have sex with girls. And when I argued with her . . . and when I told her that you really did love me . . . she told me that if you really did love me, you would have contacted me by now.

"So she told me to forget about you, that I should throw everything away that reminds me of you. And to help me along, she took my phone. So I no longer had our texts or all the pictures of you that I took on my phone's camera. And also she took away my computer and erased all my old e-mails, so I didn't have any of the e-mails we sent each other. And then she canceled my Facebook account so I couldn't even go online and look at your pictures or see your posts. Nothing personal should remain between us. She wanted everything that reminded me of you gone . . . destroyed."

A new batch of tears.

"But I still had my watch—my beautiful silver watch with the blue face that I loved so much. So every night I used to hold my watch in my hand and cry myself to sleep, thinking about how much I loved you. But then one day when I was gone, she went inside my room and took away my watch. So now I don't have *anything*."

Her crying became audible.

"So now when I cry myself to sleep, not only is my heart empty, my hands are empty, too. I have *nothing* to hold on to. And all I think about . . . before I fall into a wretched sleep is *you* . . . having . . . sex with other girls."

Yasmine clamped her hands over her face and sobbed.

Gabe reached over and pulled her fingers off her face. "Look at me."

She wouldn't.

He said, "Yasmine, I am *not* having sex with other girls . . . or with other boys for that matter." His humor fell flat. "It's all I can do to get out of bed in the morning."

"You're lying!" she sobbed.

"No, I'm not *lying!*" He tried to get her to look at him, but she refused. "I've never, ever lied to you. Take that back!" Nothing. "I'm serious. Take it back."

She continued to sob.

"I'm not this callow person," Gabe told her. "The whole thing was very traumatic. I still have terrible nightmares. From what you just said, it sounds like you're just as plagued as I am."

She was still crying. "It's . . . *horrible . . . just . . . horrible!*" She wiped her eyes. "I take it back . . . the lying part."

Gabe cracked a smile and shook his head. "Are you seeing someone to help you?"

"I tried for a while." She wiped her wet eyes and runny nose on her sweatshirt. "I stopped. I didn't like it."

"God, I couldn't live without my therapist," Gabe said. "You're stronger than I am."

"I didn't get shot."

"I didn't get kidnapped."

Silence.

Gabe said, "Yasmine, I don't want you to be mad at your mother, okay. I'm just telling you this so you'll know the truth. I wrote you at least six letters. Actually, I probably wrote you like fifty, but I tore most of them up. Your mom must have gotten to the mail before you did."

She still wouldn't look at him, but her face suddenly darkened with anger.

"Don't be mad at her," Gabe told her. "She's just being a mom. I know you can't ask her because then you'll have to explain your being here. But I swear to God that it's the truth. I mean, the last time I saw you was right after the surgery and I was loopy from all the drugs. I don't even remember what we talked about except that I said lewd things that made you blush."

She didn't say anything, but at least she wasn't crying anymore.

"I was zonked." He shrugged. "Sorry if I embarrassed you."

"I think that was the worst day of my life." She glanced at him—a start. "Do you ever get scared?"

"Like nervous? All the time."

"No, I mean scared . . . really scared about . . . you know. That he's coming back."

"You mean Dylan?"

She shuddered when he mentioned his name. "Yeah. Doesn't he *scare* you?"

"No, he doesn't scare me. Anger me, yes, but there's no fear." He paused, trying to organize his thoughts. "I lived with my father for around four months before I moved to New York. Actually three months because I was touring in July. Anyway, my dad is a total lunatic. Mostly I stayed out of his way and everything went okay." He bit his lip. "My dad did three major-league things for me while I was with him. He got me a piano . . . he got me a car after I got my license . . . and he told me that he had my back. I worry about lots of things, but Dylan Lashay isn't one of them. My dad's watching, Yasmine. I guarantee you he knows exactly where Lashay is at all times."

"He told you that?"

"He doesn't have to. I just know my dad. Don't worry about Dylan Lashay. I promise you that he's out of the picture."

"So if you don't worry about Dylan, what are your nightmares then?"

"My nightmare isn't about me getting hurt, it's about me not getting to you until it's too late." He looked at her, but her eyes wouldn't meet his. "What are your nightmares about?"

"That you don't get to me until it's too late."

He said, "Looks like we're occupying the same mind at night."

She gave a hint of a smile but still wouldn't look up.

Gabe said, "Sometimes it's so vivid, I wake up in a cold sweat. The relief I feel because it's only being a dream is overwhelming. God, I'm a mess."

Finally Yasmine garnered enough courage to look at him. In a tiny voice, she said, "Well, you're the best-looking mess I've ever laid my eyes on."

"Thanks for saying that." Gabe felt his throat swell up. "You know, Yasmine, we're not always going to be this young." He swallowed hard. "If you promise me . . . that when you're eighteen . . . you'll come to me—you'll come to New York and we can be together and we can give each other a real chance—then I swear I will wait for you. And you know what? It won't even be hard. Just like Jacob worked for Rachel, the years will seem like days because the reward at the end is so perfect."

He stroked her cheek.

"Promise me that you'll come. I don't want to go on like this. We're both in bad places right now. Let's be wrecked together."

Yasmine didn't talk for a long time. Finally she nodded. "I promise, Gabriel. When I'm eighteen, I'll come to New York to be with you."

"You swear?"

"I swear." Her fingers sifted through his long hair. "And you'll wait for me?"

"I swear I will wait." He took her hand and planted it with kisses. "I still love you madly. The more I'm away from you, the more I realize that."

She managed a tearful smile. "I love you, too."

Gabe let out an exhalation of utter relief. "New York is a good place to go to school anyway. There are zillions of colleges."

"My parents will never pay for me to go to college in New York."

"You get whatever scholarship you can and I'll pay for the rest. I have money."

"I won't take money from you."

"Why don't we worry about that in three years?"

Yasmine thought for a moment. "Maybe they'd pay for Barnard. It's a girls' school."

"Barnard would be great." He looked at her. "Did you know they have a music program with Juilliard and the Manhattan School of Music? You could study singing." A pause. "Do you still sing?"

She shook her head no.

"Now that is *criminal.* You have to come, Yasmine. Hannah goes to Barnard. She loves it."

"You see Hannah?"

"Yeah, I've seen her about once a month. She tries to feed me. If you go there, she'll show you the ropes."

Yasmine nodded, then gave out a heavy sigh. "You know, my parents will disown me."

"No, they won't."

"Yes, they really will."

He kissed her hand again. "Yasmine, when the time comes, have a little faith." She regarded his face. "Give me a chance to win them over. I can convert. I know some Hebrew, but I can learn to be fluent. I can learn Farsi. I can eat koobideh and Persian rice with a broiled tomato. I can arrive unfashionably late and give ridiculous parties where you don't start eating until eleven at night."

Yasmine laughed through her tears. "I would never ask you to convert."

"Why not?" Gabe answered. "You should ask me, because it's important to you. People are always reinventing themselves. I mean I can't change my skin color and I wouldn't give up music for anyone, but everything else in my life is negotiable."

"You would convert for me?" Her voice was timid.

"I would certainly and absolutely convert for you. My program is filled with Asians, Russians, and Jews. I might as well join a gang." His eyes focused on her face. "More than that, I'd love to be part of a God and a culture that produced a girl as wonderful as you."

She started weeping again, uncontrollable sobs that came from deep in her chest. Gabe pushed his seat all the way back and opened the driver's door. "C'mere, cuckoo bird."

Yasmine jumped out of the car, closed the passenger door, ran around to the driver's side, and fell onto his lap, crying on his bony shoulder. After he closed the driver's door, Gabe wrapped his arms around her. For the first time in almost a year, he could breathe without psychic and physical pain. "I love you, Yasmine."

"I love you soooooo much," she said softly.

He brushed his lips against hers, and she returned his kiss with a big juicy wet one. His reaction was immediate. *Hallelujah,* he thought to himself. *Yes, I'm still alive.*

She giggled when she felt him press against her.

He said, "As you can see, *nothing* has changed."

Yasmine giggled again. "Congratulations on your great reviews last summer." Gabe was taken aback. She kissed his cheek and said, "I used to google you in the library."

"Okay." He kissed her back. "They weren't *great* reviews—"

"The woman in the Oklahoma newspaper called you an exciting, vibrant pianist."

"That was the exception. One said that I showed a good deal of promise, one said that I was promising, and one said I was adequate. Okay, but not exactly stellar. But it takes time. More important is that you were interested in me. That's worth more than a thousand great reviews."

Yasmine said, "I never stopped wishing for you, Gabriel. Never, ever."

"God, I missed you, too. And I'm so sorry your mom took your watch. Looks like I'll have to start all over." He punched the button on the glove compartment and took out a wrapped box. "Happy belated birthday. I sent you a card, but obviously you never got it."

She looked at him, grinned openly, and then tore open the gift. Inside was a very thin white gold bangle studded with diamonds. She brought it to her heart. "I love it!"

"Do you really?"

"Yes, it's the most perfect gift in the world. It's gorgeous!" She laid her head against his chest. "But honestly I'd be just as happy with the box . . . anything from you that I can hold during the night."

"Okay. So I'll return the bracelet and you can keep the box," he teased her.

Yasmine's cell buzzed. "That's my carpool—"

"You have a *phone*?"

"My mother gave me a new one for Chanukah, but she still doesn't trust me. Every day, she checks my texts and my phone calls. She knows your number so you can't call me up."

"Well, give me your number anyway." When she gave it to him, he said, "Even if I can't call you, it's good to have you on my contact list again." A sly smile. "You know, I can always change my phone number. I can even do a 310 area code, and we can pretend it's one of your friends from school."

She didn't say yes, but she didn't say no. "I better go before they send out the search party."

"It's dark outside."

"Then walk me to the corner," she told him.

The two of them got out of the car, arms around each other. He said, "You know you didn't say *anything* about my spiffy car."

"Silver gray VW Cabriolet, black leather interior, carbon graphite dash with wire wheels. Very, very nice. I approve completely."

Gabe smiled. "Nothing escapes you."

"Just as long as you don't escape me." She hugged him fiercely. "And you didn't say anything about what I got."

Gabe was perplexed. "What did you get?"

She brought his hand to her chest over her sweat-shirt. "I got *boobs*."

He laughed so hard, he buckled at his knees. "We'll have to explore that much further one day." They walked a block until she was across the street from her school. When the light changed to green, she stood motionless. He kissed her cheek. "Go. I won't expect to hear from you regularly. But if you can write or text me once in a while, it'll keep me going for a long time."

"I promise I will. I love you, Gabriel. You own my heart."

"I love you, too, Yasmine, forever and always." He kissed her again. "*Go.*"

Once inside the crosswalk, she yelled over her shoul-der. "Go home and eat a steak!"

When she got to the other side, she waved and twirled and jumped up into the air, laughing and danc-ing until she faded from view.

Her own personal Viennese waltz.

Chapter Forty

The asphalt road was nothing but a rutted two-lane stretch of dust that cut a swath through the desert. The streets in the country sucked, Dylan thought, most of them studded with pebbles and potholes that wreaked havoc on the undercarriages of cars as well as the tires. Even in the major cities, the infrastructure was bad. He didn't spend much time in the cities, though. Not that it was dangerous anymore, but Dylan had lost his taste for congestion. The place where he lived was fairly remote, as was the route he was traveling—almost empty with the occasional passage of a car or two.

It had taken a while, but he felt he was doing okay, adjusting as well as could be expected. Time moved *sloooowly*. At first, he was so fucking bored he thought he was going to crawl out of his skin. But after a while—with enough meth coursing through the veins and enough whores sucking his dick—well, he kinda got used to it.

It was the springtime, which meant wind and dust and a rise in the heat factor. There were two seasons down here: hot and very hot. Today, it was cool enough to drive with the windows open. The car had AC that worked about as well as everything else did, which was to say it didn't work well at all. At least it was a step up from the junk heap he had when he first came down here. His current set of wheels still shaked, rattled, and rolled, but it could go a little faster than crawling; and it had a radio.

Dylan planned on staying here through the year—just smoking and whoring and hanging out. After that, his Spanish would be fluent and he'd go south into the bigger cities once again: maybe Buenos Aires or even Rio although he didn't know much Portuguese. But so what? With his new alias and his new passport, he knew he'd have no trouble starting over.

He'd have to get back into shape, though: take off the extra fifty pounds he packed on from all the starch. He'd eventually enter Universidad and do what he could have done in the old USA if all those fucking idiots hadn't gotten in his way.

His new car, his gap-year plans to travel the world, his degree from Yale—everything flushed down the toilet because of a few fucking idiots! Next time, he wouldn't trust anyone. Next time, he'd be a lot, lot smarter: shoot first and ask questions later. Still, an interlude of drugs and whores wasn't all that horrible.

In the beginning, all he thought about was revenge, sneaking back into the States and finishing them all off. His fantasies took on a sexual pleasure of their own. Every time a whore put her lips to his dick, he thought about the gun going off and exploding faces. To get the true sensation, he thought about Gregory Hesse's bursting face because that had been for real. Later on, he could extrapolate. First it was Cameron who blew up, then Kyle, then the rest of them. He thought about raping the little brown girl constantly and then shooting her in the face.

But then after a while, the fantasy faded and he discovered he really didn't give a fuck about any of them . . . except for maybe Gabe. For some odd reason, he still liked the dude.

The dude was cool.

The dude was *hot*.

Ah well. Time to forget the past and think about the future.

Time to think about nothing, because there was always mañana.

He jumped when he heard the pop and reached for his gun. The roads were constantly trawled by banditos and drug runners, and one couldn't be too careful about anything. But then the car started to shake and he knew what had happened.

Fuck!

He pulled over by the side of the road, got out, and immediately started sweating. He shielded his eyes as he surveyed the road. Not a car in sight.

He stared upward—a cloudless sky and a searing sun. Then he stared outward—red clay and sand and nothingness. He had a spare in the trunk, but his tire-changing skills weren't so sharp. Nonetheless, it was either waiting for someone to come around or being self-sufficient.

He'd try self-sufficient first. If that didn't work, he'd just wait. He always traveled with food and water and a gun. That was just a given out here.

Opening the trunk, he rooted around and lugged out the spare along with the tool kit. Then he bent down and examined the damage. The hubcap on the front passenger tire almost touched the road. He squinted in the sun as he regarded the tools—the jack, the crowbar, the lug nuts. He was studying the situation with such intensity that he hadn't even heard the bike pull up until it was almost on top of him.

Dylan looked up as the man gave the kickstand a whack. He was wearing a full helmet with goggles, a leather jacket, and thin black gloves.

"Need help?"

The voice was deep. "Yeah, man. Thanks a lot." The man bent down, stared at the tire, but said nothing. Dylan said, "I think I had a blowout."

"Looks like it. No biggie." The man's eyes wandered from the offending tire to the boy's back, specifically to a two-inch space of exposed skin between the waistband of the kid's shorts and hem of his T-shirt—a nice bare patch of sun-kissed tissue at the lumbar region.

The perfect setup.

The entire operation took about thirty seconds.

The man slid a razor-sharp shiv into Dylan's back, expertly driving it between the boy's vertebrae, slicing the tendons, pushing it deeper into the backbone. Several strong and deft strokes back and forth, and within moments, the boy's spinal cord was cut. Severing nerve tissue, especially the spinal cord, wasn't easy: the root was thick and strong and fibrous. It took muscle and elbow grease to slice it in half. The teen was lucky that the man had the strength and skill to sever it quickly and cleanly. It was done before Dylan could process what had gone down. With wide eyes and an open mouth, Dylan fell down onto the ground and moaned out some kind of guttural sound.

If the paramedics got to him soon enough, the kid would have a chance to live. But his legs would be useless appendages, a sickening reminder of what he lost.

Even more important, his dick would be just as useless.

The injury was high up enough that Dylan would lose all sensation as well as motor function in the lower half of his body. And that's exactly what Donatti wanted.

Wordlessly, he took Dylan's wallet and voided it of any bills. In this part of the country, robbery was always the main motive for crime.

He left the kid slumped on the ground, got on the bike, and peeled out, his destination not far from where it happened. A few miles down, he abruptly shifted directions until he was riding on the open desert. He could have found the spot without navigation, but GPS made it just that much simpler.

The twin-engine Cessna was waiting.

He got off the bike and worked at top speed to take off the wheels and handlebars from the frame. After that, he took off his jacket, gloves, and helmet. He placed everything inside the baggage compartment of the plane.

Fifteen minutes later, he was airborne.

The plane was slow, but it easily slipped below radar as he followed his carefully mapped-out route. With two practice runs under his belt, he felt confident. When he landed the plane on a private strip three hours later, he finally felt his breath come back into his lungs. The touchdown wasn't an easy one—a flat table of grass within the crags of the Sierras—and it was positively the hardest part of the entire procedure. He had bought 250 acres of forest five years ago, specifically because it contained a nice flat stretch for his unregistered plane. For business, Donatti flew either first-class commercial or on a time-shared jet. The plane was strictly for his flying pleasure or for when he did business off the radar.

And this one was definitely off the radar.

He took the motorcycle out of the hold and reassembled it, checking his time.

Two hours before the meeting.

No sweat.

He put on his jacket, helmet, and gloves; mounted the beast; and roared off until he hit the main highway. Talia, his faithful secretary and lover, was there to meet him at the secluded, designated spot a half hour later. She handed him the keys to his Aston Martin.

Donatti said, "Are you sure you can handle the bike?"

"It's not a problem, Chris."

"You're a sweetie." He handed her a cloth bag. "Take the shiv inside, wash it, soak it in acid, and luminal it. Make sure nothing glows. Be sure to rinse the drain for a good ten minutes. And do it several times. Then put what's left of the metal through the shredder and toss the shavings out in the national forest." He took off the jacket, helmet, and gloves. "Destroy all my clothing and the bag. Totally. Soak the helmet in the solution I gave you, luminal it, and if it's okay, put it back in my closet."

Talia stuffed the clothes he gave her inside the bag. Then she opened the trunk to the Aston as Donatti stripped down. She took out his suit, black T-shirt, suede loafers, and a fresh pair of underwear. "Are you sure you want to keep the helmet?"

"We've been through a lot together. If it doesn't glow, I want to keep it. But if it does, get rid of it."

Talia said, "What do I do with the bike?"

"Give it to Mason. He'll take care of it. You deal with my cell phone?"

"It was completely destroyed by the water damage so no one could get through to you this morning. I got you a new iPhone and a new telephone number." She handed him the cell. "Here you go."

"Thanks." He had slipped on his clothing, and he placed the phone in his jacket pocket. "Where am I going again?"

"What would you do without me?" she complained. "To the Barker Building."

"That's right. And what's the meeting about again?"

"It's with your broker from Utrich, LLC." She handed him a briefcase and kissed his cheek. "All the relevant information is inside here."

"Good girl."

"By the way, Chris, I did what you said . . . called in the accident from a remote source."

"Did they get him to the hospital on time?"

"He was alive when they picked him up. Last I heard he was in critical condition."

"Let's pray for a speedy recovery." He kissed her cheek. "With any luck, he'll live long enough to see what a pathetic blob he is and kill himself."

Donatti slipped into the driver's seat, put the top down, and sped off until he reached the highway. He blasted the radio on heavy metal and felt his heart's smooth and steady beat. Even hours later, he could still taste the grit in his mouth. No matter how much protection, the sand seeps inside. Talia had left a bottle of water on the passenger seat. He reached over and drained it. Hydrated now, cruising down the freeway, seventy-two degrees outside . . . life was good.

No one fucks with *his* son without consequences.

That was the self-righteous explanation.

The truth was he hadn't done a job in a long time and he wondered if he still had the touch. There were still a couple of details to take care of—payments to be made, resetting the odometer on his plane—but after the meeting, he had time to deal.

His brain ticked off items on his mental checklist. Almost everything was complete.

He felt his lips curl up into a smile.

Once a pro, always a pro.